THE

STRAW

MAN

by Jean Giono

Translated from the French
by Phyllis Johnson

North Point Press
San Francisco
1983

Le choléra n'est plus épidémique,
il est devenu constitutionnel.

PROSPER MÉRIMÉE

(to Mme de Montijo, February 19, 1848)

TRANSLATOR'S FOREWORD

Two plagues ravaged Europe in 1848: Asiatic cholera and the fever of revolution. Giono, who in *The Horseman on the Roof* exposed his hero, Angelo Pardi, to an earlier cholera plague in France, now sets him wandering in the 1848 epidemic of revolution in the north of Italy.

The secret society of the Carbonari, founded in the south of Italy in the first years of the nineteenth century, and Mazzini's largely expatriate group, Young Italy, founded in the early 1830's, inspired Italy to fight for unity, democracy, and, first of all, freedom from Austria. Directly or indirectly, the Austrians had dominated the peninsula since the Vienna settlements of 1815. However, Napoleon's regime had given Italy a taste of enlightened administration and reform which was never forgotten; in addition, the Carbonari and the "Young Italians" labored to restore to their countrymen the self-respect which centuries of foreign domination and local despotism had taken from them. In the first chapter of *The Straw Man* Giono sketches in this background to the revolution of 1848, focusing particularly on the life of the exiles in France and England.

Republican agitation in the early days of 1848 (as at Pavia and Padua) forced Charles Albert, King of Sardinia, Ferdinand II of Naples and Sicily, Pope Pius IX, and the Dukes of Modena, Parma, and Tuscany to grant constitutions in their states. However, it took an uprising in Vienna on March 8 to spark open revolt; on March 18, in Milan, the famous "Five Days" began. This tremendous, unplanned popular uprising (which forms the central section of *The Straw Man*) threw the Austrian army, led by Field Marshal Radetzky, out of the city. Public opinion in Charles Albert's native Piedmont urged him to come to the aid of the insurgents by leading his army (by far the largest in Italy) across the Ticino into Lombardy. However, he delayed, losing precious opportunities to strike the Austrians before Radetzky could reorganize his troops and send for reinforcements. In April and May, Charles Albert managed to defeat the Austrians at Pastrengo, Peschiera, and Goito, but in July his badly fed and inadequately armed forces were beaten decisively at Custoza. Charles Albert, who had dreamed of uniting all Italy under his rule, had reigned over the north of Italy for a scant three weeks. By the next year Austrian power was reestablished more firmly than ever.

However, the revolution was not the complete failure it might seem. The revolutionary fever had healthy consequences. People of all classes and from all parts of the peninsula had for the first time worked together to make Italy a nation. Giono portrays the comradeship, enthusiasm, and vitality which were suddenly released in the Italian people. These qualities did not die with 1848, but continued, carrying Italians to the final unification of their country.

THE STRAW MAN

CHAPTER ONE

O ne night early in March 1848, a calash entered Novara by the Vercelli road. It came up to the town gate at ten in the evening. With lantern darkened, it had been waiting for some time, a hundred paces away, hidden in the willows. At the changing of the guard the carriage advanced. The sergeant allowed it to pass after a brief exchange of words.

The coachman looked French. The passenger directed him in this language to proceed at a walk along the deserted avenues of the bourgeois quarter. The wind out of Lombardy, lightly mixed with rain, rocked the street lamps. San Gaudenzio tolled the hour.

"All the same, let's not wait till midnight," said the traveler.

He laughed somewhat vulgarly as very satisfied fat men do. He gave an order to turn down an avenue bordered with gardens.

The carriage entered the park of the Ansaldi house. The iron gates were opened quickly by someone who must have been waiting. Lilac bushes already in flower filled the air with fragrance. By the reddish light of the street lamps filtering through trees two people could be seen waiting on the front steps. One was a woman in a very tight short jacket and, despite the rain, a feathered hat; the other, a man in a redingote. The calash stopped in front of them. The tired horse snorted noisily against the bit.

"Good evening, Marquise," said the traveler.

He started to get out of the calash. The coachman came to help him, supporting the rear spring with both hands. The man, whose age and corpulence made it difficult for him to get down, was

Bondino, sometimes called Brutus à la Rose, returning to Novara.

He had left the city in 1821 and seen it once more for the last time that April [1]. And then it had been no more than the ghost of a town enveloped in smoke. He had been in command of a company of constitutional soldiers from Alessandria. During the march to Agogna he had told his men again and again that they were going to rejoin their brothers in Novara. Not once had he been stupid enough to believe his own words. At the first cannon-shot from the walls he realized that the light artillery was in possession of the town. One of those cannon balls might have his number on it. So he wheeled about and galloped down the entire column. He had an idea he might join several horsemen in command of a platoon of light cavalry at the gates of Vercelli. But he was in Casale that very evening, and in Genoa two days later.

He had not yet completed his schooling. An assiduous slave of the fashion-plates, he did not aspire to higher erudition. He was not the man to forget his well-formed body, and, indeed, it would have been a mistake: while carefully measuring the height of his cravat and dusting off his silk lapels with an elegant flick of his fingers he spoke courageously, making himself heard. The contrast between his handkerchiefs, colored the iridescent rose of a pigeon's breast, and the bold words he uttered with an absent-minded air earned him his nickname.

In Genoa he learned that the royal army was negotiating with Enrico, the head of the mutinous garrison, for the surrender of the citadel of Turin. Fifty thousand lire was the price rumored. As long as only the day-laborers of the port mentioned this figure, Bondino smiled. When Asinari and Morozzo confirmed that the transaction had taken place, he recognized the significance of the event.

Leaving Genoa early on April 8, he reached Turin on the afternoon of the 10th, while General de la Tour, at the head of the main body of his troops, stealthily entered the city. De la Tour did

[1] There was a Carbonarist uprising in Piedmont in March 1821. The garrison at Alessandria revolted and Turin was for a time in the hands of the insurgents. The King, Victor Emmanuel I, fled, leaving Charles Albert, Prince Carignano, as regent. Later the new King, Charles Felix, revoked the constitution, called in the Austrians to quell the revolt, and exiled Charles Albert to Florence.

not consider that the withdrawal of the constitutional forces to Novara justified a triumphal entry. A confirmed enemy of every kind of display and pomp, he gave the following explanation of the events which led him to enter Turin wearing the *bicorne* of a lieutenant general.

"Victor Emmanuel," he said, "was forced to abdicate by people who claimed to act in the name of the King. We had a few days of regency during which the fundamental laws of the kingdom were overthrown—still in the name of respect and fidelity to the King. A junta took over and organized an army corps which it sent in the name of the King to fight the King. After all these strange events I arrive, also in the name of the King, and I take the town. What will the people make of me?"

He did not arrange to have his arrival preceded by proclamations which might have won over and reassured the people. He entered Turin (he had naturally paid cash for the citadel) at nightfall. He slipped down the narrow streets with two battalions of royal light infantry. The populace gave him a cold welcome.

As Bondino also slipped into town along the same narrow streets, he was obliged to stop his cabriolet at a crossing to allow the soldiers to pass. He was sincerely displeased to give way to people who hadn't as much as a bugle for their entrance into the capital. He asserted afterward that he had seen Charles Felix following the troops like a little sutler. But it has been proved that the new king did not arrive until the next day.

However, the next day Bondino was once again on the road, the deal completed. Enrico was a man of no consequence. He had been surprised once already carrying off his hostess's flat silver in his pocket. In addition to the sum which Bondino called the people's share, the deal called for an additional sum of over forty thousand francs to be paid to a member of Enrico's family. Bondino scrawled a note on the back of an envelope: "Never put a needy man in command of a citadel."

Genoa, where governmental scenery changes with admirable ease, had reinstated Count Desgeneys after having, literally, dragged him through the mud. This general, without a man at his command, limited his activity to putting up placards prohibiting fugitives from entering the city. They entered anyway, and the best he could do was to hurry their departure. . . . Many sailed for Spain. The leaders took refuge in France and Switzerland.

On board a schooner Bondino found Charles Asinari, very unhappy but dignified, Regis, the French ex-general Guillaume de Vaucourt, Abbot Patrioli, Viancini, Castelbergo, Doctor Andreone, and even General Lisio. The last was thought to have rifled the regimental chest. He was very popular.

After five days of bad weather Asinari, who could not stand the sea, asked to be put ashore near Golfe Juan. Bondino would gladly have accompanied him. He loved victims. He had noticed that Asinari had no baggage and probably no money. He pictured him in the lonely country of the Var. Staying with him, but at a distance, he could perhaps enjoy an agreeable sight.

Vaucourt, whose face was insignificant and appearance ill-kept, was strongly attracted by the *Rose* side of Brutus. He talked about Plato. Above all, he said, somewhat coarsely but with good sense: "Keep a hold on the frying pan even if you puke." This thought, though not the Greek philosopher's, interested Bondino.

They disembarked at Marseille. Vaucourt, apprised of Bondino's deal with Enrico, decided that he wanted to settle down with him on a country estate with tall trees, running streams, and a noble landscape. He was particularly fond of the Gardanne region, where the view of Mont Sainte-Victoire on the horizon uplifts the soul.

He insisted on hiring a carriage and going at least to visit these pleasure spots. But without success.

Bondino had realized that Marseille was becoming the rendez-vous of vagabonds from Piedmont and that they all wanted hand-outs. So he found the town very pleasant to stroll in. One fine day he disappeared.

He had made the acquaintance of a certain Vendamme, a former convict pulled out of prison for the Irish expedition under Hoche in the year V and freed from Bicêtre [2] for good behavior. Vendamme, originally from Rochefort, described the western part of the country to him. There were English companies there. Business was good.

---

[2] Asylum for the aged and lunatics, constructed under Louis XIII.

Vendamme was flat-nosed and stupid-looking because he breathed through his mouth. Bondino hired him as a servant and went to settle in La Rochelle. He went into the cognac business as a representative for Marie Brizard and Roger de Bordaux. His journal shows that these houses delivered clearly forty thousand francs' worth of merchandise to him. His sales, according to the same journal, were made to Messrs. Gogué, Jagueneau, Pellier, Nicole, Lestrade, etc.

On the 3rd of October 1824, at nine in the evening, six strangers in *vestes ronde* attacked and robbed an inhabitant of the Poitou marshes. Six horses had been stolen from a Luçon farmer. After the appearance near Moréac of six men, well mounted and armed with pistols and twin-barreled guns, was reported, the police beat their way through the forest of Elven. Their search was fruitless.

About the same time, a journeyman wheelwright came looking for the police commissioner of La Rochelle with a surprising piece of news. One of Gogué's employees, Merlaud by name, had commissioned him to make wheels suitable for a gun carriage. The man had explained to him all the dimensions. He was to make the iron wheel bindings, rims, iron boxes, hubs, and axle washers himself. These articles, already begun, were found in his house and seized.

Merlaud was asked what he intended to use this gun carriage for. He answered that it was intended for a cannon which had lain buried since the last war. It was established that, despite his evident good will, he was incapable of saying where this cannon was buried. But fifty-eight bars of lead were found at Gogué's, the total weight of which was about fifty-five hundred pounds. Gogué maintained that this lead was intended for a M. Dasson for repairs on his castle, which had been damaged by fire. Thereupon, a certain Jagueneau, a priest, the brother of the liqueur merchant, declared that his conscience forced him to come clean. The truth of the matter was that he was afraid because there was a lot of talk about the lead, all the more because drawings for cannon balls had been found in a drawer in Merlaud's stable. The curé had some lead too: about eight thousand pounds. Merlaud, Jagueneau, and Gogué talked about the buried cannon so much that there was no longer any question of attaching the slightest importance to it. The drawing for the cannon-ball mold was much more interesting.

In the margin of the prefect's letter saying: "The affair of the lead has reactivated ancient enmities," the commissioner general of police added in his own hand: "The affair of the lead has not reactivated ancient enmities: it has provided an opportunity for everyone to show himself as he is: the adversaries have dropped their masks."

Vendamme, who for three years had been wearing velvet hunting-outfits with large fancy buttons and watch chains hung with trinkets, went to spend a week with some cousins who lived in the marshes and owned a large flat-bottomed barge for traveling on canals. He did not return.

Bondino, in shirt sleeves and a little nankin vest, left the wine store at about three in the afternoon, as the tide was about to ebb, saying to a clerk (a former customs employee who had been dismissed): "I'm going to Pautière's." In reality, he embarked on the sloop *L'Ambition,* out of Royan. She sailed out of the port with the tide. Besides two silk redingotes and four pairs of trousers with straps under the feet, he left, unpaid, at the shop called "La Petite Oie" on the Place Louis XVI, a bill of six hundred louis for lace, silk, and hats.

Three weeks later the brig *La Levrette,* coming from Mornas and going up the Thames, passed twenty ships of the line at Shernesse. Bondino respected all forms of force. He also loved the thick-napped greenery of English parks, trimmed by the best tailors.

There were a few Piedmontese revolutionaries in London. But no more than a few, for England called for modesty. Bondino had a talent for mimicry which could substitute for it. He had liquid cash and, in addition, a letter of credit for one hundred and three thousand francs drawn up by Cambon of Bordeaux on the house of Fabos and Feré in Paris, with a branch on the Brompton Road. He forced himself to go into retirement. He learned to go about unobserved. The day he knew how to be happy wearing a twenty-pound redingote exactly like that of a draper's clerk (except for the essentials) he understood what could be gained from the "art of life." This art could be of great use to a man with a position in society.

Moreover, while he was learning to go about unobserved, he put on weight, force-feeding himself. He had always been a greedy meat-eater. He was rapturous over a leg of lamb, even though boiled in the English fashion, as well as rare roast beef. "I need a lot to keep me going," he said to himself. He was astonished that formerly he could have subsisted on anchovies mashed in oil and bread rubbed with garlic. He recalled even polenta as a light, bodiless substance which did not *stick to the ribs*. Stuffed with meat, his body was henceforth fed. He experienced superhuman joys watching slabs of raw beef on a grill and smelling them; he drank their juice by the spoonful. He chewed stolidly, moving his tongue seven times in his mouth and then seven times seven more. He began to despise long-winded people, especially people who were long-winded out of sincerity. When he heard (for occasionally he did hear) someone speak of the happiness of humanity, he did not laugh. (He had learned not to laugh.) He said to himself: "I know what stage he's at."

Like every man greedy for power, he was always consumed by thirst. But he could drink neither hard liquors nor wine; they caused him to secrete quantities of thick saliva; he spent hours clearing his throat. He drank nothing but water—not out of wisdom but by taste and because it was not irritating. He required enormous quantities of it. In London he got the idea of drinking beer. He allowed himself to be tempted. He liked its bitterness. He also made the acquaintance of ice water. This was a supreme pleasure. He ended every meal by consuming large quantities of a certain "champagne" biscuit soaked in ice water.

Vaucourt would have been amazed. So would those others who had sometimes seen him caught in a trap of his own making, in command (for however short a time) as at Novara. If he was ever to be naïve again, as he had been about the stock-piling of ammunition at La Rochelle (and you never know, he said to himself, when a naïve action will become a necessity) it would no longer be with the likes of Gogué and Jagueneau.

Previously he had supported his trousers—like every good Piedmontese—with a belt. He bought braces.

Finally, he met Luigi Savone. He himself admired the natural way in which this long-premeditated meeting took place.

Nicknamed "the terrible old man," for years Savone had been

represented as the devil in all court circles where orthodox religion prevailed. He had started life as an apostle and had shown later that he had in him the stuff of an adventurer on a grand scale. His house in Harrington Gardens impressed Bondino. Colbeck House was surrounded by public gardens. The leafy lindens, admirable green lawns, and fragrant roses didn't cost a penny. London paid for the gardeners.

Savone had written on his door: "Believe in Heaven and love humanity." He put bread out for the birds. Blackbirds called to him from his window sill. Bondino thought this very clever. He flushed with shame to think that he himself had always taken things literally. With the exception of fear, pride, and a taste for show, he had yielded to nothing. If the truth be told, when he spoke of fighting for liberty, he believed in it up to a point! He was very sensitive to the scorn which can be expressed in a greeting.

Other very useful thoughts occurred to him. Savone had a key, thanks to which he could enjoy in perfect quiet the park which spread behind high iron railings beneath his windows. There in rustic peace he first conversed with Bondino and two other Piedmontese refugees who had come by omnibus. Despite his experience and his desire to appear a man of the world, Bondino asked several naïve questions about the gentlemen in top hats going by on the red-brick streets beyond the railings. Did they have keys to the garden?

"They don't have the right," Savone answered, smiling. "And it would never enter their heads to ask for something to which they have no right. They couldn't enter this garden unless we were civil enough to ask them in. Any invitation would surprise them, and, ten to one, they would decline. In this country no one argues about the law. All that's necessary is to have it on your side."

Bondino wrote this formula on the back of an envelope.

He also noticed that Savone never walked to the omnibus station. He remained on the edge of the sidewalk and signaled with his cane. The carriage stopped in front of him. He approached the step slowly and the conductor helped him up. Bondino underwent a vertiginous revelation like St. Paul's when he compared the old man's firm step while taking his constitutional in Green Park with his few wavering steps from sidewalk to coach step.

"I thought that I had taken every precaution," he said to himself, "but if I had been victorious at Novara, Savone would have been prime minister (or maybe more) and I, sub-prefect." Bondino learned a great deal in the course of these walks with Savone in Green Park. Very courageously he let his vanity suffer. He compared the dust of the road from Alessandria to Novara and the noise of the Austrian howitzers with the sweetness of the green walks and the nasal song of the vendors of iced ginger-beer.

Now that he used braces to hold up his trousers and no longer had to hitch them up every two minutes with an inelegant gesture, Bondino took great pleasure in walking beside Savone. The old man had no principles other than precepts of hygiene, but these he obeyed absolutely.

In April 1830, at Colbeck House, Bondino met Cerutti, a former Piedmontese officer. He brought news from Paris. There he had seen many Englishmen, especially a Mr. Folks, who was living at the Hôtel Royal, rue des Pyramides. Moreover, it was thanks to him that he had obtained, not a regular passport, but a sort of open letter which permitted him to come to London. According to these gentlemen, France was on the brink of a revolution. Charles X, who had soured, was hurting everyone's teeth just like an English sweet. All that was wanted of him was his head. Arms were entering Paris thanks to a carting-concern owned by a deputy from La Rochelle.

Savone talked of barricades and street fights. He said to Bondino: "You should go see what's going on."

"I'm too fat," replied Bondino. "Alas!" he added with a stroke of genius.

Cerutti returned across the Channel in May. His work was hard. He relaxed whenever he could. He was not foolish enough to think that he could claim an entire day of peace and quiet, let alone several. He counted his free time in hours and minutes. His London missions pleased him because of the two crossings.

Although a typical man of the south physically and morally, Cerutti loved rain, mist, veiled landscapes, and the cold. He detested the sun, especially the "full sun" as it was called. He could barely adjust to the blond light of the Ile-de-France. Summer was his worst season.

The whiteness of the Pas-de-Calais in springtime, the gray water, the cool wind blowing off the North Sea, the worn contours of the coast where the crest of the cliffs showed a little green, the flap of sails, and the indecisive tacking put him in seventh heaven. The grinding of the tiller alone suggested dryness and precision, but only served to intensify the flavor of all the rest.

As soon as he had disembarked he went to Etaples. There in a church he had a furtive meeting with Mme Vasseur, the mistress of the director of the Marine Hospital.

"I was unsuccessful," he said to her. He spoke of Bondino. He was attracted by this fat man's pallor and teetotaler's coldness.

Cerutti had been imprisoned in Fenestrelles in 1820. A certain Leblond, denounced by the Paris police, had been seized on the frontier and escorted to Turin. His carriage, which was carefully searched, concealed a great many proclamations, a letter to the Duchess Pardi, and instructions for Demetrius Cerutti and Hector Perron.

When presented with these various papers, the king had burned the letter to the Duchess Pardi without opening it, Cerutti and Perron had been arrested coming out of a ball and the government's seal had been stamped on all their possessions. This last operation was accomplished so adroitly, or so maladroitly, that during the night Charles Asinari had made his way into their room and taken everything he thought should be taken.

One summer night in 1821 a few days after De la Tour entered Turin, Cerutti escaped from the fortress. A rope was found hanging from his window, but it was established that it would have been incapable of supporting the fugitive's weight.

There was talk of a macabre escapade involving Countess Alexandrine d'Aché and another lady of fashion; without asking their husbands' permission to go to the ball given by the commander of the fortress, they had escaped about midnight and returned home at dawn in a tumbril, the only vehicle for which the drawbridge was lowered before the official hour.

When questioned, the Countess d'Aché received the investigators while still in bed, nursing her daughter. The charming, handsome baby turned from her breast for a moment to dazzle the thugs with a milk-whitened smile.

Cerutti settled in Lyon. He looked well in uniform. In civilian clothes and with a low-crowned hat, he appeared slender and a little drab. His large, dreamy eyes, full of charm when they counteracted the insolence of a bulging shirt front and an imposing ladder of gold lace, then expressed only indecision.

Indeed, he was a sensualist geared to enjoy life down to its smallest particle. He was at the same time strong and too weak: although capable of conceiving a courageous action and carrying it out, he could be turned out of his way by the fragrance of jasmine wafted over the top of a wall. His weaknesses were so understandable in relation to his feelings that his critical sense was unaware of them. When he was reproached for lying, going back on a promise, or abandoning an enterprise in which he had enlisted his friends, he himself knew that he had had excellent reasons to lie, to renege, or to abandon his friends. In reality, he spent only the surplus of his life in society. He did not need centuries of struggle and thousands of combatants to attain happiness.

For a time he led a delightful life visiting lakes and mountain valleys, sojourning on the banks of lazy streams, making marginal notes in *The Italian League, Bradamante's Buckler,* and even *Théophilanthropes.* He accepted the help of good-hearted young women, the hospitality of certain households, and one or two positions as lover in return for room and board and a little pocket money. There came, however, a period when he was almost constantly without money to pay his bills.

He took up with three former Sardinian officers, exiles like himself: Dubois, Lamurra, and Rollando. They were professional assassins who would fight anyone for pay. He himself was no amateur and acquitted himself well in five or six commissions. Following an excessive show of zeal, Dubois was arrested. Bound to the three by indissoluble bonds of friendship, Dubois gave the police their names a quarter of an hour after his arrest. Lamurra, who had a thick black moustache and a fine, lean face dark as a horse chestnut, gave the episode the loftiest possible interpretation and spoke of carbonarism. Consequently Rollando and Cerutti were carefully examined.

At that time, above Tassin-la-demi-lune [3] there was a kind of

[3] A Community near Lyon.

paradise on earth to which Cerutti had access. On the edge of an oak forest, it was the lodge owned by the widow of Roger Hue. The belling of unknown beasts sounded from the depths of the forest; the air was cool; from an arbor one could watch the lazy progress of rain and shadows along the Saône. Like all women whose bowels function freely, Mme Hue was amiable and faithful.

Cerutti found that the police viewed him with the best intentions, but wanted to make a deal. Eager to get it over with so that he could get on with his pleasures, he answered all their questions as rapidly as possible. As he had no imagination, he told the truth to make things go faster. This procedure fascinated the prefect of Lyon. The Saumur plot was still quite recent. After grilling him for several days, moving meticulously from point to point, they finally asked Cerutti what he would think of accepting a small income. That fixed everything.

However, it was not an easy way to earn money. He was obviously much freer now than before to consort with his former comrades who had gone into exile after Novara. He could warm himself at the fire of Piedmontese exaltation, profoundly happy to be among friends. But men could only be used once in his business. A few days later they were withdrawn from circulation. Others had to be found. And despite quantities of people involved in the revolution in Piedmont, Piedmont was not inexhaustible. He worked for a time among the French, but with less enjoyment: his heart was not with them.

Now that he knew that the censors were reading his letters, he renewed his correspondence with Alexandrine d'Aché. She was not the last word in intelligence, but she wrote everything that came into her head and from this he could glean extremely valuable information on everything that was brewing in the court at Turin and in the kingdom.

He could therefore be of great service. He had only one passion, but it was irresistible: friendship. Alexandrine's letters were full of names which made his heart beat faster. Nine times out of ten she gave addresses too. Because, like all heedless pleasure-seekers, he was gifted with a memory for the smallest details, he could allow himself to burn the Countess's letters and work without a single note on his person or on his furniture. All his reports were oral. He never wrote, except about the weather, to Alexandrine.

He sold friends only. His imprisonment in Fenestrelles and his forced exile following his spectacular escape had made him a hero in the most absolute sense ever since the start of the insurrection. He did not denounce the men who crossed into France secretly by the Chambéry road until he had become their sincere and true friend. Obviously he kept the wolf from the door with these secret denunciations, but money was not the source of his happiness and he would rather have died of hunger than to have deprived himself of the nostalgia, the exquisite feeling of solitude, which followed each arrest.

He returned to Paris extremely dissatisfied after his trip to London. "I didn't succeed in making Savone come to the Continent," he told his superiors, "but Savone no longer counts. He's old and he's lost all his teeth. But there's someone in his circle who can still sink his molars into a piece of red meat." He revealed the violent friendship he had immediately conceived for Bondino. "He's a man," he said, "who's not going to bother himself with anything except the real thing, and since there's no substitute for the truth, we should promise him the real thing and even *sincerely and truly* intend to stick to our promises; then at some time in the future we can help fortune thwart these intentions."

But he did not have time to bring this about. It was June 1830. In July the revolution broke out in Paris. Cerutti contented himself with observing the picturesque aspects of this entirely French affair. The workers in shirtsleeves lacked dignity. What was a revolution without plumed hats? All this crying of "Long live the Charter!" by urchins and women lacked grandeur and even intelligence. Where was the sport in all this? "We too cry out against tyranny," he said to himself, "but at least we respect it. We attack the idol of a cult. Where is the pleasure in revolting without a lofty soul and a tender heart? Do they really think a Charter can make them happy?"

About midnight, on the rue de l'Echelle, he saw shadows moving in the darkness. He approached. "Who's there?" someone cried to him. "A friend," he replied. The shadows were a barricade. He reached the Carrousel. Behind the palace railing he saw soldiers camping in the courtyard of the Tuileries. He wanted to look through the gate. A sentinel hidden behind a pillar muttered "Get on with you!" in a voice which he obeyed immediately.

The next day he could not believe his eyes: the tricolor flag was flying from Notre Dame! There was lively gunfire toward the Grève, and smoke rose in thick clouds. He took refuge with one of his clients in the rue Vaneau.

This man (Sandro), Bertolotti, had been denounced by a woman. "Don't arrest him now," Cerutti had said. "He's heavy-handed but that's all you have against him, and anyway his brutalities can be excused because they were occasioned by an almost conjugal relationship. Leave him to me. If we wait, I'm sure that he'll get himself in deeper."

Sandro had been living in France for only a short time. Cerutti had met him in the streets of Lyon. He was no more than twenty-three or twenty-four. Too young to have taken part in the events of 1820, Fenestrelles and Novara were words without sentimental significance for him.

He was handsome. Cerutti amused himself by imagining that the Countess d'Aché would not mention such a handsome young man. She did speak of him. He was the youngest son of quite a large family, the eldest of which had an income of twenty thousand francs. Sandro received an allowance of five hundred francs a year, plus room and board. He had had a *very pleasant* affair with a *very pleasant* bourgeoise from Lanzo, a small town two leagues from Castello-Maschere, the Bertolotti house in the mountains. The young woman called Clara had married to get away from her jealous mother and was thoroughly armed against the unforeseen in life. Her husband, totally lacking the good taste of a nobleman, fired several pistol shots out the window at Sandro. She could see him forcing himself—to no avail—to aim and this she thought the last word in vulgarity. She decided she had to get rid of someone so ridiculous.

Sandro went to Turin with several introductions to people in the best society. He looked well in evening clothes with his gloomy face and the abrupt gestures of a melancholy man infatuated with his own dark phantoms. In reality he was a candid mountaineer who aped no one and showed himself for what he was. But one could disregard this. He cut quite a dashing figure. He was received more warmly by strangers than by his own family. He was initiated into the charms of platonic love, listened to tercets of the *Inferno,* and saw beautiful bosoms palpitate at the word "liberty." As he had always been the epitome of the "sad animal," he had no pleasant memories of Clara's boudoir. He now shared the bed of "Free Italy." Young and pure, he confronted that ideal country like a bishop on a mission among the heathen; this afforded him a pleasure whose source would never be cut off and, even more happily, would never suffer the sadness of satisfaction.

He quarreled with a certain Manino who lived off stupidity alone —and a need to display this quality. He refused a challenge which would have compromised the entire little group of which he was a member. Thereupon, the Marquise Carrera sent word requesting him not to set foot in her house again, but continued to receive Manino. He was then possessed by the stupid idea of complaining to her daughter at a ball, but politely, asking her to end this misunderstanding. Manino, annoyed to see him speaking with the girl whom he considered a new conquest, commanded him to keep his distance and hurled after him: *"Des'no it rompo' il muso."* Sandro, in the first heat of anger, was imprudent enough to slap twice very hard (and perhaps even with a clenched fist) the insolent man threatening him. They were separated immediately and everyone withdrew. Sandro was left alone with the commandant, who, fortunately, was content to escort him home.

This outburst could have had grave consequences. Sandro's friends would rather have seen him dead. The Countesses de Croix, Montbelli, and Colbran, the Baroness Maresca, and all the ardent women of the Lotis Khon house who shared Sandro's violent pleasures had gotten the idea (or rather they had been given the idea) of drawing Charles Albert into Carbonarism. ("They" wanted to see whether he would allow himself to be tempted.) This detail was especially interesting to Cerutti. Charles Albert's sinister face was constantly marked by the vexing realization that he had placed no more than the point of his buttocks on the Sardinian throne. Bilious and believing in the Jesuits, he calculated that he could always excuse himself to women, saying he had been gallant. He pledged himself.

This pledge resulted in pistol shots being fired at Sandro once again. Those who fired them—aiming better than Clara's husband

—left him for dead on a little mountain road three leagues above Suze where he had been trying to cross the Alps on foot. He was found in the early morning by a goatherd. Without ulterior motive the man cared for him, concealed him, and cured him. Above all, deep indignation at the pistol shots and a violent desire to be henceforth on the shooting end gave him the strength to get well.

In the goatherd's cottage Sandro for the first time felt in his heart what a republic might be. The word excited both men. The rustic setting, the steep crags, and the virile air stirred them to dream of a government without hypocrisy. In the single room of the châlet the animals were the sole heating apparatus. It was a far cry from the fragrance of benjamin and musk; Sandro, who could have forgiven the pistol shots, did not forgive his fair friends the time he had lost from vapors and boudoir machinations.

He had of course known some courageous women. He knew that Piedmont was the domain of passion; that nine times out of ten, balls in the palaces of Turin were reunions of sworn conspirators; that the couples paired off in quadrilles to exchange passwords and relay instructions. He had been sent on enough missions to country estates, to small-town law offices, to merchants' houses; he had met enough people while riding along roads through woods or parks to know of the existence of serious, determined women. Without being very sure of what selfish use might be made of her, he had felt that a heroine wins every heart. But it was precisely this winning which he rejected. The blood of men was sufficient for noble childbirths. He became a "Roman."

He crossed into France, wandering in Grenoble for some time. He had no resources. He got a job as a day-laborer in a carting-business. The hard work of loading and unloading the wagons beautified body and soul. Such strong men enter the public domain immediately. Only the weak, the hunchbacked, and those who are cast off (or at least unwanted) remain intransigent.

One evening when he was returning to Lyon sitting on the barrels of a load of wine, a crowd in the suburbs forced the Chambéry diligence to stop beside the carters. While the halt continued, Sandro talked to the impatient horses in Piedmontese. A young woman looked out from behind the coach curtain and, in the dialect of the valleys, gave Sandro touching news of his homeland. She also said that she was staying at the Inn of the Dauphin. This was next door to the stagecoach office.

The "Roman" put on a clean shirt and went to the Dauphin in search of more specific information. This obtained, he got his week's pay and remained in Lyon.

As he talked in his sleep, the young woman, who was called Caroline and had coal black eyes, said to him: "You're suffering from a sickness of the mind. On my knees I beg you by the pleasures we have shared to let me help you. I too know the lines in Dante about the traitors in their city."

Caroline Sassovella revealed to him that she had been a carbonari since the age of twelve; she had regularly appeared in the initiation ceremonies, representing one of the angels of light in a white, winged costume. When she had come of age she had sworn terrible oaths and put on the plumed hat. Her father was the Sassovella who had been killed with the unfortunate Vochieri at Casale.

"With an almost incredible refinement of cruelty," she said, "they led my father beneath the windows of our house on his way to be tortured. He wasn't shot by soldiers, but by turnkeys. The governor was present in full uniform, seated on a cannon."

These details enchanted Sandro. Exile weighed heavily upon him. He asked if she had stabbed the man who had denounced her father. She said she had.

Caroline embroidered beautifully. She worked for a convent which embellished the trousseaux of girls in the best society. Sandro cared for the horses at a hack-stable. They both knew their business. The house where they lived, on the Vauzelles heights, was soon the rendezvous of all the Piedmontese in Lyon and the environs, who came to touch base and rediscover their homeland. So Piedmontese was the house that Caroline, a fertile inventor of misfortune, imagined herself neglected and repaid Sandro for some of his "Roman" indifference by denouncing him in an anonymous letter to the police.

Cerutti found Sandro's house a well-stocked fishpond. He saw immediately that when necessary he could fish the prize catch out of it in complete safety. Since the King had been murdered, its assets included an armorer capable of inventing every so-called infernal machine, women capable of sacrificing everything to the happiness of suffering humanity, noble mothers in the manner of Corneille, and even gossips. Consequently he asked that the letter be overlooked, and his request was granted. In addition he felt that he was going to love Sandro wildly. Often, admiring Sandro's handsome face, his fine ardor, and his sincerity, he savored in advance the bitter disorder which would follow his arrest.

When, for the good of his work, he was obliged to live in Paris, he took his fishpond with him. He had two or three specific threats whispered to the "Romans," spoke of a surer hiding-place, and said he would take the responsibility for finding it. They followed him.

Thus it was that during the three days of the revolution he took refuge with Sandro and Caroline. When the shooting was over, he went out to see what a capital without a king looked like. Nothing had changed except for the battered barricades making everything dirty. A few months later Cerutti asked to be transferred directly to the service of the king of Sardinia. He understood the French less and less. His *curriculum vitae,* supported by the high praise of the general who inspected gunpowder and saltpeter, was sent to Turin.

On the day of his departure, Caroline and Sandro wept heartfelt tears. Cerutti was also very moved. "Because of this damned French-style revolution—that is to say without a single noble sentiment," he said to himself, "I've flubbed it with Bondino and flubbed it with this excellent boy. Only on the other side of the Alps do people really know how to live." Finally the other "Romans" of Paris, also in tears, timidly gave Cerutti a steel watch which they had bought by subscription. They had had an intoxicating declaration of love engraved on the case, which, as Cerutti made certain at a glance, could easily pass for the declaration of an adoring woman; he slipped the watch in his fob and gave free rein to his feelings.

Benevolent autumn had come. When Cerutti plunged into the mist filling the narrow valleys on the far slope of Montgenèvre, he tasted perfect happiness. A sinister king ignorant of the use of the umbrella [4] was the absolute monarch of this haughty land. Here they knew how to live. At Suze he saw a head displayed in an iron cage

[4] Louis Philippe, the "bourgeois monarch" ruling in France at this period, was the first king to carry an umbrella.

in front of the charred walls of a house burned by the order of the police.

He had not been in Turin a week before a member of the liberal party claimed that he had uncovered a military plot. According to his testimony, twenty thousand people were to be massacred. About one hundred criminals were to be let out of prison to rush into the crowd armed with daggers and arouse the militia. The officers, warned in advance, would shout: "The liberals are murdering us" and would fire on the crowd.

The winter was bitter. With the king's money he bought a short fur cape (it would not have been possible to wear such a sumptuous garment in the streets of Paris). He was in Bologna during the blizzard which piled drifts as high as the third story of the houses on the Piazza Nettino. He spent his time with rich revolutionaries. He warmed his hands over Eleanora Regianini's chafing-dish. He met the French doctor Henri Misley, who had the title of "Professor of Street-fighting." He was often seen with Francesco Casale, Sigismondo Giberti, Orazzio Pedrazzi, and the sweet Giuditta Bellaria.

These people weren't *lovable*. And moreover, they took no risks. They were theoreticians. They drank coffee, smoked cigars, and flapped like flags.

Quite simply, he had to find out which of them would have the most brilliant idea.

In one of these drawing-rooms Cerutti was presented with an extremely curious pistol. It was the one which had been seized on Giuseppe Castello, who had been arrested in Ciro Menotti's house on the night of February third and fourth. On the barrel of the weapon was a hook with a spring attachment so that a bayonet could be fastened to it. This too was quite a brilliant idea.

At Cesena a company of young liberals armed and embellished with tricolor cockades marched up and down the boulevards of the town to the sound of a drum. In the evening, people in the streets sang the soldiers' chorus from Mercadante's *Donna Caritea:* "A glorious death is the most beautiful of fates." Only they had changed the words, and sang "patriotic" instead of "glorious." "When the people make a *lapsus* like that," Cerutti said to himself, "things are rolling."

This was a Lombard-Venetian affair. A very pretty business took place in Piedmont—a really first-class affair. "Here's where people know how to live," Cerutti repeated to himself. The yoke of the Bonnafous diligence which ran between Genoa and Turin broke on the steep descent near Novi and the coach hurtled from the top of the Rigoroso bridge into the torrent. The engineer, Lieutenant Colonel Rossignoli, the Genoese notary Sigimbosco, and Goisque the driver were killed on the spot.

At the end of a week the other travelers, all more or less badly wounded, testified that Goisque had often whipped the horses savagely while they were going downhill, that the colonel had tried to take a pistol out of his inside pocket, that Sigimbosco and the jolting of the carriage had prevented him, and that, moreover, everyone had been screaming. Only after the diligence had crashed on the rocks of the torrent had it been immensely quiet and calm.

Rossignoli had been carrying some papers. Undoubtedly they were swept away by the waters of the Bormida. A reward was promised to anyone who recovered them, the whole lot or just a few. For more than a month some kind of a wind tore loose the posters announcing the reward. Then this wind stopped. The new posters stayed calmly and silently glued to the walls of the police stations.

General Baron de Valtorren, the Austrian military attaché to the court of Charles Felix, was thrown by his horse in the streets of Turin. He killed himself on the spot. The crazed mare which had trampled her master was taken back to the stable with difficulty. The next day she had disappeared. Nothing but the marks of quantities of saliva remained on the litter of straw. Every road was searched for the horse.

Charles Felix reviewed the hussars on the Polygon. He feared that he looked like Louis XVI. He would have given anything to have Charles Albert's shrewmouse nose. For this reason he screwed up his eyes and pinched his lips: he thought that he was making his nose more pointed.

Four squadrons, absolute masters of their horses, were lined up immobile as statues. The young aristocrats who had bought their ranks had not been assigned to active duty. But they were there. They formed one detachment ranged in a square on the flank of the troops. Despite their youth (a few were scarcely sixteen), they did not move a hair.

The immobility of these young men impressed Charles Felix.

"Has learning to control their horses taught them to hit a target?" he asked the corporal.

He returned to Turin along echoing streets with the trumpets blaring the royal march behind him.

Cerutti was enjoying himself immensely. His homeland was so beautiful that he could find delight there without doing a thing. With the French or the English he always had to give his Piedmontese voluptuousness a little jolt. Here it did very well on its own. In a roundabout way he sent an enthusiastic letter to Sandro saying: "Come, you'll be worth a fortune here."

He was quick to develop the highest respect for the rich revolutionaries well-provided with leisure. Padrazzi went walking in a quilted pelisse, Eleanora sipped various infusions, Giuditta sprayed herself with violet perfume, but they all were experts in the art of self-induced fear.

He knew a little carpenter who left his house by a back door three times a week in the evening and went out into the woods. There he was king in command of five men. Armed with daggers, they roamed the roads throughout the night shouting: "Who's there?" This avid fortune-seeking moved Cerutti to tears. No one could understand better than he that an alternation between highways and carpentry was a fine mechanism for producing happiness.

Every workman smiled to himself, especially if his trade was nauseating like tanning or in disrepute like shoemaking. Never had honeymoons been longer. The young women widowed by executions wrung their hands on the public square and went home to give the polenta a good stir.

Messengers of the revolution traveled the highways in light carriages. All orders were given orally. Posts had been organized everywhere. Stable boys knew how to pronounce extremely difficult words distinctly in a low voice. A peddler of needles and threads had more men at his disposal than the prefect. The postilion of the diligence conferred with Princess Pio or Count Borromeo, who had recently been named Knight of the Golden Fleece by the Austrian emperor.

Everywhere people indulged in the study of physiognomy. Anyone with unusual features, or a strange air about him, anyone with moustaches, which had been prohibited, could not help being a carbonaro. Everyone risked passwords without obtaining any response, but not without fear.

Cerutti also saw that what would have terrified the Paris police left the Turin police cold.

"You want to avert a plot?" they said to him. "How will you know it's a plot if you avert it?"

"Then what the hell am I doing here?" exclaimed Cerutti.

"What do you mean—what the hell are you doing? It's your country, isn't it?"

Imagination reigned at the palace also; everyone was moved by nostalgic memories of illustrious misfortunes. A chill light slumbered in the long corridors of the north wing. A royal palace at the foot of mountains is always full of lamentations. The avenues of Turin, their perspectives extending out of sight, seemed to be forever deserted. Charles Felix trusted only the dragoons of the Aosta cavalry. He was afraid because he was no fool. His will to live was such that at the first sentence not concerned with himself words no longer had any meaning for him. He had once commuted a death sentence to a sentence to the galleys for life. Ever since then, an engineering-officer departed for Genoa each Saturday with the order to examine one by one the links of the chain which bound the convict to the ball.

Compromising papers were discovered in an inn on the Tende ridge. Doctor Anfossi and Giacomo Durando fled. Francesco Pastori's reading-room was closed. The schooner *Orient* left the port of Leghorn with numerous patriots from Umbria, the Marches, and Romagna on board. For four days the troops of the first corps of the Austrian army passed through Modena. There were three squadrons of hussars from Lichtenstein, a battalion of chasseurs belonging to the Empire, a Croat battalion, and a corps of pioneers.[5]

Charles Felix was said to be sick, having suffered a sudden heart attack or stroke. Cerutti asked for information at a small

[5] Engineering footsoldiers who precede the main body of the army to clear land, dig trenches, make roads, etc.

police station on the Piazza Emilio Philibert. "Yes, yes," he was told, "he had a fit of apoplexy." Then they talked of one thing and another. The fat sergeant liked this bourgeois so intent on the pursuit of happiness. The conversation turned to the most recent law-court decrees. No one had been condemned to death, but Fabrizzi and Ruffini were being investigated as was a certain Giovanni Battista whom no one knew from Adam, but who had escaped, it was suspected, from Ciro Menotti's [6] house despite the police cordon around it. And what had become of Ciro himself? They were still rummaging about searching for him. The day before in Modena the corpse of the pioneer Feritti, who had been killed in the attack on the Menotti house during the night of February 3, had been taken from the hospital of San Augustino. He had received all the honors due a hero fallen in the field of battle.

The next day the church bells rang very softly. King Charles Felix had had a bad night. It was the morning of March 28, and a rainy one. Protected by large blue umbrellas, women slipped along the small streets to Santa Teresa to pray. So much rain poured from the gutters that even the ladies were drenched to the skin. As they dripped, the large cotton umbrellas smelled of dog. The faithful, anxious for their own health, began to cough very energetically.

However, the next night Charles Felix's state improved, but his fever raged higher after dawn. About ten in the morning he requested ink and paper. He was thought to be delirious. He exploded in a sudden, crotchety fit of temper which made his eyes start out of his head, and with his hand violently pushed away Monsignore Zapone who wanted him to lie back on his pillows. At noon, Charles Felix signed a paper commuting all life sentences to hard labor for thirty years in the galleys.

Cerutti wanted to find out exactly what was up. He had heard any number of elaborate bedside scene stories. With binoculars he climbed the Santa Margerita hill as far as the pine grove which overlooked the queen's villa. In spite of a disagreeable wind off the Alps which blew the rain in his face, he could see that no one

[6] Ciro Menotti was one of the many liberals executed by Francis IV, the reactionary despot of Modena.

seemed to be inordinately anxious in the large drawing-rooms of the villa. He adjusted the binoculars so that he could see the north wing of the Royal Palace. Framed in a high window was a member of the Aosta cavalry, his bare saber in his hand, yawning, alone on guard in the long corridor.

However, Charles Felix had dysentery, and it was no joke. His valet came out for a glass of white wine in the dram-shop on the Piazza del' Palazzo near the guard house. Despite the spring rain still pouring down, he was in his shirt sleeves, and he didn't much like the cold wind off the Alps. He said that there was plenty to worry about; that things were not going well.

A parade of all the troops in Turin, Genoa, and Alessandria was ordered for the 6th of April. The King's fever was worse; his right side was paralyzed. In Turin Charles Albert, Prince Carignano, trotted at the head of the staff, in front of the lines of grenadier guards. After the ceremony he went to inspect the royal printing-press which had been moved from the ground floor of the Academy of Science to a new building specially built for it in the Via Zecca. A sestet was being printed in honor of the August Prince Savoy-Carignano. The last line praised the *"virtù dei genitori."*

Suddenly it turned hot as midsummer and Cerutti slept in the raw. One morning his landlady came into his room like a whirlwind. He somersaulted in the nick of time. Menotti had been arrested. He dressed as fast as possible and ran to the Piazza Emile Philibert. Yes (they said), he had been arrested in the marshes to the north of Mantua. At this very moment he was undoubtedly already on the road to Modena in a closed carriage escorted by twelve mounted dragoons and under the eye of a dragoon corporal and a light-infantry sergeant. In preparation, chains had been carried into the dungeon of the citadel, and the guard quadrupled. Double sentinels were to "sing out the hours," calling out to each other from post to post every ten minutes.

Cerutti knew Menotti only by the engravings which had been circulated after February 3. They obviously made him more handsome than in the flesh. But by public report he did have a small mouth and black eyes. Even if the drawing had romanticized his dark eyes and lovingly outlined his lips in the shape of a double cherry, surely behind those eyes there were wild ideas such as Cerutti loved.

Charles Felix was trying to die but his room was crowded with people and he didn't dare. He was obliged to wait until two in the morning. He was worn out. Finally, Turin went to sleep. Cardinal Zarelli tiptoed out of the bedroom. The Aosta cavalryman at the door was asleep on his feet, saber at his side. The cardinal tucked up his skirts and began to get his bearings in the corridors.

Prince Carignano arrived at two forty-five. He thought immediately of ordering the small bistro near the guard house opened. He waited until its lamps were lighted and himself went to speak to the sergeant, saying: "Let your men go get something to drink." He had taken care to put on boots that did not creak. No one had as yet begun the corpse's toilet. There was no one in the bedchamber but subordinates. Charles Albert Savoy-Carignano closed the dead man's eyes and kissed his hand. In a low voice he ordered several basins which were still under the armchairs to be emptied and also that the troops of the garrison be assembled at six in the morning on the parade ground to swear allegiance. He wrote a note in Tuscan to his wife telling her to get the children ready and come to the palace with them and the first lot of baggage right away.

Cerutti's feelings were stormy. He had heard several speeches by revolutionary agents. On the banks of the streams in the Mincio marshes (where Menotti had been arrested), lawyers and booksellers came each evening while the boatmen pitched camp to speak to them of the future. They always spoke of utilitarianism, never of dreams of greatness. He hated such prosaic schemes. What would become of the world when men who chose the red of their *chechias* [7] with such taste calculated their rights so stingily?

The military tribunal at Modena had condemned Menotti to be hanged. On May 26, 1831, at 7:30 in the morning, he was escorted out onto the Corso dell Citadelle with Vincente Borelli. Two companies of grenadiers had been lined up facing the gibbet, and in the neighboring streets, two companies of Hungarians. Menotti and Borelli, unfettered, came into the midst of this military panoply

[7] The soft red cap worn by Zouaves and various other African regiments.

like two good little shopkeepers out strolling in the cool of the day. They were so natural and obliging throughout the rest of the ceremony that everyone wondered whether the noose was not just their cup of tea. Nothing could have been more ridiculous than the movement of the soldiers returning to the barracks.

An apologetic pamphlet appeared concerning their death which spoke of outraged virtue, castrated liberty (very Piedmontese, this), the martyrdom of a just man: the father of his country, the enemy of slavery, and a monument of gratitude. This brochure was very successful in France.

Sandro found nourishment in it. He was starved. He was developing along the same lines as Cerutti. He did not like the Socialists. As he was a perfect horseman (he was even somewhat acquainted with the veterinary's art), he directed the Paris carriage stables. He had a little daughter, five years old. During her pregnancy Caroline had demanded from him and easily obtained a marriage in the church.

Sandro shivered with pleasure on going to church secretly one misty November evening. His child and his wife, who remained passionate despite the sacraments, committed him more strongly than ever to play with fire in a "Roman" manner. He had developed a bit of a paunch and wore fine sideburns on either side of his clean-shaven face. He madly loved the line by Brutus Alfieri (*"He has might; I have right."*) which had been put under Menotti's portrait. He wished he were in Piedmont. (He had never received Cerutti's letter.) Theoreticians talked of collective happiness. For his little girl, who already knew how to say such pretty things, Sandro dreamed of happiness far exceeding that which the rest of the world could expect. He had grown accustomed to Caroline. Liberty consisted in the right to stick to his habits. M. Considerant's [8] approach was wrong. Sandro remembered that he had been left for dead on a mountain road. Contented with his wife and his charming child, he was proud enough to feel himself a full-fledged revolutionary who had been over the jumps and had come through victorious, more capable therefore of looking after his own happiness than a propagandist in Condé-sur-Vesgres. Being around

[8] French philosopher and economist, 1803–93.

horses and beautiful feminine clients had given him a very handsome, domineering air. He looked at himself confidently in mirrors.
He saw in his face the mark of a soul which could combine great
deeds with his daughter's future and Caroline's passion.

Cerutti dabbled on the fringes of other "Roman" gatherings.
The well-born revolutionaries were having a bit of a rest. They
said that the new king was on their side and they were discover-
ing the pleasure of going to a ball for dancing. The people, who go
on believing in a king if at all possible, still went about the woods
crying: "Who's there?" They needed melodrama to keep them
from feeling somewhat alone. The character of Brutus made solitude bearable and even exalting.

One evening on the road to Saluces a diligence passed Cerutti.
A package was thrown from the roof to his feet. It consisted of
four or five pounds of proclamations.

*"Fettered in the bosom of corruption which despotism en-
genders,"* they declared, *"at the point of the foreign bayonet which
menaces my every heartbeat, I have always cried unto the listening nations, from the depth of prison or the height of the scaffold:
Italy lives still; she is reborn; her greatness will come forth pure
as gold from the crucible after her three hundred years' slavery.
We believe the moment rapidly approaches, my friends. The hour
of emancipation will ring out. To free national thought from local
prejudices; to bring future progress out of the first hesitant steps of
the present: these are the aims of the Italian National Army . . ."*

Its date line was London and it was signed: *In the name of the
Army: Bondino: president.*

Cerutti had a connoisseur's admiration for the scornful style.
"What fun to make a revolution with one's eyes wide open and
without the preconceived notions which make it impossible to be
witty! Savone must be dead," he said to himself, "or else the fat
man is even stronger than I thought."

Savone had died in the South Kensington Hospital. At Colbeck
House Bondino had met a young Scottish woman of the thin, pale
variety. Miss Learmonth was from Fort Augustus; she took care
of the old man's papers. In the solitude of Caledonia the pretty but
frail Miss Learmonth had gotten an exalted idea of human fear and
lust for power. She was so satisfied as secretary to the revolution

that she sometimes desired a caress or two. Bondino, whom Savone, drowsy with age, had come to call "Fido," one day rested his hand, well fed with the blood of roast lamb, on the secretary's wheat-colored neck. Miss Learmonth was undone and grateful; it was as if his hand had branded the nape of her neck. Savone was eighty-three years old. Although he didn't deserve hell-fire, she allowed him to think that the end had come at the first congestion of his lungs. Moreover, he was no longer in full possession of his senses and, before going to the hospital, he not only wept but went so far as to sob. The young woman was sweet but firm.

She had some right to Colbeck House. At the first sign of age Savone, true man of the South that he was, had enjoyed the presence of this scarcely phosphorescent pen-shaft. He had signed papers to keep her at his side. She was very happy to be able to give something to Bondino in this way. Abandoning the cause of liberty for several months, he drew on his letters of credit and visited various attorneys. In the end he stepped into the dead man's shoes and founded the Italian National Army. He thought the title over a long time before adopting it. He loved the violent, commanding word *army*. He did not want to have to argue, and he satisfied Miss Learmonth's demanding heart into the bargain.

Sandro, admirably supported by Caroline, who wanted to get her husband away from the temptations of Paris, requested and obtained the position of inspector on the three diligence lines which his company controlled: Reims via Soissons, Paris-Bourges, and Paris-Amiens. At the Marseille-le-petit stop he found a package of proclamations in a bundle of straw. It was the end of September and an enormous red sun was setting beneath infinitely empty fields. Sandro returned home with a tragedy staged against a wide horizon completely planned in his head. Caroline had completely forgotten her origins and become a bourgeoise, but a Piedmontese bourgeoise. She had great affection for the "Army." It was a rival her jealousy could come to terms with. Besides, her little girl, who would soon be eleven years old, would do very well on horseback beside her mother and father. She imagined the entire family covered with gold lace and hailed in every town.

Sandro had applied for the job of inspector with the ulterior motive of getting easily to regions where there were numerous groups of exiles. The jacobins of 1820, wild boars of a sort that were quite rare or else set in their ways, were no longer in the running. In the last years of Charles Felix's reign, the army, the magistracy, the bourgeoisie, and the trembling Piedmontese aristocracy had shown the entire revolutionary spectrum. Some had been hanged, others shot; a few, in favor with the people, had died accidental deaths. Those who were aware of the temperament of their race had taken refuge abroad. They chose out-of-the-way regions, preferably heavily forested. The moaning of tall trees in the wind reminded them of their homeland and gave them easy access to the sweet melancholy they had stayed alive to enjoy.

They all had a little money; they helped each other out quite generously. Most of them were young people living on the outskirts of egotism and mainly intent on cutting a fine figure. Those of good family were subsidized in roundabout ways. Former officers found means of getting into military circles or canteens, hired themselves out to fencing schools, or posed as mystery men and great lovers. The professional men rubbed along on very little, begged arrogantly, and discoursed in provincial drawing-rooms in return for food, coffee, and an occasional cigar. A few artisans found work. Everyone walked about in the vicinity of his lodgings to give himself the illusion of activity and to be seen by the largest possible number of people, without which it is useless to be virtuous or even to have a good reputation.

They valued Sandro highly because he could get them a warm inside seat in a diligence rather than a spot on the roof. As for his "Roman" side, it dazzled them. To imagine themselves united and free of pity lent an exquisite flavor to their situation. Sandro wrote a love-letter to Bondino. He received congratulations in exchange and ten pounds of proclamations. A postscript from Miss Learmonth indicated that if he wanted to do something at the moment, he could send an international money order for the equivalent of a shilling, that is to say, two francs, fifty centimes. Sandro gathered some cash and sent the equivalent of half a guinea. He received an immediate reply naming him sergeant in the Italian National Army. His rank was certified by a card bearing a round seal with the portrait of Menotti on it and in the exergue the motto: "Liberty for Italy and death to tyrants."

Sandro took his position seriously. First he organized the Senlis region where the nearby forest constantly murmuring helped him a great deal. He got the name of a cobbler in Crépy-en-Valois from a soldier friend he had met at one of the meetings. The cobbler, protected by his new profession and a French-sounding name, was actually a young attorney from Mondovi who had helped steal cartridges and gunpowder from the arsenal at Genoa. He recruited about ten farm workers in the region. This company of the Army met in the fields two nights a week for very serious discussions. International money orders were sent to Colbeck House from various posts in Paris, Reims and Amiens, Avallon, and occasionally even from towns like Vic-sur-Aisne or villages bordering streams like Merteuil—in this case disguised by orders for fishing-equipment.

His honesty and faith unquestioned, Sandro kept small sums in his own possession. The far away Bondino was only God; Sandro experienced the full ardor of a disinterested priest. There were expenses to be paid. Agents had to be sent into the regions not reached by the public transportation lines inspected by the "sergeant." At the end of a year Sandro had formed brigades of more than two thousand "Romans." Their names (to escape any police investigation) had simply been written in the diligence-office register on even-numbered lines, starting with the second line of each page. Three hundred guineas had been sent to London.

Sandro received a brief note from Miss Learmonth. She congratulated him. But M. Bondino's plans called for still greater devotion and sacrifice. Certain recruiting-sergeants, in regions which had been considered impoverished, had sent five hundred guineas in the same length of time. It was astonishing that a sum so much smaller had been sent by a region full of exiles which, moreover, surrounded Paris. M. Bondino did not bother himself with these details, but she, the daughter of a country which knew the price of the liberty it had lost at Culloden, felt obliged to speak up in his place. The sergeant would also understand that the Army had to be organized on a solid administrative basis. She was sending under separate cover a number of documents which he would be kind enough to fill out, date, and sign before a notary as soon as possible.

He did not receive the documents through the mail. One evening while he was drinking his soup at the "Coq d'Or" at Mareuil-sur-Matz a very well-dressed bourgeois couple beside him at table asked for some information on the connections between carriages. They wanted to go to Rennes, but in such a way that they would be able to stop for two hours in Sens. Sandro could not give them an answer on the spot. "Pray excuse me, inspector," said the woman, "we're interrupting your dinner. We would be delighted if you would accept a small rum in our room after we've had our coffee."

They welcomed him with open arms. Quite literally they embraced. After making sure that no one was listening in the corridor, the man began to talk Piedmontese and revealed a card showing that he was a lieutenant in the Army. He had just come from England, where he had been sent for orders and he had a small package for Sandro. And instructions as well. The package contained sheets entitled: "Weekly Accounting, Monthly Review, and Capital Balance."

The lieutenant and his wife had a very open look in their eyes and were ready to die for the Army. They were living in the Agen region. All the departments south of the Garonne were full of exiles who had come back from Spain. There were seven thousand adherents of the Army down there, that is to say seven thousand soldiers. Colbeck House had named a commander, two captains, and four lieutenants. The lieutenant was in charge of liaison. He spoke enthusiastically of Bondino, of Harrington Gardens, and of the house in London where before the door of the study in which he had received his instructions two uniformed soldiers already stood guard. On his way he had visited the Vendée and the part of Brittany where groups with as many as fifteen hundred men had been recruited, organized, and given their full complement of officers as well. And he had only seen the towns and villages on the diligence route. He knew, however, that all was well in the departments bordering Switzerland and in the Argonne, where, according to a captain he had met at a staff conference, the forest had attracted many Piedmontese and kept them in a state of exaltation.

He explained to Sandro how to manage accounts. The latter objected. He did not want to mark the names of his comrades on lists which could fall into the hands of the police, later to make posters in Turin. The lieutenant reassured him. He did not have to list names, but only amounts. These should be carefully listed, totaled, catalogued and sent off, no longer to Colbeck House, but to the French Spice Society, 211 Old Brompton Road, as if for regular purchases of merchandise. He would receive payment after the accounts had been checked.

Sandro admitted very frankly that he had been accumulating a cache to cover unforeseen expenses which his salary might not be able to meet. Obviously he should not have done as he had. But such an action had been foreseen: he would receive a commission of five percent on all receipts.

At about the same period, Cerutti, on a business trip through Lombardy and Veneto, the Parma States and the Riviera, met gatherings of the Army almost everywhere. Souls had been stirred by remarkable bits of literature. He admired their efficacy. These statements were obviously composed by someone with a thorough knowledge of the human heart—a very shrewd knowledge which touched with precision secret springs, usually drowned deep in shadows. They could only be the work of a man accustomed to the exercise of a caustic intelligence and who knew how to generalize from his own faults. So Cerutti thought. He was pleased to have understood Bondino at a glance. Since he had begun to work with the police of the Piedmontese government, Cerutti had lost the need to be smitten with love. Now he cared for men only as works of art in a museum. When he learned that funds were being transferred, all he said to himself was that it would be interesting to go observe this phenomenon more closely.

Sandro, somewhat irritated by the five percent, asked what all this money was used for. He received the answer that it was used to buy arms and that sizeable orders had already been placed with Sheffield armorers. At this the two men embraced, sobbing. The woman, who was French and very pretty, watched these effusions with some degree of scorn.

After this meeting at Mereuil, Sandro dreamed of a lieutenant's stripes. He sent good accounts to London, written up in a fine hand and carefully totaled by Caroline. He organized groups in Soissons,

Fismes, Orléans, Avallon, the Gâtinais woods, the plain of the Beauce, the forest of Othe, the valley of the Vesle, and as far as the plateau of Langres. He collected over five thousand guineas a year. Finally, he refused the five percent and paid for all extra expenses out of his own purse. His conduct was highly appreciated at Colbeck House. He received an adjutant's stripes, and Miss Learmonth, in a short, but very affectionate note, charged him with a secret mission.

Whereas the Army was most successful in Gascony, almost no one had been recruited in Provence. Marseille was the scene of agitation by conflicting interests. Bondino suspected the presence of jealous men putting their own interests, their own egotistical need for agitation ahead of service to the cause. The adjutant's commission was as follows: he would choose an intelligent, devoted young bachelor from among his men and send him to observe on the spot exactly what was going on. The observer also had to be armed with the seventeen proclamations published to date. He had to distribute them in the most efficacious fashion—that is to say, give them one by one to people whom a bit of previous conversation had prepared for such a reading. A gross of each of the seventeen proclamations would be sent to the adjutant in return for four shillings and sixpence, or five francs, seventy-five centimes in French money. Whomever they chose and sent as emissary should be scrupulously honest (they besought the adjutant to be careful on this score). He would take with him form no. 4 of the weekly financial situation and would send one to Colbeck House every Saturday, dated, signed, and notarized—even if blank. Cash, as usual, to the Spice Society.

Sandro chose the shoemaker from Crépy-en-Valois. He had assumed the name of Vasseur, but his real name was Doria. Provided with a travel permit valid as far as Avignon, dressed from head to foot by his brothers-in-arms, and snug in a rough woolen cape belonging to Sandro, Doria left Paris in the beginning of November.

Leaving his shoemaking shop in midstream did not make him angry. In reality his assistant, a simple-minded cripple accustomed to servitude, did all the work. Doria had chosen a trade absolutely unrelated to his former profession of attorney as a good way of keeping hidden. For the same reason he had chosen the

name of Vasseur. He had not liked any of the consequences of
the cartridge affair at the arsenal in Genoa. This affair had been
staged by five or six comrades who had been urging each other on
in conversations extending over a period of a year. To prove to
themselves that they were worth their salt, they had already attacked
and rifled the Coni-Mondovi mail coach. The carriage contained
nothing but mail sacks defended by the coachman, who preferred
a share in the loot. This expedition netted them four thousand lire
which they did not know what to do with. The cronies finally
bought silk handkerchiefs and red neckties with what they had
made off the attack, and as it was difficult to wear such badges in
Mondovi or the environs, they went to Genoa to strut about.

Doria had left the law school after a scant two years; he looked
up his friends. People were beginning once again to talk openly—
especially about a quantity of cartridge packages being stored for
the time being in a wing of the Arsenal that was easy to get into.
A master-sailmaker who was a member gave them the information.
They decided to attack the Arsenal. They formed five groups of
ten, scaled the walls, gagged the first sentinels and almost noiselessly reached the wing designated. Everything had gone very
well. It had not been any more difficult than the mail coach. By
dint of talking about courage, Doria had acquired a certain
amount of it. Reasoning danger away, he gave the best possible
proof of it. He declared that cartridges without guns were good for
nothing. This appeared so just that three groups were left to move
out the cartridges while the fourth group followed Doria in search
of guns. Unluckily they fell upon a sentinel who defended himself
like a lion, bayonet in hand, slitting stomachs right and left while
Doria, bewildered, shouted at him: "Look out, sir, look out!"

They left two dead and one wounded man, who described the
plot in order to get some laudanum as he was suffering a great
deal.

Doria was returning at top speed to Mondovi when at the
Millesimo relay he learned that his friends had been arrested. He
left the highway and slipped into France by out-of-the-way roads
above Coni. The military governor of Genoa was afraid and had
little time at his disposal. His council of war was merciless: he

condemned to death fifteen of the twenty-three accused; they were shot.

Doria was afraid for ten years with that fear which thinking increases each day. He traveled as far as he could from the frontier of Savoy. He was on his way to the shores of the Channel when he found Crépy-en-Valois, a little village with the life snuffed out of it, just what he was looking for.

But he was now much more at his ease up front in the Lyon diligence, protected by a travel permit in good order, a bourgeois redingote, a relatively well-filled purse, and a salesman's official card for the Spice Company. His courage got the upper hand. However, he was not so bold on reaching Avignon as to go right up to the Pont Bompas where the police inspected baggage. He bought a seat in a rickety old coach going to Apt and stayed on the right bank of the Durance. On the Saturday after leaving Paris he mailed in his first inventory, blank.

He frittered away two days on the banks of a small torrent of tumbling yellow water where he met an ocher merchant who was about to leave to visit his customers before the winter. For twenty sous he shared this man's buggy as far as Manosque.

This little town surrounded by elms and enjoying the last of the fine weather pleased him. He had eighty-three francs left. He lazed around for some time. In a café where he drank hot toddies every morning for a sou, he met a young Piedmontese cobbler. He took pleasure in puzzling him by talking shop in spite of his redingote, which, for Manosque, was very beautiful.

The shoemaker invited him to supper. He was called Giuseppe (in any case he revealed no more than his first name) and was somewhere around twenty-two or twenty-three years old. He had gone into exile following a military conspiracy of the 3rd Hussars of Turin. His wife, Lavinia, was extremely pretty.

Doria did not get far with her. The lovely Piedmontese girl was just a little younger than her husband, with manners much above her station in life. As she also gave evidence of the solid plebeian good sense which never bothers with politeness when defending itself, Doria thought that she must have been in service in some aristocratic household. She was molded more gracefully than most mountain people. Doria treated her gallantly, with nothing but honorable intentions, and scarcely noticed her while talking Army with her husband. He was used to workmen's wives who, especially when you take an interest in their dreams, play the fifth wheel. She knew her place, but when Doria began to lie (quite skillfully), her eyes, a beautiful mint green and sparkling, looked at him very critically. She continued to look at him unpleasantly, and Doria began to feel so uncomfortable lying that in the end he could not argue his points.

But in Giuseppe he had to do with a man both inspired and calculating, apparently delighted with the Army, obviously for many reasons other than those Doria gave him. There was something in the back of the shoemaker's mind. He gave his wife a meaningful look. Finally, he not only bought a complete series of Bondino's seventeen proclamations, but also contributed a gold louis *to buy weapons*. Doria was flabbergasted.

The gold louis kept running through his head. A shoemaker doesn't have a gold louis. In the state into which his first thoughts plunged him he almost fled. He imagined that there was a secret police, gifted with intelligence, what's more. He was so upset that it took a whole night before he finally realized that the whole reason the police were police was so they wouldn't have to distribute gold louis. He returned to the little toddy café. "I'm the only Piedmontese in the region for the time being," Giuseppe said to him. "In a little while a friend of mine, my foster brother, will come to join me. I don't know when, for he has to finish up something at home. Until he comes I can speak for him. He's a gentleman; but when I speak, he listens to me. He's a colonel in the 3rd hussars; I told you about that plot of theirs; it would have come off if it hadn't been for a traitor. I was his orderly, but we have been soul mates since we were born. This Army delights us. On one condition however: my friend's a colonel and he wants to enter it as a general at least."

Giuseppe said that even though he was a shoemaker it was politics that interested him; this was the way to great things; the army was just a part of politics. As he had grown bored here all alone for the past year, he had contacted the socialists of the neighborhood. The French were certainly preparing something very dif-

ferent from 1830. The revolutionaries from Manosque and the
surrounding region were not the absolute cream, but their very lack
of backbone meant they could lend a hand to anything. And this
was very important. There are jobs which neither you nor I would
want to do and which it's a good idea therefore to get done by
others. Finally, he gave a complete course in political revolution
in a way which the attorney admired.

"I'll keep the gold louis," Doria said to himself. He took care,
however, to make a new inventory, blank. But after thinking it
over, he destroyed this blank inventory and made another showing
five francs so that he could tell London about this strange shoemaker. Also he told himself that such an ardent man, with the proclamations now in his hands, could deal directly with Bondino.

But he had to move on to Marseille. Giuseppe advised against
the direct public-coach service. It was very carefully checked all
along the route and especially at the Mirabeau bridge. He introduced Doria to a needle and thread peddler who was off on his
little horse to visit his clientele in the Var. This good, easy-going
giant of a man agreed to transport Doria as far as Saint-Maximin,
whence he could reach Marseille by the Sainte-Beaume route,
which was not watched.

Nevertheless, at Saint-Maximin things looked very bad. Driven
by a sea wind, huge clouds from Corsica hung over the mountain
where snow was falling. The peddler, who knew the roads, urged
Doria to go around by Toulon. The messenger was not put out by
these troubles. He was in no hurry. He was not looking forward to
the difficulties awaiting him in Marseille; he was beating around
the bush. He took the Brignoles carriage and at Brignoles, the
Solliès-Pont carriage. The two nags were slowly drawing this
rickety old coach along a deep, very dark ravine when he was
awakened from his drowsing by a cracking noise, a harsh shock,
and shouts. The axle had broken and they were teetering dangerously over the torrent.

It was only two in the afternoon but the black sky, the mountain
slopes encroaching on one another, and the mist on the torrent were
hastening the day to a sinister dusk. The leaves of the thick ilex
forest pattered in the heavy rain. Doria walked two leagues on
foot to a small village lost among the tall, bare trees. Even in

ordinary weather the place was probably entirely deserted. A zinc Virgin more than three meters high, erected on the summit of a knoll, protected the houses.

In this desert, where even the peasants needed the tall Virgin, Doria's affection for the Army revived. After so many years of shoemaking in Crépy-en-Valois, he had, since leaving Paris, enjoyed the trip pretty much for its own sake. He reproached himself for the fifteen francs he had pocketed in Manosque. He feared hellfire all night. He had taken an old corn mattress for his bed, but could not sleep. He heard the rain raging outside. Before him moved revolutionaries, men like Giuseppe, deprived of guns and some with their stomachs slit open. He even thought that the axle had broken to warn him against the evil path he had started down.

As soon as morning came he felt zealous and ready to be off. It was no longer raining, but the sky was still dark; the axle was not mended and he could still hear the hammer striking the anvil. His host, an old lascar who ran the bistro, told him about a man from Piedmont who had been in the neighborhood for almost ten years. He lived at a Carthusian monastery a league away in the woods.

Doria, like everyone converted by remorse, wanted to put his zeal into operation immediately. He asked the man to point out the road to him and then, his pockets stuffed with the seventeen proclamations, he departed, already much pacified by the fact that he was confronting the threatening weather in the name of right.

He found the large dead buildings of the Chartreuse in a steep valley. Every half hour a bell rang. The little fields, crofts, and orchards were deserted. Doria met an old monk going to empty a sack of bran into the fishpond. He asked him where the Piedmontese was living. The man was deaf, and asked to have the question repeated three times. Finally, he pointed out a little house under some pines.

Doria was expecting some kind of a woodcutter. It was Charles Asinari. He was still mentioned from time to time in Turin. At Law School, Doria had heard a rather reactionary professor, a disciple of Joseph de Maistre, say that Asinari was the only one of the conspirators who was genuinely out of his head, and that thanks to this sickness, he had been able to preserve some virtue in the midst of so many base deeds. This certificate of good conduct from an opponent gave a special luster to the man.

He needed it. Cleanliness, but of the soul alone, is the hermit's first consideration; Asinari's appearance was far from delectable. His white moustache was red below his nostrils; he obviously prized tobacco. In '21 he had been thirty years old; he was a man of over fifty now.

Asinari read the first words of the first proclamation and skipped to the signature. He shouted at the name of Bondino. "He was a thief," he stammered. He shouted this word again and again, strangling on it each time. It kept his blackened mouth wide open in his beard. Doria was too happy with his rediscovered zeal; he replied sharply. The two men came to blows and finally the messenger of the army cleared out, slinking away with his necktie torn loose.

Asinari was subject to violent fits of temper. He could not bear to be contradicted or to meet with an obstacle. His twenty years' exile had been full of thorns. He had disembarked at Golfe-Juan without a sou. More than seasickness, disgust at finding himself among fugitives, all well-heeled, had made him ask to be put ashore. In port he had found the French population philosophic, untouched by the suffering in Piedmont, and very inclined to consider that anyone with a gold louis, even stamped with a Prince of Savoy, was a fine fellow. He had to swallow his speeches and his endless arguments and work for a living—work hard, for philosophers are stern taskmasters. He fished for sardines to earn a little something. He put an infinite amount of time into it. The corpulent men of the Mediterranean with whom he had come to roost did not understand this urgency. They did not expect anything from either Heaven or the King, and death, they said, always comes soon enough. According to this line of reasoning, they never had to pay up.

Asinari silenced his scruples. One hot day they left him the job of selling ten kilos of very fine fish. He pocketed the money and cleared out. It was summer. He met teams of workers who rented themselves out for the harvest; he signed up with one of them. He wintered on small farms for room and board. He lived well but was unhappy because he wanted to use his ideas. One evening on his way to set snares in some woods, he met a kind of huntress Diana. She was an old lady, but she was carrying a rifle. At first their conversation was most vehement. Asinari saw in it a chance for a little fun: he spun fine phrases. The locals hardly knew how to say yes or no, or at least lacked fire, whereas he put a great deal of fire into the expression of his ideas, now that he at last had a chance. Diana, quite harshly but congenially, invited him to the château. There he found an old M. de . . . , a very sweet man, who busied himself with geology and works of charity. Asinari was engaged to guard the woods. From woodsman he rose to game-keeper, which he enjoyed because he could have long conversations on liberal matters with his employer almost every evening. The geologist was a fine man with a good head on his shoulders according to everyone including his wife. He favored the liberty of the people as well. Every year he went on a retreat to a Chartreuse in the neighborhood. He took Asinari with him.

The steep slopes exercised an almost irresistible attraction on Asinari's romantic heart. He would have done anything to stay there. He didn't have to do much. The geologist had nothing more to say about liberty and the Carthusians were glad to please him.

Asinari was given a cabin under the pines outside the monastery buildings. He became the assistant porter. He received five sous a day which were rounded out to five francs a month. He was fed at the gate. Aside from scything the meadows, splitting wood, and cleaning the carp which from time to time were fished out of the large fishpond with a landing-net, he could devote himself entirely to his ideas. Moreover, in this desert of rocks and trees, the least idea was exquisite.

He drew up plans, organized Piedmont, won battles, and drove the merchants out of the temple. His superior in the hierarchy was an old soldier with a wooden leg. Their minds were in tune. As they were both in perfect health thanks to the good fresh air and frugal nourishment, they argued, fought, and made up over mere nothings with the greatest interest. Twice a week a little goatherd brought them each a liter of wine. Climbing to the summits over-hanging the vale, Asinari could make out on the other side the roads of Toulon and, farther off, the cliffs of La Ciotat and Cap Canaille. Asinari went to Toulon fixe or six times a year by short cuts through the mountains. There he met Livornese sailors who sailed schooners bringing pozzuolana to the Arsenal. But he didn't mince words, and the sailors were sons of the sea. He returned each time with half his beard torn out.

After Doria's flight, he read Bondino's seventeen proclamations with care. He was thunderstruck. He said to himself: "Through the sixth proclamation Bondino speaks only in generalities, but using words which hit home harder and harder. From the seventh on, he gets into the meat of the subject and talks about the distribution of ranks and pay. Finally, describing the people in order to declare his love for them, he states his ideas. He says: 'The people will be without pity.' "

Doria reached Marseille two days later. His scuffle with the old man still gave him the shakes. His understanding heightened by fear, he quickly saw why the Piedmontese of the town were uninterested in the Army. They were sitting on sacks of gold. They had started to play the finance game and with romantic hearts had adopted such strange rules that they grew richer at every turn. The oldest exiles (those of 1821, many were left on this coast), had married well-set-up Marseille girls, had taken root, and now lived on family properties on Périer hill, the Saint-Barnabas heights, and the Aygalades. They headed shiploading, brewing, carting, merchandising, and storage companies; succeeded fathers-in-law with good incomes; drove carriages, smoked cigars, settled and, up to a certain point, were satiated. After the first few years, the exiles no longer found many well-born heiresses to marry. The killing had been made. But an Italian revolutionary, with eyes like burning coals, always cut a dashing figure in the *Matrimonio*. They found a place for themselves among the shopkeepers where there were also large fortunes to be had. After 1830, those who went into exile were chiefly young men who had lost their manners and seemed to be very set in their ideas. These might not have succeeded at all. Quite a number of them had been wandering along quays for some time. They seemed either to do nothing at all or to kill themselves at idiotic jobs, but their real work was nostalgia. Prosperous enterprises, splendid families (it was odd that the Piedmontese exiles had many daughters and very few sons—and those few were always misshapen and sickly or died young, whereas the numerous daughters were sumptuous), and estates overlooking the sea did not afford happiness. One Italian oath overheard in the street ruined everything. Without speeches, decrees, armed force, with nothing but a little homesickness, Italian unity existed in the heart of the associations of Piedmontese, Lombards, Tuscans, Romagnards, and Neapolitans organized in every quarter of the city and in every suburb, uniting all walks of life. The exiles came to weep on one another's shoulders, to insult each other, and to live *alla Turca*.

Doria understood immediately how this worked. He had a flash of genius. (He was never mistaken when, to understand others, he strove to understand himself.) He made them read the last proclamation—the most violent, which spoke of pitiless vengeance—first. The first ones—which spoke of greatness, respect, the fatherland and which even said: "May good men help us with their tranquil energy; may the people trust in us as we trust them; love and blessing upon all those who gather round our flag."—followed easily. If they had not cost five sous and been included in the price of the whole set, they would have been useless.

Doria sold a considerable number of proclamation no. 17; indeed, all that he had. He reached a point where he did not know how to make out the weekly inventory. Should he tell Bondino that it had been his own decision not to sell the first sixteen proclamations? He understood that if he did this he would run into an author's vanity. But on the other hand how was he to keep the wolf from the door on eloquent prose? Necessity made him ingenious. He went quite simply and placed an order with a printer in Marseille. He swore to himself that it was not until later that he saw in this an easy way to make money for himself.

Money which he was wise enough in any case to share with Colbeck House. He couldn't keep London ignorant of his success. Every week he sent long lists of those who had enrolled and opposite certain names often inscribed sums of as much as a hundred francs! After three months he had sent off the equivalent of six hundred guineas, and the ranks of the Army had swollen by more than two thousand men.

Doria outfitted himself from head to foot, set up offices, on the rue Longue-des-Capucins, and had a copper plaque engraved with the name of the French Spice Society for the door. Director General Carlo Doria hired three Piedmontese employees, set up house and formed the habit of dining every evening at the "Café Riche." As he felt increasingly sure of his ground, he asked his table companions (all successful Piedmontese) what kind of a wife would be suitable in his situation. He made it clear that his only purpose was to hide the true state of his heart from the police.

He had had proclamation no. 18 printed, composed of a little of Bondino's first seven, a little of the other nine, especially anything that told how ranks could be acquired, and of the entire seventeenth. This one he sold for ten sous, for his own profit, for all good work deserves to be repaid.

It was wildly successful. The fair sex spoke of nothing but the gold lace which one could "win" in this Army. In the "Café Riche," Doria gave himself the rank of lieutenant colonel. Among the gentlemen who sat at Doria's table and talked gravely of liberty until one in the morning, was Luigi Balluppi, of the firm of Balluppi, Testanière and Co., importers of oranges, dates, and dried figs. He was nearly sixty, born in Genoa, renowned for always playing safe, and father of three daughters who had obstinately refused to study the piano or to paint watercolors. He had representatives in London. He asked them for information about Colbeck House. It was excellent. The young Englishman commissioned with the investigation had been received by Miss Learmonth's footman and then by Miss Learmonth herself. He had sipped fine tea before a very good coke fire. M. Bondino had for years now been a member of one of the most exclusive London clubs. There was only one blot on the picture: two soldiers in eccentric uniforms, that is to say, black and red, with feathered hats, stood guard outside the smoking-room of the master of the house.

This could be explained by the fact that Bondino was first of all an Italian and second of all was supposed to be the head of a movement for the liberation of Italy. All the same, as a member of the Adelphi Club, he was without a doubt a gentleman.

Detailed financial information followed. From a business point of view Colbeck House deserved the highest credit rating even by English standards.

Luigi Balluppi spent two hours each evening in his daughters' room. Pinned to the wall with hair curlers was a large map of Piedmont that these passionate creatures studied like a lover's face. Marseille is nothing but one big business district, and there is nothing but business in a Piedmontese heart, especially when the Piedmontese has succeeded in business. But living in a land where bare mountains plunged into the sea, they missed the aspen thickets and palings of poplars which in the plain between Turin and Novara mask the view and give no more than a glimpse of what's to come. Luigi Balluppi and his daughters had come to hate the Testanière firm and business in general. Their fortune, made from the sale of oranges, only gave them a right to egotistical, salacious sons-in-law and husbands. They wouldn't have a word to say to these mock pashas in a hundred years. Tracing the roads of Piedmont with their fingers on the map, the romantic young women and the man in the prime of life, who had not even needed to speak to his accountant for the last twenty years, galloped into towns, down the long avenues of Turin, and into adventure. They had spun a thousand dreams. But for some time they had felt that running their fingers over the roads was not enough. Doria was flashing his gold lace every evening at the "Café Riche."

Through the intermediary of his London agents, Balluppi gave a thousand guineas directly to Bondino. No sooner had he done so than, contrasting this sum with his desires, he considered it insufficient and telegraphed an order to double it.

These two payments, one right after the other, struck Colbeck House like a thunderbolt. Since his flight from the ricocheting Austrian bullets, Bondino had felt no strong emotions. Now he had attained glory. Without Miss Learmonth he would have made a fool of himself. He wanted to have a splendid general's commission engraved and sprinkled with powdered gold. This metal so intoxicated him that he thought it a good idea to give up a little dust from it. The Scottish woman had more control. "There's only one general," she said, "and that's you." She added, perhaps without irony, "And you don't need a commission." Bondino came down to earth. He sent off a commander's commission with an affectionate but restrained letter. Balluppi sent a mixed bag of a reply. He thanked him, but asked him how much he would have to pay to get "a rank at least equal to M. Doria's."

Exactly sixteen days later on a mistral-iced afternoon, a hackney carriage crossed the little village of Aygalades and drew up at the gate of the Testanière estate. Balluppi had been smoking cigar after cigar in front of the tall drawing-room window, looking out at the snow squalls. Above the tormented trees of the park, night was falling on the sea. Undoubtedly the visitor was arrogant and rotund in a way which impressed the servants. They announced him immediately without inquiring his name. Balluppi saw a man enter, corpulent but light as a soap bubble; a woman, blonder than is possible in Marseille, followed him: Bondino and Miss Learmonth.

Who was this Doria who had liberally raised his own rank, and higher than a commander at that? His name was indeed inscribed in the roll book, but as a simple soldier, a subordinate employee in charge of propaganda. Was this the same man by any chance? He feared it was. "I did not hesitate to undertake this long journey to illuminate this affair," Bondino continued, "and to cut out this infection. Our holy cause cannot permit the least failure of discipline."

This firm attitude impressed Balluppi. A languishing dusk made enthusiasm easy. Refreshments were served which, despite the proximity of the Mediterranean, found favor with Miss Learmonth. Things went further. The footman slipped a ratteen jacket over his striped vest; the master of the house unostentatiously gave the names of the horses he wanted harnessed to the break; an hour and a half later, three dock-workers, bareheaded, unloaded in the front hall vestibule the two cabin trunks which Bondino had had sent to the Athens hotel. Following a series of naïvely theatrical exits and entrances (because they thought Bondino's head, beautiful despite his corpulence, resembled that of a somewhat cruel tribune), the three Misses Balluppi had personally arranged the "blue" suite. This consisted of two rooms separated by a small drawing-room on the third floor, all on the front of the house with a beautiful view, unfortunately hidden now in the night except for the winking lights of the buoys on the bay of Estaque.

Doria was more difficult. The evening of his installation in the "blue" suite, Bondino had reached several useful conclusions about the opulence of the house which he had just entered. The next day he saw a small private semaphore signalling-device at the foot of the park giving orders to a felucca returning from Spain. A merchant with such an instrument at his disposal was surely worth more than the two thousand guineas. Bondino thus met Doria with the firm intention of getting him out of the way as quickly as possible.

But the office on the rue Longue-des-Capucins had had time to become a small capital. Recent fortune had gone to Doria's head only to make him find ways of keeping it. His former training as an attorney had made it possible for him to help exiles more or less ensnarled in police red tape. He got on with the police commissioners; his hail-fellow-well-met garrulity pleased the authorities; he could straighten out almost any problem. The young men he had helped were all between twenty and thirty; they had hardly sown their wild oats in small local revolutionary engagements and were dying to be taken seriously.

Bondino thought that he had only to appear. He was confronted by men who bluntly questioned his rights and demanded from whom and why he held them. He went home very discouraged.

"They don't know me," he said.

"Make yourself known," said Miss Learmonth.

This was easy enough to say. "It's easy to do," she said.

They reexamined Doria's dossier from the beginning and came upon the letter he had written from Manosque after his meeting with a certain Giuseppe. It was quite a specific description of a man of ideas.

"Get in touch with this man," said the Scottish woman.

The night was clear. Bondino went to the window and looked out at the slim silhouette of the semaphore at the end of the park. There was a gold mine here. A mad desire to exploit it in peace gave him a flash of genius. He remembered the dock-workers who had been bareheaded and had refused his tip. He had always known you could do nothing without the people. He understood that Balluppi had the knack. He went to awaken him.

"I've always hesitated to name a lieutenant colonel," he said. "It's such a high rank. But I'm naming you one. Now, let's get to work."

And they had a council of war immediately.

As soon as dawn had come, the footman galloped off to reserve two seats in the next day's diligence. Miss Learmonth had brought about the adoption of this democratic method of transportation. They made quite a troupe on the road. Two dockers went with them. Two were enough, the Scottish woman had said, if they were advanced in their thinking and had plenty of physical strength. They arrived at the rendezvous dressed in their Sunday best and were very gallant with the ladies.

Giuseppe was delighted to have company and to argue with gentlemen who outbid each other. He said to himself: "What's Angelo doing in Piedmont? He could be boss here." He gave a generous and spirited political lecture. The ladies and gentlemen were seated around the cobbler's bench and watched him sewing with waxed shoemaker's thread.

"My dear fellow," said Bondino, "you talk like a book. Dine with me at the Hôtel de Versailles. With your charming wife, of course."

While the party were washing their hands in a swan-necked fountain in the vestibule of the hotel, Bondino had time to ask Miss Learmonth what she thought of this individual.

"He's Narcissus," she said.

They went into a private room where they could speak freely about the fatherland and the Army.

"I am nothing myself," said Giuseppe, "but I have a foster brother. He is a colonel in the hussars and the son of a duchess. We were raised together. We have never been separated until now. He's still in Piedmont while I'm in France. I say "still" because he stayed there only to accomplish certain actions which we agree about and which will finally force him to go into exile. Foreseeing these events, he made me desert; I've been waiting for him almost a year. I can speak openly about this in front of my wife: she too was in the household of this duchess whom I mentioned to you and where we were all united like the fingers of a hand. I have never seen a better or more handsome man than my brother. Everyone loves him and wherever he goes, I follow. Your Army interests me because it doesn't belong to the King of Sardinia and because it may belong to tomorrow's King of Italy, that is, to the people installed on the throne of their tyrants. But someone's got to lead a charge, someone who knows about hand-to-hand combat.

They separated good friends.

"I was not mistaken," said Miss Learmonth to Bondino. "He wants all the power, *through an intermediary*. This will be very handy: we can play off both at once."

"I don't much like this hussar colonel," said Bondino.

"Don't forget," she said, "that he has given this little shoemaker a lot of leeway. He's in the habit of it."

Bondino loved broad certainties. Back in Marseille he asked more questions.

"We're obliged to believe what he tells us," Miss Learmonth replied. "Perhaps this colonel doesn't exist at all. I thought of this but I prefer to believe he does exist. It's so natural that the son of the wet nurse finds his own image in the aristocrat with whom he has shared his milk."

Doria got wind of the trip to Manosque. He made the trip himself. Giuseppe, who had closed his accounts, laughed in his face and did not conceal that he took him for a simpleton.

Back in Marseille, Doria was obliged to defend himself before the police. He was shown an anonymous letter in which he was accused of being the leader of a band which in the dark before dawn plundered dairies. He blew up. Then he was asked to tell what he had been doing on certain days at certain very precise hours. He was in difficulty. He was tempted to testify that these hours and these specific days corresponded not only to the hours and days he had a rendezvous with the wife of a corset merchant in the rue de Rome, but more especially to the timetable of certain planning sessions with very faithful friends. He could not speak openly of anything. He was given to understand that this was regrettable and was released, but they didn't open the door more than a crack.

Doria began to tiptoe about stiff-legged like a cat on hot coals. He lost the wife of the corset merchant and the faithful friends whom he had been looking at bug-eyed, not breathing a word.

"When we're rid of Doria, which will not be long now," said Bondino, "I don't think we should return to Colbeck House. This "blue" suite is very agreeable. The French are preparing something which will have repercussions in Piedmont. If need be, we can get there in two days, and thanks to Balluppi's carriages it will be a comfortable journey, which is most important to me. There's even a great deal I can direct from here."

"I agree with you," said Miss Learmonth. "Banking is easy here. I'm used to the French method, I lose less time than the natives; everything will be as it was in London. I can easily maintain here the secure home away from home which is the principal weapon of important men like you. The only thing we have left to settle is that order for daggers we put in at Sheffield which is still up in the air. But that's only a matter of a simple correspondence about knives and, at the outside, if there are secret orders to give, a quick trip that I can make alone, both ways in twenty days at the most. What became of your project for ordering a few guns?"

"I'm abandoning it," said Bondino. "I promised arms. One cannot decently claim that daggers twenty-six centimeters long, exclusive of the guard, are not arms."

The attacks on the dairymen continued. Even the one who supplied Balluppi with milk, and who had his farm and stables at Aygalades, bordering the Testanière estate, was rifled. Doria was summoned before the commissioner. He had been denounced again. But this time he had a perfect alibi. They seemed to be waiting for it. "I do not formally recognize the gentleman," said the dairyman. This statement contained an adverb not ordinarily used by dairymen. The fact that Doria pointed it out annoyed the commissioner, who had passed over the word without batting an eyelash.

Curiously enough, the trade newspapers like the *Courier Maritime* and the *Gazette du Port* took an interest in the affair of the dairies. They gave prominent notice that a certain Carlo Doria, *without profession,* had twice been summoned by police. Strictly speaking, this was quite true.

Another newspaper, or more exactly a sheet, but very widely circulated in the cafes, *Le Furet avant-courier,* unveiled a fantastic story. A lady called Jacquier had settled in Marseille with her husband, her mother, and her sister on a sumptuous estate in La Valentine. In confidence, she claimed that she and her husband were the Duke and Duchess de Gregorio, of Spanish origin, formerly living in Naples, and intimate friends of ex-Prince Carignano, now King of Sardinia. According to her, this liberal King, a friend of the revolution and of liberty, was in the habit of crossing the frontier in plain clothes and coming to stroll in the large park of more than two hundred evergreen oaks which covered the slopes of La Valentine, with the idea of meeting the Carbonari chiefs on neutral, friendly territory and devising with them ways of making history without shedding too much blood. The lady (Jacquier) stated that she had sacrificed the bulk of her fortune to this end. In conclusion, she asked for money.

Bondino's indignation was so prompt to show itself that it seemed to spurt out of an inkwell prepared in advance. Miss Learmonth would have preferred to have let a few days go by quietly. "It's past the time for dallying," he said. (He was in a hurry to be done with Doria.) "Let it be understood that the next time round we clamp down. I get our man."

Accordingly, the very next day after *Le Furet* published the "fantastic" story, four columns of an extremely well-composed declaration signed by Bondino appeared on the first page. It explained in careful but serious tones the meaning of "liberty," "King of Sardinia," and "spilled blood." This heroic thrust, which still covered the rear guard, necessarily fired the enthusiasm both of those who did not know how to write and of those who did. A man who could construct such a monument to good sense and generosity in the heat of a retort should be praised to the skies. The same day, at 23 rue Sainte, next door to the sorting-warehouses of the Etablissements Balluppi, Testanière et Cie, a passageway was opened. It led, by a modest flight of stairs which any workman could imagine in his own house, to a room on the first floor. There, on a table of unfinished wood and in an extremely virile atmosphere of honest poverty, men were enrolled in the Italian National Army. You had only to write your name on a list; not a centime was demanded. The 23 rue Sainte address was secret. Dockers and draymen passed it by word of mouth. Savage young men came there, so pale that it seemed as if they had lived underground until that very moment, when the pavement of Marseille had sweated them forth.

Every evening a council of war took place in the bedrooms of the young ladies. They were no longer shy.

"Ask your friends at the Prefecture if we can go there," Bondino told Balluppi. "Emphasize the fact that we are doing them a service. They'll always know where they are with us; we keep our lists up to date."

Doria was summoned once more. This time he had caught wind of it. He cleaned out his cash boxes and lit out on foot without telling his creditors. His corpse was found stabbed and half naked in the hills of Allauch. He had been robbed down to his trousers and his shoes. "Exit Doria," said Bondino.

"But don't let yourself be taken in a second time," replied Miss Learmonth.

The man called Giuseppe was invited. He saw the table of unfinished wood at work. He thought it imprudent to register his name on a piece of paper. He said nothing to anyone and watched ten or so very thin young men enroll. He was then conducted to the Testanière estate. After crossing the port suburbs, which were very dirty, and the quarters where people lived in rabbit hutches, the road climbed a low hill gilded by the sun and by reflections from the sea. They passed gardens where exotic trees and extravagant flowers had been acclimatized.

Bondino wanted to receive Giuseppe in a simple style. "That's all wrong," said Miss Learmonth. "We must have a table set with crystal and a pheasant dinner. We would have left this house long ago if we had been entertained in a simple style. Everyone is cut of the same cloth. You've got to give a man more than a bowl of soup if you expect him to knock himself out for you."

At first Giuseppe was intimidated by the sparkling table. Then he said to himself: "The flat silver is very heavy and probably solid silver, but using a hammer has strengthened my wrist. All in all, workmen are very well prepared for this life." He spoke lovingly of Angelo.

That evening when they were alone, Bondino asked: "Should this colonel really exist, what could one make of him?"

"A straw man," said Miss Learmonth.

"A straw man . . . ?" Giuseppe exclaimed later after Bondino had *frankly* explained the situation to him (the cholera was at its height, Marseille smelt terrible). "You don't know him!"

He described Angelo's character more precisely.

"But *you* know him to the core," said Bondino.

He left Giuseppe with this thought and with new images of crystal and opulence which, "whatever one may say, were a good protection against death, judging by the security of the Balluppi house on its hill purified by the sea wind."

". . . like my own pocket," Giuseppe said to himself in Manosque while packing his trunk to leave for Piedmont. The cholera was waning.

He found Angelo in Turin. He nearly told him everything. Bondino's influence was very great in Carbonari circles. People said: "He's an organizer." The outlaws dreamed of laws. The lyricism of seventeen proclamations to which, moreover, an eighteenth (this one authentic), a nineteenth, and especially a twentieth which spoke of sacrifice (in the singular, which gave the word grandeur) compensated for whatever banal dryness the word "organizer" might suggest to very humid hearts and eyes. But Angelo, theoretically still sought by the police, thought he would put his comrades in danger and no longer went to the *ventes* [9] or even the little gatherings. Among the haughty he passed for proud. But never among common people, who regarded him as a comrade and even loved him. . . .

"But if we had to care for the common man as we care for ourselves," Giuseppe, jealous of all his prerogatives, said to himself, "we'd never be done. It's all right to put your arm around him, but only to push him aside."

Reading between the lines with the greatest finesse, he delighted in Bondino's statements. His cunning introduced him to the delights of vanity.

Five or six years of plotting on the Piazza San Carlo and on the "La Brenta" estate *organized* Giuseppe's heart in relation to this vanity.

"I must keep a foot in each camp," he said to himself. And on

[9] *Ventes* is the French for *vendite* (or sales) as the Carbonari lodges were called.

remorseful evenings: "It's the same camp when all is said and done."

"How are you doing?" Bondino wrote him. "I have confidence in you and I've named you adjutant general. Don't forget, this gives you the right to write me directly, by-passing the hierarchy. Always remember, the destiny of a straw man is to be burned. All that is asked of him then is to make a lot of smoke which can be seen from a distance and under cover of which we can get to work. Don't bother yourself with sentimentality."

This last sentence was a mistake on Miss Learmonth's part. She did not know the Mediterranean soul. Giuseppe had already gone far beyond her or even Bondino. The evocation of the funeral pyre aroused many emotions in him.

The year 1847 raised the emotional temperature of all Piedmont to a fever. Everywhere chains rattled. This noise of rattling chains exalted hearts, especially small ones. The big ones began the game. They turned their attention to the pawn of Milan around Christmas.

Toward the end of February 1848, Angelo fenced with Giuseppe several times.

"You're jumpy," he said, "let's embrace. A while back I parried one of your thrusts a bit fast, but that's because you let yourself be carried away; and if I hadn't fought as seriously as you deserve, you would have skewered me. Save your skewering for later. They say that our friends in Milan are going to drive out the Austrians. I'm off. Come with me. I'm leaving tomorrow."

CHAPTER TWO

Come on now," said Angelo.

"You put me in a curious position," said Giuseppe. "You don't give a damn: you're a noble; but I know that a revolution is a long process."

They were wearing long overcoats and walking up the Via San Paolo in the rain. It was ten in the evening.

They passed low houses and garden walls. The street lamps were very far apart and dimmed by the rain. An alley crossed the street at right angles. Fifty meters to the left up this alley stood a few soldiers and local officials. The sentry was coughing in his box. Through the window of the garrison red dolmans could be seen moving under the lamp.

"It's light infantry this evening," said Giuseppe. "They'd be thrilled to get their hands on a hussar colonel. It occurs to me that they won't much like our Calabrese hats. Their orders must have mentioned Milan."

"Who goes there?" said the sentinel.

Immediately afterwards he cried: "On guard!" peacefully but in a very firm voice.

Angelo and Giuseppe concealed themselves in the recess of a *porte cochère*.

Angelo was moved by the fragrance of the gardens. "The soldiers won't fire," he said to himself. "The moment for sweeping ideas has not yet come."

Leaning on the main door, he felt that the little door set in it was not latched and that it yielded. He took a step backward and entered a wide passage which smelled of sprouting onions and harness. Giuseppe slipped in after him.

Angelo knocked on a door framed by a ray of light. It was opened immediately. Moving his head he indicated the street where the soldiers were making quite a bit of noise.

"Come in," said the man.

Beneath the lamp was a young, very pretty girl holding her breath and staring wide-eyed.

"I'm on my way to Milan," said Angelo.

"Let me hang up your coats," said the man. "I have the right to friends. Besides the soldiers never come in here. My daughter intimidates them."

The soldiers were talking loudly in the street.

"They're nervous," said the man. "A while ago some fellow with a razor came by. He cut off a sergeant's hand. The news is good, so everyone is a bit excited."

Angelo looked at the girl who was catching her breath. "There is the face that should be on the coins of a republic," he said to himself.

"Do you know whether Count Battaglia has been freed?" asked the man.

"We know nothing," said Giuseppe," but maybe you know more being right in the pocket of a garrison."

"Nothing to crow about," said the man.

"And for a Sardinian florin, maybe in gold, what would you know?"

"A lot, Monsieur, especially if, as you say, it's in gold."

"The key out into the fields for example?"

"Easy. I know where it hangs."

"Show it to us," said Giuseppe, lining up three pieces of silver on the table. "We'll see whether we'll buy the rest."

"I have a pigsty a hundred meters away beyond the walls and a little private road running from the end of my garden. Take a pail in each hand. I'll go with you with the lantern. All open and above board. There's nothing to stop me from getting help to feed the pigs."

"You get a lot of help?"

"Quite a lot."

"The soldiers know that people pass through your property?"

"They keep their eyes shut. I have friends."

"I don't much like friends who change every evening."

"I keep their palms greased."

"I prefer to do the greasing," said Giuseppe. "Give me a florin for him," he said to Angelo, "and come on."

"Wait till I light the lantern."

"Don't bother," said Giuseppe. "You've got your money. No more games; now that things are businesslike you can let us walk through the garrison."

"The fact is, it's much more simple," said the man, "and you risk nothing. Say that you saw me, but keep quiet about the florin. The tariff is two *écus* and I take almost no cut. Pardon me for mentioning the pails," he said accompanying them to the *porte cochère*. "Have a good revolution, gentlemen!"

"That frightened young girl was the very image of the people," Angelo said to himself, "but the man was the kind of rascal that always gets the better of me."

"I kept you out of the pigsty," said Giuseppe. "I lead you through the soldiers and I spend your money liberally. You must love me this evening."

"That's enough out of you," said Angelo. "I'm thinking of that young girl. Our liberty is holding its breath just as she was."

"She was holding her breath the way people recane chairs," said Giuseppe. "Because that's the way they earn their living."

They got through the barrier with no difficulty after speaking briefly to the sentry.

The road ran up hill. The lights of Turin shone on the left. They made out the phosphorescent oval of the Royal Palace and the pediment of the Opera House shaped like a three-cornered policeman's hat. The tumultuous February sky rumbled and echoed above the vast countryside.

They had been walking through the hills for more than an hour and had already seen, above the ilex trees, the two or three lights of a village when they heard the roll of quite a heavy carriage advancing at a walk.

"What time is it?"

Angelo sounded the chime on his watch.

"It's probably the old Cirié coach. It's late. And why is it going at a walk?"

By the light of its lantern they could see that the seat was empty. There was no coachman. Giuseppe stopped the horses.

No travelers in the carriage and no baggage on the roof. Inside Angelo found a woman's umbrella and an ostler's long-haired top hat.

"A nice job," said Giuseppe. "Let's not stay around this neighborhood. Is that crossroads of yours a long way off?"

"If those are the lights of Venaria we see, the road should go down hill from here on and the crossroads is at the bottom. But perhaps the lights are from the big farm at Chinsano."

"Farms aren't lighted at midnight these days. Come on."

The rain had stopped. The wind seemed to want to come up. In gusts it brought the noise of cascades from the slope of a distant mountain.

The crossroads was at the very bottom of the slope. The road was muddy. First it wound along a flooding stream. It climbed a slope, passed near a silent farm, and slipped into a vale where poplars whispered. It climbed once more and ran along a ridge overlooking a valley from which rose the noises of a sleeping town. The wind made the iron shop-signs tremble and the weather vanes grate. The road twisted and turned through a pine forest like a snake. It came out on high ground where the frozen dust of clouds scudded along level with the ground. It threaded an almost straight line across a plateau, through box and juniper, fragrant in the damp air. It smelled also of flint, and Giuseppe's nailed boots struck sparks at almost every step.

To the north there was a rumbling, a sign of the bitter north wind blowing on the heights.

A belfry chimed three in the morning peacefully. The road turned along the walls of a washhouse and entered a village, passing under a lighted lantern.

"Rocca?"

Angelo and Giuseppe slowed their paces.

"No," said Angelo. "Telleto."

It was a handsome village with beautiful houses, marble stoops, big polished doors, bronze knockers, old torch-sockets, and rings thick as an arm for hitching horses. The streets were paved with cobbles in a rosette design. Although it was night, the odor of coal fires lingered in the streets.

"There must be at least three policemen here."

"Five," said Angelo. "And they can't be bought off."

They turned onto a street that smelled of goats. Angelo scaled a wall and dropped very gently into a kitchen garden.

"I like it when you're flashy," said Giuseppe.

They crossed a plot of cabbages, jumped a brook, went along a cress bed, and after walking in a well-watered meadow, picked up the road again as it entered an ilex forest.

Here it was completely dark.

After a league, the road came out of the woods, crossed a highway, and began to go uphill once more.

They heard a river tumbling stones along its course. A trotting horse, saddle lantern lighted, pranced down the road below, heading north.

Strong wind squalls blew on the heights. The leaves of the box trees crackled like oil in a frying pan.

Cocks were crowing but the night was still black when Angelo felt before him the presence of a large breathing expanse of water.

The road ran down toward the splashing water and the murmuring reeds. A duck quacked. A bird rose heavily sending up a rending cry. A wave struck a rock. Then silence returned.

Angelo left the road. He made his way through the alders, crawling up a bank, climbed a fir grove and reached a wall. He followed it a moment to the right and went through a breach.

Dawn outlined the sharp summits of the mountains.

Angelo advanced easily through the thickets and came out on a park walk.

They reached a house. The rising sun lighted a wide, sad facade.

Angelo went to the outbuildings and knocked on a door. He was completely astonished to sense his happiness—that is to say, suddenly he felt far less happy when the door opened onto an odor of a wood fire and of coffee grounds being heated. An old man appeared wearing old-fashioned clothes with his gray hair in a thin cue.

"What have you come for so early?" he said.

"To see your master."

"He doesn't much need you these days. He does nothing but torment himself."

"Come on, give us some coffee," said Angelo. "We've come from Turin and we've been walking since yesterday evening."

"Come in then," said the old man. "Might as well be killed for a sheep as a goat. You weren't in Polissena by any chance?"

"No," said Angelo, "I have no connection with the Marquis's sister. You know me; I've been here twice before."

"Ah yes, I see," said the old man, "I remember; I didn't mind you. Anyway, I was thinking to myself that you must be pretty honest to bother to ask for the coffee. But fortify yourself with patience; my pot has the better of me; it doesn't want to boil. And I've got the fires of hell going under it. In any case, it'll be a while yet before M. le Marquis rings."

Angelo found the fire very agreeable.

"May we take off our boots?" said Giuseppe.

"If you're not afraid to walk on your socks," said the old man, "nothing's stopping you. That's what I keep saying to M. le Marquis about what's going on."

"Are we the first?" asked Angelo.

"Why? Would you want to be second? When I saw you, standing there in the dawn, I said to myself: 'Here are a couple more who are going to see what they can get out of us.' "

"He still has difficulty with his sister?"

"He has difficulty with everyone. We get it from every side. When it's not his father, it's his sister; when it's not his sister it's the rest of you."

"We're not asking for anything," Angelo said dryly.

"Yes, you are: coffee. And it's not boiling. You've all been acting like badgers, in the last few days. All underground, coming and going in the woods. Cards on the table, that's what I say. That's my opinion. In my day, that's how you got ahead. What are you people up to now?"

"Nothing," said Giuseppe. "We're not up to anything, grandfather. We want a place in the sun."

"That's normal, my boy. But why not make some sunshine instead of trying to make a place?"

The coffee had decided to boil. The old fellow went to get an old strainer and began to pour the coffee through, a little at a time. He put three bowls and a small loaf of bread on the table. He opened the drawer and brought out iron spoons and a package of cassonade.[1]

"You city people have refined sugar."

"I like cassonade very much," said Angelo, "especially this morning. My friend and I were raised together. When we had a sou, we went to buy cassonade. We stole lumps from each other's mouth."

"That's a nice thing to remember," said the old man. "Don't tell it to everyone. Go on and take off your boots," he said to Angelo. "I've still got a few minutes; I'll clean the mud off them for you. Put on these clogs. And you too," he said to Giuseppe, "why don't you put on these. I make them for myself out of the old graybeard's trousers. He dropped everything when he got stuck on his progeny. It pleases his vanity to have a son-in-law who's a Knight of the Order. I'd use him to wipe myself with."

The boots were muddy up to the strap.

"I still have some polish, and with a little elbow grease, you just wait," he said, speaking to himself.

Angelo had never drunk better coffee. He spread his big toes in the clogs. He began to enjoy a mixture of fatigue and well-being. "Here we are on our way," he said to himself, "and so far there's nothing to it. Although I must say I don't remember ever being as happy as tonight; especially when we took the crossroads and Giuseppe, not knowing the road, had to trust me; even the buffoonery at the barrier. I was a bit sad about that Jesuitical gardener, but that's because I'm inclined to give credit to everyone. It's a simple matter of a florin. When more than a florin is needed, there'll always be time for me to fly into a temper. But the game's got to be worth the candle. I'll never be able to collect ears. I could very easily have coldly cut off the swineherd's right in front of his

[1] Sugar which has been refined only once.

daughter for trying to make me carry buckets. But what would I do with them now? I'm never as free as when I have nothing to reproach myself for."

He was unaware of his naïveté. He looked lovingly at the somber kitchen, very dilapidated and even dirty, while warming himself before the hearth overflowing with old ashes.

"Do you have something to smoke?" he asked.

"I have some cigars," said Giuseppe, "but they're wet."

"If you're men to appreciate a little Tuscan one—contraband—," said the old valet, "I have just the thing for you."

"If that doesn't deprive you . . ."

"Everything deprives you," he said, "but I'm used to it."

A bell sounded from the end of long corridors.

"There he is," he said. "Orderly as a sheet of music paper."

But he passed the cigars politely.

"Don't hurry. You have easily enough time to smoke two inches. He'll drink his coffee, and then he'll want me to give him a few finishing touches so that he's presentable. He's no Romeo any more."

The old valet came down again after more than a quarter of an hour. He had exchanged his velvet jacket for a short livery coat.

"He's waiting for you," he said. "And you'll do well to put your boots back on. Not that we're sticklers for form, but appearances must be kept up."

The house was immense and dilapidated. Just to cross the hall to the foot of the stairs was a military expedition. The marble steps rose in an exquisite progression but had obviously not been swept for over a month.

In spite of what the valet had said, Count Pesaro was very dignified even in the morning. He was lying in a large curtained bed, his head and shoulders slightly raised. A torn shawl covered his shoulders; the sheets, pillowcases, and piqué cover were not of the cleanest, but he was clean-shaven and powdered and had outlined his moustache with a very black *niger*.

He greeted Angelo and Giuseppe with a long sentence in which exaggerated compliments counterbalanced a certain irritation.

"You find me in great pain; I'm nearly an imbecile now," he said.

His mouth belied his eyes which, because they were blue, seemed very candid at first; but certain glances, especially out of the corner of the eye, were not entirely at rest either. He succeeded, however, through a certain carriage of the head and a very appealing warm voice in giving nobility to what in others would have been the marks of a base hypocrisy.

He was the first to speak of the unusual animation, as he called it, of the forests during the past two days. That very night there had been a din on the lake. Yes, on this little lake not even a league long, three quarters of which belonged to him, as only three hectares belonged to the municipality of Candia, and the ownership of the rest was precisely the principal cause of the suit which his sister Polixene was bringing against him. In fact, people had been out on it in boats, shouting to one another; ridiculous, since it was so small they could have walked round it on foot.

"And why? I'm asking you! Surely, coming from Turin, you must have news? What's going on?"

"What everyone knows," said Angelo.

"Tell me what everyone knows, and tell it to me at length, I beg you. I adore knowing what everyone knows."

"Two weeks ago the Austrians had a conference in Milan; the Viceroy, Marshal Radetzky, and Count Spaus. You knew this?"

"I know nothing. The nerves in my brain have suffered in such a way that I know nothing. I imagine . . ."

"Everyone knows what I've just told you. What's less well known," said Angelo, "is that various ministries were not represented at this conference: neither the Vatican, nor Naples, Tuscany, Parma, or Modena. This is significant."

The Count closed his eyes, but he had prudently made his mouth disappear beneath his moustache. He opened his eyes once more.

"What I admire," he said, "is the certainty of your information."

"There are women in the story," said Angelo.

"Then go on," said the Count. "I hate women. They are capable of anything; but you said significant: in what way significant?"

"Count Hübner [2] arrived last Saturday in Milan," said Angelo. "That very evening he spent with an individual whom there is no

[2] Joseph Alexander Hübner (1811–92), Austrian diplomat; Metternich's special envoy to Milan in 1848.

reason to distrust, that is to say, someone who is renowned for spreading secrets as soon as they have been confided in her. She is only told those which people want spread, I imagine. Count Hübner said seriously: 'We must be prepared for intervention. If we can avoid it, so much the better, since Louis Philippe's government can create dangers about which I have no illusions. All the same, if necessary, it will take place. M. Guizot knows what we have resolved.' "

"And who is this person who is so discreet?" asked the Count after an instant of silence.

Angelo did not answer.

"Would you do me a small service?" said the Count. "Over there on my table are some little blistering-plasters of Burgundian pitch. Be good enough to give me one. I want to put one on my left temple. My neuralgia is starting up again."

Angelo went in search of the blistering-plasters. A large red-wax seal with the arms of the Ministry of Police and Justice was spread on the back of an envelope, right under his hand.

"You're there to be seen," Angelo said to himself. "Well, I've seen you."

"I am no longer anything but a pariah, an automaton, a powerless expiatory victim of divine wrath," said the Count. "They put cupping-glasses on me, compresses, patches. All these remedies make me advance one step toward health or death, God alone knows which! But where were we? With the words Count Hübner wanted to let fall on good ears, if I understand correctly. And what is Piedmont doing? This nocturnal racketing about in the woods and on my lake?"

"Playing a malicious game, at least the King is. He's waiting for things to cool off."

"Piedmont may be our country," said the Count, "but it's a puppet show. Every good Piedmontese dreams of putting on a dazzling uniform. I've never known whether you went back into uniform after your return from France."

"No. I didn't."

"Your escapade was pardoned, however."

"I don't care for the word *escapade* or the word *pardon*," Angelo replied dryly.

"I'd be delighted to apologize," said the Count hurriedly. "That's not what I meant."

"But that's what you said," thought Angelo while the Count used his most appealing intonations to coat the pills. "I know too why you spoke of puppets and brilliant uniforms, and I was wrong to bite; but beware: I learn fast."

"It is I who apologize," he said trying to round out his sentences. "I want you to know whom you're dealing with right away. Our two conversations in January did not give you a sufficiently clear idea of me, I see now. And I fear I didn't show the feelings which inclined me toward you sufficiently to assure you of the total abnegation which your courageous articles in *Young Italy* determined in me. For me, as for many other young men, you became a counselor and a kind of venerated flag. At a time when we're very probably about to see some action, I can even understand that you would call upon certain competent sources to get information about me. Even if these sources belong to the adversary. The intelligence rules all, and as you were trying to make me understand a minute ago, Piedmont is not intelligent. Nor am I, for that matter.

"I returned from France. Since then I have lived with my mother, north of Novara, where she has an estate. I did not mix with Turin society. And, I read newspapers."

"Oh, that's fine," said the Count. "That's very fine. But what makes you say that we are probably about to see some action?"

"The events on Wednesday in Pavia and Padua."

"Padua is very far away," said the Count.

"I know," said Giuseppe, "I've just come from there with the mail coach at top speed."

"And you crossed the frontier without incident?"

"Not a one."

"I don't know which is the most to be admired," said the Count, "what we might call the free and easy intelligence of the Austrians, or your luck."

"I make my luck," said Giuseppe.

"Unless events call for special guards at the frontier," said the Count.

"Judge for yourself: they can be summed up in a word," said

Angelo. "Seven students were killed by sabers in the Café Pedrocchi. But you will be far more interested in the *motives* for this house-cleaning: two Croat soldiers had been stabbed and covered with filth right in the street; they were officers, and their swords were found broken and thrown in a trash can."

"All that matters," said the Count, "is for us to stay friends. I hope you got some coffee. Do you want bread and cheese? I'm very poor, but there's always bread and cheese. In reality, I'm one of the people. And you say that in Pavia . . . That's hitting nearer home. I was awkward before, and I fear I would be so again if I repeated my excuses. Anyway, let's talk about Pavia. It's right next door."

"It was an officer in Pavia, too," said Angelo. "He was in the street. He was watching the funeral procession of a good fellow who had died a supposedly natural death. He took off his hat and was immediately crowned with a bucket of excrement. He drew his saber. Five dead, one being the officer. Kicked to death. He was Lieutenant Ferenzi, of the Ginlay regiment."

"These are sad events indeed," said the Count, "about which you unfortunately seem well informed. Let us understand one another," he added after a brief silence. "What do you want from me?"

"Nothing," said Angelo.

The mouth stopped being sly and tried to smile.

"You drive a hard bargain," it said almost without moving.

"And probably an unjust one," said Angelo.

"I don't intend to catch the stick you're holding out to me," said the Count.

"If you knew me better, you would know that I never hold out a stick," said Angelo. "Another man might, but I always feel like throwing myself in the water to save what I prize, or at least taking it in my arms."

"Let us say that you hardly prize me."

"Accordingly, I'm going to ask something very simple of you," said Angelo. "We're alone; no one can hear you and we swear by all that we hold most sacred never to reveal anything, even at the stake. Would you tell us both, in as low a voice as you please, that you love us? That would be enough."

"Ah," said the Count, "what I couldn't do if I had the time! But I'm always running after time! Let's save it. Let's stop speaking Piedmontese. I lived in London with Bondino. There's a country where they know how to do business, and all because they have a language suited to it. You don't want to tell me the name of the person in whom Count Hübner took care to confide?"

"Names are necessary only in police reports," said Angelo.

"Now we're getting to the point," he said to himself.

"You refer undoubtedly to the letter on the table? Admit that I did not conceal it. I have drawers just like anyone else, I could have hidden it. A word with any one of the boys from the village below and you would learn that very polite police officers often call on me, and everyone in Turin knows that my uncle Roberto Gerolamo is secretary general in the Ministry of the Interior."

"I told you that the forests in my part of the country make it unnecessary for me to spend my time in drawing-rooms," said Angelo.

"This has nothing to do with drawing-rooms, it's common knowledge, like the news you brought me. Except the bit about Pavia and Padua. There is only one thing you haven't spoken of: ambition."

"I have none."

"I'm not talking about yours. That's the last thing you need. I mean our King's."

"That too is common knowledge."

"Then why do you want me to say I'll go against the grain? I continue to speak frankly. Pavia and Padua aside, is it not because events are still too recent for you to know what's behind them? Although I'm in a position to tell you right now that they haven't changed a thing and, moreover, that they were foreseen and undoubtedly provoked. You still believe in the *spontaneous* wrath of the people! But why should I say that I love you? Pavia and Padua aside. There's no hurry. The victims have been buried, I imagine? They won't stink, will they? We have time. Was it the first time you saw a corpse?"

"No," said Angelo.

"You're sentimental?"

"Sometimes I wonder," said Angelo without the slightest irony.

"You confront me with my newspaper articles. Newspaper articles are excellent. I'm not speaking of mine, although I'm not trying to run them down. Remember what I'm about to tell you. You were too young twenty years ago. Right in the middle of the Ramorino fiasco when he was counting on six thousand men in two days and had fifteen a week later, three of whom were liberated convicts, Mazzini launched the proclamation: 'Whereas the moment of combat has come, etc., around the banner of the insurrection, etc., which a spontaneous glorious manifestation, etc. We decree the insurrection. Let the citizens take up arms as best they can. We will sound the tocsin, etc. signed: Joseph Mazzini, Amédée Melegori, and your servant.' Two hours later our fifteen good fellows had gone home."

"You advise us to return to Turin?"

"I never give advice and I never tell anyone that I love him. How can you tell if you love? But I know a highly-placed gentleman who would be very interested in the name of the party who knows Count Hübner so intimately. I'm at your service."

Angelo found it very easy to talk for more than five minutes about the magnificent view from the windows of the lake; then he rose quite naturally.

"Go to the village," he said to Giuseppe on the stairs, "and try to find an inn where we can eat and perhaps get an hour's sleep."

He relighted the butt of his cigar which began at once to stink. He returned to the kitchen. The old valet was scraping turnips.

"Your Tuscan is very good," said Angelo.

"This is the first time I've seen it smoked by someone who can buy fine boots for himself."

"Maybe I stole them," said Angelo.

"That wouldn't bother me."

"How does the Count send notes to Turin?" Angelo asked.

He learned that a stranger with carrot-red hair had been staying at the inn for the last week.

Giuseppe was already installed in front of some cheese. The weather was all that could be desired. The lake leaped lightly in the cool wind. Angelo had a wild love for morning light. Here it was tender and periwinkle blue.

"We're having a bacon omelet," said Giuseppe.

They cut slices of bread; the loaf made very few crumbs.

Obviously they had to beware of Pesaro. Angelo mentioned the carrot-top. Giuseppe had seen him. The man was at the other end of the terrace; he was looking at the lake as if he had been told to drink it. Without moving his head, he glanced toward the table on which the bacon omelet had just been set. At last he went down the steps to the little pleasure boat basin and walked nonchalantly away.

"No sleep for us with him gone," said Angelo.

"I've thought the matter over," said Giuseppe. "We must go see Del Caretto in Ivrea. But if we stick together, they'll easily pick up our tracks. All the more since I'm no good when it comes to words. You go there. Your shanks will carry you another five leagues. I'll go to Novara. As soon as you're finished in Ivrea—but don't rush—come to Novara. Maybe I'll be there. If not, Lavinia will tell you where I am. But what we need in Ivrea is someone made of pure gold who knows what an order is."

"Agreed," said Angelo, "but I want five minutes with you in private."

They found a quiet corner in the stable.

"First I want to give you fifty florins about which you will tell no one. I have the same amount left. As brothers, it's share and share alike. And also I want to give you a brother's embrace."

"And now," said Giuseppe, "let's not wait for carrot-top to return, and let's give him something to think about. If you absolutely insist on your Calabrese hat,[3] all right, but don't carry it in your hand. You're better-looking bareheaded and I don't like you to show off when I'm not around."

They embraced once more and Giuseppe cautioned him repeatedly to be prudent.

Angelo paid the bill and started along the little road bordering the lake. "It would be completely ridiculous to turn in order to see Giuseppe once more." He forced himself to look at the little road, very tidy with its border of osiers full of catkins. There were tea gardens along the lake and leaning against the trellised fence of one, traveling-bag beside him, was a mature, citified man.

[3] Hats in the style of those worn by peasants in Calabria were favored by Italian patriots.

Angelo asked if there was a public coach on the road.

"No such luck," said the man, who was wearing a short, furred jacket and a high silk hat." The public coach travels on the other side of the lake where the post office is. If you're interested, I'm waiting for a young sailor girl who is going to take me across for a lira. Come along; we'll split the cost."

The young lady arrived carrying the oars. The boat was on the other side of a bank in the reeds. It left shore right away with three skillful sculling motions.

"You're not from around here," said the man, "and if I'm indiscreet, pretend I asked nothing. I spent the night at the little tavern where you found me. I was treating myself to a calm night. But until this morning everyone's been whispering and conferring, coming and going, slamming doors and padding down the halls. What's going on that's so extraordinary?"

"You've fallen on the wrong man for an answer," said Angelo. "I'm in the midst of an affair which for the moment prevents me from concentrating on anything but my own heart."

"I congratulate you," said the man. "I have already noticed that the girls around here are pretty."

And he turned his attention to the sailor girl, whose ample bosom was in evidence.

They disembarked about a hundred meters from the posting-station, visible through the red branches of the willows. They took a little path leading to it.

"I'm a representative for a large hosiery house in Genoa," said the man. "We have succeeded in manufacturing very light woolen garments to be worn under a shirt; and since, by a secret process, we incorporate a certain amount of peat—but peat from very delicate grasses—in the weave without effecting either the finish or the lightness, they are true bucklers against pneumonia. If you're curious and if we have a little time at our disposal before the carriage arrives, I'll show you one. I have samples in my bag for both men and women.

"There's a lot of agitation in Genoa these days," he continued. "Last Sunday a French corvette came into the commercial port. The only thing she wanted was water. She was crowding all sails for Marseille, where it seems people are throwing pianos out of windows on top of Louis Philippe's soldiers. Everyone shouted: 'Long live the Constitution!' Some lawyers were arrested."

The traveling-salesman was going to Biella. His carriage passed through almost immediately. The Ivrea diligence was announced for noon. It arrived early. Its only passengers were three women. Angelo heard the postilion saying: "I took the direct route; I'm afraid of the woods, and I kept up a gallop the whole way." The horses were covered with foam.

The springs of the carriage were too hard for this fast pace and the travelers had been shaken up quite a bit. Two of them, certainly mother and daughter, were women of the best society dressed very tastefully. Accustomed to ruling in a world where the surest despotic power is found in the perfect arrangement of a fichu, pins, hair, and linen, they were in a murderous rage at being uncombed and brutally jolted. The younger was not even aware that her disarray, the warmth of her cheeks, her smeared rouge, and the shame which was evident in her eyes gave her the greatest possible charm. Angelo was so tired that he did not notice this. His cold civility, which seemed put on and could have passed for insolence on account of his rain-rumpled overcoat and his two-day beard, threw oil on the fire—all the more because Angelo rested his head and shoulders squarely on the back of the seat and went to sleep while the horses were being changed.

The other woman adjusted to the circumstances far better. She had a bit too much of everything: jewels, lace, avoirdupois, and malice for the other ladies; she made it plain that she found Angelo appealing.

The posting-station was at the foot of a rise, and the horses kept to a walk for more than a quarter of a league, but on the other side of the hill they were again lashed into a gallop.

Angelo was pulled out of a deep sleep by a jolt and cries. He found himself pressed against an abundant but soft bosom which smelled of musk.

"You were doing somersaults," said the plump woman, "and these ladies have entrusted you to me."

Her voice was so agreeable that he freed himself very gently. The carriage had stopped.

"What's going on?" asked Angelo somewhat astounded.

"I think we're in the hands of a coward who goes like the devil the whole time," said the woman.

Angelo stepped down onto the road in a very good humor. The coachman claimed that he had seen men and even guns.

"We might be shot, and that's not my idea of fun," he said. "I'm no gentleman."

Angelo thought this fear very reasonable.

"I'll be your passport," he said. "Wait for me; I'll signal."

He walked a hundred meters without having seen anything but the trunks of the pines.

"Did you find anything?" asked the woman when he had resumed his place.

"Enough to justify the anxieties of the father of a family with mouths to feed," he said. "He knows that there will be no one to keep the wolf from the door when he's gone."

"I like you," said the woman. "I was joking about the postilion a minute ago, but I know my way around. Anyway, I may as well tell you everything. You slept resting on me for two hours. You were so fast asleep that you didn't even realize that the jerking of the coach threw you against those ladies in a most unsuitable manner. They no longer knew how to resist your advances, and as I want you all to myself, I took you in my arms, and you started to snore like a bear."

Putting a certain warmth in his words, Angelo asked the ladies to excuse him, especially the young one. He was embarrassed to have bothered anyone so lovely; with her disordered fichus, clothing, and hair she looked as if she had sacrificed everything to passion. But he knew he spoke too well for an unshaven man, dead-tired into the bargain. He aroused no response but the wrathful look of two very black eyes.

"I know the meaning of courage," said the plump woman. "For some it's as easy as going to the water closet, and what merit is there in that! Others have to keep reviving a role which was once successful."

This thought pleased Angelo.

"I'm one of those without merit. But I know the most courageous man in the world," she said. "He's a baritone. He has sung the role of *Don Giovanni* so many times that he would kill—even at the risk of his own skin—more commandants than God could bless. He's as ugly as a flea, yet not a woman can resist him, so persuaded is he that he can win whomever he wishes. Yes," she answered, "I sing, the role of Donna Anna too. That's what makes me maternal, but you would be wrong to trust this or anything else about me. I'm on my way to join my impresario who has decided to present an *opera-seria* to the mountaineers, who are sensitive and melancholy in the spring."

At Ivrea, Angelo was pleasant and helpful to the singer, who was taking the carriage for Aosta.

"I would have loved to take you with me," she said, "if only to infuriate that slip of a girl who was devouring you with her eyes."

Angelo waited patiently for dusk before going to Del Caretto's. He bought some small cigars and carefully chose lonely roads where he could walk while smoking them.

Night had fallen when he went to knock on a charming door in a quiet alley back of the castle.

Del Caretto received him with open arms.

"How are you?" he said.

"I could sleep like a top," said Angelo. "I left Turin yesterday on foot to go see Pesaro."

He told immediately of his mishap.

"But lend me your razor, and I'll get cleaned up."

The young lawyer pushed aside the briefs cluttering his table and set up a standing-mirror and a basin of hot water.

"Pesaro is a theoretician," he said, "and you and I live with shreds of sentimentality."

"Barricades are made with paving-stones," said Angelo, lathering his face with soap.

"What do you mean by that?" asked the lawyer.

"That we're sentimental enough to make them without Pesaro's help. But there's something more serious."

He mentioned the red police seal.

"That amazes me," said Del Caretto. "I'm naïve, but that's because I have three square meals a day. Of the five thousand inhabitants here, all are in the habit of arranging their differences either amiably or angrily—but never in court. Three quarters of the briefs on the table have to do with Pesaro. I'm only a local counsel, of course. I only prepare them, and it's up to Rubini in Turin to plead them. Yet everything that I've sent to Rubini in the last three months gets through like an ordinary letter. I was beginning to think that I was a genius. I see I'm going to have to lower my opinion of myself. Obviously he's being bought off in some currency he values. Perhaps he would not have accepted ordinary money—but I'm not sure of that either," added the lawyer, "it's easy to persuade a high priest he deserves everything, and I mean everything; in the last analysis he's for order, and order means whatever's in his best interest. But I don't think that Pesaro has gone so far as to give names. Or at least I don't want to believe it."

Even the carrot-top policeman did not make him change his mind, at least not apparently.

"They're into everything in the last few months, so that I end up by seeing them even in scarecrows. We've even been graced with a little extra garrison, and we're lodging one hundred and twenty of the civil guard. Above all, I agree with you. Pesaro has outlived his time. We're going to have to pry up the pavements, and he has always been incapable of this. We'll do better at this than he could. He won't be able to understand our *whims*. He'll scream bloody murder. Maybe he considers this his right, for, make no mistake, he knows us and he knows himself."

Del Caretto was a stout young man who didn't often have a chance of speaking outside of court and without thinking of his position. He let himself go joyously.

"I see a greater danger elsewhere," he said. "What was done to this man—who was truly a friend of Mazzini's and whose writings I have quite literally devoured, as you and many others have—is being done to almost all our comrades. I've been left to one side, as have you, just as they must have left aside those they thought they could catch red-handed whenever they wished. I almost admire our Ministry of the Interior. Get in touch with our friends and you'll see the difference. They're a watered-down lot. We all have an Achilles' heel by which we could be caught, and you've got to admit they've been caught."

"Do they know about the events in Pavia and Padua?"

"The news arrived this morning, and you didn't surprise me

when I opened the door. They also know that the Cirié diligence was rifled and that the postilion who wanted to defend the mail was a bit roughed up. They're indignant and are literally crying alarm because the well-stocked wallet of an ostler on his way to the fair in Alessandria was seized at the same time. Today I defy you to make them understand that we need money to buy guns and to keep all our friends who have fallen into misfortune out of prison. This no longer affects them. What affects them is to picture themselves in the place of the horse-dealer who saw bearded faces framed in the window of the coach and had to separate himself from the *sweat of his brow*. That's the phrase they use. That's what they feel about what's close to home. As for Pavia and Padua —once the first thrill of excitement is gone, they say that it's in Pavia and Padua."

"But you?" said Angelo.

"I'm entirely at your service."

"It's not a question of my service," said Angelo.

"Yes it is, up to a certain point, a matter of your service," said the young lawyer. "This is the course we have both taken. Our happiness is fated to lie in this direction. And what wouldn't one do to be happy?"

They could not be seen together in the street: nothing passed unnoticed in Del Caretto's small town.

"If I buy two chops, they'll talk, since they know I usually only eat one. I should have thought of this and started up an affair with some widow. They would have said: 'This evening he's feeding her.' What shall we do? It's egotistical but I'd like to keep you here a little longer. Only with you do I feel free."

Angelo would have liked to make such a declaration of love.

"They don't know me," he said. "I'll go buy the chops. But I'll buy four; I'm ravenous."

"Don't think you'll eliminate danger that way," said the lawyer, who under his whiskers was still all pink with happiness. "They saw you step down from the carriage; you're a stranger; they're talking about you. But we can't keep ourselves in cotton wool forever. Nevertheless, we mustn't be imprudent. Go to Barberini; he has a shop under the arcades. He's a rabid partisan of the civil guard and he has the honor of catering to three or four high-tone families who are openly and resolutely against us. No one will ever imagine I sent you there. If you can also look very self-possessed, that also deceives people."

And he added five or six bits of advice to be followed if you want to keep a small town of five thousand inhabitants thinking good thoughts.

They cooked the chops on the embers of the fire. The odor was delicious.

"This will give us away for good and all," said the lawyer laughing. "Luckily, few people pass through my little street at this hour and the goatherds came home at four. They're the ones I fear. They're sharp as an embroidery needle. Last night an old ragpicker cooked some chops. From what they said you would have thought he was Alexander the Great. What I said before is the only solution: I must find a widow."

Their impassioned evening of conversation which ranged forward into the future and upwards almost to paradise enchanted Angelo.

"What can I do better in life?" he repeated to himself. "The terrace of a café and the established order allow for habit, but where can I find room there for more sweeping gestures? And how can I be happy if I must always be asking myself this question? Without Austria and Milan, we would be two rather foolish boys amusing ourselves burning sheep's meat."

He smoked his little cigar with extreme pleasure.

"You must stay at the Albergo della Corona," said the lawyer. It's the most expensive, but the captain of the civil guard is billeted there. No one will ever look for you in the lion's mouth. The captain won't lose a game of backgammon over you; on the other hand you may give the chambermaids food for thought."

"I can be an ailing citizen of Turin come to breathe the mountain air."

"You're pretty good if you can make them believe that. They've got much better things to imagine!"

"I can take care of women," said Angelo, "with a little melancholia and a few passionate words."

But he was received very calmly and led with unaffected politeness to a room overlooking a torrent. The peaceful mountain night, the notes of a crystalline carillon slowly tolling each quarter hour, and the noise of the rapid stream rushing among the stones beneath his window put him into a deep sleep.

CHAPTER THREE

I've got to face these dangerous chambermaids," Angelo said to himself the next morning. He wanted to get thoroughly cleaned up but he had no change of linen.

"Del Caretto's theory about the lion's jaw is all very well," he said to himself, "but if I had gone to a small workingman's hotel, my dirty shirt would have helped me and even gotten me some sympathy. Here they'll ask bluntly where my baggage is. And serving the rich makes for arrogance. I'm going to have to cope with servants who are used to being given a hard time. I don't know how to be impolite, and they'll make fun of me. And I'm not even considering the danger I'll be exposing my friends to if they start conjecturing and hit upon the truth."

Finally, in spite of everything, he took it upon himself to go out in the hall and stop a girl who was passing with a breakfast tray.

"I want some black coffee in a large bowl," he said, "with a lot of sugar and a lot of bread."

He saw immediately that the large bowl and the "a lots" had impressed her. Besides, the girl was robust, the very opposite of delicate, and didn't give a damn for a dirty shirt, for the good reason that hers was none too clean itself. She only noticed that this young man was a fine fellow and held himself somewhat stiffly.

She brought the coffee and willingly took it upon herself to go press a wide faille ribbon which Angelo wore knotted under his collar.

"I'll tie my cravat quite high," he said to himself, "no one will see that my shirt isn't clean."

He succeeded equally easily in getting his suit brushed and his boots shined. As his hat was still damp from the rain, he set it to dry on the top of a cupboard and went out.

He did not remain on the Piazza Reale for long. It was, however, very pleasant under the arcades; nowhere in the world was the sunlight so gay. In a neighboring street a hammer was beating on an anvil just loud enough to make indolence agreeable. But groups of men were standing about arguing. He spent the entire morning asking himself: "Is he a friend?" each time he met a blue-eyed mountaineer or one of their women, thin but lively as a trout.

He returned to the hotel at noon to spend a reasonable sum so as not to attract attention and then wandered in the deserted streets until twilight as suited his heart.

"How will you use this representative you mentioned to me yesterday evening?" Del Caretto asked him when he joined him.

"To receive the real news from Lombardy and transmit it to those who deserve to know it. If need be, to organize these friends and lead them wherever necessary."

"No need to search further; I'm your man," said the lawyer. "Tomorrow I'll get two members of the Vico Lodge, let us call them X and Y; they'll differ quite sharply and publicly over a fell of timber. I'll register the affair in the usual fashion in court, and X can come to see me twice a week without anyone talking. But how will the news reach me?"

They reviewed every sort of procedure, deeply engrossed. But it was out of the question to have another meal of chops.

"Since we agree, I'm going to leave you," said Angelo. "Let us act as if we frequented the best society. A bachelor lawyer goes to dine in his family boarding-house, and the gentleman from Turin returns to the Corona after a day in the fresh air. If I were a true artist I would invite the captain for a game of backgammon, but I'm not that good. I'll leave for Novara tomorrow morning. What's the safest road in your opinion?"

"On horseback or in a light carriage?"

"Neither. They expect to find me on horseback; a carriage would oblige me to follow well-traveled roads, and no matter how light, it can't leap over walls."

"Then go by Casteletto. There are garrisons everywhere, but on foot you'll get through. Are you armed?"

"I'm not that stupid. I have a little knife like everyone else."

Angelo went back to the Corona. The owner, who was presiding at the *table d'hôte,* greeted him and seated him on his right. The guests were all habitués: most probably small tax officials, notaries, or bailiff clerks. They swallowed their soup noisily and kept their noses to their plates. Angelo was the only traveler. He was an object of curiosity, but they were all adept at the art of staring tactfully. He was careful not to look about at all affirmatively for fear that the conversation would fasten on a topic of importance; nevertheless, he felt himself the focus of every sly glance.

"I'm the stupidest man at the table," he said to himself. "I'm afraid of a single topic of general interest which, after five minutes of being patient, would fire me up, whereas these good fellows eating their soup as if they were alone would know how to play with it for hours without once exposing their flank. At the slightest original idea, they withdraw into their holes and don't let anything out but the barrel of the little gun loaded with the ink which is their stock in trade. If one wishes to see them, one must talk shop and advancement list. The authorities see to it that they are advanced only according to seniority so that they have inoffensive ideas on justice. He who administers it has his hands free."

Leaving the table, his neighbor suggested they play billiards for the coffee. He was undoubtedly very sure of winning. Angelo excused himself with good grace and went up to bed.

He rediscovered the noises of the preceding night but as he was less sleepy, he took pleasure in listening to them.

He longed for some music. "It might help my wits," he said to himself. "God knows I need them!"

He was up early. From the hollow road which led down into the valley, he looked up at Del Caretto's house. The curtains were still drawn across the window. The wind had dropped. The dawn promised fine weather, but for the moment it was cold. The grass on the little road crackled with frost. Hoarfrost covered the fields like snow. Tall beeches, isolated in the meadows, reared like magnificent structures of wronght-iron against the pearl gray sky. When the sun rose everything began to sparkle. Ten minutes later fires went out; the hoarfrost had melted, and the colors took their places in violet osiers, red willows, greenish-white beeches and birches pollen-dusted by spring down.

Angelo crossed the little valley and walked toward the hill, all rosy under the dry leaves of the tall oaks. "I must be careful," he said to himself, entering the woods. He cut himself a stick from a thicket of service trees.

The ridge of the hill was long, but rising little by little to a point from which he could see, through oak branches which came down to the ground, a large expanse of low land. There, slim poplars were planted so close together, bordering the fields, or in double rows along the roads and canals that their bare branches covered the countryside with a transparent mist. The sparkling canals and the extremely white bark of the trees trembled like the sea. Dovecotes helmeted with glazed tiles threw off sparks; old farm rooms were gilded with lichen, and the towers of large estates, carefully white-washed to their summit, disappeared in the light. Thousands of larks chirped above the plowed fields.

The woods appeared black in contrast, and the moss, which covered the thick branches, was a delicious acid green. Finches called to each other peacefully, sounding like a file on iron.

From the other slope, the hill looked over a village. It was perched on a very romantic outcropping of rocks; a castle crowned with pines rested on its summit. Small orchards of fruit trees and kitchen gardens had been planted on the ramparts which supported the vineyards on the steep slopes. The village square was a terrace with a balustrade of solid stone; he could see it clearly—even the top of a café sign.

Right against the balustrade which overlooked the little valley Angelo noticed two spots of bright blue. A third could barely be distinguished beneath the pines of the castle, in a place which must have commanded a fine view. Then another blue spot slowly moved the length of the balustrade. Civil guards.

The road descended into the little valley. Angelo left it and followed the edge of the woods. He had not gone one hundred meters in this direction when he was obliged to hide behind a bush. He was just above a sort of washhouse where five unarmed soldiers were dressing. He returned to the woods and walked north. At the end of a half-hour, as the trees grew thicker, he swerved once again to the east, looking for the edge of the woods to get his bearings.

Finally, the branches parted and he saw before him a gray mountain, without sign of human life as far as he could see.

He decided to climb part-way up its slopes and cut across country. While he followed this itinerary, which he thought would bypass the village with room to spare, the air lost its morning sonorousness as the sun rose. He was walking through winter pastures soft as felt when he fell upon two young shepherds sitting eating a loaf of bread.

The two young children immediately showed signs of the wildest terror. But as Angelo stayed at a distance and spoke to them kindly, they answered him with a few words in patois, stood up, and led him to a lean-to propped against the trunk of a beech tree. There he found an old shepherd. Moving his enormous eyebrows, he looked Angelo over from head to toe without the slightest fear; this part of the mountain was no place to go out walking, he remarked.

Angelo explained that he was looking for certain medicinal plants and that on his way, he wanted to go to Casteletto. Casteletto was still a long way off and in another direction. The shepherd pointed out a spot to the south. But the plants interested him greatly. What kind were they and what did they cure? One of his knees often troubled him in the morning. Angelo described a little yellow flower which he was looking for particularly because it quieted the stomach. The shepherd then offered him some onion and cheese. With two or three well-chosen words, he sent the children back to their work and ushered Angelo into the hut.

"Your overcoat is too light for our part of the world," he said, "and, if you don't want your boots to be stolen, don't polish them."

"No one's going to get them off me that easily," said Angelo.

"The bother is that you're never attacked by one but by five or six," said the shepherd.

"I seldom pick a quarrel," said Angelo, "but, to take your boots off by force, they throw you flat on your back with your heels in the air, that's what I don't like. When that happens life is hardly worth living."

"Everyone feels that way," said the shepherd, "but if you always did what you wanted, you'd often get your knuckles rapped."

"Watch out!" said Angelo to himself, "there's something stilted about this conversation." He pulled a handkerchief out of his pocket and folded it in a triangle. The man took no notice of what he was doing.

After eating, Angelo offered one of his cigars and asked a few questions. The man's answers were beside the point.

"If I were you," said the shepherd, "I would go back down into the little valley, even though you don't find any yellow flowers. If you take care to follow the road at the bottom, leaving the oak woods to your left all the way, you'll get to Casteletto. Do you like soldiers? All right then, you'll meet them."

Angelo followed his advice and walked for more than an hour along a brook which was making a pretty noise. The road came out on willow groves and meadows. On the other side, the rough-cast of a high wall shone beneath the branches, but the numerous birds chasing each other through the willows and the jabber of many young magpies told Angelo that the building was deserted. It was a chapel. He pushed open the door. He smelt an odor of extinguished coals and found, behind the base of the font, the traces of a fire where wood had been burned, including the debris of a chair back. The ashes were cold, but the smell told him that the fire had still been going in the early hours of the morning.

"This is no civil guard bivouac," he said to himself. "They were white-collar workers who didn't want to sleep out of doors. Two or at the most three men warmed their hands at this brazier."

In spite of the shepherd's advice, he left the road which passed the chapel. He had reached a hillock bathed in afternoon light when he heard a resounding gunshot. He ran to the brim of the hill and hid behind a little wall. He looked out over a plowed field in the middle of which two soldiers in blue had stopped, guns with bayonets attached to the barrel at their side. As he surveyed the area round about, he saw a puff of smoke emerge from a bush;

he heard the report of a second gunshot and one little blue man fell. The other retreated at a run. He was fired at once more, but the shot, probably from a pistol, did not hit him. He disappeared under the trees. The soldier lying in the plowed field no longer moved.

Angelo remained on guard behind the wall. "The magpies are more cunning than I," he said to himself. "If they come back to play, that will mean I'm alone with one extremely dignified civil guard."

He did not have long to wait. The magpies soon chattered and jumped about in the very bush from which the firing had come. Everyone had cleared out.

Angelo left his shelter and went toward the soldier. He was dead. His jaw had been blown off and his throat was open. In the chaos of blood and teeth like shining kernels of husked corn his tongue hung astonishingly pink and clean.

"A bullet doesn't do this kind of job," Angelo said to himself. "That gun was loaded with shoe nails."

He saw that the fugitive had left large bloodstains behind him. He followed the track. Once in the woods, the man had caught his breath leaning against a birch tree; the white trunk was abundantly spattered with red.

"The imbecile will probably kick the bucket in some hole."

A hundred meters away where the slope was steeper, Angelo heard some rummaging in a box thicket.

"Don't be an idiot with your gun," he called out. "I won't hurt you, quite the opposite."

The soldier was wounded in the shoulder and bleeding profusely, but there was nothing to get het up about. "He's in a panic," Angelo said to himself. "And why not? It's very natural."

There were indeed shoe nails in the wound. Angelo popped them out with the point of his knife. ("A poor man's bullet," he thought, "but one that does its job.")

"Go home and pour two glasses of brandy on it," he said. "You'll get a week's leave at most, and then only if your sergeant is a good bastard."

The soldier seemed to have recovered slightly from his surprise. Above all, his blood was no longer flowing.

"Would you fill my pipe," he said, "my tobacco is in my cartridge case."

He also had jagged bullets.

"When you hit the bull's eye with these little bastards, you too must make a hell of a hole," said Angelo.

"Are you in this business?" asked the soldier. "All right, then you know it's no picnic."

"Then why have anything to do with it?"

"You gentlemen always think everything's so easy. The first thing the rest of us have to do is earn ten sous a day. We're all in the same boat. They shoot at us with anything they can lay their hands on."

"Maybe they've got good reason for what they're doing if they spend their time taking the nails out of their boots rather than going home to their supper."

The soldier drew several rapid puffs on his pipe.

"I have another league to go," he said. "They smelled blood; they'll be after me like wolves. Would you load my gun?"

"I'd be glad to, with a proper bullet," said Angelo.

"Poke around in my pack, maybe there's one left."

Angelo loaded the gun with a *proper* bullet.

"If you don't want to have a trick played on you," said the soldier before going, "take the feather off your hat. The liberal bastards wear them."

"Evening is coming," thought Angelo. "I must cover some ground toward that ilex wood the shepherd showed me; but that nervous civil guard went that way, and he didn't like my coiffure. I'll bear left and keep to the small valleys. I'll be damned if I can't find a farm where I can spend the night."

He covered at least two leagues without seeing a living soul and entered a plain crowded with poplars, like those he had seen shimmering in the morning light from the top of the hill. After crossing a few of the hedgerows surrounding the fields, he reached the edge of a canal.

He saw a horseman coming at a walk along the low path. Angelo concealed himself in the alders. The man was a lancer. He was staring pensively between his horse's ears. The endless trees were planted so close together that the countryside was hidden in a mist of bare branches.

"It looks bad around here," thought Angelo. "Generals are fools, but not such fools that they send lancers into a countryside of hedgerows and trees growing closely together where platoons can't be deployed for a charge if necessary. That means they've won. The horses are only to impress the poor whom they've already got well in hand."

Dusk was so far advanced that he could not count on picking out the roughcast plaster of a wall through the white branches. The simplest thing to do was to walk along the canal to where it joined an irrigation ditch; this would surely lead him to a farm. But on horseback you're lord and master; there's no argument. He was well aware of that. Cavalry carbines have delicate triggers. Certainly there were other lancers patroling and too much grass everywhere to hear hoofbeats sufficiently far away. Angelo continued to cross hedgerows, contenting himself with never losing sight of the canal. He heard the sound of water falling from a sluice gate into a catch basin and found a brook which ran off from the canal.

He had been following it for a while when some rummaging in the osiers caught his attention. He advanced cautiously and saw a girl on the other side of the hedgerow, putting newly washed linen in a basket. He crossed the hedgerow. The girl seized her beetle.

"I thought you were the lancer," she said seeing Angelo.

"He's far away. He's going up along the canal toward the hills."

She put her hands on her hips and waited.

Angelo asked no questions and simply said he was tired.

"Did you come from the woods?"

Angelo said that he came from Ivrea, that he had passed through the woods and that he was hiding from the soldiers.

"You won't have an easy time of it," she said; "they're everywhere."

She stooped to pick up her basket.

"Must you keep on the move all night?"

"I would prefer to sleep if I was sure of not being captured."

She looked at him carefully.

"There's only one spot," she said, "in the straw, just under the roof of the barn."

"That would suit me," said Angelo. "Can I help you?"

"It's not heavy. Let me go ahead. Follow me at a distance."

From time to time she turned to see if he was still following. She waited for him in a willow grove, in sight of an enormous farm.

"While I go in," she said, "go around behind those grindstones. The door of the barn is opposite. Wait for me at the foot of the pile of straw. For the moment you're not in any danger. Go ahead."

"The dogs will bark," said Angelo.

"There are no more dogs. The soldiers killed them."

Angelo realized that, indeed, since Ivrea he had not heard a single bark in the countryside.

The girl soon returned. A boy of fifteen or sixteen accompanied her.

"My brother," she said.

He knitted his brows. Angelo noticed that he had the somber and decided air of children who have responsibility.

The girl brought some bread, a piece of sausage, and some wine in a bottle. They conducted Angelo to the summit of a pile of straw which touched the rafters of the roof. There was a hiding-place there and even a little dormer window from which he could watch the farm.

"If you have to clear out," said the young girl, "don't go out the way you came in." She showed him a hole in the wall which opened directly onto the meadows. And he had to take the bottle with him; if it were found there it could betray them.

Angelo ate, and especially drank, with pleasure. He stretched out in the straw and a little while later saw the first star of a very clear night reach the sill of the dormer.

He was awakened by the boy, who shook him with a certain impatience.

"Give me a florin. The lancers are downstairs. If I shout, they'll capture you and you'll be shot."

He did indeed hear in the yard the curb-chains, hoofs, and oaths of a cavalry patrol.

"Wait," said Angelo, "I'll give it to you."

But he threw the boy down in the straw and covered his mouth with one hand. He drew his knife and pricked the boy's cheek.

"If you peep, I'll kill you," he said. "I've killed before."

"The funniest thing is that I'm not lying," he said to himself. He was not afraid, but sad.

He thought of the peasant girl who had turned her head at intervals to see if he was following docilely.

"Is this why you looked like a 'Roman' when you brought me the bread?" he said. "Don't you know that we slit the throats of those who betray us?"

"To make it real," he said to himself, "I should make him shed a little blood. These people only understand the real thing. But if he's a coward, he'll howl. Let's hope traitors are courageous."

He sank his knife into the cheek. The boy started but remained mute.

"Will the lancers come here even if you don't shout?"

"No."

"Think: You'll be dead before they begin to search the straw."

"They haven't come to search. They've come to drink with the boss. He's on good terms with them."

"And you?"

"Yes."

"Your sister's in on the plot?"

"We share everything."

"Will they stay long?"

"No, they're leaving."

After a moment during which Angelo wondered if it would not be better to flee through the breach in the wall (taking the boy with him), the lancers came out of the house. They spoke as if they were not even on duty and needed a "drop" to keep out the evening chill. Angelo had counted six horses in the yard. He heard six leave.

"A cavalryman, and a lancer especially, never dismounts, even to show his zeal," he said to himself. "They've left no sentinel."

He took off the boy's cravat and tied his hands firmly. He took off his belt and fastened his feet.

"You're going to keep me company. If I had given you the florin," he added after an instant, "would you have cried out anyway?"

He said to himself: "When will you ever get tired of hearing people tell you what you already know? He would have sold you because there must be a reward and he would have been able to go through your pockets. Who are you trying so hard to excuse? To know the rights of a thing is a false expression. The more you know the less content you are."

He thought of mankind with such bitterness and generosity that he did not notice when he fell asleep.

Daylight awakened him abruptly. For a moment he panicked. But the boy stretched out beside him was also asleep.

"What indifference," Angelo said to himself, "to everything except money!"

He let himself slip down gently from the pile of straw and went out by the breach in the wall.

"I'm tired of hiding," he said to himself. "To hell with Giuseppe and his prudence! Besides, flight is impossible in this countryside criss-crossed with canals and brooks which you can only cross at the bridges. Obviously, there are too many hedgerows and at any moment I may fall on a patrol which has called a halt, or even on a lone soldier. If, at that moment, I behave like a rat, then where will I be!"

He followed the road and reached Casteletto with some peasants who were going to the sheep market. He got by the sentinels by walking along with these men in work-smocks, prodding along their animals. He went to see what the town's three inns looked like. Because of the striking physiognomy of the innkeeper, he decided to enter the most popular one. It had a carriage stand.

"I had a very lively argument with my horse, and he got the better of me," he said to the man, who looked severe and frowned for no apparent reason. "That's why I need a good brushing and why I have no baggage. But if the government doesn't make us good horsemen, it does make us prudent: all my money was in my pockets and still is."

At the words "government" and "money" the landlord's face became affable and earthen-colored, making his enormous mustaches trimmed in mutton chops all the blacker.

"If your horse has lighted out," he said, "sooner or later someone will bring him in here. But I'm not so sure about the baggage.

And if your beast has gone into the woods, he'll end up roasted over a campfire. Then where will you be!"

Angelo gave a good imitation of the government employee who is in difficulty, but who hasn't given up hope of delivering the goods.

He was conducted to a light, airy room looking out on the large square. The small market town was crammed with soldiers. The chime "to quarters" resounded in the streets. Despite the early hour, well dressed young women were strolling with officers beneath the arcades. The little town, aroused at last from boredom by trumpets and men wearing corsets, was joyful, if still timid.

The man with the thick mustaches came in with some linen.

"I told my wife about you and she had a pretty good idea," he said. "Here is one of my shirts. I swear it's new and anyway you can see it is. It's too big for you, but that's all that's wrong with it. Take yours off and put it on. This window will be getting the full sun in an hour; do me the favor of taking your lunch here in front of it, and by this evening you'll have your shirt washed and pressed."

He added a few words to the effect that he paid the wine tax assiduously.

"Thank your wife," said Angelo gravely. "I'd be delighted to wear your shirt even if it weren't new. At most I would risk catching your disease of being a law-abiding citizen, and that's something I admire. If the woman who does your ironing knows how to use a damp cloth, would you have her iron this redingote as well. It's had a hard time. And in case there's some little miss who's doing nothing—which I doubt with all these soldiers—here are ten lire; tell her to go to the best store in town and buy me seven lire worth of cravats. She can do what she wants with the three extra lire, but see that she's wide-awake enough to know what kind of ribbon is right for dark eyes like mine."

He had his boots shined as well. The woman who ironed his redingote noticed the address of the tailor in the lining. He was very famous, and no one in Casteletto had seen clothes from him. All the servants and even the mistress of the house came to touch the fine cloth.

The servant girl came back all out of breath with the cravat. She didn't know how to behave in front of this young man who, accord-

ing to the innkeeper, made you laugh but didn't laugh himself.
Despite the three lire he had given for a two-sous errand, she found
him very nice.

About noon the table was set in front of the window bathed
in tender sunlight, as the innkeeper had promised. The Piazza San
Giorgio on which it looked out was surrounded by old houses
whose roughcast plaster had become pink with age. Above the
roofs, two smithies, toy figures in a clock, were set in motion in
their iron cage, and Angelo heard with pleasure the smothered and
almost clandestine sounds of their hammers on a cracked bell.

He invited the master of the house to drink coffee with him. The
man came in very anxiously. He had heard about the address on
the lining of the redingote. He thought that his books were going
to be examined. But Angelo chatted about the soldiers and, seeing
nothing else coming, the innkeeper recovered his wits. "If we
become the relay lodging-house for the public coach, business will
roll in," he repeated to himself. "Let's get it across to this gentleman of the administration that we would very much like a government friendly to us."

"Several thousand kilos of good fodder," he said, "were ruined
by nothing more than cannon wheels. You see the tops of those
poplars to the left of the belfry? Well, they've set up an artillery
range there. We're not asking anything for the damages, but since
we've put in the money, why not have the whole artillery go
through here?"

"What the hell do you suppose they're up to with all this
artillery?" (Angelo forced himself to speak like a clerk on a holi-
day who finally deals with the major problems on a high level.)

"You're really too kind," replied the innkeeper. "Here you are
shut in for three hours when you would prefer to go and join
the young people of our town under the arcades . . ."

He remarked pleasantly on the cloth of the redingote.

". . . You're bored and you seek distraction with me. But now
that I've admitted this, I'll tell you what I think. We have a king
who has set his sights high. If you had come here six months ago,
you would have met Austrian officers and their ladies (or those of
others, but that's none of my business). They danced under the
elms, relaxed in the cornfields, drank my wine, and paid their bills.

Pretty perfect you might say. But put four hundred artillerymen and six platoons of lancers in a market town like this with only three liquor licenses and replace them every five or six days with others, and right away things look very different. And do you want me to tell you how different? They look the way they do when money stays in people's pockets. If you're a friend of Austria, this is all very nice: your servant believes in friendship with everyone. They cross the Ticino in carriages; they arrive here snapping whips, fluttering ribbons, playing violins, and turning heads. All very gentlemanly and polite, but it means uncorking wine, and even then the cork's got to be perfect. But uncorking wine costs money, even to me. Whereas the artillerymen drink ordinary red wine, in no small quantities, and with ordinary red wine you can always work things out."

"Here is the Piedmontese view of Turin politics," Angelo said to himself. "This Piedmontese, like all Piedmontese, has gotten it into his head that he has the loveliest flowers in Piedmont, the most beautiful inn in all Piedmont, the best head in all Piedmont, and that Piedmont is the bravest country in the world. Moreover, he can prove to me as easily as two and two make four that Milan is nearer Turin than Vienna." [1]

"Do you think they'll declare war?"

"There are a lot of newfangled ideas," said the innkeeper.

In his fear that he might have to show his account books to a young inspector who dispensed royally with his lost baggage, he had been ready to eat humble pie. Much to his surprise, a gentleman, who was a bit serious perhaps but offered cigars and was dressed by the most snobbish tailor of the capital, was listening to him very attentively.

"Let us reason a bit," he said.

"Del Caretto is a lawyer," Angelo said to himself, "and although on one side of the family only, I have a fine position in society. All the Carbonari I know are well-dressed men who do well in drawing-rooms. When they go to Paris, they are received by M. de Lamartine [2] who does them the honor of not reading his

[1] Closer to Turin, the capital of Piedmont, and therefore more subject to Piedmontese influence than Austrian.

[2] Alphonse de Lamartine (1790–1869), French poet and moderate liberal.

verses. Sometimes they go to London, which is pretty far to still have anything to do with Piedmont. This man thinks of his wine: a powerful thought since it governs his actions and has the advantage of being homemade. Evidently, we would be capable as the next man of street-cleaning and firing guns. In any case, I would be, and I have no reason to believe that the lawyers, architects, engineers, and officers who are with us are cowards; they at least know that the first and greatest qualification for a higher rank is to stay alive, consequently they never take risks. This man who thinks first of himself before thinking of others—or rather thinks only of himself—doesn't bore me because I'm sure I'll never want to be a minister of the Republic, if it is ever created. But is this the last word in distinterest and frankness? And was there nothing more behind the fistful of nails which blew the head off the civil guard than the king's ermine?"

" 'To the King' they say," the innkeeper went on, "and I always say to myself: 'The King's a fine man! Why should he be scared of the Republic? The Republicans are his boys. Someone's got to shout "Long live Liberty!" It signifies: "Get up; I want the seat you're sitting on." Do you expect a king to shout? That would set the whole universe on its tin ear.' Whereas if it's you or me, the world doesn't stop turning. What does he want, after all? To sit on the Viceroy's throne in Milan. A man's got to raise his ass before you can take his seat. That's where the Republicans come in. They'll break a few windows; the Viceroy doesn't like draughts so he'll pack his bags. Then Charles Albert takes his seat and proclaims that shouting is forbidden because he has delicate ears. He orders soldiers to stroll before the walls twelve at a time and it's in the bag!"

The clean linen, the pressed redingote, and the polished boots were brought well before they had promised. There was still some daylight. Angelo got dressed and went out. The little town was full of soldiers and was taking advantage of them in every way. Infantry of the queen's brigade, with gray trousers and blue tunics, Sardinian sharpshooters wearing red berets, white lancers, slate-colored artillery, and "rice-bread-salts"[3] wearing the color of

---

[3] Members of the commissary corps.

sacking were all there after wine, women, and tobacco, buying everything that came to hand. Excited by what seemed to be the approach of a campaign, they were drawn to the shops like flies to sugar. They stocked up on herring, anchovies, apples, sausages, cheese and white bread and even crammed into their mouths on the spot huge pieces of a small white loaf made with oil and sugar. Officers very ostentatiously gave their arm to ladies. It was obvious that they got nothing out of it but a fleeting, intoxicating sense of show. The only true, slightly insolent joy was in the glances and demeanor of the young women of the provincial town who could at last be imprudent in the street.

Angelo strolled two or three times round the Piazza San Giorgio and a little boulevard planted with elms where the wattled pens of the sheep market still remained. He was about to enter a street leading back to the inn when he noticed in the now deep dusk the maneuvers of an ugly, vulgarly dressed girl who seemed to be signaling to him. He had turned aside several times before she decided to block his way.

"Don't go back to your room," she said. "They're going to arrest you."

She seemed about to cry.

"I've been trying to warn you for the last quarter of an hour," she said, "but you paid no attention to me. There are two soldiers in your room probably hidden behind the door. Others are waiting ready in the hall. A dried-up little man from Ivrea is in command of them. I think they want to kill you on the spot. The master of the house has already gotten the sawdust ready."

The sawdust angered but amused Angelo.

"Don't try anything. They're stronger here than you." (She went so far as to put her hand on his arm.) "I know you're called Pardi. They said your name. Come, I'll hide you."

Above all Angelo wanted to thank her warmly.

"Hurry," she said.

He followed her through a labyrinth of small streets to a low building which looked like a goat stable.

"Here's my key. Go in. Don't show a light. Wait for me. I've got to get back there right away so they won't be suspicious."

Angelo entered a narrow, evil-smelling room. He touched an

iron bed and rumpled sheets. He sat on the mattress and stayed there without moving.

He said to himself: "I have my knife." He was resolved to comport himself well before the ugly girl, even if she should betray him. At least she had gestured with real passion a few minutes before in the street. Her hand on his arm had enchanted him. He wondered too why the dried-up man of whom she had spoken had come from Ivrea and knew his name.

After waiting perhaps four hours, during which time he never once thought of fleeing, he rejoiced to hear the steps of the young girl in the street.

"They're crazy with rage," she said. "The boss was dragged off to the garrison, and the soldiers mocked him when he told the story of the horse which supposedly threw you. They said you were a colonel in the hussars."

"Not for some time now," said Angelo, "but it's true I was."

He spoke of liberty.

"I'm one of you," she said, "and my brother cleared out to have his hands free to help fashion Italy. He's not far away. Only three hours' march for someone who knows the paths. A little while ago I saw one of us: my brother will be told about you and if all goes well he'll be here in the middle of the night to help you. I have only one fear, and that is that you don't trust me and that when he enters you'll act impulsively in the dark. We must not show a light, and if a patrol knocks on the door, let me answer. I've done enough for the soldiers."

Angelo found this expression admirable; he liked her voice very much. The girl remained standing near the door. He said to her: "Come sit beside me." He asked her what had happened.

"I'm a kitchen maid," she said, "and this morning we heard about your redingote and especially about your shirt which is the thinnest anyone here has ever touched. I tried to get a look at you and when you went out I peeked out the door at you. I understood immediately from your walk that you were no clerk, nor anyone who gets thrown from the saddle, and I thought that all the fuss the boss was making over you (he was dying of pride because he had drunk coffee with you and especially because you had spoken to him as a peer) was a little risky. I often think of what my brother calls the traveling-salesmen who go from one forest to another to organize what must be done if we are to be happy. I kept my eyes open. I went into the large dining-room more than twenty times and even into the small private drawing-room, on the pretext of clearing the tables. That's how I passed this dried-up man and heard him talking about someone who resembled you."

Angelo questioned her about the dried-up man. She described a man he did not know, who did not seem to belong to the Turin police.

"Just hearing him give an order, you'd know he was important," she said. "He's scared stiff of the men who give him orders and these people are scared of you. They didn't want to cause you any inconvenience but simply to kill you. And that seems so urgent that they don't give a damn if the whole world finds out, provided they've got the law on their side. Perhaps they even need to advertise what they're doing a bit. That's what it looks like. I heard him give orders to three soldiers, who I know are in on every dirty job. Perhaps they are not even soldiers except in name. He was saying: 'When he draws his pistol,' when he heard steps in the hall and began again loudly: 'If he draws his pistols' . . ."

"I have none," said Angelo.

"They would have put some in your pockets. Anything can be done to a corpse. You can dress it whatever way you want."

Angelo found her voice more and more charming. He spoke with the most careful tact of things which were not in the slightest tragic. He succeeded from time to time in making her laugh a small smothered laugh beside him.

A trumpet sounded outside the little market town, but it was for the curfew.

Sitting as still as possible in the dark, they entertained each other for hours exchanging noble sentiments; at last the door opened just a little as if to let in a cat or as if the wind which they heard in the street had pushed it ajar: her brother had come. He struck a light, blew on his strong-smelling tinder, and looked closely at Angelo.

"I've heard of you," he said. "Obviously they want to rob us of our best brains. But we'll show them that we value them. Simply follow me as fast as you can a league into the hills without thinking of anything but putting your footsteps on top of mine. After that we're the masters and if you must go to Novara, I'll take you there on roads where we won't see a soul except for ourselves. I also understood that you were unarmed. That's all very nice, but as we're out to win (in any case, this evening) here's a carefully loaded pistol; I have two others. Be careful to hold it firmly if you fire: our charges are a bit powerful and the kick may surprise you."

Then he kissed the girl and began to whimper very tenderly against her cheek.

Instead of going out, they climbed, still in the dark, to the upper floor of the house; they crossed what must have been a henroost; the boy pushed open the door; they went along a corridor to a little frame of very bright light; the boy knocked and the door opened. They entered a room where there were three grown people, one of whom was an old woman, and five children asleep in bed. The man was in his shirt, barefoot, with a pruning-hook in his hand. He called the young man Christin as he greeted him, and looked at Angelo with amazement.

Angelo saw what his guide looked like. He was a thick-set peasant with a round head, a beard the color of maize, and a somewhat flattened nose.

"Don't bother yourself, Charles," he said, "we're only passing through. This is a friend who needs protection. But I'll take care of him; no need for your pruning-hook."

"It's very consoling," said the man.

He led them to a cupboard; by moving the board at the back they passed into the neighboring house.

Angelo climbed the stairs in the peasant's footsteps. He forced himself to make as little noise as possible.

"You don't need to tiptoe here," said his guide. "You won't surprise anyone."

The door opened on an old lady in a nightcap and bed jacket; she raised an oil lamp above her glasses.

"Is it you, wretch?" she said, "and with a gentleman too!"

"Pardon us, Signora Alicia; we're going to dirty your carpets, but we've got to pull the king's beard without letting him bite." She led them across a shabby, old-fashioned little drawing-room, where all the armchairs had lace cushion-covers, to a room where a tapestry representing Hannibal at Trebbia hid a passage to the next house.

Angelo marveled at this promenade, no longer thinking of the policeman from Ivrea. After the long hours in the dark, talking of noble, generous sentiments, the sight of the man with the pruning-hook standing against a backdrop of women and sleeping children, their throats trustfully exposed, had brought him up short. The old lady enchanted him, and he loved the fact that she had thought of the tapestry representing Hannibal. When she left them on the other side of the hidden passage, they found themselves in a large, echoing stairwell. The young peasant whistled softly. They heard a latch move, and immediately afterward, a night lamp lit the landing.

"Come ahead," said a voice.

It was an old servant in a striped vest.

"Boniface, are you on guard this evening?" said Christin.

"The Signorina went upstairs early to get rid of two officers."

"When will you learn to give them bad coffee?"

"The moment the Signorina orders me to."

"What must the Signorina order?" said a young and pleasant voice behind them.

Angelo turned and found himself in the presence of a young woman who had approached in bedroom slippers. The night lamp lighted her beautiful hair; by its light he could see that she was forcing her somewhat large but sensitive mouth into a hard expression.

Angelo greeted her gracefully.

"I heard about you this evening," said the young lady. "They're busy looking for you around Novara, where it seems the staff officer has become very touchy."

She had a book in her hand which she struck against her skirt like a riding-whip.

Angelo and his guide went down to the ground floor. Pushing a little door, they went out into a sort of garden; they stood beneath bare chestnut trees full of extremely brilliant stars.

Angelo's heart was full, as if he were about to leave home.

"Beyond that wall which we're going to jump," said Christin, "things will be a bit different, and I must know for sure whether we're in agreement. We have only three pistol shots between us; after that we'll have to make out as best we can. If there is the slightest danger of being caught, I prefer to be killed on the spot. I'm afraid I might not acquit myself well in front of an execution squad. I'm going to allow myself to give you one piece of advice which will show you I'm ready for anything: aim at the stomach. First of all, it cuts short any discussion; it hurts like hell, and we want them to howl. Nothing demoralizes soldiers more, especially at night. Things may turn out better. But this will do if they have a lantern which allows us to see their gold lace. Never fire on an officer. The soldiers hate him and are delighted to see him fall. It makes them lively. Whereas a comrade enrages them; they lose their head and that's what we need. Experience is the best teacher, Colonel."

Angelo answered tersely. The word *colonel* brought him down from the heights. He had thought no one could top the man with the pruning-hook.

On the other side of the wall they were immediately brought up short. A low voice called to them familiarly. It was the friend who had carried word to Christin.

"I knew you would come this way," he said, "but I was in a panic I would miss you."

His news was important. They returned to the garden for a small council of war.

The bulk of the patrols had departed in the direction of Novara. They were all on horseback. There had been such an uproar that they were out to do a careful job; this was both good and bad. They would not return for a long time but they would come back sure that Angelo had gained the freedom of the hills. Finally, an extraordinary bit of news which explained, he said, why he hadn't gone to bed: they were going to use the telegraph early the next morning.

"You really seem to stick in their throat," said Christin.

"About the telegraph," said his friend, "the operator, although not squarely with us, is receptive, you know, to certain arguments. We've seen to that. The dispatches are to be sent to the commanders of the garrisons at Candelo, Masserano, Crevacuore, and Ghemme; which seems to indicate that those who take an interest in you fear you'll go up toward Switzerland. Consequently, it's true they want to get you and kill you and not simply prevent you from going to Novara. The hills are the very jaws of the lion. They will besiege them one by one and get you. It's only a matter of days."

Despite the proximity of the bivouac fires which Angelo could see ruddy in the plain through the branches of the trees, he suggested smoking a cigar.

"All in all," he said, "we have some trump cards, or more exactly, thanks to you, I have some trumps. I must simply follow the policy of the needle in the haystack. As only my life is at stake, the first thing to do is not to let others get mixed up in this business. But if I go at it from this angle, you'll be determined to share my dangers on the pretext that you can't leave a friend in trouble. So get it through your heads that we can't afford the luxury of a charge. Two or fifty, we couldn't make a breach, sabers bared, all the way to Novara, in an army which is going to have a lot of fun in this fox hunt. What we must avoid above all is becoming a laughing-stock. You'll reply that if we kill ten (or even as many as a hundred), those ten won't feel like laughing. But there's the policeman from Ivrea and the people who employ him; they would think us ridiculous indeed to have thought the death of a few soldiers could impress them. They've already hemmed us in, and we'd never be able to break through."

For ten minutes, with the best reasoning in the world, he helped them choose the solution they would least regret.

"Nothing is easier to decide on than a fine gesture; it's afterwards the trouble begins," he said to himself. "If they go with me, they'll get in my way and especially curse me if, unfortunately, death leaves them time to think. I wouldn't be able to stand their last look at me."

At last, with skillful illogic that appealed to men who wanted happiness for everybody and were proud of their feeling, he spoke of nobility and generosity.

"The florin boy makes one," he thought meanwhile, "and the traitor of Turin or Ivrea who sold me to the police makes two; at the third I'm an imbecile."

"You're quite a man," said Christin. "Beyond a shadow of a doubt anyone would die for you with pleasure. And you still have time to change your mind if you want us in on the scheme. But certainly we stand to lose most by our own deaths."

"Then if you permit, I'll give you an order," said Angelo. "Leave me at the foot of this tree and get away from here as fast as possible. I'll make my arrangements after you leave. I ask only one thing of you: see that before the patrols return the rumor gets around that I have been seen in the flesh—some say around Turin and some say around Novara, and perhaps even around Ivrea where I'm supposedly returning."

After protestations and scruples which Angelo thought a bit long-winded, they decided, once he had returned the pistol, to leave.

He sounded the chime on his watch; it was a little after four in the morning. The night had extinguished the bivouac fires. The market town and the countryside were plunged deep in silence.

Angelo returned to the little door opening onto the garden. He took off his boots and went into the house. He climbed the front stairs without a sound.

"If I can find the way back into the old lady's without anyone seeing me," he said to himself, "the whole business is taken care of."

He remembered that after raising the tapestry, Christin had slipped aside a panel of canvas over the hole.

About the spot where he supposed the passage was his fingers, groping along the wall, encountered the thick frame of a very large picture. But the wall was solid behind it.

Farther along he touched a half-opened door. He was about to go on when, noticing that the door swung lightly on its hinges, he understood that they were carefully oiled. He struck a light quietly and, blowing on the tinder, saw a small rinsing room, the walls of which were hung with large miller's sacks. The passage was hidden behind the sacks. He then had only to push aside the tapestry of Hannibal to be once more in the old lady's spare room.

"Who will ever think I'm here?" he said to himself. "Now the only thing I have to do is to make a favorable impression on that spinster. Unfortunately, she's probably asleep."

He advanced cautiously on the carpet and touched an armchair.

"Far enough," he said to himself.

He settled himself comfortably and put his boots beside him.

His midday meal was long past and he was hungry, but he thought ironically of the lancers searching in the direction of Novara. He still did not understand why the policeman had come from Ivrea under such harsh orders. Unless Giuseppe had been up to his old tricks, or Carlotta . . . However, they had agreed that for the moment they wouldn't slip a powder in anyone's coffee.

In his naïveté he started to daydream of Piedmont up in arms; he thought of Paris too; although he had never visited the city, he was sure that every revolutionary password was forged there.

He imagined that he conducted a review of all prominent revolutionaries—the barricade experts, the traveling-salesmen of liberty.

He was soon asleep.

CHAPTER FOUR

He woke with a start. It was daylight. The old lady had undoubtedly been standing in front of him for some time, for her eyes no longer showed anything but a bit of malice. Although in his surprise he immediately stood *en garde,* he had the wit to make a few polite remarks.

"You've just reassured me on one point," she said. "Now I know that all the boys who go running through my apartment do sometimes sleep."

As she smiled, Angelo noticed, horrified, that he was barefoot and that his feet were dirty. He was deeply embarrassed, and murmured something in a most touching fashion about woods, long marches, and even liberty.

"If I let you stay," she said, "I assure you it won't be because I'm carefree. I have nothing to do with your revolution. Someone came and asked permission to make holes in my walls. I said yes; do you know why? Because I consider that man who thinks he's something just because he has a palace in Turin an imbecile. The rest of you have a tendency to throw out your chests too, but you're graceful about it, and you're young. Whereas that man with his beard is really past the age for foolishness. Let it be understood, however, that you're not to start spouting the lessons you've learned by heart a second time; even if the purity of your soul is at stake. I'm wary of bright eyes like yours. You're totally capable of being sincere. And at my age I don't want to be closeted with a sincere boy who shows me as easy as a-b-c that my life till now was not worth living and that spring will only begin tomorrow."

Angelo was hard put to find an answer. He could not mount any of his high-flying hobbyhorses.

She showed him a little nook where he could hide and even sleep: it contained a couch.

"A bit narrow," he said to himself, "especially if the soldiers come. There's not even room to lunge in, and my little knife will scarcely pierce a soldier's uniform unless I strike with all my strength."

He noticed the care with which the joint of the door had been fitted with a decorative line on the wall. It was impossible to detect three feet away.

The morning passed very slowly. He acted like someone on a visit.

"You look very well by my fireplace," said the old lady. "Your hair goes splendidly with the marble. But I go out every afternoon as the entire street knows. This is no time to be talked about. Besides, my wrist hurts, and that means a change in the weather. I must hurry and get some fresh air today. Go to your room. The shopkeepers of the neighborhood have known me for years and are very fond of me. The grocer opposite watches my windows when he knows I'm out, in case, I suppose, the curtains caught fire during my absence. If he saw a face at the panes or if he simply saw a shadow stirring, he would take action immediately. What's more, I'm under the impression that he's hand in glove with the soldiers, who spend enormous amounts in his store. It's not like Paris or London here."

Angelo closed the door of the closet carefully behind him and prudently remained in the absolute darkness.

He was reassured by the routine of the household. His hiding-place, although well hidden, caught every sound in the house. He heard a large clock with pompous bronze figures strike and even heard its glass dome vibrate with each stroke of the pendulum. Coals crackled in the fireplace. He busied himself studying the antimacassars which decorated the chairs. They were carefully crocheted of extremely fine thread and represented an acanthus jungle—or simply volutes such as a woman sheltered from the slightest passion might dream of.

·　·　·

"You're the subject of every conversation," said the old lady when she returned. "I've never seen anything stupider than the faces of the police looking for you. They must have been hand-picked to act like imbeciles when you're taken. A patrol of lancers is said to have just missed catching you this morning upstream from Arboro when you were crossing the river. You fired a pistol which sent several pieces of iron chewing into a young boy's artery. The tourniquet they fixed for him got out of place and he made as bloody a corpse as you could wish. They threw him on some straw in front of his comrades, who had seen him leave hale and hearty the evening before. It seems that he spoke very touchingly of his wife and children before he died. People are quoting very edifying words. He was certainly the personification of honor and duty, a man of the people, wrenched from the bosom of his family to serve his fatherland; to cut a long story short, the least I can say is that you choose your target very badly. The soldiers are furious. Four or five hotheads among them have gone to ask the colonel for military honors for your victim. It seems that the colonel is very broadminded and overlooked their impoliteness. People even claim that he had tears in his eyes. Just now I saw a charming barouche leave empty, escorted by three lancers in dress uniforms. I presumed it had gone to stock up on handkerchiefs since the entire army is in tears. I was corrected: it's going to fetch the widow and orphans from a farm near Borgo. They'll be made to parade dressed in black. The spectacle is going to be very well organized."

"I wouldn't want to bring the wrath of the gods down on this house for all the rice in China," said Angelo.

"This house is as innocent as a newborn lamb," she replied. "It could bear witness—if testimony differing from the whims of public opinion were of any use—that you were asleep in one of its armchairs at the precise moment when, seven leagues from here, you committed this crime which is so useful to the King. But it's a fact that soldiers on the eve of battle won't hesitate between the truth and a widow clawing her face (because, make no mistake, she will claw her face: they're obviously getting set to do things up brown), and a little town earning its bread and butter won't hesitate either. The seven leagues don't matter. You could easily have wings under your redingote. It's in the best interests of everyone to believe it. In fact, things have come to such a pass that today no one puts any stock in the story told by several peasants (they were very timid anyway) who claim to have seen you in the flesh around Ivrea. Without the widow you could easily have been around Ivrea. But at an opportune moment the lancer's artery was in the way of a little bit of ironwork, which, by the way, is said to have been very jagged. It was extracted from the wound. It's on show. It makes one quake. You've got to admit that Charles Albert knows where to put arteries."

"I've put you in great danger," said Angelo. "Everything they've rigged up can be demolished by your simple testimony. That'll be their first idea if they find me here."

He unburdened his heart with rhetoric worthy of an ancient orator but a bit ridiculous to this woman, who was the epitome of common sense, and whose cheeks, he had to admit, had flushed in the fresh air.

He was sincere. He even put his hand on the door knob.

"Leave that knob alone," said the old lady. "I expected better of you. I formed a more flattering opinion of your wits while watching you sleep. I never thought that once awake you would reason so unimaginatively. As soon as I start having some fun, someone always spikes it. First, on the pretext of prudence, then on the pretext of kindness, now on the pretext of generosity or I don't know what other synonym for pride. You're the worst yet! Aren't you ever going to stop talking? Are you, or aren't you a revolutionary? If you are, then admit the revolutionary spirit and let it go at that. And don't stand with your jaw hanging open just because an old lady speaks energetically, or I'll begin to swear. I was completely forbidden to use my mechanical hobbyhorse on the pretext that my long hair—which was very beautiful at the time of the mechanical horse—would catch in the gears. Ever since I've had a wild desire to stuff lots of things in lots of gears."

The next day was very hard for him.

Starting in the morning, drums veiled with crepe rolled in every street. They were carried by soldiers walking slowly and rolling their drumsticks on the stretched hide. They had to keep to the rhythm of one roll every two steps, as for a general-in-chief. This funereal rhythm was intended to provoke very egotistical, black ideas.

Angelo didn't dare admit that he was greatly shaken by these measured beats. He discovered that by moving a large Venetian mirror slightly he could see in it everything going on in the street without running the risk of being seen in the window. He put an end to this arrangement when he found himself face to face, in the mirror, with three drummers walking toward him at a slow pace, rolling the cylinders of their drums. Following orders, they gave a good but unimaginative imitation of profound grief: that is to say, they stared.

Angelo generously misinterpreted this complete lack of expression. He put it down to an imbecile state induced by excessive grief, as in Ariosto. It made him very unhappy. He didn't like to see people suffer.

His unhappiness was augmented by a large bell which began to toll the funeral knell. A cannon was fired also, as if to make known to the populace that all the dapper officers, who only the day before had gossiped with the townswomen, were now in mourning; then came the musket shots of the soldiers paying the last honors.

The widow had arrived during the night, without any escort, not even in the barouche which had ostensibly been sent for her. Naturally she had been lodged in the inn where Angelo had stayed —a useful contrast. She was a thick-set little woman, strong as a horse, who cried out from time to time as if to call sheep or wake a mule.

She was silently having a drink when three children were brought to her.

After the drummers' tour the townspeople began to gather under the arcades of the Piazza San Giorgio. The women, with the soldiers in mind, had dressed in their best; gay ribbons fluttered everywhere. A little bell, more piercing than the one which had sounded the funeral knell, began to ring excitedly; two panels of the church door folded open and all the preparations for a mass *praesente cadavere* could be seen. Thus it was a serious occasion and everyone spoke in a low voice. The attitude of the officers was significant as well. Grouped around the lancer colonel, the representatives of each corps of troops held their heads high, grimacing like pictures of men defying death. The artillery commander's absence was noticed, however. It was said that he had fired his cannon with bad grace. Besides, he was much given to the bottle and had unburdened himself of unsuitable remarks concerning the ceremony. It was whispered that he was going to be cashiered, even that his loyalty to the king was in question. People pointed out a man whose unpleasant, severe face made him seem in deep mourning, despite his shabby clothes. He was the policeman who had sworn by the body of the soldier not to drink another drop of brandy before putting an end to the crimes of the republicans. Those who didn't tread the straight and narrow path would have to reckon with him.

The officers had lined up on the side of the Piazza San Giorgio, facing the church. The guard of honor gathered on their left and sounded a very impressive "Order arms!" Shoulder straps slapped wood as gun butts sounded on the pavement, and then all was quiet, except for the clatter of sabots in the neighboring streets where six platoons of lancers waited and the regular tolling of a shrill bell. The bell disturbed the horses, making them nervous.

The widow appeared in the recess of the inn doorway. She let out one of her cries but was hastily pulled back by someone who seized her arm in order, as it later came out, to put a hat with long veils on her head. But in any case, the body had not yet come, and the colonel was growing impatient. He appeared to say something rather sharp. At that moment the command "Present arms!" resounded. The officers at attention raised their hands to their kepis, men removed their hats, women crossed themselves, and the hero of the day (or at least the white pine box containing him) made his entry into the square, carried by eight of his comrades. A moment of true sadness followed, unprovoked by the solemn display or by the large bell which had begun to ring loud and deep once more.

The widow, completely equipped, came out of the inn. She walked a little too quickly perhaps, dragging along a child with each hand. The rumor went round that the third child, terrified by the death of his father, had been seized with convulsions and that the major of the light-infantry regiment was at his bedside. Everyone felt very sorry for this little woman who with her long black veils and short-legged body looked like a hedgehog. Every five minutes, with absolute regularity, she exhaled a peaceful peasant cry.

"I must be seen at this ceremony," said the old lady, "and anyway, I don't want to miss a bit of it."

Angelo was in no humor to find things amusing. In the mirror he saw the deserted street and all the closed shops. The neigh of the horses, the chiming of the bells, the noises coming from the Piazza San Giorgio gave him food for thought. He had reached the conclusion that a man had been killed because of him and perhaps even by his fault. His imagination was vivid: he pictured all the details, especially the most horrible. He saw before him an unquenchable stream of blood flowing from a displaced tourniquet; he saw it reddening and soaking the uniform, hardening on it, the equipment, and the leather of the saddle down as far as the saddle blanket, splattering the dust of the roads and the fields. He said to himself: "Without me, that man would still be alive and would not have suffered that long agony" (the spectacle of which, minutely reconstructed, he contemplated). He went so far as to add: "That *innocent* man!" He was stupefied by the ease with which you could kill through an intermediary.

In this state of mind he heard the *Dies Irae* intoned very lugubriously. He looked into the mirror. There he saw the cross appear carried by a little choirboy black as ink.

The clergy had put on a big show. Their stoles, lace surplices, and copes were of the best. He wondered who was going to foot the bill. The commissariat, probably. This first-class show included singing by the full choir throughout the procession. The choir consisted of the butcher's eldest son—who had a very beautiful bass voice—and two young pupils of the Jesuit college: chubby boys with a suspicion of beards but endowed with extremely pure, somewhat reedy, girlish voices. The three acolytes were on hand, sumptuously dressed, affording the greatest possible enjoyment to both eye and ear. As the order of the ceremony had been planned so that the flag-bearers of all the chartered societies of the region would walk in the van (just behind the three singers), many had intrigued up to that very morning to be up front in order to enjoy the hymns.

This advance guard of the procession, setting its own slow pace, moved very solemnly. Completely occupied with the profound enjoyment of the three singers, who were delighted by the harmony of their own voices, these music-lovers stared with the fixed eyes and immobile features of egotists at work. There could be no more perfect imitation of the inanity of grief.

"These men are not sad according to orders," Angelo said to himself. He was above all impressed by the thick mustaches of the peasant citizenry. Their surly whiskers lent a certain virtue to the entire scene.

He heard wide wheels grinding with a muffled noise as they rolled slowly over the uneven pavement. He expected to see a small caisson arrive; instead he saw a plain truck on which flags had been draped. Riflemen, their guns pointing to the ground, escorted the bier which had been very bizarrely perched on top of a sort of catafalque. The desire to show off the *corpus delicti* was too evident and smacked of the police.

At last a reasonable, even somewhat useful idea occurred to Angelo.

"Is there really anybody in that coffin?" he asked himself. "If the coffin's empty, what a splendid hoax!"

The old lady returned with some news. "What a coronation!" she said, taking the pins out of her feathered hat. "You were publicly crowned werewolf. They gained time with the ceremony. Here where people know life for what it is, it's twenty years before they label anyone a murderer; until the tenth corpse he's just a poor fellow. But with these goings-on, you've been tagged at the first offense. An officer sporting four medals delivered a discourse at the tomb, explaining everything: your cowardice, your way of creeping up in the dark, and especially your habit of attacking *the people*. He emphasized the fact that you killed a soldier, saying that you were very careful not to fire on the officer commanding the patrol. He didn't dare say you were afraid; this would have tended to rouse the sympathies of the shopkeepers who are also scared; but he pointed out that you were a former colonel and an aristocrat. Now no one will be astonished if you're killed at sight.

The police have a free hand now: that's what they were after. I think they were after something else too, but had to give it up. The officer read his discourse so slowly that I wondered if he wasn't hoping someone would contradict him. When he said you were a coward—and the word came up more than a hundred times—the police and the staff looked all around above the heads of the crowd. They looked as if they were waiting for someone. I promised myself to ask you a question. Do the police know the workings of your heart? Or if you prefer, couldn't a friend have explained your small bit of interior clockwork to them? Whoever's looking for you seems to be banking on a certain knowledge of your weaknesses."

"I have few friends."

"One is sufficient."

"None of them would sell me."

"It's obviously not a cash deal. Besides, what you just said was stupid. Don't you know that a friend has a hundred ways of hating? In short, are you a man to answer any provocation, whatever it may be, without hesitating; or to put it another way, can people hit you where it hurts?"

"It's true I don't stop to think," he said, "but I would hate to. If I didn't let myself be carried away by an instinct for actions which bring immediate happiness, I would be nothing."

"You're a child," she said, "and they know it."

"But they don't know that I've been keeping my eyes open."

And he mentioned the probable emptiness of the coffin.

"I don't agree with you," she said. "The coffin was full as an egg. It was a mass *praesente cadavere*. And a mass with an open casket is a windfall for the clergy: there's nothing like it to encourage the fear of hell-fire. The clery wouldn't botch its best trump, *even* to help set a trap."

Angelo was touched by the little adverb. "That 'even' is something I can appreciate," he thought. "It makes me happy—no belly-laughs or ecstasies either, just happy."

The weather was gusty during the night. Coming out of his retreat, Angelo heard hail striking the window panes.

"I went to the neighbors for news," said the old lady. "At my age a woman alone has the right to be afraid, especially when the wind rattles the doors. The artillery commander is in hot water.

He had a violent argument about you yesterday evening with a lancer captain. It seems you were partly right. Maybe there wasn't much in that coffin. There was a corpse all right: they had one on hand, there's no doubt of that; they were careful to show it off, and fifty people incapable of a concerted lie saw it. But when the so-called widow got back from the cemetery, she had a couple of drinks, and when they tried—without using kid gloves either—to get her to go to bed, she demanded a certain sum of money they had promised her. People go so far as to say that the children were borrowed. First there were to be three; only two were seen. There's a lot of embroidering going on. A scandal's a ceremony just like any other. Your artillery commander has put his foot in it, whereas the lancers were like cats, lapping milk without wetting so much as their whiskers. They were starting to behave like boors when some-one pointed out to them that they were wearing sabers. There's talk of a duel."

"I'll be there," said Angelo. "It's up to me, not him, to fight."

"Where are you going?"

"To that artillery officer's. Perhaps at this very moment he's dead or wounded. They've certainly matched him against some trickster who'll get him in no time. I have only one skill: I know how to use a saber. A half hour from now, there'll be at least one lancer who won't feel much like laughing."

He put on his coat and repeated: "Is there any way I can get out of this house without compromising you?" five or six times. The last question was so loud that he was ashamed of himself. He asked the question again very sweetly.

"And if this is another trap?" she said.

"I'll have to accept it," he said.

She conducted him to the ground floor where a servants' passage led to a little alley. She opened the door and smiled prettily. "I love women," he said to himself. "They understand everything."

It was early. The wind and rain had the free run of the streets. He walked for ten minutes, head lowered, before finding a man sheltered under a sack, trying to clear a drain stopped up by large hailstones. He asked him where the artillery commander lived. With a timber merchant, he learned, who had a beautiful house next door to his warehouses. Angelo knocked on the door which was opened immediately by a young, frightened servant girl who had been weeping. Sniffling between each two words, she said that the commander was in, that he hadn't gone out.

"Don't worry," said Angelo, "I'm his friend. Take me to his room."

The commander was in slippers. He was smoking his pipe and looked at Angelo with astonishment.

"I'm the man who did not kill the lancer and I'm sorry," said Angelo. "I've been told you were to fight because of me. You'll understand very well that if it's a question of dispatching one of yesterday's comic-opera impresarios, I want to do it myself."

"I thought Piedmont was no more," said the man. "Make yourself at home and have some coffee with me."

He was a short man, a little corpulent but robust. His eyes were amazingly blue.

"As for taking my place, you can forget about that. My gunners would never forgive me. I'm no novice. From seeing us with dirks you'd think a cavalryman's saber would make hash of us. But they'll strike bone. Anyway the duel has been put off till tomorrow because of the bad weather."

"That's pure malice," said Angelo. "A point of honor can't be put off. I know full well what your adversary's going to do today."

"To hell with what he's going to do today; I have a pretty clear idea what I'm going to do tomorrow. Do you know what I was saying to myself, a half hour before you knocked on my door? They know you're still in town because they've combed the fields with a fine tooth. I said to myself: 'If the fellow is worth anything, you'll know it. If you hadn't been worth your salt, I'd have fought anyway; but now, allow me to tell you, it's a treat.' "

He went to the door and called his servant softly. She must have been waiting, she came so quickly.

"My sweet," he said, "go make us a big pot of coffee."

"There speaks an artilleryman," said Angelo to himself.

"She seems to care for you a great deal," he said aloud.

"Annette? She's quite a girl. I'm a father to her. She's an orphan; that's why she dissolves into tears."

"This is the first time I've ever let anyone fight for me," said Angelo, "but you've said enough in the last quarter of an hour for me to recognize your right to. However, there's one thing we both want: to live, if only to show those who want to see us dead. But this depends on a few flicks of the wrist; I must know ten of them. We mustn't leave anything to chance. Ask your master-at-arms to bring two cavalry sabers and I'll show you two or three little tricks a lancer would never suspect.

"But," he added, "perhaps you find me imprudent? I'm your guest; maybe you would like me to remain unknown to everyone except you and the little girl who worships you."

He thought that he had never seen anything more handsome than this hero in bedroom slippers.

"I'll call not only my fencing-master," said the man, who had a large household, "but five or six of my officers. If we were the jokers these parade cavalrymen are, I could have you stroll by all the batteries bare-headed without a risk. To handle cannon, you've got to muck up your hands with grease and strap a lot of junk on your back. That's why we're all republicans. The King would have done away with his police long ago if he could count on his cannon. But he can't."

The girl brought the coffee. She had stopped sniffling, although she was still a little short of breath.

"Go get me Bartholomew, my sweet."

The orderly arrived ten minutes later.

"I won't tell you who this gentleman is unless you carry out my orders carefully," the commander told him. "Hurry to the friends whose names I'll give you. Tell them to come round as fast as possible; it'll be worth their while."

Angelo tasted almost indescribable happiness. He was no longer alone; his passionate nature had found a kindred spirit.

Soon there was a knock at the door: the two lieutenants who had been summoned. They had taken just time enough to throw a coat over their fatigues. Then a captain, an adjutant, and a corporal entered. Angelo was introduced to them; for ten years they had been waiting for a bit of madness and, despite the disparity of ages and ranks, they all began to talk somewhat extravagantly and laugh as if for the first time.

"Above all," Angelo said to himself, "don't mention fraternity or any feeling that is easily come by."

"Gentlemen," he said, "when I find a friend I tremble for fear that I don't deserve him, and here I am with six. . . ."

"Anywhere else I would be ridiculous," he said to himself, "that's why we're in revolt."

"Not all of your friends are here," said the corporal; "go search the batteries and you'll find others. Besides, I know you, Colonel: I was serving in Count Avogadro's squadron when you left for France. This isn't the first time I've had the pleasure of seeing you."

"I've never been more than a comic-opera colonel. Now I'm earning my real stripes."

Finally they talked about the duel. At the back of the courtyard were the wood merchant's warehouses.

"Let's go find ourselves a quiet little spot there," said Angelo, "and get to work. Put on the trousers and boots you'll be wearing tomorrow, Commander. You've got to break them in. In this kind of business things sometimes hang by a thread. You can be sure your adversary knows this and is counting on taking advantage of it. They've only put off the encounter in order to play *big*."

They found a suitable spot in one of the timber warehouses. The corporal had brought sabers of the right weight and length.

He blushed with pleasure when Angelo congratulated him on having left nothing to chance.

"I'm of your school of thought, sir," he said.

"I'll see about that," said Angelo. "Let's have a little set-to, just the two of us. First, I want the commander to watch. It's easier to copy tricks one has seen."

"How shall I attack you?" said the corporal.

"As violently as possible, and if you can bring yourself to hate me a little, that would be perfect. Wait till I make myself clear. This is no game. Let's try to reproduce tomorrow's combat as exactly as possible. We won't stop till my thrusts could strike you. I'll hold back; I won't touch you. Don't be afraid: in reality I love you and you love me. Even if you kill me no wrong will have been done."

"You're asking too much of me," said the corporal.

"Nothing is too much to help our friend."

"You're quite a man," said the commander. "Do what he says, Hector. Today is the finest day of my life."

The corporal was a former hussar. He began with a few flourishes. They were forceful, but still too decorative.

"Stop," said Angelo. "You'll never beat the lancer fighting Italian style. Listen: while I was in France, I stayed in Aix-en-Provence for more than a year. I got bored. I frequented a fencing-school run by a certain M. Bisse. I've never met a person with a better feeling for the weapon. He told me something very true: 'By its form the saber encourages feints. These must be cut short.' He also said: 'No Italian will ever cut his feints short.' I was annoyed. I learned to cut them short. In the end I cut them short before he did. *En garde* now, and you'll see! Attack!"

In the midst of a great "show of steel" Angelo executed an effortless backhand thrust which could not be parried.

"The devil take me," said the corporal, "if this doesn't interest me."

He set to work much more heatedly. He parried wildly—backhand thrusts, straight ones, disdainful lashes, easy at first, then tougher, increasingly unforeseeable and even coming from where his adversary's blade *wasn't*. He was talented himself. His inventions were happy. Angelo urged him on and he went to it, giving himself completely. When Angelo thought himself hermetically sealed off, he executed a *divine* hit with the point of his saber; it rang on the buckle of the sword belt and stopped short an inch from the skin of the man's stomach.

"Let's catch our breath!" said Angelo.

"I've better things to do than catch my breath," said the corporal. "I've had enough. I did everything I knew how, and more, enough to bag three carloads of fencing-school assistants. But I prefer you in a picture rather than in the flesh. If we began again I'd really hate you."

"Then let's embrace right away," said Angelo. "I did my best too and you stood up to me."

The two little lieutenants were fresh out of school. They were full of the wonders of the world and this was the first fight they had seen which wasn't straight out of a logarithm table. Their comments were wildly enthusiastic and beside the point. The captain and the adjutant, however excited, spoke like men who know that there's many a slip between the cup and the lip. They were old friends of the commander and they didn't hide it.

"You're very good," said the latter, "but I'm of age, am I not? You're coddling me. Do you know what's going to happen if you coddle me too long? I'll become a doddering old man who can't hold his water. Come on now, let me get into the act. I'm dying to be put on trial."

Angelo found him better than he had thought and even quite cunning.

"Don't wear yourself out; just warm up."

"Here's a very fine fighter," he said to himself, "who doesn't shirk and who takes risks courageously. If tricksters hadn't taken up the art of the saber, his would be the way to fight. But the tricksters exist."

"You don't cover yourself sufficiently," he said. "You go to meet the thrusts. It dazzles me, but you're going to have to cope with a lancer who first of all is under orders—don't deceive yourself on this score—and, second, is in no way magnanimous. He has been ordered to do a job; he's going to try to do it as fast as possible and in such a way that he won't have to do it again. He wants to please his employers and get the job over with so he can go back to his card game. You acted with honesty and courage and you continue to act with honesty and courage. But these qualities are against you because they're known. You must apply them to things they don't know and would never expect."

For three full hours, but with judiciously timed rests which conserved all his pupil's vigor, Angelo tried to show the commander that he should operate like the works of a clock.

"I'm very unhappy," he said. "I value your esteem above that of any other man. However, I'm doing everything possible to make you scorn me. This clockwork is the diametrical opposite of the soul. But I want you to live and this is the only way."

They threw themselves into each other's arms. "I haven't given my heart an airing in a long time," thought Angelo. "How wonderful these embraces are!"

The thrust, he explained, was not treacherous but simply very beautiful, so beautiful that it bordered on the most unexpected trick, for tricksters only.

The young men saw only the beauty of it; Angelo's sincerity had overwhelmed them. The commander and the captain were thrilled to rediscover the absurd reasoning of youth.

After another hour's work into which everyone put heart and soul, the commander stopped and said he was hungry.

They were all astonished when they came out of the shed to find that the weather was still bad, gusty with hail and heavy rain that fell almost horizontally in the wind.

They lit a good fire in the fireplace, drew the table into the middle of the room and sent to the mess for lunch. A fatigue detail of three soldiers came with flasks of wine to lay the table. Everyone was happy; it was like a picnic in the country.

"Today," said the captain, "let's say to hell with the police, the lancers, and everyone who's not on our side. There's not a single bastard in the kingdom of Sardinia who would dare stick his nose in our business."

Angelo asked permission to give two florins to the fatigue detail to buy themselves wine.

"If my commander agrees," said the adjutant, "I'll give the order to buy wine for all the batteries. I get a cut."

They had to show the lancers that the members of the artillery were men. Was there any better way than by blithely drinking?

An orderly was told to go get some volunteers and roll out some kegs.

"I don't know what we've started," said the commander, "but I'm delighted. I've had enough of demanding salutes. Our house of Savoy, although until now it has had no more than bourgeois privileges to hand out, is horribly afraid of a night like the 4th of August.[1] This is one, and nothing is finer."

It must be admitted that Angelo was afraid of this enthusiasm. After a while he saw a somewhat sad, or at least serious look in the eyes of the commander.

However, lunch was very gay. Indoors it was warm while outside the rain beat against the windows; arms and hearts had been well exercised in the morning.

[1] On the night of August 4, 1789, the French Assembly revoked all feudal privileges.

"I left Turin a week ago," said Angelo; "I have no idea of what's been going on. All these troops in Casteletto surprised me. What's up?"

"What you see are only the reserves," replied the adjutant. "All the active army of the kingdom of Sardinia is lined up along the Ticino. Their cartridge cases are full. They have three days' provisions in their packs. We have twenty rounds for each piece in our caissons. The cavalry has half its forces in the saddle and on guard in rotation day and night. And we've been ordered to follow the instructions of Secret Circular No. 4, which, as everyone knows, authorizes requisitions and gives military justice precedence over civil. Although no more than a simple adjutant, I've had the right for the last five days to give orders to the syndics."

"Everyone has huffed on his spectacles and wiped them clean," said the captain. "All eyes are fixed on Milan and it's said that there's going to be an outburst there. If that ourburst comes, it'll mean war with Austria. We'll take Lombardy."

"We'll get a good kick in the teeth first, Achilles," said the commander. "In Turin they think Radetzky will throw in the sponge the minute three pistols fart off under his officers' noses. But that's not the way to skin a cat."

"Radetzky is eighty-three years old," said one of the lieutenants, who had a charming blond mustache carefully twisted above very thin lips.

"My dear little Alexander, you're mistaken in your judgment. When our monarch played the perfect lover to the Viceroy (not so long ago as all that) you dined at the field marshal's table just as I did. Did he seem so moldy to you then?"

"No, Captain, but war is for the young."

The commander guffawed.

"They're blushing," he said. "They're both blushing. The other one hasn't said a word, but they're thick as thieves, as usual. They're trying to get it across to me that I'm an old crock. That's what they mean, Achilles, and it goes for you too."

The two lieutenants protested but they had indeed reddened to the roots of their hair; their peach fuzz showed against their scarlet cheeks.

"No, my little ones, you can't pull the wool over my eyes quite so easily. I used to think as you do. Once I was of an age where I thought a man of thirty old, and now as I'm forty . . ."

"What beautiful eyes he has!" Angelo said to himself. "They're so frank! Should I teach him to be deceitful even to save him?"

(Angelo thought himself a monster of duplicity because he knew thirty secret ways to kill a man with a saber in single combat.)

". . . an old monkey who knows how to make faces. Anyone who gives you three cock feathers has got you in the bag, my children. You'll say that the same goes for me, since I lead the column. But no; it's discipline and habit which hold me. I'm told, 'March or die' and, since this is one of the precepts of my trade, I march and if necessary die. It's all in a day's work. Or rather it's all in the name of an old trickster."

"What trickster, my dear Ajax?"

"Why Charles Albert, my dear Achilles! Our beloved monarch; the progenitor of the house of Savoy, the future King of all Italy, the old gossip of Turin, the tall, dry-as-dust mummy who is preparing to rule, among other subjects, three hundred thousand Carbonari like ourselves, and especially like our two little lieutenants."

"If we leave aside our need for happiness," said Angelo, "it's evident that we're seated at a gaming-table with Charles Albert and Austria."

"Each man is playing for his own skin," said the commander, "but what does our happiness consist of? Liberty?"

"No," said Angelo. ("He has those blue eyes," thought Angelo, "and he *reasons* into the bargain.")

"That's more like it," said the latter. "Come let me embrace you. After this morning's display of steel I no longer knew whether you were Robespierre or the honest fellow who entered my house at daybreak. I've been a Carbonaro for seventeen years. That makes me ready for a pension. I was Achilles's, Hector's, and the adjutant's godfather, and all of us together have been godfathers to all the Carbonari in the batteries. Only Alexander and his buddy came out of the Politecnico already baptised. It seems that the younger generation learns to hate tyrants along with their multiplication tables. But if you wanted me to send the self-respect I owe myself packing, you'd have to fight me till my last gasp. Our happiness lies in our humanity."

They embraced after wiping their mustaches.

Night fell sooner than usual; extremely black clouds pouring forth heavy rain rolled by level with the roof tops.

"Do you know why they're trying to keep you from going to Novara?" asked the commander. "It's because our side has the initiative there. Conspiracies go on right out in the open. Meetings with all the chandeliers lit, cabals at the Prince's, or rather at the Princess Pio's, while carriages block the street in peace. And our staffs are obliged to stand all this. Imagine what a blow would have been dealt this ardor if you had been hanged! Because they didn't intend to shoot you but to hang you on the Piazza San Giorgio and to leave you hanged in a most ridiculous posture for everyone to see while they pulled your tongue and mucked up your trousers. That's why we've got to get you out of this wasp's nest, and I have a trick to parade you out right under the nose of the wasps."

The trick was to give Angelo an artillery captain's uniform and send him out at the head of a small patrol. No one would look under the kepi of an officer obviously on duty. And this very night, gusty as it was, was suitable for his departure.

Angelo didn't like the idea of the disguise.

"It's not a disguise. You were a colonel in the hussars. You can very well come out in favor of the artillery and honor this branch of the service by accepting the rank of captain. But joking aside, I'll tell you why you must do as I say: you've got to stay alive, you told me so yourself. You've taught me your tricks; here's mine. You're about Achilles's height. You'll wear an exercise uniform which will fit you loosely. We'll mount your little cavalry detachment on four or five of the most high-strung horses we own and then, off you go! We've had a good day but we'd better not strain our luck too far. Think how we'd look if the lancers got you in the end. . . . !"

Angelo objected to the soldiers escorting him.

"They won't escort you, they'll justify your presence on the roads. After what you've shown me of your talents, don't think I want to protect you with an escort. Hector will be your corporal. He'll choose three friends who'll take to you like ducks to water. You'll be in command of them. Should you wish to commit suicide in the course of the journey, they'll love you sufficiently to let you do it. But in that case I'll think you were fibbing when you said you wanted to live, and I'll ask myself scores of questions about the spot you were in such a hurry to occupy in Paradise. It could be very bothersome in the future, and I won't think of you with any pleasure."

The slate blue worn by the Piedmontese artillery didn't have much life to it despite its piping, but the captain went to get his full-dress uniform with gold epaulettes, a purple lanyard, and a shako with a green feather. Angelo cinched in the sword belt over the tunic which was a little too full. He looked most impressive. The corporal soon arrived with three soldiers who were obviously in seventh heaven.

Angelo wrapped himself in a heavy raincoat. It was a moment when the heart alone could speak.

"Stay on the defensive," said Angelo in a small, trembling voice. "Don't use what I taught you unless you're very hard pressed. Exercise two hours more this evening, then go to bed without either alcohol or coffee."

He could not go on.

"You do your job, old man," said the commander. "We'll do ours."

The minute he was in the saddle, Angelo knew his horse was spirited.

"What do you think of the nag, Captain?" asked the corporal. "Ours are of the same temper. That's in case you want to get fancy while we're strolling to Novara. The men would love that. They're all former hussars and I promised them we were in for some sport."

The wind had extinguished all the lanterns in Casteletto. When the riders were out of the town, it struck them harder, but the rain was to their backs.

Angelo approached the corporal.

"Do you know any house about a league from here where we could spend the night? I want to stay in the neighborhood. The outcome of tomorrow's duel doesn't strike me as certain."

"I was worrying about exactly the same thing," said the

brigadier. "The commander has always been quite a man. We're six men and six horses. The best idea is to push on as far as the posting-station."

This was two leagues away, at the Buronzo crossroads. The station's broad, lighted windows made it possible to see the start of the Novara road, bordered by tall, wind-tormented poplars. There was no one in the main hall.

"The couriers have been by," said the innkeeper, "and in this weather, no one would travel except the regular services. I was about to go to bed."

"Go ahead; don't bother with us," said Angelo, "close the shutters; give us some wood to keep up the fire, some rum, sugar, and your punch bowl. I'm paying and I'm generous. You don't have to wait on us. Just get what I asked for."

Their host had little cigars as well.

"I haven't smoked one for five days," said Angelo.

"Buy yourself a bunch," said the brigadier. "Today you scarcely had time."

Before a good blaze the soldiers began to talk politics in the manner of the people, that is by proclaiming their likes and dislikes. They were happy to be able to argue without having to think of the consequences, and to be sitting by a fire on which punch was cooking.

"But we're making too much of a din; the captain must want to sleep."

"When I sleep nothing bothers me," said Angelo. "Go right ahead."

"You should take off your boots," said the corporal. "Let me bring this chair up to your armchair. I want you to stretch out your legs and rest them. As far as we're concerned, there's more in two well-strung thighs and sound knees than in a thousand professors' heads. Let me coddle you. We don't often have a chance for hope, especially a hope that stands on his own two feet."

The simple soldiers, still deep in their stupid talk, wrapped Angelo carefully in dry coats.

He awakened, summoned by the corporal.

"It's four o'clock. The duel is on now. There was a small scare about midnight. Quite a large party of lancers is ferreting around in the neighborhood. There must be about ten of them. They went by once at a gallop, taking the Novara road. They returned at a trot a little later. We heard them once more going along the road at a walk. We've taken precautions. Things have been calm for some time."

An artilleryman was on guard near the door, musket in hand.

"We won't leave," said Angelo, "until we know—perhaps I should say until we are reassured—about the fate of that fine blue-eyed man who so wanted to hold a saber in my stead. Without even a cup of coffee, one of you must go to Casteletto immediately for news, and come back as fast as possible."

"All right, I'll go," said the thinnest of the soldiers. "If it's a question of speed, I can beat everyone by five minutes because I'm the lightest."

Dawn broke in a calm but cloud-encumbered sky. Angelo smoked a little cigar on the doorstep. The Novara road, still glistening with rain, floated over fields swathed in mist. Around the inn the poplars, tranquil once more, raised their long, bud-starred branches in the pale light. Groves of sycamores black as ink, red willows, and aspens whiter than snow, disposed like stage sets far away on the plain, appeared as the mist shifted. The peaceful morning stillness gave a strange sharpness to every noise: the drip of water from the roof tiles, the wing-beat of a silent crow, the sigh of the earth sated with water. Far away to the east a trumpet sounded the four acid notes of reveille.

The Arona diligence arrived. Angelo looked at his watch. It was five-thirty. He walked round the house. Behind the stables his little troop was ready.

"Perhaps it went on longer than expected?" said the corporal.

Finally, after a quarter of an hour, they heard the sound of a fast gallop. The soldier had returned.

"He was done in!" he said. "No one knows whether the bastard who did him in really was a lancer. Although he was wearing a lancer's uniform. They stuck the old man in front of some guy who couldn't possibly miss him. They didn't leave a thing to chance."

"To horse!" said Angelo.

He took the Casteletto road and started to gallop immediately.

The corporal had trouble catching up with him.

"Albergo della Corona," he shouted. "They're celebrating."

Then he restrained his horse and got back into line.

Angelo stopped at the entrance to the town.

"Straighten your uniforms," he said, "chin strap as if on parade, kepi straight and proceed at a walk behind me."

Casteletto was still asleep. Above the roofs Angelo noticed a very beautiful, green wing-shaped cloud in which the first rays of a pale sun lighted golden feathers one by one. On the deserted Piazza San Giorgio only the Albergo della Corona had its large rose windows open; the lamps were still lit in them. Behind the panes red and white uniforms could be seen.

Angelo greatly loved the noble, measured noise the horses' hoofs made on the pavement of the square. With a simple gesture of his hand he stopped his little troop so that they faced the windows, five paces away. The twenty-four horseshoes halted at exactly the same instant. He could not have felt more exalted.

Inside they had been watching his maneuver. Faces had approached the panes.

"Give me a musket ball," said Angelo.

He threw it like a stone against a pane which flew into splinters. Someone opened the window.

"There's a swine among you," Angelo said calmly. "I'm spitting in his face and if this bothers him any, he can come and politely tell me why in the hotel stable where I'll be waiting."

He awarded himself the luxury of remaining a few seconds longer, immobile and exquisitely happy, before the dumbfounded faces; then with a mere pressure of his knees he turned his horse.

He thought, almost casually, of a thousand noble and pure things while the horse wheeled with perfect grace.

After setting foot in the stable, he immediately took off his tunic and shirt, drew his saber and waited.

"Two sentinels at the *porte cochère*," said the corporal in a low voice. "Stand by to fire. Keep your eyes open. Don't look at the spectacle; look where that little street opens; that's where the police may appear. If they arrive, fire into the air. That'll shut their traps. Keep the horses, you. Orson, stay with me: you'll be a second."

The lancers were somewhat in disarray, but rollicking. They pulled themselves together once they saw Angelo bare-chested. A tall, thin captain, moving with all the suppleness of beasts trained to dangerous games, advanced, dragging his feet elegantly.

"Are you the one who did the spitting?" he asked.

Angelo didn't answer. He felt a shiver of pleasure.

"Not so talkative any more, are you?" continued the other. "I admit it's tough luck to kick the bucket as young as you. But, you shouldn't have played with fire: it burns."

He took off his overcoat and his shirt; someone handed him a saber; he stood *en garde*.

Angelo ostentatiously placed one foot beside the other and stood stiff as a sentinel.

"Idealist!" said the lancer with a little smile. His lips were of the thin variety so useful for expressing scorn. He attacked impetuously. Angelo, feet together, parried without moving. The smile disappeared from the lancer's lips. He forced his performance, lashing one after another with three backhanded thrusts which were almost impossible to parry but which met with ringing steel; he opened his mouth, perhaps to cry out. Angelo lunged as far as possible, as if he had been fighting with a sword. The sole of his boot resounded like a pistol shot on the beaten earth. Half his blade penetrated the lancer's stomach. The man belched. With a sharp turn of his wrist Angelo sank his blade four inches deeper. The lancer uttered a little, trembling, feminine cry; at the same time his body exhaled an enormous organic noise. His knees folded and he fell slowly.

"For God's sake, stay at your posts!" the corporal shouted to the sentries.

"Next!" cried Angelo.

He still felt an exquisite sensation in the palm of his hand: the small leap of the supple blade bursting the skin.

The climax had been so rapid that the lancers had not yet moved. They looked at the captain stretched out full length; he was twitching horribly.

"No fooling around, Colonel," said the corporal. He helped Angelo into his shirt.

Angelo took the time to button all the buttons of his tunic.

"You enjoyed yourself?" asked the corporal. "We did too. Now we must clear out."

Once out of the town, they left the highway and started across the fields.

In the limpid air the mountains seemed near; the line of their peaks bit incredibly sharply into the clear, linden-green sky. In the hollows of this line the ice and snow of Switzerland were heaped like powdered sugar. Villages ordinarily hidden in the blue distance showed every *génoise,* tower, and battlement as they gripped mountainsides, perched on rocks, and spread over alpine meadows skirted by shining ilex forests. The rain of the day before varnished their tiles; the first rays of the sun made the rough-cast of their walls blossom rosily, lighting the gold netting of their old ironwork.

The countryside stirred at the tender touch of the breeze, chilly and acid one minute and the next, caressing the land with warmth. The horses trotted through the meadows, scaring up masses of finches, all singing, and heavy, solitary crows which rose silently on great felt wings. Patches of narcissus whitened the grass.

Angelo felt detached and at peace.

"At any other time a morning like this would have made me happy," he thought, "but I killed that man with pleasure, perhaps with too keen a pleasure."

A few birches already displayed leaves light as glass baubles; tall aspens planted in rows around the fields tossed up a soft green foam from the tips of their branches; the proud peaks of the ancient poplars were still colorless. The orchards, crisscrossed with new red wood, laddered their way from terrace to terrace up the slopes of the hills. On the steep mountain the oak groves were refreshed by the vermilion of new growth. Blue down, which, from where they were, looked like the fuzz between a kid's horns, filled the valleys.

Angelo's little cavalry troop followed a road flanking the hill. On his right began the plain down to Vercelli.

The tents of the Piedmontese infantry dotted the fields as far as the eye could see. Some were topped with banners. Officers in shirt sleeves smoked cigars while pacing back and forth. Fatigue details wearing short gray-linen tunics went to and fro from the fountains with canvas buckets. Greatcoats were airing on ropes strung between poplars; men were beating blankets with willow branches. Small groups of soldiers took up their guns to go on guard; others made the rounds of the camp fires, which were not yet flaming but only smoking a great deal. A courier, recognizable by the red feather in his hat, strode through the fields, leaping brooks; a sentry, bayonet in hand, kept company a flag planted in the ground before the open door of a staff pavilion. Orderlies were sitting on the grass, shining boots. A regimental barber was drumming up trade by clicking his scissors like a dog-shearer. A patrol strolled home.

It was the bivouac of the 22nd Light Rifles. They were holding a line from Serravallo to Gregio along the Sesia. It's easy to see when a corps is in third or fourth position back of the front lines. The soldiers had constructed huts of branches and thatch. They had been careful to place them on knolls, hillocks, and the lower slopes of the hill (some of them were even near the road Angelo was following), so that they looked stylish. At the moment they were all busy grinding coffee in mills which sounded like grasshoppers. They were heating water in pots set on three stones over heaps of glowing coals.

The five horsemen, with Angelo in the lead (holding himself stiff as a sentinel) crossed the Sesia at a ford above a mill. Some unarmed soldiers had settled themselves like vacationing bourgeois for some quiet fishing along the canal paralleling the river. Cloddish peasants that they were, they dropped their tackle dumbfounded to give this snooty artillery officer a strictly regulation salute.

Across the river the Novara road wound its serpentine way through the willows. In this narrow valley which caught the full sun, the spring was more advanced. The vines were beginning to weep. Their owners, wearing drugget redingotes and with spectacles on their noses, had come out to examine the vinestocks. They had parked their carriages under the elms to keep the road clear where the commissary wagons, small caissons in convoy, and also freebooting soldiers of every variety were passing by. When the latter saw Angelo with his shining gold lace and curling feathers on his hat, they took to the bushes; the rogues, who had slipped pieces of white paper up their sleeves so that they just showed over their cuffs, as if they were carrying orders, stood at attention and saluted by the side of the road.

The hawthorn trees smelled strongly. Also Angelo caught the appetizing fragrance of hot bread coming from the regimental bakeries installed in the meadows, the perfume of aquatic grasses, damp stones, and fish which all streams exhale, and the incense of trotting-horses. The cloth of his borrowed uniform, the visor of the kepi, and the sun-warmed plume showing his rank also had an odor which Angelo inhaled in small draughts.

Dazzling clouds raced across the blue sky. Bugle and trumpet cries rang out around the entire horizon. An armed company came out of a cart track and broke ranks to climb the hill. The silver catkins on the long willow branches sparkled in the sun. A small boy (armed with a wrought iron bell from around a ram's neck) stood by every hen house guarding the poultry. Seated at the foot of an oratory, a goosegirl wrote in the dust with her staff.

The five horsemen passed through Romagnano. A military band with drums and bugles was practicing the Royal March among the trees planted quincuncially at the entrance to the town. The main street was blocked by peasant carts and military vehicles. But people gave way—without cursing—to the little troop. The five men were obviously on duty; and meant business, to judge by the way they had their chin straps fastened. They were riding very fine horses; they used them insolently; the least you could say was that they were in no joking mood. A sergeant major going by on the side walk with an account book under his arm even went so far as to tell people to move along. Angelo returned his salute so politely that the delighted officer continued, for the fun of it, to tell them to move on.

Beyond Romagnano, they resumed a walk on a crowded road. They seemed to have left the bivouac region for an area occupied by mobile troops. A reserve company was dragging along through the dust. Its men, part of the Coni brigade, had left home hardly a week before and were in a rig more civilian than military. For some unknown reason one of them had tied a small child's chair to his pack. As soon as the sergeant of the rear guard saw Angelo's gold lace, he barked out commands and began to run like a sheep dog around the flank of his flock. The mountaineers were overburdened with equipment: long guns and dirks, pots and pans, basins, soup ladles, and thick blanket rolls. They looked enviously at the horsemen.

The 7th and 8th infantry of the line regiments of the Coni brigade were moving toward the Ticino. The battalions had been tramping for more than four hours up the gradually narrowing valley of the Sesia along a rocky road hemmed in by wooded slopes. At that very moment a staff meeting was being held at Ghemme. They couldn't go on pouring six thousand men and materiel down a narrow road which buried itself in small valleys that resembled flytraps and were impossible to escape from. The pace of the columns had been slowed; then they had been told to halt while awaiting orders; these still had not come. The soldiers did not understand why they had been stopped and kept standing, pack on back, guns slung over their shoulders, under orders not to stack arms.

Two leagues from Ghemme the disorder was aggravated by an engineering-company dragging along mules loaded with pontonier's materiel. They came down an intersecting road and tried to start up a steep road which scaled the elm-covered slopes. The entire population of the surrounding farms and hamlets gathered under the trees to listen to the shouts of the officers, the neighing of the mules, and the cudgel blows which sounded on the hollow bellies of the beasts. This wasting of good teams interested them greatly.

A multitude of people could be seen moving on the summits of the hills. They were in rear-guard companies which had disbanded; with their officers in the lead they were striking out through the woods.

Urging his horse through the mob one step at a time, Angelo succeeded in making room for himself. The corporal and the three artillerymen followed him like his own shadow. Simple men, accustomed to the vicissitudes of military life, they modeled their behavior on Angelo's. Not uttering a word, they took great pleasure in maintaining a haughty air. They urged their horses inexorably forward and even made them prance a bit.

The pontoniers were not as easy to intimidate. They made their mules back-step in the forecarriage of the caissons so that the long beams they were transporting swung about dangerously. In this way they had already wounded several footsoldiers, who were swabbing their faces with bloody handkerchiefs. A lieutenant of the line, a short man bristling with feathers like a cock, had taken aside the fat sergeant major in command of the maneuver. The sergeant was a placid fellow who had re-enlisted and seemed to know all the dodges; he told the lieutenant to mind his own business, that he knew what he was about. Angelo seized him by the epaulette and pushed him against the wheels of the wagon.

"Stop, stop," shouted the sergeant major to the soldier holding the muzzles of the mules.

Once they had passed the crossroads, Angelo put his horse into a trot despite the crowd, all the while keeping him on a short rein. The beast, which understood his rider's mood marvelously, sneezed with rage and impatience.

"Let's cut through the woods, Colonel," said the corporal. "If we've got to take each of these little cats and rub his nose in his crap, we'll be here till Judgment Day."

They made their horses prance; the crowd gave way; they climbed into a chestnut forest.

As they rose they saw that the road was blocked with an ant-hill of uniforms as far as the outskirts of a village. A beautiful standard floated from the belfry of the village church.

The floor of the woods, although quite steep, was easy to ride on and soft-piled as a carpet. The horses took advantage of it to lower their heads and seize a few tufts of nettles, very appetizing with their spring fuzz.

At the summit of the hill, the woods parted around a glade covered with flowering thyme. They could make out the entire plain. Beyond the village, dust smoked beneath the wheels of a long convoy of baggage wagons. A platoon of red dragoons was trotting across a field of sprouting wheat. The reflection of the sun on the helmets jumping up and down rhythmically flew over the heads of the horsemen like a flight of larks. Jerking along to the loud roll of drums, the weighty ingots of another infantry regiment advanced, company by company, the length of an earthen embankment. Peasants in bright blue blouses were guarding the light grayish-green rectangles of their vineyards. Patrols, foragers, and processions of small black caterpillars with yellow trousers went to and fro in the fields; green flies in riflemen's uniforms swarmed around the farms. Over the entire plain as far as the eye could see the army wound along, flashing its scales and its weapons in the glancing light of the young aspen leaves. The noise they made, like that of water rolling over a gravel bed, was suddenly emphasized by the tolling of a large bell which began to scold far to the east, probably in Novara itself.

A faint track led along the peaks to a small hermitage. A lean-to supported by four pillars and, above all, three slender, extremely black cypresses accentuated the white of the well-plastered walls, making the chapel look like a Greek temple. In front of the peristyle, half-recumbent on a carpet of thyme, a Franciscan monk and a *bersagliere* [2] cadet were warming themselves side by side in the sun. The young officer had rested his two-cornered feathered hat on the grass. He had handsome blond hair and a finely chiseled hawk-like profile. His company was making a halt in the circle of shade beneath a large oak. He had ordered them to stack arms. A few soldiers were eating.

The woods went down into the deep valley of a torrent. In this narrow gorge, which was sheltered but exposed to the full sun, spring was more advanced than elsewhere. Bouquets of wild roses flowered in the windows of a little hamlet of three charming houses, hidden under the mixed greenery of willows, chestnuts, and creepers. Silence reigned there, hardly stirred by the cackle of hens. At the noise of horses on the highway a girl rinsing linen sprang up like a hare, abandoning her basket, and ran toward the houses. As she ran, she lost her sandals, which Angelo's horse sniffed.

As soon as the horsemen had passed, two men came out of a stable and, armed with cudgels, went to take their posts beside a small vineyard. Behind one of the rose-filled windows the girl leaned forward to look at the soldiers.

Angelo and his troop made their way through a thicket of flowering reeds to the edge of the torrent. Swollen by the rains of the day before the muddy waters were overflowing. Crossing was out of

[2] Italian footsoldier.

the question. They retraced their steps and followed a little road bordered by flowering hedges and young ash trees. At times birds sang all about them and at other times the silence was so complete that they could hear the rumble of the torrent.

After an hour's march in this secluded area, they heard the sound of a hammer on an anvil, coming apparently from a grove of entirely bare and leopard-mottled plane trees. They turned in its direction. Under the vault of a sturdy, square building covered with clinging ivy they found a forge. The sound of the hammer stopped, then that of the bellows. The blacksmith looked at them.

"Subject to your pleasure, Colonel, we should rest the horses here," said the corporal; "not to mention that a bite to eat would be very pleasant."

Angelo dismounted and went to cool his hands under the spout of a fountain. The water was overflowing the basin and running over cress which seemed, so invisibly clear was the water, to be waving in the wind.

The corporal explained to the smith that they would pay cash for the bread and wine; thirty or forty centimeters of sausage, if he had it, would make life perfect. The little boy who pulled the chain of the bellows stretched out his hand asking for the money first.

The square building had evidently once been the country retreat of a gentleman who, although misanthropic, had been a lover of the fine arts. Although the balustrade was in large part destroyed, the front landing still had great dignity, and the bare facade was exquisitely proportioned. Wheels, iron bars, slabs of rough-hewn ash, and decorated wheelbarrows now leaned against the walls.

Following the cress brook, Angelo reached a bower of hazelnut trees. The water, still invisible, cooed around some stones. The bushes showed no more than a few little gray leaves, casting a pale shade. Angelo lay down on the ground. When he came to bring him some food, the corporal found him asleep.

He awakened an hour later feeling bitter. The artillerymen were smoking their pipes. The forge was extinguished; the blacksmith seemed to have gone off in a hurry, leaving hammer and iron on the anvil.

"It seems," said the corporal, "that we don't need to cross the torrent. It flows down to Novara, and level with the town there's a bridge."

Crossing the little valley, they saw a few more large, lonely houses. On the balconies, wash had been put out to dry.

After traversing a gravel heath where only tufts of furze grew and passing the slopes of a bald mountain, they found themselves once more on the edge of the plain. The tracks of numerous baggage wagons and the large wheels of cannon marked the meadows. Two sappers in white leather aprons were chopping down a poplar. A munitions caisson was stuck in the mud of a near-by rice field. They had to make blocks quickly and get it out. They said the Piedmont brigade was behind them, moving in a line to the left toward Galliate to protect Novara. *They* were in the half-brigade of guards, including the first and second regiments of grenadiers, which, somewhat late, was wheeling to align itself on the north along the Bellinzago-Cameri road.

Angelo went across the fields at a fast trot. On the outskirts of a large farm, a peasant woman, raising her arms to heaven, cursed them. Coming out of a grove, they heard to the west the rumble of the brigade on the march and, to the south, the high chirp of bugles probably entering a village. The good clay soil made it possible to gallop. Angelo gave his horse a kick.

They came out onto open ground to find the front line of the troops solid black to their right, two hundred meters away. They were advancing in formation, officers first, flags unfurled. Before making a detour to the left and spurring on his horse, Angelo saw a mounted courier leave a group marching along a little road and gallop toward him.

He was a staff lieutenant.

"Good day, sir," said Angelo, "I'm on my way to Novara."

"Begging your pardon, Captain," said the young lieutenant, "but if you want to cross the bridge, you've got to step on it. Our right wing is already in San Pietro."

He pointed to where the bugles were sounding.

He added that the battalions were deployed along a front six leagues long, in a semi-circle, with the left wing conducting a forced march toward Castignana. Right here the captain was in the center of a pocket and he was in danger of being swept away by the movement.

"We're going like a bat out of hell," he said joyously.

He had a slight speech defect. Making his horse rear, he saluted with a flourish and returned to his post.

They galloped toward San Pietro. The village was occupied by the commissary department of a division and especially by slaughterhouses. The butchers had set up their blocks in the streets and were busy moving them to allow the infantry to pass. Drummers, in formation on a threshing ground on the edge of the village, were getting ready to drum the troops into town. Three soldiers, hampered by their guns, were trying to subdue an infantry commander's horse. The odor of the quarters of beef had frenzied the enormous bad-tempered beast. From the other side of the village the bugles continued to ring out a joyous little march.

Angelo rode out into the open country and took his horse's thoughts off the beef by making him jump some brooks and finally a hedge, behind which he just missed landing on top of the regimental band sucking their clarinettes.

Beyond San Pietro, Angelo could see vast free territory. Instinctively he and his men galloped in that direction as fast as if they were charging. It was rice fields they had seen. half-submerged so that the infantry could not march there. They could be seen occupying the entire south, as far as the eye could see, and forcing what the staff lieutenant had called their right wing to flow and pile up on the highway, whose only issue was the single street of San Pietro. The tired soldiers rested on their guns around the commander whose horse had finally been quieted; farther off, other companies were putting down their packs.

Ferreting around the immediate outskirts of the village, Angelo found a narrow passage between two houses. They entered it Indian file. Their boots scraped the walls on each side, but they came out in this way on an empty part of the street ahead of the troops and then galloped toward the bridge.

They reached Novara at dusk. Strolling up and down the spacious, vague terrain on the edge of town, the citizens were enjoying the last rays of the sun. Spring was not yet sufficiently advanced to warrant shirt sleeves; men in redingotes were playing slow games of base, and battledore and shuttlecock. A young, well-powdered woman watched the five horsemen crossing the playing field. The officer seemed abnormally sad to her.

CHAPTER FIVE

There were no soldiers in Novara. Angelo conducted his troops to an inn where he was known. Everyone there was amazed at his uniform.

"What happened?" said the owner. "Have you gone over to the other side?"

Angelo, who for the last few hours had been reproaching himself for everything, was naïve enough to take offense.

"What's so extraordinary?" asked the man. "Everyone knows where his bread's buttered."

As soon as they were out of the way of indiscreet ears, in a little room with nothing in it but an iron bedstead, the corporal announced that the three men and himself were set on throwing in the sponge—that is to say, without mincing words: they were going to desert.

"If they've played it right, you're not the only one in this little performance they've been staging," he said. "They've gotten every liberal in the army into the act. They wanted to unmask them all. The police thought: we'll kill two birds with one stone. Hang one big bird, and the little ones start peeping. They didn't hang you, but we peeped loud enough for them to know our tune henceforth. In short, what the four of us should do is to have a drink with you, if that's all right, and then take to our heels."

Angelo was anxious about his uniform, which he wanted to return to its owner, and about the horses, which belonged to the army.

"These are bad times for anyone who owns something," said the corporal. "The big birds lose their feathers, which go to feather our nest. The captain who lent you his Sunday overcoat is a good bastard and knows how things go. But, if you want your conscience to rest easy, let's not joke. For example, we can agree to reimburse him when we see him again. As for the horses, let's be realistic: I've got to sell them to whoever will take the risk, and people always exaggerate risk. We won't get anything worth shouting about. And we each need the clothes of liberals. A white shirt and a cravat cost money. Besides our weapons are what's noble in all of this, and we're going to hold on to them."

Angelo had some wine sent up. They talked in a very friendly fashion but the corporal watched for nightfall.

"Let's not go to sleep on the job," he said when he saw that the lamps would soon be lit. "Good evening, Colonel. If things really start moving for the happiness of the people, we'll be in the front line; and if you have tough going, we'll know about it, to judge by the way you run your business. Maybe we'll be in the neighborhood."

After their departure Angelo began to suffer from scruples once more. He started thinking of details. However, he hadn't eaten all day and wasn't hungry, and when you've had your shoulder to the wheel, it never pays to slight the body in favor of the spirit. He thought of the ease with which he had killed the lancer and even of the shivers of happiness he had felt in his wrist. Finally he called for some harness-maker's thread, a bobkin, and some mattress ticking. He had concluded that he should carefully wrap up the officer's uniform.

The owner brought him the stuff and a candle.

"I've arranged about the horses," he said, "but the lads didn't want to handle yours. What'll we do about him?"

"He's not mine," said Angelo.

"It's no use getting wrought up about it," said the owner, "but he's certain to give us some trouble. If I sell him for whatever I can get, he'll bring a nice little sum like anything else."

"I don't have the right to dispose of him," said Angelo.

"Questions of right can always be settled," said the owner. "All that's needed is a little time to think them through. Think about it. There's no rush. Do you want to eat?"

"No. I'm leaving," said Angelo, who was doing his best to sew the package with neat stitches.

"I was talking about you lately with a certain Borgès. You know the fellow?"

"Who is he?"

"A Spaniard. He came from Naples. He's been here some time."

"In the police?"

"Not at all. Everything quite in order."

"What did he want of me?"

"Nothing special. Your name came up in the conversation."

"Has my brother shown up in town lately?"

"He could have without my seeing him; I haven't set foot out of doors for a week. In any case he hasn't come here. I only know that the group met Thursday, Friday, Saturday, and Sunday at the Ansaldis'."

"Why the Ansaldis'?"

"Last Monday a fellow from France came to stay with them."

"The Ansaldis have always minded their own business."

"But it seems that this fellow is worth bothering with."

"Who went to these meetings?"

"The front-liners and second-liners. The reputation of being a republican town was not enough for them; it seemed to me they went a bit far. Especially Thursday. From what I heard, there were carriages lined up all along the park fence. People came from five leagues around; even from Lombardy it seems."

"Do you know the man's name?"

"No one breathed a word of it. An old 1821 man, it seems, who commanded a company of constitutional soldiers from Alessandria at that time. If it hadn't been for my work I might have gone to see him, but as long as I'm in danger of running into the fellow who caught us rifing the stores of the 4th of the line, I'm an in-doors man. What I saw with my very own eyes was part of the going and coming. The town was full of liberals."

Angelo had made a very pretty package.

"I'll take care of that if you want," said the owner. "You can leave it with me. An artilleryman's braid is seldom made of real gold."

"I'm taking it with me," said Angelo.

He settled his bill and went out into Novara. Fog had invaded the streets. The town had come gently to life beneath the lamps. He came out onto an avenue bordered by bourgeois houses and gardens. An empty calash waited without a coachman in front of the Ansaldi gate. Angelo examined the horse carefully; he had never seen it before. Through the branches of the trees he made out the facade of a proud little château; the doors and windows were closed. Lights shone only in one round attic window. He hid in the shadows and waited. The light was extinguished after a moment, and he heard someone open a door onto the front steps and carefully relock it; then steps scuffed the gravel walks of the park and he saw a man come out carrying a heavy chest. It was undoubtedly full of silver. The man loaded the strong box onto the calash, turned the horse, climbed onto the seat, and went off down the Vercelli road.

Walking down little alleys full of the fragrance of the first lilacs, Angelo made a tour of the Ansaldi domain. The stables and the servants' quarters were deserted. In the bright light of the moon, now high and piercing the mist, he saw that a carriage with a broken axle had been abandoned in a courtyard. They must have cleared out in a hurry. In this neighborhood, on the outskirts of the town, he heard the confused rumble of the army. To the north in the milky night, sparks of light gleamed on the mountains.

Angelo crossed the canal on the old bridge and took the road through the osier thickets. Soon he heard only the croaking of the frogs and a muffled plop as they dived. On the other side of the swamp he made his way around a large farm. He was about to come out of a hedge when he saw a man on the other side in the meadow, walking along beside a road parallel to his. He let him get ahead. The man (who was a civilian) was carrying a gun; when he reached a large poplar marking a crossroads, he climbed onto the road and turned left, toward the Ticino.

Finally Angelo came to a mass of trees silhouetted against the gleaming fog. The grove marked the beginning of a park of ilex woods and somber pines. He entered the park and after passing two ha-has, he reached the front of a house flanked by two square towers. He heard water trickling into a basin.

On the corner of the steps he found a key wrapped in an oily rag. The lock itself had been freshly oiled. He entered the house noiselessly. The half-moon of a white-glass fanlight lighted the vault of the hall. The copper of a newel post, the filigree of a bannister and the spine of a marble step shone in the background between the bluish glimmer of a mirror and a gilded frame containing a very pure blue.

He put the package which he had carried so lovingly down on an armchair. He had almost finished lighting the candles when he heard clogs clattering lightly behind him. It was Lavinia.

"You have sharp ears," he said.

"I was waiting for you," said the young woman. "There's a lot of coming and going on the roads tonight."

"Where's Giuseppe?"

"He left day before yesterday by carriage with the man from France."

"Did he tell you where he was going?"

"No. He got dressed up and they took the road over the bridge."

"Has my mother shown any sign of life?"

"Yes, the day you left for Turin. She sent word to me through the miller: 'Starch my son's shirts.' "

"Carlotta hasn't come?"

"The Countess slept in the master bedroom Thursday, Friday, and Saturday."

"She went to the Ansaldis'?"

"Everyone went there. She reigned there all three days."

The young woman asked if he wanted anything to eat. He wasn't hungry. He went upstairs to the room Carlotta had occupied to see if she hadn't left a note about the Ansaldis. He looked under the candlesticks, saucers, and the glass bell of the clock. He found nothing but a box of little cigars she had, as usual, left for him in plain sight on the marble top of the bureau. He smoked one right away. The very first puffs gave him a pleasure he didn't have the heart to begrudge himself. He went downstairs to his own room and opened his closet to get out fresh linen. Giuseppe had taken three of his shirts ("undoubtedly starched," he said to himself), his thick black silk necktie, and his stylish redingote.

"He always wanted that redingote, although it has a horrible fold in the back when he wears it," thought Angelo to himself.

He pulled off his boots and walked about barefoot with such unequaled happiness that he was prompted to light a second cigar. He seated himself in an armchair. He didn't dare go to sleep for fear of hearing once again the little, feminine cry of the dying lancer. But he had enough sense to know that his lips would let the cigar fall. He put it down in an ash tray. He went to sleep and awakened in an instant. His hand was still on the ash tray, but it was dawn.

He was as hungry as a horse. He went downstairs to the kitchen. He rummaged in the dresser, found a pot of milk, and drank it without taking breath. "This is the first time I've drunk this stuff they've always tried to palm off on me as cream. I would have understood better if they'd told me that anything fills the stomach; but I was right, it's not cream."

He looked through the drawer of the table, found three eggs and then three others in a box on the mantel; he blew on the coals, put on some dry wood, and fried the six eggs in oil with a trickle of vinegar. He made as little noise as possible. He was doubtful how placid Lavinia would be this morning. Then he drank some wine, mixed some with a handful of cassonade in a bowl, soaked some bread in it, and ate it with a spoon like soup

He went back up to his room on tiptoe. There was no more light in the vestibule than when he had arrived the evening before. The house was still. It was four in the morning. The dawn was dirty. He could hardly distinguish the tops of the trees. To his pleasure he saw that Giuseppe had not borrowed, or rather had not been able to find, a pair of very supple half-boots. He chose a hunting-costume, put it on carefully, and selected a beautiful scarf. To the sixteen florins he had left, he added fifty Turin louis in his belt on the right, and fifty on the left. After folding twenty Sardinian *écus* in a piece of paper, he took two pistols and noted with pleasure that his pockets did not bulge. Downstairs, he put the little package of *écus* on the kitchen table and went out the back door.

"Lavinia can't see me from her windows," he said to himself, "and if she's awake, she won't think right away of looking out the shutter of the black bedroom. I wouldn't know what to reply to her cold eyes this morning."

Besides, he was quickly hidden by the thickets of the park. The resin of the pines was like incense. He could also smell the musky odor of the ilexes and the spruce grasses awakened by the coolish air.

"If Giuseppe crossed the bridge in a carriage, I can certainly cross it on foot. Unless that famous bourgeois of his from France is an Austrian general in disguise who came to open the gates of Lombardy to my starched shirt and my redingote."

But he played it cautiously, and, a hundred meters before the bridge, hid behind a willow. He saw what he thought was clearly a shako and the point of a bayonet showing over the parapet. There was not yet enough light to make things out clearly, and the river wafted vapors with it. He approached, staying hidden in the osiers, until he could see the waters of the Ticino. It was indeed a shako, but the bayonet resembled a pikestaff. Before he had even time to think, he saw a small, towheaded cowherd wearing a shako, getting ready to go down the bank.

Angelo went up onto the highway.

"If you want one of the emperor's helmets," the boy said, "you have only to take one, there are three more in the sentry box."

He was watching the cows of the monastery, whose belfry could be seen, white and thin above the Lombardy pines. The Austrians had departed two days before, abandoning their arms and baggage. The monks had taken fourteen guns. *He* had picked up this hat.

On the Piedmontese shore not a sound was to be heard except the sourish cry of larks, numerous at this season and hour on the gravel shores of the Ticino. Obviously, the army Angelo had seen moving the day before had stopped a good distance from the river. The fog prevented him from seeing if there were any campfires in the countryside, but the wind carried no trace of the unmistakable odor of dry wood brasiers.

"I know by experience how hard it is to keep soldiers from blowing trumpets," Angelo said to himself, "and you can hear one three leagues away in calm air like this."

He didn't try to explain to himself why the Austrians had packed up.

He crossed the bridge into Lombardy. For a moment he wanted to go see the monks. Finally he thought of Giuseppe's carriage and began to walk along the road at a good rate.

"How often you dreamed of penetrating enemy territory when you were a two-for-a-nickel colonel!" he thought. "Well, now here you are in enemy territory. Yesterday when they staged an entire opera to hang you, you were still in your own country."

He found everything charming, and, above all, the pack no longer wounded him. The flowing water sounded lovely in the silence of morning; tall green canebrakes with leaves like banners escorted the road, and the light, increasing every moment, throwing blond patches into the mist, was completely glorious.

The sun was rising when Angelo reached a crossroads and an inn. A woman, whose singing he heard, was washing the floors and sending floods of dirty water leaping over the sill. Angelo was still hungry, and nimbly avoiding the broom, he asked for a hot toddy with bread and cheese.

The servant girl looked at him as he had looked at the Lombardy morning.

"There was a brawl last night," she said, "and it's going to be a job to find a bowl with its saucer. If you'll settle for your toddy in a glass, it'll be quicker. I'll fill it twice so you'll get your money's worth."

She also advised him to put his feet on the rungs of a chair so as not to wet his pretty boots.

She related that the previous evening she had been alone with a boy who had been flirting with her a bit, and that she had been just about to lock up for the night when an Austrian soldier had entered. "For the past three days we'd been seeing all sorts of soldiers going by, heading pretty rapidly in the direction of Milan, but this one seemed to be going in the opposite direction. Runaways like that are usually no good, and this man asked for some peasant clothes in exchange for his uniform. The boy who was with me is the son of a farmer who has his nest better feathered than many landowners; he's not the man to boil over like milk on a fire. Besides, he's on the thin side, with sweet manners and that's why I like him. To cut things short, they came to blows, and I cried out. The boss came, but strong as he is, he had to go some because the other man had taken his gun by the barrel and was turning it this way and that. The lamps and the china jumped around a lot. Finally, Charles waked up even though he was sleeping in the stable; he was the one who carried the day by striking the soldier a good blow on the head with a stick. We took advantage of the time he was out to tie his hands and feet and throw him in the dirty clothes tub. This morning when I got up I heard him snoring very happily. Come and see."

He wasn't snoring: he was dead.

The girl didn't want to believe it, claiming that Charles wasn't generally heavy-handed and that this wasn't the first time he had made a little order with his staff, but she refused to touch the body and when Angelo raised the soldier's head, taking it by the ears (because the hair was cut short), she turned to the wall and began to vomit.

Neither did the landlord find the business to his taste. He was a fine fellow, very red in the face, with a body so big that he blocked the door. He made it very obvious that he didn't like this stranger poking his nose where he had no business and darted several furtive looks at Angelo which said a great deal.

"Don't get any ideas about me," said Angelo. "First of all, I bite, and second, it's not my job to count the Austrians who don't show up for the roll call. You've already got one fellow on your hands, stiff as a board. What would you do with me? That is if I let you get me."

"You've shut me up," said the man, "and you're right. Usually I'm not so nervous but lately with all that's been going on, I've lost some of my grip."

Angelo accepted a glass of wine with good grace.

"Toss the soldier in a hole and cover him with dirt," he said. "Before Radetzky's army balances its books, a lot of water will have gone under the bridge."

"That's what I was thinking," said the fat man. "I'm going to stuff him in . . ."

"Don't tell me," Angelo cut him off dryly. "Otherwise, you'll wake up with a start every night imagining that I'm selling you to the police."

"Small risk of that," said the innkeeper. "Now that I've got my eyes lined up with the holes, I see what kind of man you are; I'll stick my hand in the fire that you're Piedmontese. Quite a few have been by since the Austrians cleared out."

Angelo asked him if he remembered having seen a carriage with a bourgeois and a very nattily dressed man: a starched shirt and a redingote which had an awful pleat at the back.

The owner began to joke. A redingote with pleats?

"Starched shirts," he said, "usually go at full speed to Milan to take office. No one sees them. They slip under your nose like rats."

He made a pretty declaration of liberalism and added that he was going to take care of the Austrian right away before the first customer arrived.

Angelo left the highway and took a dirt road. In this way he thought he could sooner reach the path of the mailcoach coming from Switzerland and going to Milan; but he was still a half a league from the crossroads when he heard the rumble of a huge, rickety old coach. It passed its stop without halting and continued on its way at a gallop, raising a great deal of dust. When he reached the crossroads, he found an old lady, very richly dressed in violet faille, seated under a willow beside a large valise. The sun flashed off her long watch chain and off the ball-fringe on her little jet purse. He approached and asked courteously if he could be of any assistance.

"No, my friend," she said, "unless you load me on your back and replace this carriage which has ceased to be public without anyone deigning to warn us."

She explained that the diligence had been loaded to the roof with officers and that it was a uhlan in green who had been whipping along the horses.

"Do you understand it?"

Angelo admitted he didn't understand any of it. He suggested that the soldiers and, more probably, the officers, had to get somewhere in a hurry.

"Of course, my friend," she said. "For the last month while our ears have been tingling with the war Sardinia is going to declare, the military think they can do whatever they please; but I'm in a hurry too; and would I ever think of seizing the mailcoach? My son said to me: 'Don't go tripping about these days: your heart is only hanging by a thread.' Perhaps my heart only hangs by a thread, but it's an iron thread, sir! Soldiers are not distinguished by courage, so much as by bad upbringing!"

"It happens, Madame," replied Angelo, "that I too must be in Milan as quickly as possible. I was intending to take the mail coach, but since it's been whisked out from under us, I'll go to the village with the red roofs you can see over there. I'll be damned if I can't unearth a carriage there. I offer you a seat, if a voyage in my company doesn't frighten you."

"You're a true gentleman, my friend," she said. "I'll wait for you."

The village consisted of about ten houses around an enormous church with a green copper dome. There was no coach stop but instead a sign showing a horse painted on a panel of wood. Angelo recognized an ostler's stable.

"You're asking for the moon," the man said to him. "Maybe I could try for that, but as for a carriage, that's more than you can ask of any man. Revolution has broken out in Paris and we're all trying to save our belongings."

Angelo succeeded in uttering a few indifferent words; secretly he slipped a finger into his belt and aligned three gold louis on the palm of his hand.

"And for this," he said, "could you get me, if not the moon, then a light carriage, a fast horse, and a groom?"

"God," said the man, "are you trying to make an astronomer out of me! Here are three charming coins showing a handsome king. If there were four of them, I believe I might make an effort. Now that I come to think of it, there's always a buggy."

While he was harnessing the horse, Angelo forced himself to look detached. He paced up and down very clamly and even smoked a small cigar.

"I see that you're in a jam," said the man, "but don't worry: this little mare will get you out of trouble in a jiffy. And as for the groom, that's me. This is no time to lose sight of one's possessions."

The old lady was no longer under the willow. Angelo called and looked everywhere, but in vain. She had disappeared.

"You've been fleeced," said the man. "Someone cut the ground out from under you. But there's plenty more where she came from. It's the old lady who's losing out. Let's not take root here. From now on, days are only going to be twenty-four hours long."

The little mare was full of good will, and after warming her up a bit, the man put her into a rapid trot.

Angelo risked talking about the revolution in Paris.

"I was making a deal with a Hungarian colonel for six remounts. He was rude enough to offer me no more than a centesimo for them. Day before yesterday in the evening, they came to drag me away from my supper, pressing cash into my hands. 'Joking aside!' I thought to myself, 'They've come into a fortune.' Yes, it was a pure case of panic! They heard by telegraph that Louis Philippe had come unglued. Now it's all over town. You should see how all these boys with their gold lace and their family crests embroidered on their shirts have started to run from one side to the other. All the more because if anyone just says the word we'll be in for some real fighting. Some soldiers are already looking at crowned heads as if they were ninepins. They may want to start bowling."

There weren't many people on the road. They passed through a village which seemed almost deserted. In Magenta the shops were closed and the carriage rolled through strangely echoing streets. After Sedriano, they saw Milan on the horizon.

At about the same instant, a puff of white smoke rose like a balloon above a large black crenelated building the brow of which rose above the roofs of the city; immediately afterward they heard a muffled explosion. There was a second puff and a second explosion, then a third and a fourth at regular intervals. It was the alarm cannon.

"Colleague," said the man, "I smell something burning. I've got to go home; the soup's boiling over."

He stopped the carriage.

If Angelo had not been in such a state of exaltation, he might have made a fool of himself; he jumped down onto the road and walked about ten steps before thinking that as liberty dawned he should share his happiness and embrace the ostler. The man had already turned the horse around.

In spite of the delicious, well-rounded explosions, Angelo somewhat recovered his wits.

"I'm still at least a league and a half from the city," he said to himself. "Running is out of the question. What good would I be with a stitch in my side? Besides, these cannon shots are not hurried: a corporal spaces them regularly according to regulations with a watch. They're not under seige."

He entered Milan by an interminable carting-road. The long avenue of beaten earth bordered by wooden fences and small low houses was also almost deserted. But the few people strolling along the sidewalks did not seem to take seriously the emphatic detonations which shook the window panes every two minutes.

Besides, after each cannon shot, the cocks in the henhouses sang at the top of their lungs.

Angelo was much put out. He had been expecting noble gestures. Only one thing was certain: someone was frying onions. He had such a need for decorum—at least for a certain kind of wind furling and unfurling draperies—that he was moved almost to tears by plain sheets moving slightly as they dried on a balcony clothes line.

He reached a stone-paved city street. Numerous women with baskets of groceries and even children were still about, but they trotted along, sticking close to the walls and turning abruptly into passageways. Suddenly, at a crossroads, Angelo was confronted with a dead horse stretched out in the middle of the street. The beast was harnessed in the Croat manner. All its saddlebags had been rifled and the boot was empty; even the saber had been taken, leaving the scabbard empty. Three paces farther on, the horseman was hidden behind a milestone. He was a courier killed by a pistol held to his chest. His boots had been stolen and his pockets picked. From this point, three streets opened out, entirely deserted. The cannon no longer thundered.

"It was murder," Angelo thought, "but we've all known for a long time now how many eggs have to be broken for an omelet. Even I do. I should get to the castle or the cathedral as fast as possible. That's where equilibrium will be re-established."

He wasn't going to start finding flies on the first corpse that pleased him. In any case, he believed that liberty is just.

However, he had the distinct sensation that his boots made a lot of noise as he walked around the soldier, looking at his pockets, everyone of which had been pulled inside out. The only sections of Milan he knew were very different from this. He chose a street at random and advanced somewhat cautiously.

All the shops were closed. On the upper floors the shutters barricaded the windows. He noticed the lamellae of the blinds and, within, furtive white glimmers which he took for faces.

Before turning the corner, he hid in the recess of a doorway and looked up and down. In the direction of the crossroads where the Croat was, as well as in the opposite direction, the way was entirely free. He came out onto a little square. The four or five outside tables and two charcoal bins of a cookshop had stood where there was now nothing but an elm, its branches moaning, and a fountain spurting water which struck the basin repeatedly.

It was a setting for noble passions. But Angelo left the fountain quickly. The noise of the water prevented him from hearing things. He was listening for the crackle of a full fusillade.

"When I heard it on maneuvers, I used to say to myself: 'Try to remember that noise. Will you recognize it when it echoes in the streets?' "

However, the streets echoed nothing but the flap of an immense flag, made of thousands of densely massed pigeons still crazed by the cannon, wheeling level with the rooftops.

Angelo heard someone rummaging in the cookshop. He knocked discreetly several times.

"Go around to the passage," cried a voice.

He then saw that a bit of paper had indeed been glued to the shop front to this effect, with an arrow pointing the way.

Inside, the owner was standing on a chair, regulating the wick of an oil lamp which had been smoking.

"If you'd come ten minutes ago," he said, "there were some gentlemen here who wanted to fight too, and they looked as if they knew their way around. I'll be damned if some more don't turn up any minute."

Angelo asked him if he knew what was going on.

"Not much," he said, "except that I had an idea: I cooked some tripe this morning, all you could want and I'm selling it for three soldi a portion."

But what about the cannon!

"I admit it makes a lot of noise," he said. "People always go for wholesale. But in this neighborhood we prefer retail."

Nevertheless, he knew some dandies had been up to something at the town hall. What exactly? Well, he couldn't say. Some customers had been talking about it.

"I see plain as the nose on my face what's getting you," he said. "The cannon has made you ambitious and you're looking for the bridge of Arcole.[1] But just let me tell you something: I've never known where it was."

Angelo drank a glass of wine for the sake of politeness and then went back to surveying the deserted town, this time striding down the middle of the street.

He had been going along a paved street for a good half hour when he was suddenly grazed by a burning bullet. A report sounded. He threw himself down flat on his stomach. Obviously, this was a time to listen not for the crackle of the fusillade he had been hoping to hear, but for a bullet aimed at him.

He was playing dead in the middle of the street when he heard an amiable voice saying to him: "Don't move, little one, or else you'll really get it."

He risked a sidewise glance and saw someone taking refuge in a passage.

"You've given him time to reload," said the voice, "I'll make him think I'm coming out. As soon as you hear the shot, leap over here under cover."

The man made a quick feint to come out. The ball struck the corner of the door and flew mewing across the street. At the same moment Angelo leaped into the passage and fell into the arms and onto the very comfortable stomach of a little man with a mustache.

"You saw how nervous the bastard was?"

"Austrians?" Angelo asked.

[1] Arcole is a small town in the north of Italy, the site of a French victory over the Austrians (November 17, 1796) and the scene of one of Napoleon's great personal triumphs.

"I don't really know who it is," said the other, "but he's got a full gut. It's really me he's after. You're to amuse the gallery or else he's taken you for one of my buddies."

"Would death be stupid?" Angelo asked himself. He realized that he had just missed being killed.

"We're in the same boat," said the other. "If we stick so much as a nose out, they'll snipe at us."

Angelo was horrified that he had just thrown himself flat on the ground. He asked heatedly and a little insolently if nothing else was going on in Milan.

"Why yes," said the little man, "and I was just on my way to it. But that's exactly what they wanted to keep me from doing. Are you armed?"

Angelo was completely happy to show his pistols. He was in the process of getting seriously angry over that idiotic gunshot which had bowed him to the ground.

"Unfortunately they're handsome," said the little man.

"They do as much damage as the ugly."

"That's what I think, but they're not as easily borrowed."

He spoke very cordially. Angelo gave him one pistol.

"A cinch," said the little man. "I'll tell you what's going on. Let's get the hell out of here."

He led Angelo to the end of the passage.

"I don't know who lives here, but now that we've got something to do the talking for us, let's go up."

The stairs were quite plushy.

"Is this a kind of courier chase; does this man prefer retail too?" Angelo wondered. He found the little man congenial. Besides, he held the pistol very badly.

"I'll fire twice as fast as he," Angelo said to himself. Above all he was favorably impressed by the man's little stomach and by his clean shirt, from which emerged a clean, well-shaven neck and chin. "He looks like a cooper, and he's over forty."

From all evidence he had good manners in addition. He knocked very politely on a door which opened and greeted a thin man behind whom a woman was hiding. They stared and gaped a bit.

"Nothing to worry about, ladies and gentlemen," said the cooper; "we're not after much. Only be so good as to tell us if this hole has a back door. My comrade and I want to get to the via Rastelli but we can't get out of your passageway. A fellow's firing on us. Do you think we could get through the courtyards?"

They had heard the gunshots. What was going on?

"Nothing. Don't be afraid; get us out of here and go back to your soup."

The table was indeed very neatly set.

"Who is he?" Angelo said to himself. "The head of an office, probably . . . and there's gunfire two steps away from his pitcher of clear water."

"From the bedroom window you can climb down into a courtyard. You gentlemen won't hurt anyone?"

"Certainly not," said the cooper. "Today everyone is nice."

The bedroom harbored a little maid and a boy of seven or eight whom they had hidden at the sound of the knock on the door. A clock under a glass bell rang noon. The curtains and a heavy bedside carpet made of goatskin muffled its ring.

Climbing over the balcony, they found themselves on the roof of a shed.

"Go to the end of it," said the man, "there's a terrace below. The courtyard is beyond."

The woman closed the window. The little boy, very interested, crushed his nose to the pane. The courtyard was narrow and green with moss. A passage opened into the back hall of a bourgeois house.

"Easy there," said the cooper.

"What do you want, gentlemen?"

A tall, English-style valet had just risen out of a low door and drawn himself up to his full height.

"The way out," said the cooper.

"This way, gentlemen."

He went ahead, swinging his stiff arms ceremoniously.

"The eldest son of our house fought this morning on the cathedral square," he said. "He has come home for a rest. The Hungarian sharpshooters are occupying the roof of the cathedral and doing a lot of damage it seems."

He opened the door onto the street and got out of the way.

A woman's voice asked from the top of the stairs: "What is it?"

"Some gentlemen going to fight, Madame."

"Splendid!" said the voice.

Angelo was cross as a wet hen.

"Go your own way," he said to the little man. "This is more than I can swallow."

"The bit of lead you almost swallowed would have been much harder to digest," the man answered; "and besides, maybe your way is my way—unless you're from the upper crust, too."

"I'm what it pleases me to be," said Angelo in an icy tone.

From deep in the town came the rapid cannon shot; then two others: the dry thunderclaps, this time, of a field battery firing balls.

"That takes care of it," said the little man. "The old Austrian is ringing the dinnerbell with four-millimeter pieces. Every eldest son will gallop home for his lunch. We'll be left with the bottom of the barrel."

"I'm Piedmontese," said Angelo, "and I don't know Milan well enough to get around in the deserted streets. I've been wandering for more than an hour now trying to get to the fighting. When I get there, I'll bet you anything the bottom of the barrel will be twice as full as you think. I know workmen who are dastardly and even cowardly. And many too many who think themselves big cheeses because they discovered their heart could palpitate. I've been turning their palpitations to my own ends ever since I could walk."

He strode along, followed by the little man, toward the rolling drums resounding in the neighboring street.

At the crossroads they found themselves face to face with a tall boy, pale but powder-blackened; the big drum he carried gave him an awkward rolling gait.

"My friends at last," Angelo said to himself.

He looked passionately at these hollow cheeks and dull eyes.

"Where can we get guns?" he asked.

"Via Dante."

Angelo began to run.

"Not that way," shouted the little man running after him and dragging him down the alleys. A trumpet rang the cry to horse. A large bell sounding the tocsin answered the trumpet.

Via Dante was battered by cannonfire. The thick towers and black walls of the castle appeared at the end of the street, through the torn smoke. The artillerymen fired low to sweep the glacis clean. Grapeshot could be seen jumping off the roadway like hail, and balls bigger than a fist rebounded off the paving stones and scraped the facades. Arms were being distributed in a billiard room, somewhat out of the firing range of the Piazza Ronda.

Angelo was given a gun and a knapsack full of ammunition. He was so happy that he allowed himself a bit of irony.

"Happiness at last," he said to himself.

However, he noticed, as if it were part of another world, that it was raining. Only his passion was natural: the pack and the gun which weighed on his shoulder were more real than the rain.

He left with three young bourgeois who sported enormous cockades made of tri-colored ribbon, scarves, and hats with feathers. These *Signori* said that they all should go to the town hall as fast as possible, where for the last hour the chiefs of the insurrection had been besieged.

The tocsin had begun to toll throughout the town. Despite the loud ringing of the bells, the cannon, and the crackle of gunfire, they could hear the cry of trumpets.

The alleys around the town hall were cut off by barricades. Young girls and boys of ten or twelve, armed with axes and iron rods, were prying up the long white paving-stones.

The dignified *Signori* swung their arms like fine fellows while women and children, garnishing the balconies despite the danger, applauded them.

Angelo was somewhat offended by the feathers and by the ladies watching and applauding as if at the theater. One of his companions wearing a Hernani hat called it to his attention, saying that he wore it in honor of Verdi so that the great man could thus be present at the liberation of Milan.

"What have we to do with a great man represented by a hat?" Angelo asked him.

And to see what was happening, he climbed onto a barricade.

The Piazza Broletto, of which he could see a part, was full of smoke and red uniforms. It was impossible to know what was best to fire at. Besides, the Austrians, who were no fools, had buried their cannon in a shop and were going about their business out of range of the continuous heavy volley from dormers, windows, and even roofs.

Angelo was deeply moved to be taking part in events which from one minute to the next might make him happy. He did not immediately understand that the main concern of everyone on this side was to make a lot of noise.

Accordingly he loaded his gun and fired at random on the red uniforms. It was not until after he had fired that he was ashamed of such vanity and of the pedestal of carts, carriages, furniture, and kitchen utensils on which he was perched.

He was climbing down from the barricade when he heard an uproar which filled the entire sky. The crackle of gunfire, the cannon, and the applause had stopped abruptly and the tocsin continued alone. There were cries of "Run, run," that the Broletto had been taken, that the Croat light infantry had entered it easy as pie with bayonets on their gun barrels. Everyone disappeared from the windows and closed the shutters.

The buildings emptied, and out of passage doorways issued a crowd of extraordinary characters: clergy adorned with cockades, bare swords or sabers in their hands; *Signori* in jerkins of black velvet in the style of Veronese, or wrapped in *capas,* their entire brows shadowed by a sombrero or an ostrich feather; bourgeois wearing Calabrese hats; women rigged out like Belgiojoso.[2] They scattered as fast as their legs would carry them, shouting orders.

Angelo looked at a group of simply dressed workers; among them was the little man with whom he had had sharp words. They were not fleeing: their retreat was orderly. They were holding their guns primly and dragging along the powder kegs.

He joined the group and helped carry a box of very heavy cannon balls.

One moment trumpets rang out. There was a shout: "The hussars!"

"That was just the 'on guard' ringing," said Angelo. "It always takes a minute before a platoon 'on guard' is ready to charge, especially if they're fighting for their lives, as is the case now."

[2] Princess Christine Trivulzio Belgiojoso (1808–71), Italian patriot.

He noticed that "for their lives" did wonders.

"If we went only as far as that *porte cochère* between the pharmacy and the grocery," he continued, "of the house facing the street where hussars are going to come out, we could, just the six or seven of us, fire at them in rotation; they wouldn't feel much like laughing then."

They rushed to the door he indicated, opened both panels wide and barricaded it with a dresser, straight chairs, armchairs, and tables which they dragged out of a room which seemed to be the concierge's apartment.

There were eight of them. Half were nominated to reload the guns; the others, of which Angelo was one, lay flat on their stomachs, ready to fire. The end of the street was full of smoke. A captain in Radetzky's hussars, who had taken particular pains with his appearance, emerged from it. He advanced at a walk, carrying nothing in his hand but an exercise switch and smoking a cigar. He was several lengths ahead of his men and for an instant he seemed to be alone. Then the platoon appeared behind him, in lines of four, sabers bared.

Angelo aligned the officer with the end of his gun. Despite the rain which made it hard to aim, he forced himself to sight the man's chest exactly; Angelo liked his looks and noticed that he was wearing a gold *fourragère* and several medals. When he saw that he was level with a sign representing a *Gambrinus* [3] lifting a stein of beer, he began to press the trigger very softly, following the precepts of the rifleman's art. Finally, the gun fired and he saw the bullet hit its mark. His companions began to fire with great composure. But they were dealing with a well-disciplined troop, their professional vanity roused at the idea of fighting civilians; they advanced vigorously. One of the horsemen even came within five paces of the barricades; a single bullet plowed through his horse's forehead and struck him on the chin. The entire edifice, with its jutting saber, toppled to the sidewalk. The defenders of the barricade took the reloaded guns handed to them and fired without stopping. The horses began to waltz and rear, and as soon as they

[3] The legendary Flemish or German king supposed to be the discoverer of beer and the founder of the town of Cambrai. He is still sometimes depicted on European tavern signs.

could turn them, the platoon cleared out at a gallop.

About ten men and a horse lay flat on the street, no longer moving. Another horse, wounded in the rump, was trying to get up, scraping the pavement with his shoes.

It was a rapid victory leaving no savor. Angelo was astonished not to be content. He had kept firing throughout the combat, sheltered behind a cauldron.

"That officer was magnificent," he said to himself. "He offered himself to my shots with intelligent scorn."

"Where are you going?" the little man said to him. "That's not the way to light out."

"I'm not lighting out," said Angelo. "I'm going to see the officer."

"Leave him be," said a tall redhead who was biting a quid of tobacco. "He has pistols like everyone else."

Despite the tocsin which continued to peal furiously, Angelo found the silence of the street disagreeable. The captain was stretched out on his back. His open and obviously living eyes looked alternately at the heavens and at the closed windows. His blood was beautiful against his medals and aiguillettes.

"I hit the bull's eye," Angelo said to himself, but he corrected himself and thought: "He's wounded where I aimed. He's not dazzlingly vain as I thought. Now that he's lying in the mud, I see he's a melancholy soul."

He bent over the officer.

He then noticed that the courageous man's eyes had become unbearably intense and that his hands were trembling.

"He thinks me a coward come to finish him off," he said to himself. "He doesn't know that he acted like a man after my own heart."

Perhaps he was about to kneel near him and gently caress his hands when he heard one of the large, lively flies buzz by him as they had since morning.

He leaped to the shelter of the walls. At the end of the street appeared heads in kepis and gun barrels. A sour Hungarian cornet was stirring the footsoldiers to charge.

Angelo entered a passage, closed the door, and slipped the bolt.

On the second floor, he found some women weeping.

"We can't take any more," they said to him. "Whoever you may be, sir, Austrian or Milanese, have pity on us. Our house has become the thoroughfare of the insurrection. People are always going and coming on the stairs. A while ago men wearing cockades gathered on the roof. They made us keep the doors of the apartments open. Now soldiers all in green are camping on the roofs across the way, riddling our blinds with bullets. All the panes have been broken and the bedroom is full of smoke. This very instant, a bullet shot by one of those soldiers crossed the drawing-room a few centimeters from the cook as she was leaving the room, pierced the panel, and landed here where we've taken refuge. And if we're taken in an assault, what will become of us?"

"Probably nothing," said Angelo, "but I'm not certain."

He inspected the location. He could indeed see Hungarian sharp-shooters crawling on the roofs across the street. In the drawing-room the only safe spot was between the windows, which unfortunately came down to the floor. The old lady who had done the talking was one of those opulent matrons who in ordinary times rarely throw in the sponge. A very pale young woman and two girls kept close to the shelter of her skirts. The weak arguments with which Angelo tried to reassure them had no effect. They wept and shivered pitiably; the sobs of the cook crouching under a table mingled with their moans.

Were they alone in the house?

No. On the floor above there was a French dressmaker; higher still, a Swiss woman whose profession one did better not to examine too closely; a few other women of the Milanese lower bourgeoisie and two or three old men who, as they were hardly appetizing, risked nothing.

"The profession you speak of and the old men seem to me perfect for the present situation," said Angelo. "Come with me and invite all the ladies of the house to follow."

The Swiss woman was from Fribourg, spoke German, and was no more than reasonably bothered by the idea of receiving soldiers.

Angelo had them construct a shelter of straw and hair mattresses in a dark room on the third floor.

"The bullets won't reach you here," he said. "Stay hidden. If you hear a hubbub on the stairs, the most courageous of you— or the one with the least to lose—should take courage and look out to see if it's the soldiers. If that's the case, Madame should shout in German. There will be a moment's pause. Then those who are eldest should show they are fearless. The soldiers disdain old people completely and the important thing in an attack, where no one's got a moment, is to be disdained at first glance. As for me, no one will believe I'm innocent. You'll be in the greatest danger if I stay with you."

"Go down to the floor below," said one of the women. "Cross the drawing-room and go pull out the big bed in the bedroom. You'll see that behind it the partition wall is pierced. Six months ago we took these precautions, here as elsewhere; that's the way my husband and my two sons took off about an hour ago. But it's no good unless you can fight because after passing through four or five similar holes, you'll be out in the street again."

Angelo easily found the passage.

On the other side he came upon large apartments, deserted and in great disorder. The blinds had been shredded by bullets which had then burst the bell over a clock, shattered a large pier glass and plowed up some lovely stucco moldings. In the corner of a window, the plaster was spattered with blood. Someone who must have been wounded in the shoulder had leaned there and bled quite abundantly on a very fine carpet. Taking all the customary precautions, Angelo looked out onto the street. The soldiers were going along touching the walls. The shots of a platoon crackled in a near-by quarter, but here the firing had ceased. There was no longer anyone behind the barricade. The only commands he could hear were brief and unintelligible like dogs barking.

"Croats," Angelo said to himself. "The Swiss woman would have bawled German in vain, they wouldn't have understood a thing."

He was on the point of going back to the woman. But he noticed that the soldiers were not trying to enter the houses; undoubtedly they had been ordered to seize the crossroads only and as they met with no resistance, restricted themselves to going along the streets. Besides, they had already passed the door of the passage.

Angelo found more bloodstains in a little boudoir and even on the stones of a second opening hidden behind a dainty easy-chair.

He started into this opening which penetrated a thick wall. It came out near the vaulted roof of a vast stable, three or four meters from the ground but only about two meters above the top of a traveling-coach just beneath it.

The round windows let in hardly any light. The sky must have become more overcast, or perhaps evening approached. Angelo leaped onto the roof of the carriage, but as he climbed down onto the coachman's step he saw a face thrown back on the cushions of the carriage. A boy of about twenty. Angelo thought he was asleep, but he was good and dead. He had a very nasty wound at the back of his neck. He smelled of gun powder.

"A young bourgeois," Angelo said to himself. "He must have fought single-handed in the apartments up there and come in search of the cushions of the carriage when he felt himself dying. Perhaps he had one of those feathers in his hat which you don't like, but which as you see don't get in the way of anything."

Angelo was still thinking thoughts strangely lacking in virility when he heard a door open and saw an old man appear, holding a lantern high in his hand.

"You fell out of the nest too," the man said to him without manifesting any particular emotion. He was wearing a long jacket with horn buttons such as are worn in coach offices. "I heard the noise you made. I thought you were my little customer. But I see he has kicked the bucket. I came to see him a while ago: he was still moving. He's from this neighborhood, but I don't know his name."

Angelo was too moved by the head sleeping in its little collar of blood not to say stupidly that he had to finish what this boy had begun.

"I won't contradict you," said the old man. "It's a long time now since I've contradicted anyone. But anyone who can let himself get shot up like this fellow just to put Charles Albert in Ferdinand's place must be cracked, with all due respect."

"We're not looking for power," said Angelo. "Our army is not trying to put its commander in chief on a throne. We obey only the best impulses of our heart."

And he went on as if the town were not already full of people changing laws.

"I'm not arguing with you, Prince," said the man, "I spent fifty years of my life on the coachman's seat getting slapped on the ass each time the wheels went round. Nothing like that to open up the old mind. You're ready for some more? This way out?"

He made him cross one after the other two long stables, which smelt of horse manure, and conducted him to a little door.

"Here you are in the Contrada delle pesche. Turning left, you'll come out opposite the Palazzo Reale. I advise you to stay away from it; there are still snipers on the roof and they don't give a damn whether you're for or against; the moment you move, they'll shoot. While they've got a chance! If I were you, I would go over by San Ambrogio. Any moment now it'll be time to eat. You may find a little cookshop over that way where they make soup. A little while ago I heard some young fellows talking about it."

Night was falling. The street was deserted. The tocsin continued to toll without pause, but its knell was carried away by harsh gusts of rain-weighted wind. Isolated gunshots crackled. A large cannon grumbled, solitary and majestic as thunder.

"Above all, I must not die from scorn," thought Angelo. "That would be the stupidest way to leave the world. But as soon as it's dark, there'll be a grocer out shooting on every street corner. In my case the safest thing to do is not to pop up unexpectedly in front of anyone."

Consequently he walked resolutely down the middle of the street making as much noise as possible with his boots.

During the afternoon the Contrada delle pesche had undoubtedly been the scene of a serious skirmish. Corpses of soldiers lay across the sidewalk and even along the walls. They had been sniped at from windows without being able to take shelter. The street was heaped with oddments with which they had also been stoned: bricks, tiles, pot covers, pieces of coal, and even bronze plaques of mythological scenes, the upper parts of clocks, furniture, and foot warmers. Facades of the houses were torn by bullets and grapeshot; shutters and blinds, torn from their hinges, had fallen to the ground; the iron balustrades of balconies were hanging loose, a few shops had been staved in by cannons. The street smelled of pickled herring and gunpowder.

Angelo asked himself whether behind the gaping windows and broken-down doors snipers on his side were still watching. The position seemed to have been abandoned by everyone. The corpses were all those of tall soldiers with long Ukrainian-style mustaches. The uniforms were well cared for. It seemed that a de luxe battalion, some sort of guard, had charged in the area. Did Radetzky or the Viceroy have a personal guard? In this case the fact that they had been thrown into battle seemed to indicate that the Milanese had done more than flee in feathered hats.

"I saw the Broletto being taken," Angelo thought. "I thought we could hold out till the bitter end there, but I saw the Austrians force the walls of the old building. What have I done to offset this except fire a few shots, perhaps ten at the most, at a platoon of hussars?"

He reached a neighborhood of little alleys, then a church square. He heard a gust of wind whistling in the iron cage of the belfry and the squalls hurling themselves across the sky. The seeds of a downpour pattered on the tiles. The tocsin was no longer ringing.

The return to the extraordinary disconcerted Angelo. He noticed that the rain wet him and was cold. He raised the collar of his jacket. This neighborhood too seemed abandoned.

"Everyone has closed up shop," he said to himself.

The rain, the night, the silence, the deserted streets in which he walked hunching his shoulders did not agree with the idea he had formed of a glorious revolution. At the end of the cross-street he was following, the wind wailed like a lost soul. The street came out onto the esplanade of the Castle. The old fortress, with bright lights in all its dormer windows and flickering rosy glimmers behind its crenelation, reared its large shoulders but seemed calm.

He retraced his steps.

"If I knew how to find my way back there," he said to himself, "I would very much like to see the Contrada delle pesche again. Perhaps not a single one of those corpses with long mustaches ever existed. Perhaps I never aimed through the rain at that very likeable captain's chest, and perhaps the alarm cannon didn't thunder around here this morning? You who always fear to be duped, what have you fallen into?"

Finally, after what seemed a long time—and as he was crossing the church square for the second time—he heard someone call and saw a little bar of light from a half-opened door.

A man in a dressing-gown called "Sir" to him two or three times before asking him if he knew what was going on.

"No," said Angelo, "I've been asking myself the same question. It seems to me that I knew once, but I must admit that on my life I wouldn't dare claim I know now."

His interlocutor was obviously a bourgeois. The oil lamp he had put down on a console in his hall cast an artificial glow on his silky beard, full cheeks, and well-trimmed whiskers.

"It's a great bother," he said. "The blacksmith of our quarter has spent the whole day up in the top of the belfry ringing the tocsin by striking Santa Gudula (excuse me: that's the name of our bell) with his hammer. I could see very clearly from my house. I questioned him when he came down. He saw nothing but smoke, except, he told me, grenadiers camping on the roof of the cathedral! Is it possible?"

"I was told the same thing," said Angelo. "I didn't go see, but I suppose it's true: it's a strategic position."

"You must admit, sir, that it's a strange time when soldiers are obliged to perch on churches."

"That's because they're getting a hard time of it in the streets," said Angelo.

He mentioned the Ukrainian-style mustaches.

"Things have gone that far?" said the man in a low voice.

"You heard the cannon and the gunfire didn't you?"

"God yes, sir, I heard huge explosions and I thought they were most probably cannon. I even mentioned it to two little neighbor girls who were going out in high spirits and laughed in my face. Well, as you see, I was right."

"More right than you can imagine," said Angelo. "They were shooting grapeshot."

"But come now," said the man after a moment's silence, "I'm a customs' inspector. I've had to deal with Austrians of all kinds fifty thousand times. They've always been polite and well brought up. For them to start shooting grapeshot, they must have gotten it pretty bad. I'm afraid," he added, "that all this will come out badly."

He had already closed his door a little more. Angelo asked the way to the center of town and departed, striding along in the direction the man had rapidly indicated.

"Decidedly," he said to himself, "I must have been dreaming: there was no boy sleeping the sleep of the just in the coach."

But he soon heard deep in the town a chirp made, it seemed, either by acclamations or shouts; coming to a crossroad, he saw, at the end of a long street, red glimmers dancing.

Signori, their Calabrese hats pushed down on their foreheads, armed to the teeth, sword in hand, all wearing cockades and tri-colored scarves, were directing the construction of a barricade. The structure consisted of carts, straight chairs, sofas, armchairs—larded with numerous copper basins and warped with straw and hair mattresses, was already up to the imposts. People continued to drag out furniture. Two fat men in work smocks, using the points of picks as levers, were prying up the large marble tiles of the street. Rain-soaked children, young girls and women with hair disheveled—but who were not of the working-class and who stopped what they were doing in midstream to draw shawls tighter across their breasts with a charming gesture—pushed these heavy stones against the barricade to shelter the sharpshooters. The scene was illuminated by big fires on which they threw light pieces of furniture, wicker objects, and even prettily-made chairs which must have come from a boudoir. An herbalist in a green apron, but wearing a Neapolitan sombrero on his head, threw bunches of medicinal plants into the fire to stir up the flames. He seemed to be acting in a dream and laughed blissfully as he rid himself thus of his stock; besides, he often put his hand to a pouch pocket from which emerged the butt of a pistol. People in the windows applauded, shouting "viva."

Angelo came to warm himself beside an old man, dressed soberly but elegantly with the look of an English coffee shop. He asked him where the soldiers had gone.

"The imperial soldiers have returned to the castle," the man replied gracefully; he had a nice round beard like Raspail[4] and seemed to take infinite pleasure in putting his thumbs in the arm-

---

[4] François Raspail (1794–1878), French chemist and statesman active in the revolutions of 1830 and 1848.

holes of his vest, despite the wind and rain. "The marshal probably didn't want to expose his troops to street-fighting ambushes during the night. We're taking advantage of this to block the routes down which he will be forced to throw his horsemen tomorrow."

"It would take just one good policeman in disguise keeping his eyes open and going to the castle two hours from now to report," Angelo said to himself, "and that would be that! We'd have had it."

He shared his thoughts with the old gentleman.

"Allow me to give you a bit of advice," the latter said in a low voice. "Don't get angry; I could be your father. Don't, whatever you feel, stop their fun and give them food for thought. Remember that the hero Ajax, for all his strength, had a bird's brain. I see that your hands are blackened with powder and I don't suspect you. But they wouldn't be able to see that you're a fine fellow and probably a brave one. Or they might see it and instantly close their eyes to it, or even take an exceptional, new pleasure in keeping their eyes open and disregarding it anyway. A while back two unfortunate men were killed right here who were no more spies than you or I. Lean over and look this way; you can see their boots. Heaven preserve you from seeing their faces. The only thing they did wrong was to be on the spot at the precise moment that these upstanding fellows you see with guns slung so dashingly over their shoulders, decided to make up for years by the fireside in their nightcaps. Perhaps you're an exception because of the look in your eye, but I'm here like the others to kick up my heels."

"Your confession pleases me," said Angelo. "Now I can ask you a question I would have been ashamed to ask otherwise: where can I get a loaf of bread?"

"Why, in Milan, sir—that is to say anywhere in a town where it's been in everyone's interest since morning to feed anyone who pays by fighting. I live close by. Come to my house. You can eat (I've already eaten, please excuse me). And rest assured: so you don't make me lose my esteem for you, we'll settle right now that I'm to show you to the door ten minutes after your last mouthful."

The Raspail-like beard's apartment was spruce and smelled of furs. Prints of race horses decorated the walls. Cleanliness and meticulous orderliness denoted the feminine egotism of a man who was a confirmed bachelor but well brought up and well-heeled.

Angelo recounted his day very timidly in a few words and out of simple politeness. He insisted only on the fact that he was a Piedmontese liberal who did not know the town and did not understand a thing of what was going on.

"You're not the only one," said the old man. "One thing is clear as crystal: we can do absolutely nothing without the aid of your king and his army. The revolution in Paris in which the French threw Louis Philippe the hell out, and the one in Vienna, of which less is known, but where the students seem to have broken Metternich's window-panes—have thrown oil on the fire here. The revolt has been advanced forty-eight hours to force Charles Albert's hand."

"I happen to know that our army was on the move yesterday evening," said Angelo. "They were lining up on the Ticino."

But he remembered the larks singing above the gravel banks of the river.

"They shouldn't be on the Ticino," replied his host, "but across the Verona road. Two rebukes from a cannon talking Piedmontese, a party of your cavalry at the Porta Tosa, and Radetzky will hoist the white flag on the castle and, if he doesn't have one, he'll hoist his shirt."

They agreed that today the fighting had been aimless.

"However, this was the honeymoon," said the old man.

He spoke of the slander that goes on in political parties.

"The elite are working for a chair to sit on. They've been sauntering in the streets this afternoon the way people pace up and down an antechamber."

From a high window he had seen the prisoners coming out of the Broletto, surrounded by the grenadiers of the Paumgarten regiment. They weren't the real insurrection committee but the Cafe Cova insurrectional committee: the offspring of great Italian families in which plotting is traditional and an end in itself.

Counting noses, he had seen at least two hundred and fifty come out of this communal fortress, the walls of which are more than three meters thick and which thirty resolute men could hold indefinitely even under cannon fire.

Only a ninny would be surprised at their lack of resistance to soldiers who were evidently a bit nervous but who would have been patient if anyone had explained to them what was at stake.

"Our gentlemen cut a fine figure while they were being driven towards the castle like a flock of sheep. They sang splendid subversive songs and shouted words that will go down in history. They'd been wanting to do just this at least once."

The old gentleman asked Angelo's pardon for making him eat his bread flavored with words alone, which, all in all, had nothing to do with the magnificent burst of heroism which today had thrown all classes of society after the heels of the occupying army.

In the course of the morning, children, from ten to twelve years old at most, had been seen approaching Croat sentinels guarding the Scala passage and, when they were near them, shooting them in the stomach with pistols. Very judiciously, as a shot in the stomach is fatal, and the stomach is the only spot where a wound immediately causes such pain that you cannot think of retaliation.

"In addition," he said, "the children pretended to be naïve. We're learning a lot, but we'll forget it."

"A rounded beard, especially a white one, gives a great air of wisdom," Angelo said to himself while looking at his host's face. "But his eyes are too bright for a man who can no longer hunt: that's why he's over-meticulous. Preserve me from being ridiculous this way at my age."

He thought himself capable of simulating naïveté, and then some, if need be.

Aside from the seizure of the Broletto, where they had tried to engage in a pitched battle using only undisciplined popular troops, all the skirmishes had turned to the insurgents' favor. No cavalry platoon had been able to hold its ground in the streets, under the rain of bricks falling from the rooftops and the bullets spurting from every window and smallest transom. The infantry, even though deployed as sharpshooters, had met with no greater success. On the Via Montenapoleone after three bayonet charges, the men of Reisinger regiment, abandoning their wounded, had been forced to retreat down little streets where all hell had broken loose. Soldiers who had lost their way, batmen, families of Austrian functionaries besieged in a house in the Custercio area had finally surrendered, despite the efforts of the adjutant general himself to deliver them. A group of mountain peasants who had reached Milan in the afternoon seized the small doors of the cathedral, scaled the interior galleries by knotting ropes around the bodies of the statues, climbed along the gutters, and, suddenly appearing on the roof, began to clean out the grenadiers who were occupying it, forbidding access to the square of the *Duomo* by their gunfire. The combat had lasted till nightfall; finally, in the shadows of dusk, the last soldier, larded with knife gashes, was hurled all disjointed onto the pavement of the square. Everyone stood at the windows shouting *"viva"* with such ardor that it took more than ten minutes to see that those shouting *"viva"* were dying like flies. They were being picked off one after the other by grenadiers hidden behind the chimneys of the Palazzo Reale.

On the Corsia del Ciardino a priest came out of the crowd to bless the barricade that was being built. He uttered several fine phrases, giving heroic significance to the pile of mattresses. He was recognized as the Archbishop. Everyone wanted to join the group escorting the prelate back to his palace, applauding wildly. The barricade was left to the protection of a few idlers, and a statue of the Virgin was placed at the crossroads. Nevertheless, it restrained, with this slim garrison, a dozen or so dragoons who did not dare approach, but turned helter-skelter down a little street where two horsemen were dismounting on the slippery pavement.

Following this conclusive operation to which His Excellency declared himself to have been impelled by a kind of interior revelation, priests began to bless barricades all over town. They had in any case been on the scene since morning. Never had so many abbots been seen, pistol in hand.

Troops clashed more violently around the East Gate. The Austrians were occupying the bastions, but the little bridge across the ditch had the stylish air of historic sites. The handful of townspeople who had reached this spot, after exalted comings and goings under balconies full of pretty women in the throes of delirium, knew that the taking of a bridge usually decides the outcome of a day. They attacked courageously. Fifteen were killed, and they were half driven to retreat. They were angry and made repeated assualts. Finally, a journeyman mason who had just arrived was the first to cross the bridge while the Austrians withdrew twenty paces to a corner house they had fortified.

The dead and wounded were collected. They were found everywhere and carried to the home of Comte Uboldo degli Uboldi, whose collections of ancient weapons and historic museum had been pillaged early in the morning by workers searching for guns. Thus the Milanese doctors and society ladies cared for the wounded beneath standards taken from the Turks (but bought from Jews during a whole lifetime of collecting) and panoplies of Albanian halberds. Here too, as at the East Gate bridge there were many of those fine sacrifices which distinguish the first morning of a combat. Strips of embroidered sheets had been torn to make bandages, and *silk* lint made of the raveled chemises, corset-covers, and drawers of marvelous women lay in piles higher than a man.

About noon ambulances arrived bringing middle-aged bourgeois, clean from head to foot, wearing clean shirts, and then younger bourgeois occasionally with three or four wounds, some bandaged hastily with handkerchiefs. All were very stoical under the scalpel, their faces stern and savage; it was hard to know how they had stood being drapers so long. In the course of the afternoon, workers arrived carrying their wounded on ladders and improvised litters. From that moment till evening, more and more working-people were brought in, almost all of them cut to pieces with sidearms, as often happens in furious hand-to-hand combat. Finally, the corpse of a priest chanced to be brought in. He had been killed by the explosion of a holster which had broken his superciliary arch and chewed up his brain. "It often happens that you spring a rattrap on your fingers while baiting it," said the chaplain. But the dead man, who, after his inside pockets had been searched, was established as being the vicar of Santa Maria delle Grazie, had the sleeves of his soutane fastened up and the blood which stained his arms to the elbows was not his own.

"And there are nothing but larks along the Ticino," Angelo said to himself. "Not even the little bugle and trumpet notes an army in the country always sounds."

"Let's prolong our agreement for the length of time it takes you to smoke a cigar," said the old gentleman.

"I'll accept your cigar with pleasure," said Angelo. "Mine, which were in my pocket, are in bits. But I won't compromise about our agreement. Let's say, in order to avoid rhetoric, that I like to smoke while walking in the fresh air."

He excused himself for smelling like a wet dog.

"To tell the truth," he said to himself when in the street, "if I could buy happiness utensils as one buys cooking-utensils, what I would need now is a madman certified as such from a good asylum and guaranteed incurable. That would be the man with whom to exchange ideas. With these people who claim to kick their slippers over the nearest windmill but in reality put them side by side on brand new bedside carpets, I can't think of a word to say and I look like a fool. Whereas with my madman we could *settle in for a good gossip*! But it's undeniable that this coal-black city with flames flickering in its depths and people shouting and especially applauding to burst your eardrums is no sight for a family man."

It was no longer raining. Aside from the murmur of the crowd gathered wherever barricades were being built, the only noise was that of the wind, very strong and quite cold.

"It's completely ridiculous to go on wandering about in such weather on the pretext of having played a few jokes on the Austrian army yesterday afternoon," Angelo said to himself. "Would you be afraid to sleep, like all these fine fellows who, ten-strong, perch soapboxes on retrenchments which are already too high? Look for some place to sleep."

He was in a neighborhood where numerous fires had been lighted in the streets because the near-by square was being fortified. The flames lighted the facades of pampered houses which seemed deserted and even pillaged; undoubtedly the homes of high functionaries who had taken refuge in the castle and whose property had been thrown into the street.

Finally, in one of these palaces, he found a vast drawing-room hung with somewhat faded red damask where an old armchair still remained. He dragged the armchair in front of a large carved-marble mantel and made a good fire as if he had been the owner. He fed the fire with the debris of the furniture, thick papers bearing enormous signatures in Chinese ink, and fluffy bits of mattress wool. The wind moaned in the unhinged blinds and the odor of burned wool evoked proud mountain peaks. He fell almost immediately into a sleep that heard and enjoyed everything.

He was half awakened at various times, first by the hollow roar of high-rising flames and a sensation of excessive heat on his legs. He half-opened his eyes and saw five or six men around him feeding the fire with boards, some in workmen's smocks and caps with flaps, others in redingotes and Neapolitan hats. He pulled back his legs, turned on his side, and went to sleep again. But the noise of a long animated conversation with, from time to time, the pathetic solo of a bass voice, speaking the Paduan dialect, prevented him from completely losing consciousness.

He wondered what was going on in Venice, and if Modena and Parma had been swept along with the rest. The old connoisseur of horse prints was right: a cavalry troop across the Bergamo road. But there was no cavalry troop across the Bergamo road.

Then he was awakened by silence. The fire had died down. Among the men sleeping on the stone floor near the chimney, which one was the Paduan with the deep voice? Padua is the fatherland of lawyers. What a weapon for persuasion to know how to speak dialect, especially one that sounded like snoring! People used it every day to say "Good morning" and "Good evening," and now suddenly someone was using it to sing: "To arms!" His cup was full to overflowing. But the uhlans from Verona were galloping unrestrained on the Bergamo road.

The wind which had come up grumbled in the silent town. Angelo dreamed of the mountains. The rearing heights covered with brown forests put him to sleep.

Finally the beating of a drum awakened him completely. All the men had departed except one who was heating coffee on the coals.

CHAPTER SIX

The coffee-lover (who asserted that he was making it "Turkish style") said that he was a stonecutter—a journeyman, of course. He didn't look any too well: his cheeks were green and his eyes red from breathing marble dust all day. This aside, he found plenty to laugh at in life.

Day had not yet dawned. The drum rolled in the streets, departed, and then drew nearer again. Angelo no longer wanted to fly into the fray.

"It takes all kinds," said the green-cheeked man, "and we haven't done such a bad job; the proof being that the Ostrogoths have gone back into their shells. Listen, if they'd had the best of it, you wouldn't have slept in that armchair. I agree: these days you can't fly into things. You weren't on the Piazza San Lorenzo yesterday evening, were you? The word went round that there's one of Napoleon's generals on our side. He's set himself up in the Palazzo Borromeo. I'm going to have a look there."

Angelo didn't believe in the Napoleonic general but he followed the stonecutter.

The Piazza Borromeo was full of famished Austrian prisoners. They called for food in lugubrious voices. They were foot soldiers of the Vienna corps who had put up no resistance. Torchbearers escorting baskets of bread came out of a street where bakers had been set to work.

The balconies of the palace were crammed with people. The lighted windows, wide open, exhaled thick tobacco smoke. Men you could call men, with lovely hunting-pieces on their shoulders, crowded the hall. They spoke little, displaying a calculated impassiveness. Moreover, they were accompanied by grooms and snapped their fingers from time to time to ask for their *briquets* or handkerchiefs, or to call them to order.

"If Giuseppe is anywhere around, he's here," Angelo said to himself, making his way among the groups.

But all the neckties were too whimsical.

"Giuseppe is incapable of understanding the divine inspiration in the fingertips of those who can tie such flowing knots, especially at daybreak. He must be in the back room of some café with a group of people who've got everything down to a system, especially neckties. Unless he died to the cry of 'Long live liberty!' That's not completely out of the question. He's not always in command of himself."

Angelo went up to the first floor where someone seemed to be making a speech. There, men who were not as fussily dressed (many were armed with a gun, a dagger, and a saber all at once) were listening to an invisible orator who seemed to be talking about battles with a degree of common sense. Angelo tried to get up to the front row. He was allowed through politely.

The speaker was a small, strong-backed man in green kerseymere britches and soft boots. He looked about fifty, but physically very strong. In place of a jacket he wore a sort of heavy sailor's sweater which swelled his thick arms and broad shoulders so that his small, bullet-round head seemed to grow right out of them. He spoke very well, but with a foreign accent.

"Could this be the famous general?" Angelo said to himself. "In any case he knows the tune and he's spicing it up."

He was happy to hear someone talking shop at last, because, basically, if they were going to fight, it came to this. But he understood why the gathering had made way for him so politely. The man was constantly making sarcastic remarks which did not spare anyone.

"An army undertakes a campaign. An army of the people undertakes a country jaunt. If it's a question of aimless sniping and killing soldiers for the sake of killing, I say to hell with it. I'll stay home with my pipe and slippers."

"I'm a liberal who fought with you yesterday," said Angelo, "and

I'd like very much to know if something coherent is to be done at last."

"Something coherent will be done when there are fewer liberals and more people who consent to obey."

"As far as I'm concerned, I'm not only consenting, but trying, to obey," Angelo began.

But he was interrupted: buckets of coffee were brought in. In the uproar that followed, Angelo found himself side by side with the little man, who was blowing on his coffee like everyone else.

"I spoke a little harshly, sir," the man said to him after drinking, "but that's because I'm having a hard job of it hitting these heifers where it hurts. You answered like a soldier."

"I am one," said Angelo.

"I'm not surprised," said the man.

"Civvies never realize that an exact maneuver saves bloodshed. Where have you served?"

"Kingdom of Sardinia. Colonel in the hussars."

"Charles Albert sent you?" the general asked. He added immediately: "Pardon the irony."

"I left the service more than ten years ago."

"You can't have been a very big colonel at the time."

"You can't have been a very big general in 1805 or '06 . . ."

"1812. Under Napoleon there was no such thing as a big general. I'm sixty-three and I have all my teeth. I crack lobster claws and chicken bones. Your king is a blackguard."

"You can say whatever you want: he wanted to hang me."

"Better if he had hanged you: then at least he would have been doing his job; one could have hoped for some feeling, but what can you expect from a horse trader? . . . He got us all worked up. I thought he was a *king,* and this little word still meant something to me. Now he's got us where he wants us, that is burned to a crisp if he doesn't make a move, up to our ears. He's holding all the trumps, and if we want to see them we've got to force his hand.

"The army was on the move yesterday."

Angelo recounted once again, but in military terms and without a single excess word, what he had seen between Casteletto and Novara. He even permitted himself the luxury of using technical language.

"Here at last is a precise report. The first in twenty-four hours," said the little man who had listened very carefully. "It doesn't give me a farthing more hope, but I know where I am, and anyway I know my way around this country."

He asked for the names of places and roads. He drew Angelo aside and with a pencil sketched the maneuver on a piece of paper.

"Good," he said, when he had drawn his little rectangles. "In addition to being a blackguard, he's an ass. Why did he gamble all his cavalry on the right? What does he want to make of them? Pancakes? We've been cheated from beginning to end."

Angelo, seeing the Milanese citizenry all about him armed to the teeth, spoke of the heart and even of putting one's heart in one's work.

"Agreed. A handful can do a job but to get a handful, you've got to have a hand that can grab. When the Broletto surrendered, if Radetzky had struck while the iron was hot, he could have walked over us with two battalions of Hungarian infantry and a squadron of uhlans! I was in a cold sweat. Don't push us over the edge. We won't be the ones to beat the Austrians; the Austrians will give themselves a beating. Yesterday evening when I saw them riding their nags back into the castle I sighed with relief. Thank God, St. Fright be saved, and all of that! But it's going to be tough to win the dolly twice in a row, believe me."

Angelo offered his services.

"You're one in a million; did you think I was going to let you slip through my fingers?"

"Don't take me for a great captain. I've never been in combat."

"There's nothing magic about a battle. It's like anything else, you've got to give it a try. Once you know water wets, you know everything. But stop a minute: let's be frank. My authority grew bit by bit because I talked shop to young fellows who were throwing their gunpowder at sparrows. There's no money to be made in working with me. No, good accounts make good friends. If you want the list of prefectures, you'll have to go to another window. But if you want to see the country and get rid of black bile, I can promise you this much and stick to it."

The little man, who was called Lecca, explained the situation. Radetzky had ordered the entire garrison to return to the castle.

But his provisions were scattered throughout the town. They had to seize them, set ambushes in the streets leading to them, and stand fast. "Fatigue details must transport as much flour, munitions, and forage as possible to places we control, burn the rest, and especially not trouble themselves with anything picturesque. What the hell do you expect us to do with the Viceroy's palace, for example, or the hundred and forty-three portraits of archdukes in the Palazzo Marino? People have been gargling with this loot, but I don't have a sore throat: I have a hot seat."

"Give me ten men who will obey me without my having to be coarse," said Angelo, "and I'll take care of the stores if you'll tell me where they are."

"Why not? Ten is a good number. I like modesty. As for coarseness, the only justification for it is that it drives men better than a good reason. But you're free to try your method as long as you don't come back to cry on my shoulder."

Angelo heard the men moving ammunition chests around him say that a very handsome fellow had just arrived who had campaigned for two years in Algeria against the Arabs and that with him you could be sure of success.

"With me you're sure of nothing," he said to himself.

He inspected the weapons of his little troop and asked why the packages of powder were not according to regulation. They replied that they had the new smokeless gun cotton from France. He was very proud to leave the palace and to cross the square at the head of his party, but on entering the dark streets he said to himself: "I've changed souls." Almost immediately a cannon shot coming from the castle tore and shook the night; the bells began to ring again.

He decided to go first to the store containing flour. He found a barricade in the vicinity of the store and a crowd of men, women, and children, very excited by the cannon; not knowing what else to do, they were throwing wood on the fires, which already rose in flames five or six meters high.

"Put that out," he said in a voice that he found with surprise to be very powerful. "Right now you're a target for the artillery, and you'll be even more of a target if the soldiers start slipping down the narrow streets, staying maliciously in the shadows. Besides, you've built your retrenchments all wrong. Instead of leaping like goats at the explosions, look at the trajectory of the bullets: that's the way horsemen with sabers and foot soldiers with bayonets will come. And then you don't need many people to break their ranks. Try to find me an ironmonger's or an edge-tool maker's in the neighborhood and bring me some bags of nails. Let the women go collect all the empty bottles in the near-by houses. I'll show you how to knock down ninepins."

His little speech worked miracles on the crowd, who were tired of outwitting a little morning cowardice and ready to be told what to do. The women immediately found a St. John Chrysostom in this tall youth who had, in addition, a very delicate mustache.

While they hurried to do his bidding, Angelo gathered the men on the steps of a little church from which the street where the warehouse was could be seen.

"The Austrians may have left a sentinel in the store," he said. "And since yesterday evening he's had plenty of time to load a number of guns and arrange them around him. By calculating his shots he can cut us in half if we advance with what Napoleon's general would call an excess of confidence. Those who are unfortunate enough to return empty-handed will have to hear how the French take redoubts. Therefore I'll go first, alone. When I've reconnoitered, I'll whistle; you come join me one after another, being as careful as I was. I may be killed. If so, this gentleman will assume command." He indicated a man with a very dark complexion. "Perhaps he too has campaigned in Algeria," he said to himself.

"Three of you will stay here," he continued. "Two will collect fatigue details and bring them to me over there to move the flour. The third will organize our defense. As soon as the nails and bottles are assembled, he should see that the nails are spread and bottles broken on the ground a hundred paces up each of the three streets that come out here. If we're attacked, I want you to kill and especially don't applaud: we're not at the theater. If someone applauds, that's because he's not doing anything and there's work enough for everyone. Send him to me; I'll make him carry flour sacks."

Thereupon Angelo plunged into the shadows, following the walls. But the store was not guarded, and it was very easy to lift the simple bar of wood closing the door.

While the sacks of flour and beans were being dragged to a stable in the neighborhood, Angelo went back to the square in front of the little church. He found the sentry posts well established and defended; everyone was silent and resolute. The man he had left in command was carefully searching the gloom before him with the intelligent look of a brigade commander. Only the enemy was lacking; for the moment they seemed happy to restrict themselves to hurling ridiculously small bullets at the town.

"We're not going to await the pleasure of these gentlemen in the castle," said Angelo. "Hand over your command to whoever you think is best qualified and bring him to me."

The transfer of authority was accomplished with a ceremony invented instinctively on the spot, but possessing the finish of a priest's gesture.

Angelo gave instructions to the new commander of the fortress of furniture, nails, and broken bottles. Although he was a timid man who chewed his thick red mustache, he was reassured that the game was finally being played according to the rules.

"It's no treat what I've landed you with," Angelo said to him. "I'm leaving you responsible for moving the flour. As soon as they've finished and the store is empty, set fire to it with something which flames well. Probably you'll need straw sprinkled with oil. I want the entire shed to burn so that the flames can be seen from a distance. The enemy must feel the blows we're giving him. When everything is burning well, line up in columns of four and come join me in your best order on the Piazzo San Ambrogio where I'm going to take care of the engineering-depot. Don't dawdle, I need you, or more exactly, liberty needs you."

The engineering-depot occupied vast, dreary buildings.

"The Austrians are no fools," Angelo said to himself. "They didn't guard the flour because they know they can always send foragers and carts to the mills in the area, but this Arsenal contains powder, and in times like these the nearest gunpowder is farther than a horse can travel. Surely there's a guard posted."

Accordingly he approached with infinite precautions. He did

indeed see a little halo of light at the end of the street, probably from the guardhouse lantern concealed in the corner of the square. Other reddish glimmers flickered on the main facade of the Arsenal.

One of Angelo's men said that if they advanced fifty paces more in Indian file along the walls, they give each other a leg up and jump into the cloister of the Theatine monastery. The monastery church was on the Piazza San Ambrogio; they could thus go under cover to see what was happening and even, he said, occupy a strategic position. (Since the seizure, without a single blow, of the flour store, everyone was for technique.)

While the Austrian sentinel at the end of the street let his coat float over the lantern, they edged silently along quite a high wall and fell into a courtyard without a cloister, but filled with sharp odors of cooking, especially of frying.

They found five or six monks breakfasting on thick slices of bread which they dipped in a frying pan of eggs. These holy individuals *ex abrupto* declared their unswerving loyalty and, hardly taking the time to wipe their beards, brought well-oiled guns and no small quantity of ammunition out of a chest. They were dying to use everything and told the Signor Commandatore that their belfry contained a little gallery made expressly to keep the Piazza San Ambrogio under fire in total security.

The passage was indeed pierced by loopholes. Just below, five vans and three caissons were visible, which the soldiers, coming and going, were loading with cannon cartridges and sacks of cannon balls.

Angelo had all the loopholes occupied and as many guns readied as would be necessary for several minutes' continuous fire. Then he gave precise orders in a low voice. Each man should choose a target; useless for two to fire at the same man, but each man should hit his target.

"At the first shot," he said, "we should be rid forever of the officer in command, of the coachmen on the seats and of the individual you see down there in the open door holding a bunch of keys in his hand. You must then fell as many soldiers as possible, but especially those who try to seize the horses by the bridle or who rush to close the door. Take care not to wound the horses; we're going to need them." He told them several times more to aim carefully as on maneuvers and pointed out severely to the monks that it was no joke.

"I'll wait as long as necessary," he said, "for you to get cold as snakes and ready to carry out my orders to the letter with no flourishes. This is no place for people who are a bundle of nerves or hysterical because until now they haven't had enough entertainment. Get it through your heads that I have a job to do—and you too, moreover—and have got to do it as well as possible. A pair of shoes is not made by luck."

When everyone was frozen by his clipped, decisive voice, he ordered them to fire. There was no need to keep it up long. The soldiers spared by the first round fled immediately, fearing that the carts would explode.

"There is always a decisive moment, and probably this is it," Angelo said to himself as he stepped onto the Piazza San Ambrogio. "I must not let it slip by, but I don't know how to catch hold of it. I'll never get used to these rapid victories."

He found the large, dark house very large and very dark, the wide-open door too wide open, and the bloodstained corpses too bloodstained, and above all too still.

He was probably about to do something heroic and stupid, for example throw himself all alone into the jaws of the lion, when he heard the rumble of troops on the march in one of the streets which opened out onto the square.

"I'm about to die," he thought.

With terror he felt that under the circumstances he would undoubtedly be obliged to do so somewhat pompously.

But it was simply the timid man with the red mustache who, carrying out his orders to the letter, was coming to join him with the entire troop after setting fire to the flour store. These subordinates, who till then had succeeded in everything by obeying orders, no longer had a single doubt; and it was following them, although at their head, that Angelo made his way into the Arsenal.

The small squad of pioneers guarding the engineering-depot had taken refuge at the start of the combat in a little fort at the back of the courtyard. Since the day before no one in the Austrian army had liked the idea of dying. Seeing nothing more than a few hesitant shadows outlined in the doorway, they had fired a few gunshots.

But before the numerous, resolute troop they ceased fire; however, their shots had not been ineffective: two of Angelo's men had fallen.

Angelo had got hold of the bunch of keys. But all the inside doors had been opened for the fatigue detail which had been loading the wagons. Two unarmed soldiers were taken prisoner trying to slip down a long corridor, and, leaving marksmen at the windows with the order to prevent the little post, which was still barricaded, from coming out, Angelo made his way into the workshops. They contained wheels, gun carriages, and even a little mounted cannon.

The men went wild over this powerful weapon. In an instant they saw themselves drawing it through the streets. Angelo had a world of difficulty re-establishing order among the men; they had learned in school that seizing cannons is synonymous with victory. Violently he pushed aside those who had already put their shoulders to its wheels.

"And I don't like the feathers you're sporting on your hats any better. If the only thing you can think of is a parade, take this cannon which any imbecile will be only too glad to applaud and get out of my way. It's men I want. When we've won—if we win— you can amuse yourselves as you wish. Until then I have some say in the matter. Is there a stoneworker among you?" he continued when order had been somewhat restored.

Two men came forward.

"I appoint you captains," said Angelo, "you have authority to shoot to pieces the first man who disobeys you. I've decided to shoot you if, after accepting your rank, you don't fulfill all your duties. I need a device which only you can set up perfectly."

He wanted to blow up the Arsenal. This was a far lovelier idea than the cannon, and they began to speak in low voices.

The stoneworkers, who were accustomed to explosions, were to go reconnoiter the store of gunpowder and practice their trade. This turn of events, making them bosses more than captains, gave them a certain bite and severity. They asked for only two men to help them and were malicious enough to suggest they didn't want simpletons either.

Someone came to tell Angelo that the little fort was waving a white flag and asking to surrender. In consequence he led the rest of the troop into the courtyard.

The adjutant of the pioneers was deathly pale and seemed in a hurry.

"We know full well what you're going to do," he said. "I'm from Lombardy and I don't want to be buried under ruins for nothing. All we ask is that we're gotten out of here fast, as far away as possible. The powder kegs won't giggle when you tickle them."

Angelo sent the vans, the caissons, and the prisoners to the Palazzo Borromeo under escort. He lined up his other men on the Piazzo San Ambrogio, stationed them in lines according to height, counted them, checked the ammunition bags, and asked a few idiotic questions in the tone of a drawing-room conversation. He had noticed the hangdog looks the working-class soldiers were casting on the corpses of the Emperor's soldiers heaped on the pavement.

"If you don't do something good and stupid right away to stop them thinking about naked death, you'll have had it," he said to himself. "Don't forget that you're driving simple people to a relentless effort (and an effort in which they must forget themselves); until now they have never worked more than ten minutes without drinking a glass of wine, whistling a little tune, or putting their feet up at home."

Finally the captain-stoneworkers came out of the Arsenal unwinding a sulphured fuse. They were in an excellent mood.

"There are sixty kegs of cannon powder which, at your command," they said, "are going to go up like crazy."

First Angelo ordered all the soldiers commanded by the red mustache to go to the Via Beatrice where the fate of a forage store had to be settled.

"Are you sure it's going to explode?" he asked the stoneworkers when they were alone.

"Commander," they said, a bit mockingly because they were talking shop and read the passion in Angelo's eyes, "if it doesn't blow up, it'll only be because the good Lord no longer exists."

They mentioned all the precautions they had taken, and even all the imprudences they had committed. Besides, they had experimented with a bit of wick a foot long: you could count three before it had burned. Thus the wick was very fresh and could not go out on the way. There was a little over two hundred feet, counting stairs and corridors, from here to the pile of powder.

Angelo lit the wick and stood stock-still watching the little red flame race like a rat and enter the door of the *conciergerie*.

"We ought to get a bit of a move on now, commander," said the stoneworkers.

Suddenly Angelo was glad to run.

They had only just joined the troop, which had left ahead of them, when the engineering-depot blew up. The detonation, the spurting of the flames, and the general conflagration were beyond anything Angelo had imagined. They had really tied a tin can to the tail of a very big dog! Debris of all kinds fell on the roofs and in the street. They had to take shelter in doorways. A beam flying with red wings landed and capered about on the pavement like a wool carpet. All the windows had opened without a sound on people who had come from God knows where (probably their beds) and were gesticulating wordlessly. Finally Angelo's ears unstopped and he heard the fire-alarm drum, the crackle of the blaze, and the shouting. There was no "Hurrah!" People shouted "Fire" with piercing, practical voices.

Angelo had some trouble regrouping his men. They had struck up passionate discussions with the population in the windows. As the fire continued to jump about, cut to pieces by dry or extremely glorious explosions, the flames leaped to great heights. This time the shouting was operatic. By grappling with his men, Angelo nevertheless tore a large part of his troop away from the spectacle and from their arguments. The laggards ended by joining them.

Altogether, guns slung over their shoulders, they were crossing a large, deserted square bordered by noble houses when Angelo noticed out of the corner of his eye a red-and-black mass moving in a street to his left. At that moment enormous horsemen issued from the street with sabers bared. Their gallop was comical on the slippery street, but they advanced quickly, looking very heavy. There was not even a cry of "Look out there!" Angelo was rushing behind the base of a lamp post when he was hit on the forehead by an object which was at the same time hard and sticky. He fell without losing consciousness. He heard the nutcracker noise of sabers cutting on heads and the whinnying of horses wheeling.

He remained stretched out on the ground, his cheek glued to the pavement. A voice near his ear said: "They're gone, Commander. You've been hit."

"I don't think so."

His voice had a curious ring to it, and no matter how wide he opened his eyes he only saw red.

"You're covered with blood."

He wiped his face. He saw the deserted square, the dawn, the corpses on the street. His blood continued to flow, burning, into his eyes. He tried to get up and got on hands and knees. "I'm as ridiculous as those horses a moment ago," he thought.

"You can walk?"

"Certainly," he said.

He struck out firmly and took a few rapid steps. He would have fallen head first if his companion had not held him up in his arms.

"We've got to clear out as fast as possible," said the man, "otherwise they'll come back and cut off our ears."

Angelo felt that he was being supported. He concentrated on taking little steps, carefully putting his feet flat down. He had five or six thoughts in his head, especially this one: he who goes slowly goes far. All these thoughts made him feel sick as a dog.

When he awakened, he was lying on a couch. He said to himself: "They've shut me in one of those quarantines where people die in filth." But he saw a bourgeois drawing-room around him. A young woman, ugly, but for that reason determined to be known for her "character," was soaking compresses in a basin from which rose a strong odor of camphor. Near her a bald old gentleman in a dressing-jacket with braid and a breasty matron who breathed very rapidly seemed caught somewhat short.

Angelo said good day nicely; everyone was delighted by this presence of mind. A man who must have been at table somewhere rose and came forward with his mouth full.

"Then, Commander," he said, "you're back in the land of the living."

"I recognize your voice," said Angelo, "it's you who helped me."

"I was just in time," said the man. "The dragoons returned while I was pulling you along. Luckily I was able to stuff the two of us into a passageway. These ladies and gentlemen have been very kind."

Angelo thanked the young woman with the compresses. She replied as he might have expected: "Don't get excited," and leaned against Angelo's elbow to make him lie down again.

"But there's nothing wrong with me," said Angelo, resisting the pressure of this egotistical hand. "What happened to me?"

"The officer fired at you with his pistol," said the man. "The shot squirted off at an angle. It hit the bone but went no farther. The Signorina had a good look."

"You must stay quiet," said the Signorina.

"You must sleep," said the lady with the large bosom, "and I'll make you some chicken broth."

"I'm going to see if I can stand up," said Angelo.

"Young man," said the old gentleman, "I fought in Mantua on the 29 Fructidor, and I know what a head wound's all about. You think you can stand up, but in reality you can't."

"However," said Angelo, "here I am standing up and thanks to your care, I'm steady on my pins."

He took several steps with great assurance. He looked at himself in a mirror, saw enormous brilliant eyes, cheeks eaten away by a green beard and a bandage as regular as the finest embroidery.

"Have I been here long?" he asked.

"A brief half-hour," said the man. "The minute you sniffed the sedative water, you began to fidget. You were just knocked out. Besides, the dragoons are still patroling all around, and they just charged five minutes ago, out there in back."

Dawn was rising in a beautiful sky, clear of clouds but blackened by the fire. Through the masses of smoke which the wind beat down on the roofs, he could see the blue of a calm morning. The tocsin rang out; a large mortar on the citadel rumbled at regular intervals; the town was full of shouting.

"I must say something nice to the young lady who undoubtedly sacrificed a piece of her trousseau to make such pretty festoons for my forehead," Angelo said to himself.

"I know very well," she replied to his words of thanks, "that men have important work to do."

Her voice was pretty in contrast to her face.

"But come now," said the old gentleman, "there's time for everything."

"On the condition," said the lady, "that you have a bite to eat and drink something."

"I'll go along with that," said the man. "That's a fine little white wine you served me, and God knows, I know the stuff! I don't drink wine like that every morning!"

Angelo needed no further urging to eat. However, he remained standing, both to try out his legs and to get it across that he had no time to sit at table. He did the honors of a peppery tripe sausage and some ham smelling of violets. The first mouthfuls were in a way intoxicating; he no longer thought of anything but stuffing his cheeks.

"I'm a connoisseur all right," said the man. "God knows, sometimes life is no joke."

The old gentleman was very proud of his white wine. He had a vineyard in the vicinity of Milan, toward Serto.

Angelo explained that he had been ordered to set fire to the enemy's stores and that he was going to do so.

"You've not done badly so far," said the man. "From time to time the Piazzo San Ambrogio still gives out with a good blast." Anyway the gunpowder had been doing plenty of talking.

There were still two food depots, and, above all, the forage stores. Horses must eat. It would perhaps be less spectacular, but destroying the forage would in a way clear the streets.

Despite the engineering-depot which continued to explode bit by bit, and the smoke torn by the vivid red conflagration, it took Angelo five whole minutes to calm the egotism of these people who through him were at last involved in the events of the day. In sum they were telling him that the weather was bad outside. He mounted some pretty big hobbyhorses and talked about one's native land. They were so proud to hear something witty that they abandoned their prey with a certain pleasure.

"Don't think yourself obliged to follow me," Angelo said to the man who had gone out with him. "Just show me the way."

But the man followed close on his heels, remarking all the while that this business of forage was exactly his meat and that he wanted to have a hand in it now that the troop, that is to say, collective responsibility, no longer existed.

He was a thick-set man, broad-shouldered and a little heavy, wearing a sack overcoat and a hat with a flat brim; he walked like a sailor.

At the first barricade, the bandage, which was beginning to show a star of fresh blood, worked miracles. Also his jacket of bright velvet was all stained by the hemorrhage. There's nothing like blood on a tall, pale young man to win people.

Angelo asked to see the commander of the square. There was one, there were even two, for the man pointed out came up, followed by a woman. She looked at the blood with affected indifference and spoke like a man despite her lovely lips, which, nonetheless, she had reddened somewhat.

"Madame," said Angelo, "this is a trade in which one must be an apprentice before becoming a master. The dragoons are good workmen. It won't be long before they find the little street you're turning your back on."

He mentioned nails and broken bottles. These techniques were instantly to everyone's taste; they all had seen bits of broken glass on the tops of walls.

"Finally," Angelo continued, "I have been ordered to set fire to the forage store in your neighborhood."

On the morning of this second day of fighting, the insurgents were expecting to be attacked, but had made no plan of their own. They were right in thinking they had seized the town. It was now the enemy's play, as in a game of dominoes. Could you pass up your turn in this game? They asked Angelo very seriously whether the Austrians weren't going to get angry.

"If they get angry," he said, "they can get out."

"They may get insulting and set fire to the town."

"Milan is rich enough to burn and be reborn from her ashes."

This was pretty strong medicine.

"Sir," said the male commander, "you're under orders and obviously you want to carry them out. But who gave them to you, and have you got them where we can see them?"

These last words were wildly successful. They were already

sprinkling nails and breaking bottles in the little street Angelo had pointed out, but as for the orders, they wanted to see them.

"If I mention the general, they'll claim they're obeying another," Angelo said to himself. "I won't even be firm."

"Gentlemen," he replied, "obviously you are free, as we're fighting for freedom. But if you demand of me what I don't demand of you, we'll come to blows.

"My orders are sufficient and I'm going to blow up the store without asking your permission. However, since I like you and since I have some idea of the way things work, I warn you that when I set fire to the haystack, the cavalrymen won't be any too happy and will try to shake the fleas off someone. As you're in the area, they'll probably think of you. But for all your good will, you haven't constructed anything to win their respect with these cupboards and mattresses."

He gave a rapid demonstration of the weaknesses of their retrenchments which could be maneuvered around on all sides and even easily taken from behind.

They swallowed their pride immediately and asked his advice. He perceived that they were worth more than their words. He mustn't repeat too often that they should hold out till death: they were capable of doing so. These swaggerers didn't give a thought to their skins: they were simply intimidated by the public. Women they had always seen washing the dishes were walking around with sabers. Housewives who had never thought farther than the linen closet and the soup kettle displayed the prodigal faces of great passion. They feared that in the end they would not be masters of the upheaval.

Angelo found volunteers to go with him. All together they courageously assaulted the dozen or so stable guards defending the hay. The latter at least had the merit of playing out their role.

At noon all the forage stores were vomiting fire and flames, covering two thirds of the town with heavy smoke full of flying coals. Each street was black as pitch. The stifled tocsin seemed a great way off; it rang high in the sky. Cavalry platoons in disarray could be heard trotting about haphazardly.

Angelo returned to the Palazzo Borromeo.

"We've become the top brass," said Lecca. "You roused them

so they've sent us some men, fine ones."

Angelo was naïve enough to believe he meant Austrians.

"The Austrians are out of it. Better than that: they've sent us the cream of society and they're the people who are out for the top positions. We're not making this revolution all alone, old man. They even thought we didn't have a thing to do with it. They dropped everything and came to see whether we were sheep or goats."

He took Angelo by the arm and conducted him up to the third floor of the palace where the state apartments were.

"Is that real blood?" he asked, indicating Angelo's bandage.

He asked the question very jovially. The drawing-room on the third floor, far from the crowd which had overrun the lower floors of the palace, was the setting of a charming scene. Unfortunately, the well-bred conversation taking place in this vast, gilded room inundated by Venetian mirrors was marred by smoke, especially the black, burning smoke from the stores where the forage, still a little oily, was burning without flames. Moreover, since five, while explosions continued to shake the furnace of the engineering-depot, the fire had spread to the huge drug and pharmaceutical warehouses where sulphurous substances had started to burn, spreading their acid vapors. Torches hurled great distances, or perhaps people acting on the spot had lighted the grass and groves of the western road around the city where redoubts stuffed with infantry ammunition had caught fire and crackled like pine cones. If you cared for the spectacle, you could see the whole thing from the third floor of the palace.

The three people, obviously strangers to the house, conversing with a fourth person, no less obviously at home, looked as if they did not like the kind of thing going on before their eyes.

"They look like people who come to complain that our cats can't make love without howling," Angelo said to himself.

In reality these people were forcing nobility upon themselves. The one who succeeded best was wearing a soutane and shamelessly sporting violet stockings which he had quite clearly borrowed. He was addressed, nevertheless, as Monsignor.

He was talking about Christian charity in a high voice.

Angelo once more understood the advantage of wearing a jacket that looked as if it had been dragged through a slaughter house. At the sight of him the conversation ceased. The prelate hung in mid-air as if floating, despite his heavy face of Roman marble.

"Here's the artist," said Lecca. "He won't bite."

Angelo was immediately showered with compliments in such a way that he replied: "I'm under the impression you're holding something against me. Let's be frank."

Since early morning he had become so accustomed to striding fast wherever he was going that he had entered the drawing-room like a light infantryman. Everyone had expected a finesse which he indeed lacked. His brash manner gave them pause, especially to a tall, handsome man with curly hair and lips like Diana's bow, resembling Ugo Foscolo,[1] minus the eyes. His, which he narrowed, were immobile.

"You've destroyed a great many provisions," he said. "We'll forget about the hay; we don't eat that, believe me. Not everything is accomplished with gunfire. Think it over and you'll even see it proves nothing. We've got a town to feed. Wheat doesn't grow on sidewalks even if they're sprinkled with blood."

The little round gentleman with whom the prelate had been talking about Christian charity prevented Angelo from replying, asking pardon for his interruption with a pretty gesture of his pudgy hand: "I'm a very bad host," he said. "Lecca, have we any more of those hot *croissants*? The neighborhood bakers have been sending them in all morning."

Lecca knew enough to smile a crooked smile; he assumed the air of a good fellow who is being kicked under the table.

"We're past coffee time," he said, "but I saw some baskets of Turin *flûtes* arrive a while ago."

He went out to shout an order down the stairwell: "Have someone send up some baskets of good, crisp, Turin bread sticks."

"You're right, sir," said Angelo to the handsome man, "people eat a lot during revolutions. I've eaten in various neighborhoods— on invitation, I'll have you know, and as recently as two hours ago. I saw no sign of want anywhere. All the same, since I don't eat hay either, I took care, before setting fire to the sheds, to have the flour

[1] Ugo Foscolo (1778–1827), Italian Romantic poet.

transported to citizens' houses where it's being stored. I can give you the addresses."

"Do no such thing," said Lecca, "because it's too bad if we don't take your word and you're the kind of man to get good and mad if doubted. We don't claim the flour belongs to us. It belongs to the entire populace. I'll be the first to say so, before Monsignor, who would hesitate, I'm sure, to be a false witness."

"I have downstairs," said Angelo, "a man who looks like a sailor. He caught me in the act of honesty. He's been with me every step of the way. He was present when I was wounded."

Lecca savored this word like a sweet and winked.

"When you want flour," Angelo said, "come see me. I'll sign your chits."

"There's nothing we need to ask you for," the monsignor said somewhat hastily. "Not right away, in any case," he added. (Against his will a trickle of impatience had flowed into his voice.) "The only thing we've come to talk to you about is smoke," he continued, indicating the windows. "The only thing that has moved us is the misery of this town facing imminent suffocation. We're spending too long talking about flour which belongs to no one. The soldiers will easily find the supplies deposited with citizens."

"They'll have neither the time nor the desire to look if they're busy with other things. Get them busy."

"Your use of the imperative is all very well, but who will occupy them?"

"Monsignor wants to expose us to the temptation of pride," said the little round gentleman.

"God forbid! I generously supposed that this imperative was addressed to Milan in general. But your Excellency's palace is somewhat out of the main current. You're pretty far from the news coming from Piedmont. The news is bad. We can't count on the liberal King. We were the only ones anyway, I imagine, not to see up to now that these two words contradict each other. We're thrown back on our own resources. They're meager, including a small talent for finesse, much scorned in heros, but with which we can repair passably whatever we have taken care not to shatter."

At this moment the Turin bread sticks arrived. The men carrying the baskets looked like rogues.

"They weren't here this morning," Angelo thought, "or else they were kept hidden. If the general didn't invent them, he chose them. It would be difficult to be more ignoble."

They looked as if they were in the police. No one took the slightest notice of the delicate golden sticks, which cracked as they cooled in the baskets, giving off an exquisite odor.

"We have, alas, passed the age of discontent and jubilation," the monsignor continued. "We know that it's almost impossible to do a good job of doing good. In my opinion, we must negotiate tomorrow or the day after, let's say Thursday if you want. The people, whom you are now using to do your errands and to unseat the authority of Austria, won't recognize yours any longer than that; they won't get any fun out of coming to look us over as soon as you're obliged to demand of them what the Austrians demanded. The people always discover they're tired *ex abrupto*. If you need proof that they're tired and just don't know it yet but are going to sit down on the job before long—which is all the more serious since they only stood up yesterday morning—reflect on the success of your recruiting: those who are tired imagine that with you they'll finish off the work on the double. They leave our service where everything moves at a snail's pace to enter yours, where everything seems to move at a fast clip. They're in a hurry. I'm sure that the Arsenal explosion put the town in your lap. That's because they think you delivered the death blow and that the job is done. You've fought Austria on infinitely vaster battlefields, general, and you know the work is not even begun. Your Excellency was with us two months ago when we opened negotiations with his majesty the King of Sardinia," he continued, addressing the small round gentleman. "At that moment the Austrians had decided to make war on liberalism simply for the sake of economy, to avoid the expense of maintaining an army in Lombardy. The loss of an arsenal isn't going to ruin them, and it was only an engineering-depot. I admit that the powder made a noise. There's a great difference between cutting off bridges and blowing them up. We've killed soldiers: a matter of sergeant majors. We've killed officers: a matter of the rank list, and the chancellery disposes of pretty jewels for widows to pin to their bosoms. You set fire to powder; it's heard a long way off; it's no longer something to be dealt with in an office; the detonation gives you a head start; this head start is irritating. In brief, if I were a field marshal and wanted to give myself the right to put up a gallows, I would first send some kind of turnkey to blow up my own arsenal."

"I won't lose my temper," thought Angelo. "Someone lent you some violet stockings, you think they fit, you want to keep them but you're too impatient."

Besides, everyone pretended not to have heard the last words and the prelate did not even seem to have uttered them.

Lecca and the round gentleman answered at the same moment. Their sentences tangled farcically. They stopped short, offering each other the floor with good grace.

"Go ahead; go ahead."

"No, no, we were talking about the position of my palace. I can only think step by step. This is ancient history. I meant (just a word on the subject) that although I am indeed out of touch with the news from Piedmont, I am, on the other hand, at the heart of the Milan news. I know that yesterday at nine the field marshal opened the door of the castle and liberated the prisoners he had taken in the Broletto. They returned to the bosom of the church if I can permit myself—please don't think I take a light view of sacred matters—an allusion to the fact that they are at present at your house, Monsignor."

In addition to violet stockings and the imitation Ugo Foscolo, there was in the camp of morality a third person, who did not utter a word, but was making a good meal off his mustache which was very black and stained his lips with die marks. He was anxious but no less avid for hope as he searched his partners' faces. Stiff as a judge in an unnatural, military posture, he was trying so hard not to look at Angelo that he squinted.

"We're soldiers," said Lecca, with a studied edge of vulgarity. "When the enemy smiles at us, we take advantage of it to steady our grasp on his throat. It wouldn't enter my head to preach in praise of method, but on the battlefield it's too late to forbid the use of the seven capital sins. You order your buckled shoes from a shoemaker; order your wars from a soldier: it's his trade. While you were receiving the Sistine Chapel singers the marshal sent from the castle, I was talking to a peasant who had come at full speed from Bergamo. All the roads are cut off, the bridges destroyed, the villages barricaded; the Austrians cannot get a single order through. The Bergamo gardeners drubbed the battalions of Archduke Sigismond's regiment as they were leaving the town to come fall on our necks. The commander, Lieutenant Colonel Baron Schneider, was wounded, thrown from his horse, and taken prisoner. The troop went around the countryside looking to see if I was there."

"But they arrived in good order in Milan this morning at three under the command of Colonel Heinzel," replied the tall, handsome man.

Monsignor could not keep from dreaming a bit over the buckled shoe. He knew, moreover, that it was extremely politic to show that he dreamed. He looked in the direction of the dark windows against which pressed smoke so dark that it pattered against the panes like hail.

"What a horrible business!" he said.

"The most horrible of all would be a fratricidal struggle," said the small round man.

The north wind filled the streets with smoke and drove it against the Palazzo Borromeo but left the castle clear in the sunshine of a fine March day. Field Marshal Radetzky had passed without transition in the last forty-eight hours from study to battlefield. All night, in the mud among the mass of cannons and caissons, his eighty-two years had wrought miracles. When the engineering-depot blew up, he had just closed his eyes. For an instant he thought of blasting the town. But he didn't have the siege artillery necessary for a bombardment. He possessed only twelve howitzers and, it's true, quite a considerable quantity of rockets. He was no longer in favor of extreme means which, moreover, would not have settled the question here. The Emperor had not charged him to destroy Milan, but to save it for him. He liked orders from which there was no way out.

"I don't like to argue," he said. "I've had enough of it."

He dozed as he did each day at noon, but this time on a chair which had been placed in the courtyard of the castle in a spot where the sun warmed the wall. A visit of the consular corps in full-dress uniform was announced. He opened his eyes to see the English consul straddling the stewpots of a rolling-kitchen, his long legs encased in tight, beef-blood trousers. The French consul spoke first and protested in the name of his government against the damages a bombardment would cause his nationals.

"Would cause," the field marshal said in French. "But I'm not bombarding a thing," he added in German.

He closed his eyes. He liked the heat of the sun. The consuls were doing their duty; he was doing his duty (besides he didn't have the equipment); these duties did not exclude each other. Everything was perfect. He opened his eyes once more. "A question of humanity," he said in French, smiling to the French consul. He indicated with a gesture of his hand that the interview was closed. He rubbed his upper lip with his index finger. For the last week he had been growing a mustache and the short hairs itched him.

In the city, the cavalry patrols wandered through the town in search of adventure. You couldn't see past the end of your nose. The men were coughing, weeping, and sneezing; the smothered horses reared or threw themselves into fantasias which had to be restrained with both arms. No enemy to charge. In contrast, hell-fire poured from the windows. Half Radetzky's forces were being lost for nothing.

A corporal in the Croat dragoons dismounted. He had noticed that the noise of the horses attracted gunfire. No use going on being bowled over like ninepins. He had given his platoon an order, but at that moment the drug warehouse caught fire; you could have cut the smoke with a knife. His order was not carried out. The others said: "Let him go to hell." It was each man for himself. He discovered he was alone. A cavalryman never abandons his horse. But he abandoned his. The smoke was acid. He could not get his breath; his eyes were as big as eggs. He ran under a *porte cochère* and caught his breath in air which was a little less thick, coming out of a large dark passage. He heard his horse being killed. On his way out, slipping along the wall, he bumped into someone also slipping along the wall to enter the passage. He had only his saber, but he felt a bodice under his hand. The woman spoke to him as to a friend. About groceries. He caught only the word "milk." He answered: "Ja." The woman screamed and ran into the passage. He left his shelter hurriedly, moving along the walls and wandered aimlessly off.

The troops inside Milan had exhausted their ammunition. Those who could have sent them some were in danger of falling into the hands of the insurgents. Every convoy needed an escort, so that each time a certain number of soldiers had to be sacrificed. In the field marshal's situation every man killed was a great loss. He decided to recall all the troops fighting in the streets. He did not see the advantage of holding the corner houses and the palaces, or of charging on the boulevards. He sent couriers and bugles out into the smoke. He went out onto the glacis to watch them depart. The vast castle square, with all the little three-foot bushes he had had planted the preceding autumn, was deserted. It resembled a field, and he, an old peasant on his doorstep as he stood in the postern gate. The tocsin sounded furiously.

"You who have good ears," he said to the aide-de-camp, "try to hear my bugles under all these bells." After a quarter of an hour, the young officer said: "I hear them, your Excellency."

There was no difficulty evacuating the center of the town. If the populace ravaged it, Milan was rich enough to pay. Many of the emperor's subjects were still hidden in houses. The young wife of a high functionary of the Lombard government and her cook, Viennese like her mistress, had been hiding for forty-eight hours under the stairs in the broom closet. They ate a little chocolate that the cook had in the pocket of her apron. Great numbers of armed men circulated in the house. An immense quantity of stones had been transported to the roof and the upper floors. Guns had been heaped on the stairs and in the corridors. A little after the explosion of the engineering-depot, Trabant dragoons had charged and cleared the street. The valet had appeared. He had been looking for Madame everywhere in the house. The fact that he was French and a wide tricolored ribbon worn as a sash served him as a passport. He had finally had the idea of looking into this well-concealed closet. Monsieur sent word to Madame that a friend, a little banker, a native of the Italian Tyrol, in whose house he was hidden, offered her a sure asylum. But how to get there? The last Trabants had just disappeared when armed men made their way into the house shouting ferociously. The valet inserted himself quite brutally between the two women and drew up his long legs which stuck out of the retreat. If they were recognized as Austrians they might be seized as spies and treated accordingly. "Pardon me, Madame," he said five minutes later.

The buglers had entered the thick smoke two by two. Before putting their instruments to their mouths, they took shelter in doorways. Many dismounted cavalrymen had lost their way. Coarse pontonier's gunpowder was burning. Contained in sacks, it did not explode but dissolved, spreading fire all about and giving off black smoke. The enormous heat had made the kegs of sulphur burst. The bugles sounded with the small, strangled voice of cocks. They were sufficient to rally the lost soldiers. The Croat corporal, who had bared his saber, exclaimed: "The old man's going to pull us through! He gets the prize!"

The cavalry platoons which had not broken their close formation had taken refuge on the squares. The officers thought it was the moment to shout brief, refined commands, as on maneuvers. The second-class cavalrymen carried out their orders, much amused. They jabbed each other with their boots as ordinary people jab with their elbow.

It was, however, very difficult to find their way. They went toward the bugles, but the buglers wandered haphazardly. One, who came to the end of a street where it opened onto a square, blew vigorously on his instrument, turning his head from right to left and from left to right to disperse his call. His short concert came to an end when he distinguished in the turbulent smoke the porch of a church with the columns and pediments in the shape of a policeman's hat. He recognized the Palazzo Borromeo. He cleared out at top speed.

"Does that bugle belong to you?" asked the prelate, who was coming downstairs at the head of his delegation.

"Whose do you want it to be?" said Lecca.

"It's an Austrian tune and it's coming from right near here."

"If I'm polite to you—and apparently I am—it's because you're not in any danger," said Lecca. "The days of the Borgias are past."

"I don't like your incendiary," said the prelate.

"He's a good bastard."

.   .   .

"Signor," said the short round man to Angelo in the large salon where they had remained alone, "we stood by you the best we could. If the praise of a second-hand soldier who, however, served acceptably at the battle of Arcole is agreeable to you, you have it entirely."

"They don't much like us," said Angelo.

"They don't like us at all. They prefer us. Besides, they don't count. They called me 'Excellency' and I'm only a count."

Lecca came back up almost immediately.

"Obstinate bastards," he said. "The Monsignor, who is only a canon, stayed downstairs on the pretext that he heard a bugle. In reality, he's looking for that sailor you mentioned a while back. He hopes to get the truth out of him about the flour stores."

"The sailor is dead," said Angelo.

"God, you're sure?"

"Yes, unfortunately. I was very fond of him. It was he who dragged me out from under the horses' hoofs when I was wounded. He was killed at my side charging the last flour store, which was strongly guarded. I could give you a few details to calm your imagination. He received three bullets in his chest. Everyone was firing at him, I don't know why. He had finally gotten a taste for our little business. He didn't even say 'ouf.' Three holes big as a fist. The Austrians were Hungarians. They were firing jagged bullets."

Lecca seemed disconcerted.

"I prefer to be precise," Angelo said in a natural tone of voice. "You're the one who's looking for the sailor."

"You're not as dumb as you look," said Lecca, laughing frankly. "I wanted to spare you the bother of writing on a bit of paper the list of places where you deposited the flour. With so many of us, it won't be long before our stomachs start rumbling."

"Admit that this morning you used me for your own purposes," said Angelo.

"You don't say!" said Lecca. "When did you catch on?"

The wind had freshened and the smoke was dispersing. It no longer lay on the roofs, plastering the streets like black mortar; the wind billowed it upward and scattered it. Large patches of blue sky appeared. The sun struck the red tunics and gold helmets of the dragoons. The cavalrymen fled at top speed, bent low over their horses. Gunfire burst out at them from all sides along their way.

The field marshal gave a general order to retreat to all the troops holding the center of the city. In no special direction: just get to the ramparts and gates that they had to occupy and hold. Reinforced by the Maurer and Strassoldo brigades, which had entered with two batteries, the castle was strong enough to repel any attack by the insurgents, and could almost hold the town.

Maurer, his unalterable good temper and irritating mania for smoking a long, white clay pipe aside, had not brought very good news. He also had a passion for intrigue and supported an entire mob of spies, cheaply, moreover: he paid three soldi for each piece of news. Despite this relatively low price, he received some, even a lot of news. Bits of this news were useful. According to him, the Ticino district was marshaling its troops, armed volunteers were harassing the frontier. "I entirely stripped it," he said, winking (no one could tell whether the wink implied malice, or if it had been provoked by the bitter smoke of the new pipe he had pulled out of his trunk immediately on arrival).

He added that in Piedmont the hatred of Austria had reached its peak, the leaders of the secret societies were preparing to rush to the succor of Milan; the troops were making for the Ticino; free companies were being formed. They had to reach a definitive decision.

"There is never such a thing as a definitive decision," said Radetzky. "If you imagine you've made one, and believe it, you're unbelievably weak. If Charles Albert doesn't make a move, the surrender of Milan is a matter of days. Civil war is a question of patience: the sleeping dog wins. There are good beds in the castle, thick walls and drawbridges. But perhaps the surrender of Milan is just what Charles Albert is waiting for. Kings never put a shoulder to the wheel; the carriage might get away from them. But when the horses are dead, they can always mount the seat before hitching up the others they've got right at hand. As soon as I've received the burghers of Calais,[2] he'll sound his trumpets, and I don't have enough ammunition to withstand another attack. I've asked the general in command of Verona for a convoy. But has anyone seen such a convoy? Did Heinzel see it on his way from Bergamo or hear mention of it?"

All Heinzel had seen was Colonel Baron Schneider hit by a bullet, then by a pruning-knife, and carried off like a rabbit. The field marshal rubbed his upper lip with his index finger.

The afternoon had turned out fine. The mixture of sun and cold wind induced languor. General Baron Rath was in the process of losing half his forces in the neighborhood of the criminal prison. He tried to withdraw toward the ramparts. He was under heavy fire from the round windows set in cellars and roofs. Marching, sometimes under a rain of stones and boiling water, he had nevertheless been able, up to now, to take his wounded with him. But now he no longer could. He had to defend himself constantly. He could not do so like a *mater dolorosa,* his arms borne down by bloody men. He himself knocked on the door of a church. He had massed his Trabant grenadiers in a square. While the transshipment was taking place, he saw his best soldiers fall before his eyes. They were old hands and remained calm. As soon as he could, he ordered an attack on a house. It was taken in no time, from top to bottom; the men shook off their numbness with unequaled joy. Insurgents thrown from the rooftops and windows were crushed on the street. Women were killed. Rath's good old mug was impassive too. He noticed that killing women was an excellent antidote to the long slaughter they had suffered. Unfortunately, there were only two in the house. He urged his soldiers on with guttural cries that exasperated the romantic Croats. It was imprudent perhaps to let himself loose while leaving the wounded in the hands of the enemy. But above all he wanted to go on scratching where he itched; he went on shouting louder and louder until he was wounded in the shoulder. He put his hand to the hole. The blood flowed between

[2] "As soon as I've received the burghers of Calais" equals "As soon as Milan has surrendered." In the Hundred Years' War, Edward III of England promised to spare the town of Calais if its six most prominent citizens brought him the keys of the city. They had to walk barefoot in their nightshirts with chains around their necks.

his fingers. The narrow streets would be hell on earth, but he ordered his troops to retreat down them.

In the evacuated center of Milan the revolutionary tempest doubled its fury. A tricolored flag had been hoisted on the Palazzo Reale. The archbishop came out *impontificatibus*. His hood was lowered in a hurry. The streets and squares which until then had been echoing and deserted filled with a crowd shouting muffled cheers. In reality everyone was shouting as loud as possible. But the streets packed by the crowd no longer echoed. Everyone was disagreeably surprised by the lack of resonance in the shouts of "hurrah!" The rumor went round that General Rath was at bay, that there was an unhoped-for chance to annihilate a whole battalion and that they should run in that direction. Everyone was spared the need for courage.

Rath, harassed without respite, withdrew into twisting alleys. His most violent assailants had not left him since he had come out of the Palazzo Reale; they were tracking him with unheard of boldness. It was no longer a question of the conquest of liberty, but of a hunt. They too were losing a lot of men. They no longer took shelter in houses, but advanced step by step along the streets in order to enjoy the spectacle fully: the enormous grenadiers of the Viceroy's guard retreating before them. Rath had arranged a shrewd system of rotating gunfire which left practically no time lag during the loading. A marvelous tactic in his position. The insurgents died without knowing it; their wounded, besmirched with blood, remained standing. Under gunfire so heavy that not so much as a thread could have gotten by, shopkeepers and bourgeois advanced for the sheer pleasure of advancing, until the shock of the bullets made them spin like tops. They did not fall until they had lost every semblance of humanity. Despite this marvelous tactic, there was hand-to-hand fighting several times. The soldiers turned to the general with astonished looks. Rath ordered them to cut the bullets so that they were jagged. It was no time to be romantic. This was a man's work. He trusted the tricks of the trade. He ordered his men, who were not at all inspired by events, to fall back whenever necessary.

By chance the field marshal learned of Rath's situation. He ordered cannon balls fired on the town. The crowd dispersed, searching for shelter in cellars and closing their street doors in great haste. The cannons grumbled isolated shots at first, then almost uninterrupted detonations. Soon Milan was enveloped by concentric fires in the castle and outer walls.

The two Viennese women and the French valet hidden in the broom closet were frightened by the deafening roar of cannon fire and the staccato rebound of the balls. Despite the tumult, the Frenchman, moved by the warmth of the two women (one still smelled nice) and by their abandoned fear, had wits enough to hear a noise of sobbing and weeping in the hall. It was a young woman, quite crazed by the detonations, followed by an armed *giovinetto:* husband, brother, or lover . . . She refused every consolation that he lavished on her. Eyes closed, arms crossed on her breast, quivering at each explosion, she held herself immobile at the foot of the stairs. In the end the young man, obliged to rejoin his band of revolutionaries, kissed her tenderly on the forehead and departed.

Bad news of Rath was brought to the castle. Exaggerated by the breathlessness of the couriers, who had for the most part been unsaddled and had come running in their heavy boots, it presented the situation as desperate. The Trabant grenadiers had been halted and encircled in the neighborhood of the Lombardy stage-coach office: a neighborhood that was all alleys and dead ends. The field marshal refused to send the cavalry to free them. He had already lost a third of his hussars, and the platoons of his dragoons had returned worn to the bone. The men were beside themselves to have left their wounded. The field marshal stepped up the firing on the neighborhoods near where the Trabants were fighting. "That's the most I can do," he said.

Above all he was anxious about the fate of the fortresses occupied by small garrisons, not in the least organized on a wartime footing. He saw himself obliged to undertake a defensive war in a Lombardy lacking all the necessary forces. Milan and its insurrection were of only secondary importance from now on. Rath had only to practice his trade.

He was doing so. Blood no longer flowed from his wound. He knew that after they had gone over the jumps for a while the dogs would have to stop for breath. He had not once lost his way. The soldiers trusted him. This made them willing to expose themselves to death. The reinforcements his assailants received were part of the crowd which had invaded the center of Milan, evacuated before the cannonade. It was hard for them to come down to earth; as far as they were concerned, the day's work was done. They had found the Archbishop and the flags very agreeable distractions. They no longer had much desire to get back on the job. They didn't understand that one can waltz joyously to the lash of bullets.

Rath abruptly got clear and occupied a little square a hundred paces from the ramparts. There he was attacked by what remained of his first assailants; *they* were not one bit less intoxicated. They ran so furiously that three of his artistically disposed lines were broken through. The grenadiers were even obliged to fight with their fists as at a fair. They were men chosen for their stature and physical strength. For a long time now no one had been fighting for either liberty or emperor. The hand-to-hand brawl enchanted everyone. Rath drew his saber and began to hack great slices; his shouting did not smack of either romance or tactics, but of plain personal feeling.

The field marshal was looking through opera glasses. He saw the last puffs of the volley dispersed by the wind and turned to his aide-de-camp with a questioning look. Yes, he too no longer heard the noise like a sheet being torn which the fusillade of a well-commanded platoon resembles. Finally, after a long interval of what might have been called silence, and despite the hundred bells ringing the tocsin as loud as possible, there arose a distinctly Austrian din of rejoicing and "hurrah!" Rath had just entered the ramparts.

The sun was setting. Long thin clouds burst into flame like live coals. On this windy day the sky was an intense blue. It reflected light like a mirror. Oblique rays and even reflections coursed through the deserted streets. The cannonade continued. The fighting had stopped. Everyone had gone down into the cellars. Major General Baron Rath was recovering his strength in his cell.

Night fell. Trying to hide, the insurgents found the hiding-places of the Austrian civilians. A few policemen, disguised but well known, were disemboweled *morti popolarmenti*. Nooks and crannies, areas under stairways and broom closets were searched, most of the time simply for the pleasure of scaring people, especially women. Nevertheless, the generosity of grown men searching for amusement at home while it thunders outside cannot be counted on too heavily. Although they only went as far as murder seven times out of ten, they always forced themselves to vex and humiliate. Two hours ago they had thought themselves victors without further fighting, and the mouths of a hundred or so cannon were now gaping fire at them.

Rather than risk having their ears torn off by people who had had their cake taken out of their mouths while they were eating it, many Austrian subjects chanced it in the street under cover of night to go take refuge with friends. A functionary of the state chancellery, who till then had been crouching in a closet, ran to the home of a man from the Italian Tyrol with whom he had done business. He was ushered into the presence of an old couple. He suffered a second of intense fear: he did not recognize his client, whom he had only seen twice. Philemon was a man far into his sixties with a sweet, open face (which meant nothing); Baucis, his wife and about the same age, was Milanese. "I think I'm as good an Italian as all these noisemakers," she said, "but I've always supported Austria and I always will. My husband has declared his allegiance to the new government. Thus you're safe and you can stay with us as long as you wish." Thereupon she gave him supper and made his bed in a little study.

The field marshal's cannon did little damage with a lot of noise. The artillerymen had been ordered to spare the cathedral, the churches, and the public buildings. In return they could amuse themselves on the houses of the main leaders of the insurrection. Cannon balls struck the windows of the Palazzo Borromeo. Everyone had taken refuge in the enormous cellars. "The marshal goes to bed every evening at eight-thirty on the dot," people said. "No one will fire while he's resting." But at ten o'clock Papa Radetzky had not gone to bed.

"We've got to form the provisional government right here with Casati, you, me, and a fourth if absolutely necessary," said Lecca.

"Have you the list of flour stores?" asked the little round gentleman.

"Yes, written out neat as a copybook. Angelo's a boy who can send the whole world to hell."

"I don't agree. He doesn't understand the whole world. Or else he understands too much. What did he have undèr his bandage?"

"A wound in the flesh and bone. His kind always play a straight game: I know them."

"Someone should have taken care of him."

"Useless. People have been beginning to die natural deaths here and there ever since this afternoon."

The field marshal first thought of heading toward the Adda; but beyond the fact that this position did not constitute an adequate military position, the news which reached him at six in the evening from the interior of the kingdom made him abandon the project. The entire countryside around Bergamo was coming to a boil. At Lodi, Archduke Ernest *personally* in command of his forces, had been drubbed in a pitched battle by peasants led by a notary. It would be a close shave if he could hold, as a hanged man his gibbet, one bridge across the Adda. You can't resist madness. The field marshal decided to withdraw toward Verona. He disclosed this decision to his staff. He ordered Strassoldo and Manner, who had been sent out to reconnoiter, to return. They had reached Milan at eleven in the evening without too much damage, but dumbfounded. They were wondering, if it ever came to pass, whether they would sell clothes with as much dash as the drapers made war.

As secretly as possible, all necessary measures for departure were taken. Generals Clam and Wohlgemuth were ordered to clean out the buildings from which the insurgents might disturb the troops on the march. What bothered the field marshal was the lack of transportation. He was afraid to leave the sick and wounded in the hands of the enemy. But if he carried off the sick and the wounded, he would be obliged to leave the state valuables in the lurch. The valuables, God knows, could be justified, but there were also the state funds in the Palazzo Marino.

He could not let himself be influenced by his more tender feelings. One quickly falls into regrettable excesses.

The massive edifice of the Palazzo Marino, carefully bolted, could be opened only with the aid of a cannon: all the employees had fled or were in hiding. This was no insurmountable difficulty, but once the treasure was retaken, where to put it? On ammunition vans? This was perhaps the only solution. But in the present circumstances his cartridges were the apple of the field marshal's eye. After all, they would need cartridges to guard the money. If the money was lost . . .

"Let's put it in the simplest terms," said Maurer.

"Let's not complicate what's already very complicated."

He was in favor of loading the soldiers—with cartridges, of course. Three extra kilos per footsoldier, six per horseman. This way there would be space on the vans.

Clam was in charge of breaking into the Palazzo Marino. He ordered a fieldpiece advanced at a full gallop. He expected the kind of resistance Rath had met with, and his detachment consisted of gay blades who were very resolute, all volunteers, and enchanted by this attack by main force.

The artillery van made an infernal noise on the pavement of the deserted streets. The drivers strained themselves hoarse, cursing the horses to keep them nervous. They saw no one; the insurgents obviously disdained the Palazzo Marino and its environs. There were several million florins in this lugubrious barrack. This disinterest made Clam far more anxious than any furious assault. The deserted streets, the empty houses, the millions which they obviously didn't give a rabbit's fart for, seemed to scorn him. The volunteers, although they were far from romantic and knew the value of gold even in affairs of the heart, felt a little ashamed, as if held to a job unworthy of a man's interest.

They leveled the cannon. The door flew to bits at the fourth shot. The fieldpiece was pushed through the breach. They rolled the coin along the corridors. They had to lower it with ropes down a cellar stairs. While these maneuvers were executed, four squads of crack light infantry, judiciously ambushed in the street and main door, stood ready to face their Maker in person. Each soldier had three guns and two men to load them. He was armed besides with the canisters used by pontoniers in river combats. It was a case of chasing butterflies with seige mortars. They didn't see as much as a cat. Clam began to understand why one notary was enough to light a fire under Archduke Ernest's ass.

They fired with their guns touching the door of the strong room. The detonation in the confined space made the ears of the artillerymen bleed. They had to fire fourteen times. The basement was full of bitter smoke. Upstairs, the light-infantry guards were furious. They wondered when the useless noise would be over. Finally, they carried off four million florins in gold and silver ingots. The soldiers insisted on saving the cannon. They threw themselves into this work as if at last they had found something honorable. The expedition then returned at a walk.

The field marshal spoke of military servitude.

Fortunately he had something else to tell them. Wohlgemuth had already gone into the town to carry out his house-cleaning mission. Clam assembled his entire column on the parade ground and inspected it in a very surly manner. This comforted everyone. The artillery was ordered to set fire to several houses in the area Clam and Wohlgemuth were to clean out. This time gold ingots were not at stake, and Clam, hardly out of the castle, was assailed on all sides. After battling for more than an hour, literally to get through the tumultuous streets, he ran into Wohlgemuth's column, their progress halted also, surrounded by bourgeois facades spitting fire like cats.

In the Piazza Borromeo, the insurgents had seen the field marshal's maneuver without understanding in the slightest what motivated it. So the Austrians had once again sent two columns of grenadiers out into the streets of Milan. They paid no particular attention to the fact that there were generals in command of these columns and that these generals were apparently intensely interested in the mass of houses around the railroad station and in the neighborhood leading to the Porta Romana. The insurgents thought they were simply little boys stealing apples. Without preconceived plan, without asking orders of anyone, and, moreover, without warning anyone, the insurgents slipped down the streets in sizeable, and then very sizeable groups, into the houses and upstairs. As Wohlgemuth's grenadiers demolished and burned the barricades in the streets, they built others on the stairs, the landings, in the drawing-rooms, and even on the roofs. As soon as the general, disturbed by the fire which was picking off quite a number of his men, wanted to capture the houses barring his route, he ran into a well-organized worker resistance set up inside the buildings. He entered thickets of gunshots. Bursting forth on all sides at very close range, they inflicted such horrible wounds that the soldiers, completely shameless, began to scream with terror. They were fighting an invisible enemy in total darkness, and it was only in the yellowish flash of the gunfire that they saw death and their own spilled blood all in one instant. They ebbed back in disorder onto the little square, and Wohlgemuth found himself in the situation Rath had been in during the afternoon.

But now it was night, and there was nothing about the butchery glimmering in the firelight to incline them to swagger as men always do a little before a tactical rally.

Clam came into the midst of this. There was some disorder and, deceived by the dancing shadow of the flames, the soldiers were shooting at each other. But the Hungarian general roared like a lion. He was going to make someone pay for his humiliation at the Palazzo Marino. He didn't want to be called a burglar. He had thought of nothing but this for the last two hours.

With a group of soldiers he made his way in person into the house from which Wohlgemuth's grenadiers had just been repelled. Stimulated by his voice speaking as if on maneuvers and in their native tongue, the Hungarians took advantage of the interval between two charges to throw themselves into hand-to-hand combat. Silence was restored in the house from which only prolonged cries like the creaking of a door issued, and, after a long interval, the troops appeared at the windows and signaled with sweeping gestures that it was all over. Finally they came out, so pleased with themselves that they dragged along by the collar, as proof of their victory, the soft little corpses of shopkeepers and craftsmen still wearing their aprons. Thus equipped, the soldiers no longer looked like butchered sheep, but like the butchers themselves. This change of situation was striking and in itself most hopeful.

Squads of house-cleaners were organized on the spot, in the shadows. Clam regretted that he hadn't long ago made bast sandals such as shepherds wear in the winter mud part of every soldier's equipment: they would be just right for slipping noiselessly up on any good fellow who needed butchering. In the absence of bast sandals, he nevertheless stripped the house-cleaners of the complicated harness which binds grenadiers. Like all soldiers freed of part of their uniform, Clam's Hungarians and Wohlgemuth's

Viennese began to find things a great deal easier. To kill, free of a neck piece and responsibility, has great charm. They began to joke into their whiskers and jab each other in the ribs. Finally, teams commanded by ordinary soldiers—which made them ready for anything—left the fires which lighted the scene excessively brightly; in Indian file they went to begin their work in the darkest parts of the battle.

Before blocking the passages and stairs with barricades, the insurgents had done their best to find shelter for children, and old or delicate women. The other women naturally fought with them and there was nothing to be done about their fate. But the very blond ones or those with the lovely kind of chin you want to hold in your hand preferred to remain hidden. They were stuffed into attics. They had immediately invented the art of hiding under old clothes. Others, on the contrary, among the most terrified, had seated themselves near a bit of lighted candle. In tragic moments, vivid imaginations spend themselves madly like pyrotechnic suns and then leave their world in darkness. It is then that the fearful become indifferent.

A little servant girl from the Ticino, fifteen years old, Tessinoise, with burning eyes and black hair, but too young to feel with empathy, had gone to bed in her garret. "Intrepid," her employer had said when he saw her pick up her candlestick. *He* had piled up tables and chairs and toppled a mirrored wardrobe across the doorway. His wife was grasping a gun in her arms while saying timidly: "Don't go away, Giovanina." The people across the landing could be heard carting away furniture. Gunfire crackled in Wohlgemuth's direction. Incendiary rockets were falling on the Como Gate. But Giovanina took her candlestick and went to bed. She undressed, because you had to act as if nothing were going on; otherwise she would be obliged to scream, and what good would that do? When the boss decides to burn down the barn, that means the fodder's used up.

However, she pulled the sheets up to her chin when she heard a noise right above her head. The skylight leading onto the roof opened; she saw a little pair of boots come down and two long legs in yellow velvet britches. A man leaped into the room. He was young but white as linen under his dirty beard. A bloodstained bandage encircled his forehead. The blood did not frighten the girl, still less the boots and the young man. She had an answer for all this, especially in her bedroom. She made a bluntly coarse remark.

"What the hell are you driving at?" Angelo said to her, laughing. "This is no moment to play the lady. Don't you hear the Hungarians firing?"

They were doing more than firing; they were breaking in the street door with axes. Two other boys had come down through the skylight. They told the girl to put on her skirt and stockings as fast as she could and stop acting like a ninny. Their words were reassuring. All three went out onto the landing. She leaped into her clothes.

Gunfire broke out on the lower floors, followed by the cries of rats; then the Hungarians called to each other peacefully as in a Hungarian home. The garret was reached by a stairs made of a miller's ladder. Angelo and his two companions stationed themselves along this stairs, backs to the wall. They had no guns, but pork butchers' knives.

Clam's soldiers came upstairs, talking of coffee and schnaps. That was all Angelo could catch. The first didn't even have time to shout. The second let out a weak cry as he tipped off the stairs. The knives, extremely pointed and sharp, causing absolutely no pain, entered as if in butter. They aimed for the stomach only. The cold steel penetrating this otherwise hot area was the only surprise the soldiers felt. They didn't shout; they clucked. Their bodies crashed to the hall below with a noise which at last bore some relation to the circumstances.

This well-bred battle continued a moment longer, however, without haste or jostling, full of terrified cluckings; then the Hungarians went hurriedly down the stairs again. They could be heard striking a light.

The three men returned to the garret on tiptoes. They lifted the little girl out through the skylight and climbed onto the roof. The fires gave a little light. The tiles bathed in dew were slippery. They had to proceed on all fours.

Clam and Wohlgemuth were cleaning out the houses methodically. They both would have agreed that they were not losing too many men, especially if you considered that they were doing a good job. Daylight would perhaps reveal more considerable losses, but the result would justify everything. They already had a firm hold on all the buildings in the neighborhood of the railroad station; in the streets leading to the Porta Romana, floors fell one after another at the rate of one every ten minutes by the clock. There was still a full hour of night left.

Along a chimney Angelo found the iron spikes used instead of a ladder by chimney-sweeps. They climbed down these to the roof of a small private mansion. Light showed beneath the panes of an open skylight. Soldiers seated around a lantern were guarding the top of the house.

Angelo had been fighting since well before midnight. He had first defended dining-rooms, like everyone else, but, after the first hand-to-hand combats, he had understood that a gun is not much good indoors. With four or five comrades he had gone to a pork butcher's to get arms. Two of these comrades were later stopped en route. One had the misfortune to thrust a knife at a sturdy Hungarian's belt buckle; to judge by the little cry he let out afterwards, he must have been seized by the neck and strangled. The second had fallen in the street. He didn't know about the others; perhaps they had gotten disgusted, or butchered without complications. They were stretched out on the landing.

Despite the pleasure of killing in the dark, which always charms passionate hearts (they delight in rising up like justice), they couldn't kill the whole Austrian army with three knives. For the last forty-eight hours Angelo had been telling himself: "No silliness now!" He could not keep from admiring, although he did not understand them, the brief Hungarian orders which resounded in the streets.

One of the three men stayed watching the soldiers through the panes of the skylight. The other two and the little girl slipped noiselessly to a dark dormer window. Angelo whistled softly. The man on watch joined them. "They didn't budge," he said.

First Angelo crawled down into the house through the dormer. The others lifted the girl down to him. They were in a junk room. Through the brick wall they heard the conversation of the soldiers.

The house was well kept; the doors of the attic rooms did not even creak. They leaned over the stair well. All you need for sharp ears is to have to risk your skin in the dark. The young girl was so quiet that only the man holding her by the hand knew she was there.

Downstairs, the street was lighted vaguely a little farther on by a barricade which had been set on fire but was dying down. In the doorway stood a sentinel.

They killed him very simply, without a sound. Faultless work which satisfied the spirit.

It was hard for Angelo to leave behind such a blow, struck without animosity, or indeed any emotion whatsoever.

Nor did his comrades and the young girl feel like running.

CHAPTER SEVEN

Angelo had been back at the Palazzo Borromeo since dawn. The cannonade had ceased; the fighting had not been resumed; the tocsin rang no more.

"Do you want to do me a great service?" Lecca asked him.

"May I keep my eyes open?"

"Wide open. A gig left last night by the Porta Tosa. Going toward Verona. In it were a man and a portfolio. I don't give a damn for the man; I'd give away the portfolio; but I'd love the papers it contains. And when I say 'I'd love,' I'm talking rather modestly."

"I don't see why you're sending this boy after those papers," said the little round gentleman. "They're details."

"There's no such thing as details," said Lecca dryly.

"It happens that I feel like a stroll today," said Angelo. "How will I recognize this fellow?"

"By the fact that he has passports."

"What means of persuasion do you wish me to use so that this individual with passports will be kind enough to give me his portfolio?"

Lecca took time to think.

"In other words," Angelo continued, "if need be, do you intend to disavow me totally or in part?"

Lecca blew his nose solemnly.

Angelo achieved a superb candid look.

"Remember, my boy, that I advised against the whole affair," said the little round gentleman.

"Obviously I advised it," Lecca said. "Everyone is in danger right now. But, I won't say anything more."

"Nevertheless, could you perhaps go so far as to lend me a horse for a stroll? I can be someone in need of an airing, whom you're being kind to . . ."

"It's common knowledge that I have very good horses," said the little round gentleman, "especially a royal white-foot named Sultan whom I never lend. He must thus have been 'pinched' off me if it's proved that someone else was seen riding him. In place of kindness, which is always a little ridiculous, you can have learned of the existence of this white-foot (which is altogether possible) and have thought that liberty gave you the right to take liberties. In any case, with a horseman such as you must be, the horse is capable of making up a five-hour handicap. My stables are in a little street behind the palace."

He added that, by the most extraordinary luck, he had needed his grooms this morning and that the coach houses were unguarded.

Angelo was going downstairs when Lecca ran after him and took his arm.

"Come, we'll eat," he said.

He took him to a baker's in a near-by street. There was a crowd there; the baker's assistant winked when he saw Lecca and conducted them into the back of the shop.

"They claim our government had been formed," he said, "and that you're in it?"

"We'll all be in it if it's a republic," said Lecca, "but that remains to be seen. Give us something to eat, so that we can keep up our strength."

There was naturally bread in abundance, but also salami, anchovies, oil, black olives, and chianti.

"Count Borromeo is rotten to the core," said Lecca in a low voice when he was alone with Angelo. "If it weren't for politics, of course, he would have killed me a hundred times over. He needs dummies to take the knocks in his place, otherwise we would have been out the bottom long ago. No matter what power you dangle like bait in front of him, he strikes like a pike. Just think, last night at a certain moment, someone, I don't know who, some trickster maybe, spread the rumor that Radetzky had been taken and was being brought in. He rushed out like a madman shouting: 'Make way, make way for the marshal!' I'd be crazy not to have my police. You remember those three characters who didn't like the smoke? That's not the only thing they don't like. They're the black band who shipped off the gig. Who's in it? I don't know, but someone who's going to Verona armed with every possible passport: Austrian and ours. It's the same old story: to deal directly with Radetzky, or for Radetzky to deal directly with us, either way would be too hot, but through Verona both sides can get a pincer hold. The fellow who's going to get hold of the pincers will undoubtedly have letters of credit. Often letters of credit are signed. If his aren't, they'll be in the right style anyway. If they've taken the precaution of dispensing with the style, we can go so far as to put in whatever's necessary. We won't finish up this job in Milan without an argument. I can then bring those papers out of my pocket in a dignified manner and say: 'Gentlemen, you're big talkers and cheats and here's the proof!' In any case, I'm capable of doing so. Borromeo no, but me, yes. If we were stupid enough to give him such a weapon, Borromeo would make a deal under the table, and the rest of us would be the laughingstock of the whole town. That's why I'm going to give you a bit of friendly advice; on your way back, before coming to the palace, stop here and send me word. We'll have a chat. One more thing, between the two of us, now that no one can hear me: the fellow in the gig may want to defend his portfolio with his life. At least we must hope so. In fact, we've got to pretend he did if hope doesn't get us anywhere. You kill him in the heat of action: we can always find an extenuating circumstance."

Angelo left by the Porta Tosa, which had fallen into the hands of the insurgents during certain night combats. Corpses still littered the roadway. The horse took advantage of this to cut up a bit.

"This is no longer an avenue, old man," Angelo said to him. "This is the boulevard of liberty."

The animal was too much of a thoroughbred not to feel to the extreme the gentleness of his rider. He gained confidence and allowed himself to play with his fear like a grownup.

Angelo was in an excellent mood. He had something nice to remember. He had awakened this morning in a room where everyone was sleeping on the straw mattresses of a drawing-room barricade. The girl curled up next to him was snoring with her mouth open. Her delicate lids were like violets.

Now he breathed the white spring air.

The deserted road revealed the tracks of a great many carts. Colonel Heinzel had brought his troops along this way.

"In this flat land criss-crossed with hedges, you stand out like a sore thumb," Angelo said to himself. "If you want to amuse yourself for any length of time, make a sacrifice to the god of prudence."

The lilacs and hawthorns were in flower. A tender sea-green sky shone beneath the slender curtain of Lombardy poplars. The confused contour of the Alps rose on the northern horizon. A dirt road led Angelo to a village, the entrance to which was barred and guarded. He asked the man in command—a young but capable carrot-top—if he could be conducted through.

"We got a signal you were coming," the man told him. "Which proves we take good care of ourselves. We have little boys posted in the trees and, if you didn't see them, it's because they love their work. Without that bandage on your head, and your bloodstained jacket which the messenger has already told me about three times since he arrived, or if they had made out the slightest military touch in your equipment (and their eyes are not in their pockets), you would have been stopped way back. It seemed you were out for a stroll."

"I was looking for someone who could give me some information, but not just anyone," said Angelo. "You can do it. I've come from Milan."

"Have we a government?"

"They're working on it," Angelo said, "but you and I certainly wouldn't want to exchange a one-eyed horse for a blind one."

In exchange he received the most detailed information on the situation in the region. Not a single footsoldier remained in Bergamo, where the inhabitants were the masters of the town. But the cavalry corps stationed in the area of Lake Como and Lake Iseo still controlled the countryside. They had not yet foraged this far, but around Bergamo there was not a wisp of fodder left. Every night pistols were fired and horses galloped by. Angelo would have to look out as he advanced.

These military considerations reminded the carrot-top that for the past three days he had been general-in-chief of his village with the right to sign an X mark on official documents. At all costs he wanted to sign his client's passport.

"If I don't, you might get your finger caught between two stones."

Angelo reached Bergamo at three in the afternoon without having seen hide or hair of the Austrian cavalry. The town was in a great state of agitation. He circled it through the hills to the north.

He would gladly have remained in these charming hills covered with terraced gardens and perfumed by the springtime; but despite the sun, which was still high in the heavens, and the lilacs, men and women, loaded down with their worldly goods, were hastening to the outskirts of town. They had the look of people saving their clocks and saltcellars by main force.

He slipped down into the plain and took the highway which ran straight as a die. Darkness had come when he was stopped at the entrance to Brescia.

"Perhaps what you tell us is true," said the guards at the barricade, "but you've got to come repeat it to our commander."

They escorted Angelo down a zigzag passage to a noble house exhaling a great deal of candle smoke from its windows. It seemed there was an important staff of some kind within; there were a great many very animated shadows on the front stoop. A lantern was pushed under Angelo's nose, and after they had taken a good look at him they pushed him a little more brutally than necessary into a hall, in front of a man who with regal dignity took up the entire room, wearing a costume that was at once civil and military.

"Contrary to what these men claim," said Angelo, "they didn't arrest me. I presented myself and asked for passage. They told me that I had to come repeat my demand to you. That's what I'm doing."

"They're right, I'm in command here," the man said, looking in the direction of a large mirror in which he saw himself reflected.

"Would you then be so kind as to allow me to enter this town?"

"What for?"

"To eat and sleep. I can't see what else I would do."

"Nor do I," said the man. "Conduct him to the Albergo Reale."

Angelo took this "conduct him" for the formula of a great noble in embryo. "The people are having a good time," he said to himself. "But the men, who have already driven them a bit hard, will encircle them tightly once they're in the saddle. One of them is taking the horse by the bridle right now."

The town presented a strange spectacle. The people had undoubtedly been ordered to light the houses. On every balcony and in every window he could see candles, torches, and Venetian votive lights. This abundance of light high up contrasted with the darkness and emptiness of the streets bristling with barricades. Stopped every moment, the little troop was obliged to go around them by passing under the arcades of the houses. Each time the password had to be given and the man on horseback they were conducting had to be explained and discussed.

Angelo heard one of the men escorting him say: "He's a runaway."

He touched the man's shoulder.

"If you go on lying, you'll be sorry," he said.

The other man began to curse the *tedeschi,* but he calmed himself when he perceived that the man he was insulting seemed to ignore his presence.

It took almost three-quarters of an hour of this kind of shilly-shally before they reached the courtyard of the Albergo Reale. Angelo was most astonished to find an ugly crowd gathered there. Their faces expressed famished hatred. The innkeeper, surrounded by his boys and a crowd of idlers, received Angelo severely, not to say insolently. Without saying a word, he led him indoors to a reasonably clean room. When they were alone, he told him with a deep bow that the Viceroy and his august wife had spent the night in the room on their way to Verona.

"I'll put up with it then," said Angelo, "but whom do you take me for?"

"We know very well," he said. "You're a high-ranking Austrian prisoner. We were warned by a messenger from the town gates."

Their private conversation was interrupted by some men armed to the teeth. The innkeeper changed his tone and stance immediately. He tried, however, to rid Angelo of this company but could not prevent two of these individuals—one was the liar whose shoulder Angelo had touched—from stationing themselves before the door of the room, which they ordered left wide open.

"Here's the other side of the coin," Angelo said to himself. "Here's what our enemies see, and why they scorn us. They'd have to pay me well, and in coin they have no idea of, before I would consent to say a single reasonable word to such mugs."

He walked up and down the room affecting the most marked insolence.

Finally the curious crowd blocking the passage fell back hastily and an officer appeared. He at least was evidently at home in a uniform. Moreover, he wore a tricolored sash. He dismissed everyone, the two sentinels above all, and closed the door.

"I'm more humiliated than you," he said. "The guard on the Bergamo road has just sent me a paper telling me that he recognized and arrested Count O'Donnell fleeing. The national guard is dying to get into the act. You're Count O'Donnell, as I would be ten leagues from here if I fell into the clutches of those seeking to be heroes cheaply. You don't know how carried away they are by this idea. People commission themselves general. I haven't seen an admiral yet, but I don't know why not. In any case I know some fellows who have fourteen gold stripes stuck on their sleeves. Why fourteen? Because they've seen their friends stick on thirteen. I don't have to be first in the class at the Politecnico to know you're one of us."

"How can you be so sure?" said Angelo, regretting his insolence immediately. After the usual grandiose coquetry which mainly consisted of being ostentatiously modest, the two men ended up by talking like comrades.

"They're dying to hang and gut. It's the first time they've tasted the pleasures of kings," said the officer.

Angelo told the story of the gig. "I don't put much faith in it," he said. "Everyone's kicking up his heels. If we were philosophers, there would be cause to laugh at the spectacle the clever boys have been putting on lately. But if we were philosophers, we wouldn't be taking part in the fighting."

The officer, on the other hand, took the gig seriously.

"The clever, such as you speak of, will go so far as to shoot their friends joyfully in the back. That's why, in spite of everything, I can't help taking a liking to the ragpickers standing guard in front of your door. You're the rabbit in their stew, and they're not going to lose sight of you. But they don't look beyond their immediate appetite; they do just enough to be sure of two, or let's say three, meals a day. The clever are out for an income; they think of what they're going to be eating ten years from now. If you weren't afraid, or, pardon me, if going two or three hundred meters down streets held by these lovers of rabbit cooked in its own blood didn't bother you, I would suggest your coming and talking to the provisional government about the gig. It's really only a step away."

Angelo replied that nothing would give him greater pleasure than to limber up his legs.

The members of the provisional government were in session. More exactly, they had been in continuous session for three days and nights, for fear of "get-up-so-I-can-sit-down-in-your-seat." Their session consisted only of occupying their places in a vast hall where six candelabra could light neither walls nor ceiling. The bare table on which these candles sparkled seemed to have been placed in the midst of a limitless night.

At a glance Angelo realized that he was in the presence of true notables. Brescia was no Milan. Here the face of the town still reflected two periods of its history: the municipal element dating from its days of greatness as one of the free Lombard cities and Venetian influences dating from its vassaldom to the Most Serene Republic of Saint Mark.

The story of the gig carrying off a trator reached these men, trying to justify themselves in their grandiose circumstances, in the nick of time.

Once they had paid tribute to republican indignation, they busied themselves with details from which something could be gained perhaps. Could they lay a hand on the man in the gig? Nine times out of ten traitors are too hot to touch.

"A big fellow doesn't run risks; consequently, he doesn't travel about. They sent some small, ambitious type."

"Not necessarily small."

"They promised him a lot and he believed them. You call that big?"

He hadn't necessarily believed them.

"But he set out to cover forty leagues and cross three bridges!"

"He's a confidential agent, gentlemen, that's the point. He'll commit treason as his bosses have ordered him to do. Then, he'll betray his bosses to suit his own interests. No one knows better than he the importance of the papers he's carrying. We're only running after them. *He* has them in his pocket. That's where they'll stay."

"He won't come back to Milan alive. This gentleman may miss him," said one of the notables indicating Angelo, "or we may miss him, but his friends won't. That's part of the contract. It might almost seem you had never used confidential agents."

Finally, they began to bring up their guns and especially their famous cleverness. A tall, handsome man who seemed to possess fingers solely to roll the ends of his mustache asked the question which was on everyone's lips.

"Does this gig really exist?"

"That's just what I asked myself before leaving Milan," said Angelo.

"I don't suspect your good faith. Perhaps they wanted to direct your attention elsewhere. Which puts you in a pretty high bracket. Or deflect ours. Did they mention Brescia?"

"Not once."

"How did you get through? The bridges are guarded."

"I took cross-country roads. I only reached the highway after Bergamo."

"You went through Rovato?"

"I took a detour around Rovato as around Bergamo. I was on horseback; I could follow my fancy. But the gig, if it exists, couldn't."

"How much of a head start did it have on you?"

"Five hours, I was told. They weren't trying to sugar the pill."

"On the chance that they were playing a straight game, which would astonish everyone, the gig would have reached here at six in the evening. I'm counting the detours you made."

"You're not making enough allowance for them," said Angelo.

"I have a high opinion of myself and I accept orders only on very special conditions. I'm just as doubtful as you about the truth of what I've been told. I thus allowed myself to stroll through every lilac grove, even stopping to pick bouquets."

The bouquets were hard to fit into a plot. The gentlemen were embarrassed.

"It happens," said one of them with a fearful look, "that your pleasure (I don't dispute it!) served your interests. We never thought of posting sentinels among the flowers. Perhaps you lost less time than you think. My colleague estimates two leagues an hour for the gig, and that's high."

"I don't count two leagues an hour; I count three. I said that it should have arrived at six, let's say seven. You may think it lost time at each bridge, I don't. You don't have to have been around long to know that even a really tough sentry can be bought off any time for forty soldi."

Several voices protested, naming Rovato. The town of Rovato was guarded by Brescia men, consequently incorruptible.

"The changing of the guard took place an hour ago," said the officer. "My adjutant who is in command at Rovato is down below on the square. Let's have him come up; perhaps he knows something."

"We did indeed stop a gig at four in the afternoon," said the adjutant. "The traveler was a man of about sixty, very much afraid. He was brought to me and I questioned him. He is a certain Sanviti Bernardo, some kind of a marchese from what he told me. He claimed to be on his way from Parma to the Ferrarolis' in Rizzato. These statements have three out of ten chances of being correct because, while I was holding him, his carriage was searched and his baggage opened; a letter was found from Comte Ferraroli, inviting the marchese to stay in urgent and friendly terms. We found as well an account begun in 1845, apparently proving that the marchese is the proprietor of four buildings in Parma from which he collects regular rents. His face is clean-shaven except for two thin little gray sideburns which come down as far as his ear lobe. It's easy to read his thoughts. He was livid with fear, and he only got his color back while I was interrogating him. He welcomed my questions and seemed reassured to be in our hands. This total absence of character put a flea in my ear. I told him that the Austrian outposts were at Lonato, that is to say hardly three leagues from the place he was going. This piece of news had a great effect on him. He begged me to give him a paper permitting him to return to Milan immediately. I replied that it wasn't in my power. I advised him to push on this far, to stay at the Albergo Gambero, and we'd see about the paper. I kept him more than an hour longer, and as he never once stopped trembling from the most genuine fear, I sent him on his way. He must have arrived here between eight and nine."

Officers were ordered to go to the Albergo Gambero immediately.

"Bring us the good fellow. Let him have a taste of something really dangerous on the way. We leave you to choose what. In a word, frighten him, rough up his necktie and even go a bit farther. We want him ready when he gets here."

"Here's a government that's going to govern," Angelo thought. "I've got to get it across to them that you mustn't mix the napkins with the dusters. Let's see if I correctly interpreted certain looks of that young officer who spoke to me so honestly at the Albergo Reale."

"One moment, gentlemen," he said. "While we were conversing politely five minutes ago, one member of the honorable government assembled around this table slipped away in the direction of what I now, as my eyes grow better accustomed to the dark, see to be a handsome door. Perhaps he quite simply went out to take a leak: I know that the allure of gain sometimes has curious effects on the bladder. Perhaps he went out for something entirely different. In that case, I want to see that you're not making a mistake. You have revealed yourselves somewhat to me, which is of no importance, but you would prefer to think otherwise if only to appease your pride. Henceforth you're going to think of me as a bothersome witness. But should you know a hundred ways of getting rid of me, I would know a hundred and one for taking care of myself. Just for trying to rough up my necktie, you'd pay dearer than for seizing the town hall of Brescia."

"We don't deserve your suspicions," said the man with thin whiskers when the officers, both very red, had gone out. "You noticed our colleague's departure; more important, you saw we weren't in on it. Whatever he went to do (if he went to do anything), he kept secret. Besides, he's a man who weighs his actions; he's been a draper for thirty years, and his business has done well."

"I have nothing against drapers," said Angelo; "I've even been in the habit of buying cloth from them."

"Far from wanting to get rid of you, I express the general feeling in saying that we shall always understand each other. If we're thrown out, evil men will replace us. And I'm sure that you're on the side of the good."

"The documents don't interest me," said Angelo.

"They're going to wonder from now till doomsday just what does interest me," he thought, "but I'll be damned if I've the slightest desire to mention my heart to people whose 'businesses do well!' "

They did indeed question him very kindly, talking at length of noble ideas, but as of tops to a child.

The handsome door half-opened noiselessly. The draper came to take his place once again somewhat too naturally. He was on his guard as soon as he heard high-flown words; furtive looks warned him to be prudent. He remained standing at the edge of the shadows.

"These gentlemen are asking you to be somewhat discreet but not too," said Angelo. "How's the weather outside?"

Finally the officer returned. There was no gig at the Albergo Gambero. Investigations were being pursued as the sentry precisely remembered a pale man, trembling with fear, whom they had allowed in about nine in the evening without formalities by very reason of his panic. All the same, something serious was up, and the officer gave Angelo a wild-eyed look.

"The absurd rumor that you are O'Donnell continues to spread, sir. There are violent discussions about you in the cafés along the Corso. I got nowhere stating what everyone knows: that O'Donnell is fifty years old, that he is short and fat, and that he has no reason to come here. They won't let go. I gave my word of honor and was insulted in reply. I would have had to slap three hundred people. The least frenetic say that O'Donnell or not, an example must be made, and the calmest speak of limiting the fire. People have been working on them for some time, there's no doubt of that. I disapprove of this procedure which is the lowest of the low."

"I'm going to have a look at his," said Angelo.

"I beg you to do nothing. I shall never forget your words of a while ago. I'm no murderer, and if I knew that the victory of my ideals demanded that I become one, I would kill myself."

In his exaltation he spoke somewhat pompously, choosing his phrases well, however.

"In spite of everything I must go to bed," said Angelo. "I fought yesterday. I'm tired and I haven't eaten this evening."

"My room is right here," said the officer. "I'll give you my bed. Don't try to prove to me that you're capable of confronting this imbecile crowd which is so easily deceived. I'll be happy to put you up for the night; it'll be a real revolutionary act. I'm not doing it for you. So you see you can't refuse it."

"It would be hard for me to indeed," said Angelo, "but I can't help telling you that I'll be anxious about my horse; I left him alone at the inn. Aren't the people in your street capable of going and shouting insults at him? He's a very sensitive being for whom I have the highest esteem."

"I thought of that," said the officer, smiling at last. "Two of my boyhood friends who share our ideas are standing guard over him in the stable. I'm sure they've already spoken tender words to him."

"Those tender words have decided me," Angelo said.

He was happy.

"Tomorrow no one will remember this blunder," said the man with the thin whiskers. "Basically we like your way of seeing things; we need your emotions; you take us back thirty years."

He excused himself and the entire provisional government: in the heat of conversation no one had thought to congratulate the honorable horseman from Milan for his bandage and bloodstained jacket.

The officer conducted Angelo along the passages of the Bargello.

"I only precede you, sir," he said, "in order to lead the way. Do me the pleasure of walking beside me."

The room, hewn out of enormous walls, was tiny and contained nothing but a folding bed. Its small barred window looked out onto the church square, illuminated like the rest of the town by votive lights. The officer pointed out to Angelo groups of men and women who seemed to be very calmly enjoying the cool of the day.

"They're waiting for you," he said. "Others are hidden at the foot of the stairs, and there are at least twenty under the vault of the large courtyard. The women are armed with those horrible sticks used to kill rats."

"I'm unarmed," said Angelo, "except for a little pistol, and it's a long time since I checked the cap."

"That remark repays me for the shame I've endured for the last two hours. That swine of a draper did plot all this: I have proof of it. The people listen to him because, being his father's son, he always pays his bills; around here that's called honoring your signature, and the public considers it the last word in probity. He appealed to the element which trembles at the idea that the Austrians are only three leagues away. Think what a treat it is for cowards who know they're cowards to play he-man a hundred to one! Your corpse hanging on the Corso would have represented a great victory, the image of their virility."

"I have no idea what I represent," said Angelo, "but this revolution seems to have a disturbing and overwhelming need to see me hanged. This is the second time it's been suggested to me most insistently. The third time, I'll start keeping a track."

The officer went to look for something to eat. He returned with two bottles of good Piedmontese wine, and in addition some delicacies, especially some duck pâté which had been dressed with the head and tail of the animal; he also brought slices of peppered haunch of venison.

"Right now nothing is too good for the people. They've been mad for such things for the last two days. They want to stuff their hats with food as if tomorrow were the end of the world. A man who runs an eating house in the lower town understood the way people were feeling and is making his fortune with thrushes served on toast; moreover, thrushes aren't any good at this season. But they don't give a damn; anything goes."

After eating heartily, the two men pulled off each other's boots. Angelo refused the cot.

"Take it without scruples," said the officer. "We're friends, my adjutant and I. We've set up our headquarters in this part of the Bargello, where political prisoners were kept in the days when Brescia was a free city. I'm going to get a straw mattress from the cell next door. Do me the favor of sleeping in my bed. You're my guest.

"At my father's death," he said when he had blown out the candle, "my sister and I kept the estate where we were both born undivided. I grow grapes and wine. I live a family life with my wife, two little girls, and this sister to whom I am very close. I need a clear conscience to savor unreservedly the beautiful mornings on Lake Garda. About ten years ago I took part in an African campaign as a volunteer with General Trézel in La Malta. I want to have some say when laws are passed which can wipe out my happiness and that of my family with a scratch of the pen. If we lose our political hopes, our life no longer has any meaning. Perhaps you're astonished to see me associated with rascals? That's because they please the majority, and I have no choice."

The next day Angelo categorically refused to be escorted the short distance to the inn as the officer wished.

"Pardon my frankness," he said, "but I'm not used to being chaperoned. I always have to confront things myself. That's my Lake Garda. If I lose my self-respect no more beautiful mornings!"

In the same way he dismissed the men standing guard over his horse. He asked for some hot water to unstick his bandage, which was beginning to pull. He was washing in the main hall when he heard an uproar in the street and saw that some idlers were gathering in front of the inn.

"I've been ordered to prevent you from leaving," said the innkeeper.

"Then take off your apron; we'll fight it out."

"Make fun of me as much as you want," the man replied, "but this time your friends in the town hall have nothing to say. General Allemandi's arresting you, and you can start saying your prayers."

The "friends in the town hall" put Angelo in an excellent mood.

The wound, which was far from lovely, interested the chambermaids. They looked at it, chewing their fists, keeping their eyes on this dark handsome man, sure that he was about to meet a tragic fate. They gladly furnished two clean little handkerchiefs and a scarf to make a new bandage.

However, the crowd had swollen and even made its way into the courtyard. Everyone seemed uncertain as to the line of conduct he should pursue. One of Allemandi's officers arrived; to relieve their consciences the crowd shouted a few isolated cries of "Death to the *tedesco*!"

"The commander general of the mobile Lombard columns wants to see you!" said the officer, not bothering to be polite.

"I'm flattered," Angelo replied after a calculated silence.

The officer was a pale, emaciated young man with a pointed beard. An enormous tricolored scarf and numerous ribbons in the same colors covered his chest; a little yellow-leather cartridge case jiggled on his stomach; an ostrich feather crowned his hat.

"Without those ridiculous ornaments he would be the epitome of the kind of fortunate man I always want to embrace," Angelo said to himself with a trace of amused tenderness. "He doesn't know what more to do now that he's been insolent; nor do I for that matter. How would it be if we burst into tears?"

"Lead the way," he said, "I'll follow."

Allemandi had served the previous year under General Dufour in the Sonderbund war. He had an unwavering idea of what a town owes a staff. He had set up his quarters in the loggia. The morning sun played gently in the double-arcaded gallery along the facade of the palace.

The general was at first as insulting as his courier. He spoke loftily of suspect comings and goings, and heaped quantities of threats on Angelo's head. As he spoke, gesturing mightily, his voice cracked on the summit of pomposity, and he was left in the ludicrous position of having to draw breath.

"There is no great difference of temperament," said Angelo, "between you, who are from the Ticino, and me, who am Piedmontese. You would certainly be astonished if I pretended to be impressed by this accumulation of death sentences, when in general one's enough."

"You don't understand the first thing about all this," said Allemandi. "You're back in the days of the gallows. We no longer set men sentenced to death up on platforms. If you think your life is the only thing I've got to take from you, you're blind. You've been stupid enough to show me that you're proud. Pride, too, can be killed."

He was genuinely angry. His face, which he had been handling carefully, decomposed.

"There's a dirty beast under those clean-shaven, even talcum-powdered cheeks," Angelo thought.

Allemandi mentioned the gig, demanded the papers, uttered the word "unpack" and repeated: "Unpack your bag."

"I have no bag; God knows if that's any way to talk! . . ." said Angelo, but his voice, which had quavered slightly, displeased him and he didn't finish his sentence.

"Those two little bastards in ostrich feathers are going to come and frisk you," he thought during the silence that followed.

There was no weapon within reach for him to seize.

Allemandi left the room without giving any order, as if subsequent events were all determined. Angelo remained alone with the two officers, who were paring their nails.

"We're going to have to wrestle it out," he said to himself. "They're counting on an ugly fight. Even if you kill one—and you must—it'll have to be with your teeth. Besides, after these two, twenty to a hundred more will appear. They won't have to do more than break one of your arms and keep turning it and you won't be able to keep from shouting, weeping, and even licking their boots, if they wish. And they will wish."

The idea that courage was not sufficient for everything terrified him.

"All right, let's get at it," he said to himself.

He never dreamed of deliberately insulting people who had not yet laid a hand on him. He thought himself pretty insolent just to go sit in an armchair as if he were in his own house.

For more than an hour his imagination tortured him, showing in detail humiliations he could not have withstood.

Finally Allemandi returned.

"We've all been taken for a ride," he said. "The traveler in the gig was the very opposite of a coward. I've just learned that this morning at dawn he forced his way past our outposts, pistol in hand. You've been cuckolded as well as us, young man.

"Let him go," he said to the officers, "he's free."

Angelo seriously asked himself the following question: "Must I make him pay for the tortures I've just suffered in this chair?"

He departed regretfully.

The square was crowded with people. Angelo, making his way among groups of workingmen and armed peasants, recognized certain individuals with the look of hangmen, who, on the evening of the previous day and even this morning, had caught his attention in the courtyard and in front of the door of the Albergo Reale. For the moment these arch-revolutionaries had their noses in the air and seemed above all to be interested in the course of a few clouds, which, for that matter, shone brightly. Nothing could have been sweeter or better, nothing less bloody, than the expressions of these idlers. Allemandi's officers, leaning on the balustrate of the loggia, were exchanging jokes with the wags of the crowd about the weather, saying that it would be very disagreeable when it changed for the worse. They talked about "kicking the bucket" and about "giving up the ghost."

"These astute double meanings seem to concern you," Angelo told himself. (He did not give a single thought to the little loaded pistol in his inside pocket. He allowed himself nothing but a bit of irony about the suffering he had endured in the armchair.) "These people have never been able to afford the delicacy of expensive passions," he said to himself. "Now, they're glutting themselves."

He had reached the middle of the square when he was insulted in a mild way by a sort of government clerk. Audacity gave character to a physiognomy made to have none. Angelo wanted to move on, but he was restrained and even pulled back violently while other filthy insults were whispered in his ear. He tried to get free, but a pair of extremely brawny arms closed about him. This physical strength was a hundred times greater than his; there was no way to resist. Everything happened with impressive silence. Only the words "This way, this way," repeated a hundred times like the chirping of birds, could be heard and a few brief orders to "push the swine into the narrow streets."

More carried than pushed, uplifted by the big red-haired arms which encircled his chest, touching the pavement with his toes only, Angelo was obliged to waddle in a most ridiculous fashion.

The big fellow whose arms were around him made him advance by goosing him with his knee.

The very absence of tumult and concerted action made it clear that the crowd might risk doing something rash at any moment. Guns, bayonets, picks, and forks began to appear above the mob. A gun fired *by chance* could become the signal for a massacre.

The women, moreover, had changed into furies. Panting, wild-eyed, as if about to satisfy some imperious desire, they extended sharpened fingers toward Angelo's face. They were repelled by men shouting "Wait! Wait!" They didn't want the fun to start in the main square; the narrow streets were much more suitable.

There the balconies and windows were packed with women and girls. Angelo was not suffering; he didn't have a single idea in his head. As he had nothing else to do but continue to waddle stupidly with each knee-blow, his eyes engaged in a brief conversation with a young woman; she obviously belonged to that part of society which takes no part in street-fighting. Her face, her bosom, her body were abandoned to passion. He could have lighted a cigar from her burning eyes.

"What a spectacle for you!" said Angelo.

"It's what I like. It enchants me," replied the eyes.

She looked him up and down with hatred which in the end was quite flattering.

He was consequently in the process of thinking, not exactly of love, but of the sweat pouring abundantly from the entire crowd when he felt a sharp, piercing pain in his shoulder. He had just received the first knife thrust and his jacket was stained with fresh blood.

A hoarse voice shouted: "Let go! Let him go! Move on! The people mustn't kill him themselves; they have executioners; they have judges; they can give orders; justice is in their hands. Make way! He's an example; everyone must know it. Wait! Don't ruin what we've already accomplished!"

The man doing the talking was waving a bare saber and seemed to have taken it upon himself to speak without stopping. He broke through the crowd. He was followed by four or five deserters of Archduke Albert's regiment, still in white uniforms, but trimmed with tricolored ribbons.

They let go of Angelo.

Angelo had read in Lamartine's *Les Girondins* that the September victims who tried to protect themselves against their murderers died slowly in atrocious agony; those who welcomed the blows expired immediately without suffering, the poet said. Consequently he took advantage of his relative liberty to clasp his hands behind his back.

"I'll get you out of this," said the man with the saber.

"For God's sake, leave me in peace," Angelo replied.

"Come now, sir," said the other, "you're not the only proud man in the world."

The man was a sleight-of-hand artist: he continued to proclaim in a loud voice that the people were king, meanwhile swiping their bone.

Angelo was now surrounded by thirty or so Lombard deserters; the Austrian uniforms they were still wearing seemed to give them the right to enforce the law, whatever it might be—on this occasion that of the man with the saber.

The latter gave several orders from the manual of arms. Guns crawled up shoulders; hands slapped butts. It was a pretty sight into the bargain. There were shouts of "bravo!"; the balconies applauded. Surrounded by soldiers marching in time, Angelo was conducted to a bourgeois house from the pediment of which floated a large, brand-new Italian flag. The soldiers deposited their weapons in the hall in a rack of unfinished wood which, it seemed, had been nailed to the wall only a few hours before; the mirrors and pictures taken down to make room for it were still leaning against the furniture. A large door with glass panes in it opened out into a garden. To show some kind of will, even idiotic, but to make it quite clear that he intended to obey no one, Angelo, with his hands still behind his back, walked slowly toward the garden.

One thought dominated every other: "Anyone, if he's stronger than you, can make you into a coward, that is to say, kill your soul. Physical strength is enough to do it. If he's ignoble, he can force you to be that way too. And he will be ignoble, because if he weren't, he would respect you.

"Worse still," he went on, "the mob is going to be giving the orders. The mob will always be the tool of a whim. (The whim can be an idea or a constitution.) And it's to this whim that you must bend.

"The alternative leaves no room for hope: to become common, abandoning every personal ideal, or die, and at that with physical suffering organized to deny every dignity, all in the name of a 'good tyrant.'

"What an abomination a dirty death would be," he said to himself.

He suffered because he was reasoning normally yet imagining horrible things. He had gone so far as to think that the people are not necessarily the *ne plus ultra,* when he heard the crunch of gravel in the garden. It was a gentleman the likes of which he had seen over and over again in the last twenty-four hours.

"That wound you just received should be disinfected," the aimiable individual said to him. "The people out in the street at present stab with the same knives they use to cut pretty powerful nourishment, rotten cheeses in particular. The last fellow they killed turned completely blue."

"I'm not afraid of dying, even blue," said Angelo, "but I'm afraid of dying stupidly. What frightens me is the brief moment three seconds long before kicking the bucket, in which I'll become sure of the general stupidity of the world."

"My good fellow, they say that in order to live in peace in a country of one-eyed people you must keep one eye closed. Admit that it's not very difficult! And that's all there is to it, I assure you! The butcher's boy who had a hold of you treated you as he treats his pigs or his fiancée. He's a good boy; I know him like the inside of my own pocket: he wouldn't hurt a flea in ordinary times, but what do you expect him to make of your haughty silence? You're making too much of him. As for the fellow who knifed you, he's a nice little notary clerk to whom I would willingly entrust my fortune, except my political fortune. He didn't know you disdained him. He saw only the throat and a chance the like of which he had never had. Nothing ruins people like misery."

This charming man had one of those faces "which command respect and make sympathy certain." His noble features were embellished by an extremely sweet expression; a lively glance animated his fine-drawn, witty face in which nothing was exaggerated except the vivacity in his eyes. Only this could be disquieting, especially when you noticed that it never showed itself unreservedly.

Angelo had other fish to fry; he was busy practicing the art of loving.

"However, sir," he said, "I'm not cold-hearted. I dream like everybody else, especially of giving your butcher's boy and your knight of the knife the character which makes happiness possible. I don't think you're one of those who think that a more exact division of beans will bring the golden age to pass. They should be divided, of course, but the soul should be divided as well. Here also some have too much and others not enough."

He spoke of the people as a Roman does of his mistress, that is to say very badly. Anyway, he was not cut out for reasoning.

"We've come a long way from the few drops of alcohol we were going to pour into the hole the notary clerk made in your skin. What good is a tragic view of life if you don't think first of all of yourself? Come on then. If the world is a world at all, it's because the egotists made it so."

The charming man made Angelo go up to the second floor.

"Obviously," he said, "you can always shut up shop and let others do the talking if business seems bad to you. But in that case it won't be long before you look the way you did a little while ago."

The rooms on the second floor (there were three of them, proudly opening one onto the other) were quite small, but made to appear larger by mirrors; they were for the use of the local bourgeoisie. Consequently, they contained the portrait of the first owner of the house to have ten francs to pay for a portrait of himself, a figured stucco panel, a scarf with ball-fringe on the mantel, and, in the corners, false columns of real marble with wooden entablatures supporting pots of greenery.

A woman, pretty and young but buried in fat, cleaned Angelo's little wound very industriously. Her thick blubber and combativeness made her short of breath and quick in her movements. Beside her was lint enough to stop the bleeding of several slaughtered steers.

"Note that my daughter is not afraid of blood. Moreover, you are no longer bleeding. You were lucky enough to have come up against a knife that had been freshly sharpened. No one's afraid of blood in this house."

The man with the saber came to look at the wound. He had changed into a lounging-jacket.

"Here's the man who saved you: my son-in-law."

Angelo asked pardon for the somewhat sharp manner in which he had welcomed him before.

"I confused you with these rogues."

"They're no rogues. I know them all. I sat beside them on the benches of the primary school. But today anything goes. What would we do if we were aware that anything was possible? It's simply a little harder to persuade us that the route is entirely free. A question of education more than temperament. It's our job to educate them."

He was obviously very proud of his little demonstration in the street. He uttered the word mission. He seemed to be speaking to someone beyond and above them.

"To whom is he talking?" Angelo wondered. "Is there a tall person standing behind me?"

He was happy to find something to joke about once again. He listened with every evidence of the most flattering attention to the man affording him this happiness. To tell the truth, he had also just noticed that his arm functioned as before. He had feared that he would not be able to handle a sidearm.

"That's the thinking of an exceptionally talented man. His clairvoyant eye is fixed on the future," said the charming man. "Today's spectacle is mere dust! The violent enthusiasts are out beating the pavements; much good it'll do them! The pavements of Brescia aren't made of flint; they won't strike sparks. Let's keep down the damage as best we can—above all, when it's a matter of men like you whose intelligence—allow me the word—can be seen in their faces. Let's look further. A central government will be necessary, and a representative from Brescia will be elected. It's good to be able to say on an election day that you were instrumental in preventing a mob prosecution, that you freed an innocent man from the clutches of . . . My son-in-law is called Dossi. Remember his name. I have too high a respect for the liberty of each and every man, especially in political matters, to tell you to

'Remember too the moment you would not have given two soldi for your skin.' Dossi! A lawyer, like me; for that matter, he followed my example. We need the enlightened talents of moderate men. We belong at the head of a troupe which, without us, would go God knows where. What did I say as soon as I saw we were winning? I said: 'We must make a flag, as big as possible.' My wife and daughter spent the whole night sewing the colored strips of the standard which now floats on the facade of my house. My two sons bought uniforms from deserters. They put them on, sir. They thus enlisted twenty or so of these unfortunate young men who yesterday while still serving Austria—very much against their will, be it said—were learning to obey without argument. Supposedly well informed minds have told me: 'You won't be able to hold onto them: liberty will seize them like the colic.' People are always deluded about the desire for liberty. It's not a physiological necessity. One jump doesn't get you there. It must be invented in order to be possessed. These men will invent it four or five days from now; between now and then a lot of water will have gone under the bridge. At the present moment they're very happy still receiving orders. Besides, I feed them decently."

This speech amused Angelo. He had completely forgotten the butcher boy's brawny arms. He said to himself: "This naïveté is charming. Basically we all take each other for imbeciles." He had finally noticed the vivacity playing on this face, otherwise completely suitable for an ancient laurel-crowned bust. "He doesn't yet know how much I can swallow but just let me put on my dumb look. . . . There was more to him a while ago in the garden. He even had some fine things to say about misery. It was a good start. Is he letting himself go now because he sees his daughter making a mess of my shoulder? In any case his scorn is so kindly that I can't get angry at it because he admits to me that he wants to be a little Medici. . . ."

The fat young woman found some pleasure as well in Angelo's handsome shoulders.

"How can I thank you?" he said. "Rest assured, Signorina, that I will remember the light touch of your hand. Men would pay a high price to be wounded if they were sure to get your care afterward."

He raised the collar of his shirt.

"Perhaps I'm treating her bandage a bit lightly, but what the hell! She doesn't even notice," he said to himself.

A loud explosion echoed among the hills of Brescia. The sky shook like a sheet and a cannon ball whistled through the air.

"There are still a few detachments of Austrians in the castle and from time to time they bombard the town a bit."

Roof tiles were breaking from the cannonade, but no one seemed anxious. However, the street, still murmurous as on a market-day, grew quiet.

"I have a little request to present to you," Angelo said.

He looked at the fat young woman with what could very well have been taken for a spark of passion; since caressing his shoulder, she was beside herself.

"You must have bought weapons and equipment from the deserters," he continued. "Perhaps this equipment includes a saber like the one your husband used to deliver me. If you would lend it to me, I'll slip it into my belt, and it will take care of me on my way from here to the inn where I left my horse."

"It's very dangerous," said the young lawyer.

"I don't think so," said Angelo, "for the good reason that these days anyone who is obviously armed is classed *ex abrupto* on the right side. Also I give you my word that I'll be content just to carry the saber; I'm under the impression that will be enough. My testimony on your ability as a moderator will be useless unless I return to Milan alive!"

"That's a thought," said the charming man. "With whom are you in contact in Milan?"

"Odd or even, whatever number comes up."

"That is to say?"

"No proper names." ("Am I enough of a Jesuit?" Angelo asked himself. "But I've got to lead them on.")

They went to get him several sabers and were malicious enough to want to make him choose.

"It doesn't matter which one you give me; I'm not a warrior."

"That wasn't even a lie," he said to himself once in the street. "I'm a civilian who doesn't want to get stepped on any more, even in the name of justice and liberty. Let 'em come!"

But no once came. From time to time more cannon balls whistled above the roofs. The street was almost empty.

He was astonished to reach the Piazza della Loggia almost immediately. He was under the impression that a long time had passed between his exit from Allemandi's and the knife thrust. In reality the citizen who took himself for a Medici and the general of the militia were separated by no more than a few houses.

The officers were no longer leaning against the balustrade. After each cannon shot, flights of pigeons swooped down on the deserted square.

Groups of men were still standing under the arcades. Angelo took pleasure in slipping between them to enter a tobacco store; he bought some little cigars. He lingered in the doorway drawing a few puffs. The men looked at him indifferently. The saber never even crossed their minds.

"Here's how, once satiated, they digest your perfectly useless death," Angelo said to himself. "I have better things to do than haul their ashes. In any case, I won't do it for free next time."

He was now somewhat angry.

The innkeeper was almost mute and courteous. His only blunder was to refuse payment. He got a gold coin thrown in his face. He stooped to pick it up.

Once on horseback, Angelo somewhat regretted this insolence, but said to himself: "You always lose too much time carrying coals to Newcastle."

At the edge of town, the sentinel instinctively opened the barrier for the melancholy rider advancing at a walk as if leaving Brescia with regret.

Despite Angelo's indifference, the horse turned coquettish. The day threatened to be stormy. A towering edifice of clouds was building up toward Mantua. Blue vapors slumbered on the plain. The sun stung like a gadfly, but a light, cool air graced the heat. Spring had crushed gold chalk on the hills. The air was perfumed with lilacs and broom. The delicate footsteps of the wind traced shining furrows in the meadows.

Angelo was weak enough to say to himself: "What use is virtue? If Austria had collared me, she would have stuffed me in one of these prisons where you end up by coughing your heart out. Piedmont wanted to hang me as flypaper. That butcher's boy wanted to make a toy of my bare throat; all he ever got out of thwacking his pigs was good strong arms.

"Today as in the past, the strong must be pampered. But this never used to amuse me; why would it amuse me now? I'm not trying to wear the starched shirts of the new regime."

He thought he was doing some sound political thinking.

Basically, he was jealous. The revolution was giving itself over to the first comers. He would have wanted it to remain wise just because he himself was not interested in profiting from it. He did not know that necessities existed.

He avoided Ospitaletto by making a detour across fields honey-sweet with willows. Back on the road once more, he encountered several men strolling along carrying guns with bayonets on the barrels. They appeared to be enjoying the spring weather; they gave friendly salutes to the rider wearing an unsheathed sword slipped through his belt. Little shopkeepers from Brescia, they were undoubtedly from the same street for they called each other by their first names as they went into ecstasies over the flowers in the fields and the sweetness of the air. Angelo stayed with them, and they gave him some bread and sausage. They looked apprehensively in the direction where the clouds were darkest. They wondered if it wasn't thunder they heard; they listened hard. It was a wagon rolling along a rocky road to some farm.

Angelo explained why there was a chance it wouldn't rain before evening. They were greatly touched by his explanations and repeated what he had just said about the hot air rising and the cold air coming to take its place. They were prodigiously interested; it was easy to see that they hadn't the slightest desire to exchange their present situation for combat. They were going to guard a bridge across the Oglio, beyond Chiari, for a five-day period. They wanted very much to see a big storm, but without getting wet. They went into ecstasies over everything. Angelo, who in his youth had known the language of flowers, pointed out various plants by name.

When they were in sight of the first houses of Rovato, Angelo said he was going to leave them and make his way around the mass of buildings because he didn't like formalities.

"It's very simple," they said. "Don't do that. You go first. You don't have to say anything. You're our leader. Once we're lined up behind you, we'll get through all together like a letter in the mail."

They did indeed pass through Rovato without any difficulty. People even looked kindly after them.

They were not going to guard the main bridge across the Oglio—which since the start of the revolution had been held by a garrison from Chiari, very high-hat about its prerogatives—but a kind of heavy footbridge above Palazzolo; it could support light carriages and the government hoped to use it as an important pawn.

They were going to show the men from Chiari, who had always had a high opinion of themselves, that in reality they *naturally* depended on Brescia. They thus took the Palazzolo fork with Angelo, who preferred this route because it took him nearer the mountains, where it's always easier to hide if need be.

It was a little after noon. The light, cool wind had ceased to blow. The sky was almost entirely overcast except for a small spot of blue which persisted toward Bergamo. It was hot. Angelo's horse sneezed frequently. They stopped to eat beside a stream.

However, their pleasant stroll came to an end; they reached the famous footbridge and had to start taking things seriously. The light but solid bridge crossed the river at the very place it came out of the mountain, a romantic spot indeed. Here in the flesh were those intensely black rocks which one likes to contemplate in etchings, peering over the quilt from a downy bed.

"Whoever sent you forgot only one thing," Angelo said, "and that is that there are only five of you. If he had seen the bridge as we see it, he would have realized that five is insufficient to guard it properly. I've been in the service; do you want me to give you a piece of advice?"

He made them cross to the other side and set up their post in the mysterious rocks. From there, hidden in the high broom and rock ferns, they could overlook a quarter of a league of the road.

Evening was coming, and with it the storm. After a dry thunderclap, which rolled endless echoes around the mountain, a heavy downpour began to fall. They went to take shelter under the bridge, for lack of anything better, when by chance they found a grotto at the foot of one of the rocks. It was a hole hollowed out when the stream was high, but its opening had been considerably enlarged by a road repairman who undoubtedly came by on his rounds to check the cables. Even the horse could be sheltered in it. They piled themselves in. They were only on the edge of the storm; it struck violently in the surrounding area. Big drops of rain came only in squalls like flights of sparrows, but the thunder roared continuously and the lightning lashed the dusk and then the night.

"Stay with us," said the man who was supposedly in command of the squad. "Leaving aside the fact that, as you say, there are only five of us, I'd be the first to admit that in such weather I don't feel in the slightest like going and shouting: 'Halt there!' to someone who, if he's out now, knows no fear and wouldn't give a damn for me any more than he would for an old sock. This is no work for a family man."

Angelo understood this line of reasoning very well. He said that he would gladly wait in their company till the end of all this commotion and that he too was not dying to go for a stroll in the lightning. He distributed a few of his little cigars. The six little red coals made the hole a little cosier. The horse had seen others like these and did not move.

The storm circled the brambled slopes for a long time, still making a great deal of noise.

Despite the lightning which flashed brilliantly yellow, they had to blow on the coals of some tinder to check the time on a watch. It was ten o'clock. At almost the same instant the horse stretched out his neck and caressed Angelo's ear with his cold muzzle.

"We've got visitors," said Angelo. "Come with me. Above all don't fire. You might kill a friend or someone who isn't hurting anyone. Perhaps it's a farmer or a shepherd from the neighborhood. We'll soon see."

They climbed back up onto the road, bending low in order to stay hidden by the broom. Between two thunder claps they heard some pebbles rolling down the slope of the mountain.

"A troop," said the corporal.

"No, one man alone," Angelo murmured, "but he's leading a horse by the bridle."

At last a glimmer of lightning showed him an Austrian dragoon. When the soldier was level with him, he jumped on him and, de-

spite his helmet, belts, and straps, was lucky enough to get a grip
on him at the first try, immobilizing his arms.

"I've got him," he said. "Don't shoot."

He feared only his companions, whom he heard shuffling and
sniffling like cats.

"Take the horse."

He thought of the saddlebags, in which there were undoubtedly
papers. The soldier did not try to free himself or utter a word.

They made him crawl down to the grotto. The men had candles
in their packs. They lighted them. He was a young cadet. He looked
at everyone, blinking.

"I speak Italian," he said.

"But, do you understand the Italian we're going to speak to
you?" said Angelo. "We won't hurt you, sir, but we want some
information."

The horseman's boot and his cartridge box contained nothing but
some papers written in German.

"I was not told to get myself killed for just anything. I'm a
forager. I lost my party in the storm, and I've lost my way. We're
reconnoitering for Clam's advance guard. The platoons are ten
leagues from here; I heard them forcing their way across the stone
bridge at Chiari. The information I'm giving you won't do you
much good."

"If it will set your conscience at rest," said Angelo, "realize
that in some situations . . ."

"Don't get in a lather," said the young officer. "It's wartime."

He took his mishap well. Moreover, he was pleasant, ruddy, and
obviously determined not to complicate his existence.

He saw no reason why he should hide what everyone was talking about. The field marshal had left Milan and was withdrawing
toward Verona. Clam was now in command of the dragoons; with
a light brigade he was protecting the old boy's left flank while he
skedaddled with all his guns and equipment.

"Radetzky left Milan?"

"And how! Walking stick in hand, my boy! There's a character
for you!"

"There's nothing more for you to guard here," said Angelo to
the Brescians. "Of course I can't give you advice, but in your place

I would go home right away, taking this young man with me, even if the road I traveled this morning farted a few shots at my heels. You have his horse; you can take turns resting."

The young officer begged Angelo to explain to these gentlemen as well that they had nothing to worry about, that he was a good fellow.

"I fear amateurs like the plague," he said. "They don't know that once a bullet is fired, it's tough to get it back. You can't whistle for it like a dog. It would be too bad if they got it into their heads, just because of some little word I said, that I wanted to give them the slip."

After bidding a republican farewell to his companions, who, in spite of the thunder and the prisoner, showed themselves receptive to his words, Angelo, pulling his horse along by the bridle, wandered for more than an hour on the mountain side. The lightning flashes peopled the solitude with tall pines; the road petered out among ferns. At last the moon appeared from behind ragged clouds and he saw the first estates of the plain and a little hamlet enveloped in mist.

Naturally, everyone was barricaded. However, as he seemed to be determined to break in a door by beating on it with a stone, an uncertain voice tried to frighten him. He asked for the road to Bergamo.

The moon permitted him to gallop. A clock chimed once as he was passing through the deserted lower town: a half-hour, or one in the morning. Once out of Bergamo, he resumed a fast pace.

He could see his way clearly. He had put his horse into a military pace; professional cavalrymen recognize this noise anywhere, especially on a lonely night. From a distance his bandage could be taken for a helmet. If some dragoons still remained here and there in the fields, they would take him for a courier.

He was no more than three leagues from Milan and day was about to break when he heard on his left a noise like that of distant thunder. But the rumble was continuous: a cannonade. Advancing a little farther, he saw on the horizon, despite the dawn which was just beginning to break, palpitating sulphurous glimmers and blazing trajectories. Angelo noticed, however, that these trajectories all started from the same point and met with no reply. The cannons were thus all on the same side. In any case, the engagement seemed to be getting hotter all the time.

He reached Milan at daybreak. The town was pale to the point of being green, without either noise or smoke. It seemed deserted, like Bergamo or any of the villages he had traversed; worn out. At the Porta Tosa on the boulevard which circled the town, Angelo saw three horsemen preparing, like himself, to enter Milan. The dawn obscured their silhouettes; he made them out with difficulty; nevertheless, they seemed a little stiff and over-starched. They were proceeding at a walk. Angelo reached them in front of the gate; a standard-bearer and two men of the 4th Sardinian lancers. The Piedmontese army was arriving. He passed them without saluting.

CHAPTER EIGHT

Angelo stayed for a week in an inn, eating and sleeping. Entirely naked, he rolled up in the sheets with nothing but a little wool throw, and when he had enough of sleeping on his right side he turned on his left, his back or stomach. He had the owner bring him up small bites to eat.

He had not gone to report after returning from Brescia; he had contented himself with returning the horse to the stable guard. Besides, the Palazzo Borromeo seemed deserted. After the three horsemen Angelo had passed, the Piedmontese advance guard had made its entrance accompanied by a fanfare. Indeed, it was the fanfare that came into town, pure and simple: fifty or so bugles swelled cheeks, as many drums rolled, and a tall drum major tossed his baton as high as the second floor.

The streets filled with a crowd dying to do some kissing; they kissed the drums and the bugles; they kissed the horses, the coachmen and the officers arriving by calash. The houses were decked with all sorts of flags, ribbons, and red and green material.

A tired, sullen infantry company stacked arms on the cathedral square. The soldiers did not look very affable. They demanded wine.

A rumor went round that the King of Sardinia was coming and from every direction at once. The crowd ran to the Porta Tosa—each time to find *dandylike* officers slowly dismounting and looking off down the streets of Milan with an absent air at God knows what horizon.

General Bentz was taken for something he wasn't. He entered the castle, lumbering a bit like a bear. The shouts of "hurrah" surprised him as he was putting his foot on the drawbridge. He wheeled sharply: "What's all this now?" he said. The square was black with people. The blue dolmans of a platoon of hussars danced above the heads.

A true military band with trombones and double basses transported on little carts tried to make its way down the Corso del Giardino. As it wasn't playing, it had the greatest possible difficulty getting through the idle, excited mob which included young women of the highest bourgeoisie, dressed in their best, their cheeks rouged, waving little perfumed handkerchiefs, paper flowers, feathered hats, and fichus above their heads. The musicians, hampered by their instruments and by the dirks they wore, which got caught between their legs, lost their kepis in the general embracing. Their leader ordered them to sound the cymbals. The crowd parted and lined up nicely on the sidewalk. To the satisfaction of all, the soldiers played a march, marking time in place. Their dancing movement, making the pretty plumes of the recovered kepis oscillate and bringing full tones out of the brasses, gave spirit to the entire street. They sang Mercadante's *Die for the Fatherland*.

General Passalacqua waited in vain for his band in front of Santa Maria delle Grazie. Against his will, he decided to enter the town with his three orderlies without either drums or trumpets. These four horsemen were rapidly surrounded by working-girls dressed in their Sunday best and shouting in high-pitched voices. The horses became agitated. "Come now, that'll do," said the general, who didn't care for equine whims.

The two first battalions of the 14th Royal Piedmontese brigade commanded by Major Bès camped outside the walls in the commons. They covered the Melagnano road. The little town had been set on fire and pillaged the evening before by the cannonade, the last rockets of which Angelo had noticed at dawn. An engagement was feared in that quarter in the immediate future. The fourth infantry regiment, to which a Sardinian flag adorned with tricolored scarves had been given on the spot, reconnoitered along a road smelling of burned rags.

The street noises, the tra-la-las of music and the cries of women, which a footsoldier can recognize from afar, could be heard in the Royal Piedmont bivouacs. A corporal who had decided they should be called "unlucky" tore up a garden stile and began to hack it to pieces with an ax to heat his soup. He was in a very bad mood. He imagined a civilian telling him not to break everything and himself replying: "What's your sister breaking?"

The horizon in the direction of Melagnano was mired in red smoke. The rest of the sky was sparkling and limpid throughout the day, and the heat, almost as intense as in summer. The town smelled of leather, uniform material, leg bindings, rice powder moistened with sweat, and camphor—for carefully stored and even historic redingotes had been unpacked.

"What's called the Piedmontese Army consists today of nothing but de luxe officers," Angelo said to himself, looking at the soldiers, who were thin, tired, and above all melancholy. They didn't relax. The mountaineers from Coni didn't understand their prerogatives as liberators; moreover, they missed the cool air of the Alps. The young ladies went back to their world. They were replaced by biddies who obtained a few gray smiles.

Angelo went to a pharmacy to have his head wound bandaged correctly.

"You've been in the fighting the last few days, sir?"

"No," said Angelo. "I ran into a door a bit hard."

"An iron door no doubt," said the pharmacist, washing the wound.

But he showed that he understood.

Angelo first slept twenty-four hours straight. After this double turn around the watch face, he felt somewhat less bitter and completely in agreement with his comfortable bed. He struck his boot against the floor of the room to summon the innkeeper to come upstairs.

"You're under no obligation to trust me," he said to him. "Here is some money in advance. If I please you and you please me, it'll be a good deal for us both. I want to sleep and eat, period. Sleeping is my business; eating is yours. I like good substantial dishes. Kidneys, sweetbreads, grilled liver, tripe with tomato and cheese.

When I've had enough, I'll tell you and we'll go on to another kind of exercise. I want cool water, Asti wine, and will you buy me five packages of small cigars."

"This is just my line," said the owner. "You can sleep like a top, sir; I'll take care of everything."

So well was he taken care of that a plump chambermaid came in without knocking and murmured throatily: "Tell me, young man, don't you ever . . ."

"I said I wanted to sleep," replied Angelo, half-opening one eye.

She went out on tiptoe. She had seen his bare shoulders. This gentleman obviously had no difficulty getting for nothing what she was selling.

"It was a mistake that will not be repeated," said the owner bringing up skewers of lamb's liver. "I see now what you're up to: you really do want to be put out to pasture. Don't judge me on the basis of one slip; I'm your man. And do you know why? The world is the way it is, and that's exactly what I hold against it. If I wasn't obliged to run this business, you'd see. The fact is that right now it's not running anymore. It's racing. It would be a shame to miss."

"Keep me company while I eat. Pour yourself some wine. And tell me the news," said Angelo.

"True or false? There's some for every taste. The Austrian army has ceased to exist. Forty thousand prisoners have bowed to Italy's great sword. Radetzky had his legs shattered; he was tied to his horse's tail and dragged along to the applause of his army. Verona surrendered. All the enemy flags, cannon, and baggage were seized. No one knows how many casualties there were. The Piedmontese army moved cautiously. Day before yesterday strong patrols were seen leaving in the direction of Lodi. They returned in a hurry yesterday evening. It seems that the Austrian army is impolitely and resolutely occupying the bridges across the Adda. The soldiers spoke of atrocities."

After three or four days Angelo took pleasure in strolling about his room a bit, still completely naked. Hot weather had come suddenly. The cold stone flagging under his feet and the little tongues of wind blowing through the blinds caressed him agreeably. He then went back with pleasure to his wool cover, his little cigars, and the intoxication of sleep. The owner had reached the stage of calf's head fricassees and was talking about *coq au vin*.

After the *coq au vin* his inspiration seemed to waver. He was, moreover, very busy.

"They're all like you, busy getting rid of something that's sitting heavy on their stomachs," he said; "they don't use real remedies, just stopgaps, but it's the same story. For them it's ordinary red wine, beef stew, and flirting their way up under Martha's petticoats. If they could only afford to sleep! . . . But that's a luxury."

They heard the soldiers singing and the girl crying out with a good facsimile of conviction. Each of her cries provoked a cheerful "hurrah" in which there was much good will as well.

Angelo had some clean shirts bought for himself. Finally he got dressed with the idea of going out and getting himself spruced up in suitable clothes. The blood on his velvet jacket could no longer be considered anything but dirt.

The streets were full of officers strutting about. The thinnest, who had sunk a lot of money into their uniforms, walked alone with an extremely virile step as if hastening to an important rendezvous. The most aristocratic did not give the women so much as a glance. They seemed to say that they were henceforth going to busy themselves with work badly done until then. Nevertheless, they ordered the movement of their backs, buttocks, and necks in such a way that they resembled male peacocks. Others paraded in groups of four or five, with less refined audacity. Every officer kept a finger to his mustache as if to the trigger of a gun.

Angelo went to a stylish tailor to order himself a myrtle-green planter's jacket and trousers of thin cloth. He tried on boots. He bought a hat to carry in his hand: his forehead was not yet cured. He was tired of Verdi felts; he chose a hard-brimmed Bolivar.

He would have been much astonished if anyone had told him that he, too, was sacrificing to the god of show. In reality he did not want to look like the "old soldiers" he saw everywhere, proudly sporting bloody tatters. Couldn't all these men take five minutes to clean up and put on a clean shirt? He did not remember ever having met so many heroes. With a quarter of the virtues he saw shining in their eyes, they could have built a hundred Italys. He had his beard shaved. While he was sitting in the barber's chair, shouts of "viva" rang out in the street. He went out onto the sidewalk, towel around his neck, with the other clients and the barber. It was a troop of Neapolitans led by Princess Belgiojoso. This beautiful woman had grown thin, but her long legs still made her working-class petticoats billow bravely. Every carriage had stopped to let the procession pass. The Princess herself carried, unfurled, a large flag with the Italian colors. In the windows and on the balconies, innumerable handkerchiefs waved.

"I'm really in the *theater of operations*," thought Angelo.

"So you told the mirror where to get off," the innkeeper said to Angelo when he returned to the inn in his new suit. "This is more like it. And what are you going to do with your old jacket? Give it to me. You know that you can't get blood out of velvet."

"Wonderful," said Angelo, "I'll have it framed!"

"Joking aside! That was my idea," said the innkeeper. "I know it could be very handy around the home, especially if the little woman starts trying to wear the pants; but in business, mine especially, you can't imagine what it would mean. I'll offer you forty soldi for it."

"You're always too formal," Angelo said to himself. "Why wouldn't this jacket make a good cabaret sign?"

He let it go in exchange for some stuffed pig's feet.

He took his meals in a small private dining-room which looked out under a trellis onto the courtyard. While he was eating, the plump chambermaid came out to joke beneath the window with the boy delivering beer.

"She's not bad," he said to himself, "and she knows how to show off a pretty bosom. That's better than marching about with flags unfurled at the head of young men who are going to take a beating. I was unjustly vulgar the other day."

When the brewer had finished rolling his kegs, Angelo called to the girl.

"You don't recognize me," he said to her, "because I've had my beard shaved. I'm the fellow who wanted to sleep. I spoke inconsiderately and I'm sorry. Go around by the kitchen and come pardon me by drinking a glass of wine with me."

Her name was Lucia. She was from Alagna at the foot of Monte Rosa. With the exception of several swaggering phrases, spoken with a good accent, which were the tools of her trade, she uttered her naïve feelings slowly like a mountain girl.

"Why have you been so kind to me?" she asked one morning while they listened to the pigeons cooing. "*Up our way* I have a boy friend who's sweet too, but he doesn't have black eyes like yours or this delicate skin you let me be so brutal with. I don't understand everything you tell me but it's very nice to hear. Men usually don't court me."

"That's because they're mistaken about what they want or else don't want anything," said Angelo.

"Oh, no," she said, "they want what you've got, but they can go hang."

Angelo said to himself: "I need a little acid conversation. I must go see my mother. Perhaps she's still at La Brenta."

He bought a horse and tried it out on the Corso. Many people noticed his vigorous horsemanship. He looked morose; he had pushed the Bolivar down to his ears to hide the bandage he was still wearing. He was honored by the salutations of the many parasols lowered to watch him pass.

The morning of his departure Lucia drew him into a corner of the stable and said to him: "I'm going to speak to you as if you were my brother. A lady would hide it from you, but *I*'ll admit to you that you're exactly what a woman needs. This is rare, and there's a lot of money in it. Make them fear you."

She managed a few tears.

Angelo took the road to Switzerland. Clouds swollen with light followed the road too. Spring flowered all around him. Aspens sparkled like mirrors set to catch larks. The silvery leaves were so smooth that they reflected the blue sky. In place of the mountains still covered with mist, these reflections off innumerable rows of trees extended the horizon to infinity.

Angelo kept to a walk for a long time, completely absorbed in the pleasurable swaying motion of the horse. The foliage slipped by beside him, murmuring and glimmering like a brook flowing over pebbles. Villages on the heights coiled like snail shells around old belfries crowned with Spanish lilacs. On the first dips of the plain, market towns spread their purple-plastered, laundry-decked arcades to the sun. Farms, all straw without, sheltered sheep and blue carts in little hovels of rose-colored earth. There was no wind, but the fallow fields covered with borage, poppies, daisies, and centauries were snuffed out when cloud shadows passed overhead and then rekindled like coals on which one blows.

From the top of the high earth embankments Angelo, lulled by the cracking of the new saddle, the click of the curb chain, and the dull noise of horseshoes in the dust, picked out, beyond the trees, blackish-green clover, sprouting wheat all vermilion, violet plowed fields, blond oats, heaths burning like coals, the scales of roofs, and the blue panes of rice fields extending into the distance until they mingled with the gray of the horizon. The horse chewed his bit and pricked up his ears.

Completely irrespective of political events, flags of all kinds and even simple bright colored skirts or gaily striped material had been fastened to the peaks of the highest poplars. At the entrance to lanes leading to estates just recently in the hands of the Austrian soldiers, greatcoats, helmets, and broken side-arms were abandoned on the grass.

The bell of a monastery chimed. Angelo put his horse into a trot.

He ate under a trellis in a little country pothouse after the Parabiago fork. A large woman made him a breast of pork fricassee on a charcoal fire.

While sitting cross-legged smoking a little cigar, he saw the stragglers of the Piedmontese army pass by.

He resumed his journey. Several leagues farther on the landscape changed. The clouds which had risen revealed the mountains. He could see the dark mouths of small valleys. The birches and aspens had disappeared, replaced by large oaks; regulation flags fluttered like little spitfires from their tops. The ochre color of the pebbled ground concealed low houses constructed of cobbles; a rainbow played on their walls exactly as it did on the grass.

As evening approached, Angelo was drawing near what seemed to be a mass of silent houses when he was passed by a gig which was going along at a good clip. A man leaned out from under the hood and shouted some incomprehensible words at him.

As he came into the village square, he heard someone calling him from the door of an inn.

"Come in!" (It was Lecca.) "I won't insult you by giving you explanations," said the general.

"Nor will I," said Angelo.

"I recognized you just now by your green jacket. I'd heard about it."

"No one knows I have one."

"You were seen on the Corso. You don't pass unnoticed, old fellow. The ladies have an eye for you . . . When the sight was described to me, I said 'It's him.' Devil take me if I thought I'd meet you. However, I had several things to reproach you for. Why didn't you tell me who you were? If I'd known, we wouldn't be where we are now. I was so alone, I had to beware of everyone. All I needed was a faithful Achates."

"I don't see what my name would have changed?"

"Everything. In the job we're doing you must never believe what's staring you in the face. You see courageous fellows: you must always ask yourself why they're that way and what's in the back of their mind. The moment you need them most they always rap your knuckles because in reality they've always been minding their own onions, not yours. A name, old fellow, why it's everything! It's a trademark. What makes one buy iron from one man rather than from another? Because, as far as the public knows, it's always one-hundred-per-cent iron in the store you patronize. No, if I'd known, you would have seen something."

"What I saw wasn't bad," said Angelo.

"Don't be naughty. How did you finally make out with those papers which, in any case, existed? I was determined to defend you if you brought them back, to make a bulwark of my own body. I've been told some delightful things about you on this score."

The general was very much at his ease. The peasants looked with admiration at the Napoleonic cross he wore on his redingote. He had succeeded, thanks to it, in getting himself served some wine—and, by God, not bad stuff either—in this hole, which seemed to be better stocked with large blue flies than anything else.

"Did you finally succeed in getting that Prince Borromeo in the bag?" Angelo asked.

"What? You didn't know? But first of all, he's not a prince!"

"I know. He doesn't try to hide it. He told me."

"So he gave you the treatment too? He knocks himself out to get a title, which he then refuses with pride. All in all, it's very complicated. He's not the only one. They're all running wild worrying how to fart higher than their own ass. But he takes the cake with his prince bit. In reality he's I don't know what, let's say a man of independent means, and he palms himself off as a modest man whom the *vox populi* forces to the rank he deserves: the highest, of course. But what astonishes me is that you don't know what happened to me? For three days I was general-in-chief of the forces of the provisional government of Milan!"

"That's quite a job."

"It was a job in which I could do a lot. But your little Piedmontese comrades turned up."

"It took them long enough."

"I don't hold anything against them. They behaved correctly. I saw Passalacqua. He's the right sort. I think he's the chief of staff, at least that's what he claims to be, and there must be some truth to it because I saw him giving certain orders that he would have done better to keep to himself, but that's another story. Just because he has a tongue that can wag . . . He told me.

"I saw Bentz, too. He has a pretty high opinion of himself. There he was, installed in the castle, setting up a hue and cry for the field marshal's apartments, bellowing like a calf. What kind of a fellow is he? You should know, you're his countryman. But I didn't tell you the best thing of all: Passalacqua, who swallowed his saber, and the other one, the foul-mouthed one, came to blows with the Milanese—what am I saying?—with the quintessence of Milan, who had succeeded in getting out of the raffle by dragging the other fellow through the mud. My friend, there's nothing I haven't seen in the line of bastards! That's government for you!"

"Piedmont is poor. We certainly lack finesse, but we've got character."

"Come now! Aren't you being too kind? Call it character if you will; where I come from it's called a good appetite. It's clear to me they didn't come for love . . . I'm an old dog . . . but soft pedal, Jack! let's have a little modesty! Can't do the whole job the first day. A four-year-old could have . . . It's not finesse they're using now, old fellow. What they're using you can learn in kindergarten. They had only to say the word. *I* was there. They didn't say it. I would have shown them how to tie the whole deal up. Instead of that: the brotherhood of arms! My children, you can argue about brotherhood like everything else till the cows come home."

Angelo made a declaration of republicanism.

Night had come.

"Let's go piss," said the general.

The wind-filled sky was white with stars. On the southern horizon rosy glimmers palpitated.

"Let's stay in this hole," said Lecca. "We're the masters. The bistro people have never seen a jacket like yours (nor me either for that matter!), and they heard me say I was a general. They'll take care of us; we'll be pigs in clover with them taking care of us. The next dump is God awful, they told me at the posting-station. Now I've got you I'm going to hold onto you. It's a piece of luck. Trust to luck, I always say. I've got a lot of serious stuff to tell you. In a word, I gave up the whole business, threw in the sponge. You might say I went to Moscow with the old *bicorne* himself and made it back. If you change masters, you may as well . . . But I've got to fill you in on the whole story. Let's eat first."

The peasants were terrified by the idea of serving a meal and preparing beds for these two gentlemen, who spoke familiarly of big issues. Finally they got used to the idea.

"Does he think I have a particular talent for being duped?" Angelo asked himself. "Is this what they call the soul of a leader? Men like him took the French army gallivanting off to the four corners of Europe, but they were served by peasants like these who have just served us such a good dinner on a white tablecloth. Etc."

"Here's Pavia," said the general, pushing away the plate on which he had just eaten his cheese. "Here's Lodi. And this bottle is Verona. I speak to you frankly. Do you know what Bentz was doing when I left Milan? He was engaging his footsoldiers there! He was stuffing his baggage train in here. He was starting his cavalry off on the hunt this way, and his pontoniers, his pontoniers

and the whole works . . . A large-scale campaign is one hell of
an obstacle course, that is any one worth shouting about, one of
which you can say 'Well done.' Do you know where those pontoniers are? Me neither. There aren't any! I didn't see any. And
when I say I didn't see any, I speak as a specialist. I went to see
what was going on. They were singing victory songs. We've taken
Lodi. Just so *we*'re the ones who've taken it. Last Tuesday a fellow
called Manara—who, I was told, was the last word in heroes because he had left his supposed wife and daughter and the joys of
life (Of course, Signor Manara's joys consist precisely in bartering
his wife and daughter for a good something or other—well, skip
it)—then this fellow, Manara, brought me one hundred and twenty-
nine young men armed with kitchen knives (I'm not joking) in
order to *pursue the Austrians*. I'm quoting him. One hundred and
twenty-nine, not one more. He had called them the Army of the
Alps. All right, fine. We took Lodi. I answer: 'Perfect, I'll see.
Let's go.' What do I find next? Mules on their way home with
corpses in their panniers! I say: 'What's this new-fangled way of
taking good folks for a stroll? They do better stretched out on the
ground!'—'Ah!' I'm told, 'but they're officers!'—'Ah!' I reply, 'and
you think they're ever going to serve again?' I hadn't gone ten
leagues when this time I met a cart with a tall fellow laid out on
the straw: General La Marmora who had just had his chin removed. If it hadn't stuck out so far, the bullet would have gone
by right under his nose. That's what you get for fighting. Near a
bridge, a company with arms stacked and a sergeant with a pipe
in his mug. 'What the devil are you doing here?'—'We've taken
the bridge.'—'And so?'—'We're guarding it.' What were they thinking of doing with a bridge? Making jam out of it? The Ostrogoths
have reached Pamplona. Why have we taken Lodi? Because the
Austrians don't give a damn for Lodi. What interests them is
Verona. Lodi let itself be taken. Two clerks with pencils and port-
folios. Old daddy thing-gummy, what's his name? Radetzky—is no
fool. If we'd limit ourselves to following him, he's putting up some
pretty fine resistance with his rear guard. You're crazy if you think
he'd ever engage unprovoked in a pitched battle with those carriages full of crockery, women, and children he's been dragging
with him since the evacuation of Milan. He's driving the whole

works as fast as possible to the fortresses of the Lombard quadrilateral, Peschiera and Verona. Once there, my children, you can start running—away from him. That's where the cavalry around here should be. And not playing the trumpet. Lancers, dragoons, hussars, even cuirassiers, anyone who's got something for the glue factory between his legs—I'd throw in the whole works, fifty squadrons of extra-light foragers, no supplies, make out as you can, sabers, cartridges and off we go at a gallop. There aren't a whole lot of orders to give. Charge their flank till they cry shit. I'm not going to make my infantry lose time carting all their junk around the countryside. March or die. In four days they'll be here. Then the fun begins. I'm bringing up my infantry. What did you say? Let's talk about you."

"You embarrass me," said Angelo. "I'm no strategist. Nor do I agree with you about my fellow countrymen. They're good fellows, and courageous too. It seems to me you're right about tactics. But the King gives the orders. And you'd have to be mad, that is to say not plan ahead, to get rid of him now. But we're as Italian as the Milanese. For that matter, isn't it this which makes the idea of unity legitimate? Get rid of Charles Albert and all our generals will start toting up apothecaries' accounts; our officers will take sides; even the advance guards will start plotting. We'd be farther still from your death charge. As for me, I prefer your procedure. I'd love to charge."

"Tell me about yourself," repeated the general.

"It's a subject I know even less about than the preceding one. Certain things give me pleasure, others leave me cold or bore me. I force myself to have to do with the former more often than the latter."

"Italy?"

"I love her."

"Add 'a lot' and call it a day?"

"No. I love her without qualifications. I only wonder if she will be as beautiful as people believe."

"Be a minister and you can deck her out. Now's the time to stake your claim."

"I don't like surveyors or ministers."

"God! It's asking a lot to be anything more, but it would suit me even better. The claims can be staked for you. The Piedmontese are good for six months. After that, they'll be taken for their shirts. If we wash our hands of them, the war may well end up under the walls of Turin. What's needed (not right away, but in a while) is a man the people can think of when they dream. Cincinnatus, but handsome, because of the women and children. At fifteen, children want to join the fight when some character pleases them."

"I don't see myself in the role of Cincinnatus. I don't see myself in any role."

"If the public sees you in one, that's enough. You don't have to knock yourself out. They always add whatever's lacking."

"I don't want to be fabricated in this way. I'm not blaming anyone. I'm no monster of virtue myself. If you need a horseman for your famous charge, I'm your man. The rest bores me. And that's the end of it."

"You have a great many friends in the Piedmontese army."

"You astonish me."

"It's a fact. I was told of a recent affair in which you played a role made of solid gold. If you don't like the word role, let's say that you conducted yourself well; it's all the same to me. The lancers say you sent someone who was passing himself off as a lancer 'to join his fathers.' The phrase is pretty and now that they've found it, they want to justify themselves to you. A fellow to whom a cavalry corps wants to justify itself is quite something."

The next morning the gig was hitched up. Angelo was already in the saddle. The general came and stood by his stirrup.

"Then you're fleeing?" he said. "Poor France!"

"I'm not fleeing; I'm going home to La Brenta."

"The river Brenta! But come now, that's near Venice!"

"My mother was very happy one day on the shores of the Brenta. She later gave this name to our ancestral estate. In our family we're very skilled when it comes to prolonging our happiness."

"I've heard about your mother."

Angelo smiled at the idea of a battle of wits between his mother and the general.

". . . I admit she scares me. And your pseudonym . . . where is it?"

"In the mountains on the bank, not of a patrician river, but of a torrent which is called Mastellone, a good name for a highwayman."

"Good. All right, I'm going to Switzerland to try to talk to someone who understands. Unfortunately, not of your stature."

Angelo let him go. That evening he spent the night in a beautiful, severe market town living soundlessly in the midst of an ilex forest. The next day, riding down to the small lake Osta he crossed fields of narcissus. This valley, like that of Aosta, still sheltered a few lepers or at least people who spread this rumor in order to live protected from the police in huts of unmortared stone. The gardens surrounding the huts were very beautiful. Carpets of every kind of flower, and especially excessively bright and leafy sweet peas, marked the steep slopes with tiny strongholds of liberty.

Coming back to these spots, Angelo more than breathed the air of home.

Little vineyards supported by low walls scaled the slopes of the mountain. Wooden canals trickling white water ran along the summits of the cliffs. The forests were hung on the walls of the little valleys like the fleeces of wild beasts. The faintest noise struck deep echoes.

Villages covered with bark or flat stones, hidden among the rocks, raised thin stalks of tall, transparent belfries.

When the road left the bottom of the valley to bypass excessively narrow gorges or rockslides, Angelo noticed men and women below bending over the spring hay like ants. He heard a solitary muleteer, fearful in the full daylight, singing high on the mountain. He came upon calvaries with Christs of the South, red-bearded, full of physical pride, as if they had been fed constantly on meat and on which the holy wounds seemed to be traces of rouge. He knew the far more realistic ex-votos at the corner of the woods, in the fields, and beside the road where children of this world had met with sudden death, by accident or murder.

Here he had thought his first thoughts.

He did not find his mother at La Brenta. She had departed for Turin.

CHAPTER NINE

Angelo spent several voluptuously peaceful days.

"The adverb is not too strong," he said to himself. "It literally describes my pleasure in the company of women who have a passion for the present, like that little mountain girl in Milan who in the end made an honorable declaration to me. I breathe by talking to them. What revolution could ever give me similar pleasure?"

He was in love with everything he saw.

"But," he continued, "a revolution could deprive me of this happiness, which doesn't bother anyone. One calculating opportunist like Borromeo or one butcher's boy from Brescia, for that matter, would be enough. The one wants to be prince at any price, and the other has his own idea of a good joke, and anyway is so strong that someday he may think it witty to sink his knife into solid wood."

He went for walks among the rocks which supported the castle. The granite, piled nearly five hundred feet high, overlooked a beech wood famous in the region and a gorge where the waters of the Mastellone boiled. The trees rooted in spongy meadows shot up their branches to dizzying heights. Spring made rosy the tips of the branches which were supple as threads, starring them with varnished buds.

Like all lovers, Angelo saw in them more than was there. The wind stirred their silken lace shining in the sun, but he was naïve indeed to catch gusts of pride from it.

One afternoon Angelo climbed into the eaves. Up there were

routes he followed each time he came to La Brenta, especially a narrow stairs which gave him access to the platform of a tower. He heard the cries of a coachman who was urging his horses up the ascent to the castle. He peered out of a loophole and a traveling-coach came out on the terrace below; a man with shapely legs climbed down and a woman with ballooning skirts. He recognized Carlotta and her husband.

Carlotta always dressed in slightly lemon-colored materials. This artifice was sufficient to put a charming blush in her cheeks. She had the most beautiful pale complexion in all Piedmont. She knew, too, that this trace of acidity brought out her brown hair, which she wore in the style of the Duchesse de Berry. Her somewhat too wide mouth, on which the least emotion trembled, contrasted in a piquant manner with her fine black eyes which seemed the enemy of real sensations. She had decided that her heart should be haughty, but by nature it was disposed to tenderness—"Alas!" she was accustomed to say.

Her husband, Count Gianpaolo d'Aché concentrated on emphasizing his elegant svelteness with close-cut clothes. Despite the thinness that thus resulted, he had the foppish face of a blond, but as witty a blond as a man can be. Obsessed by honor, he searched for it in places where he alone could find it. When he entered a drawing-room, everyone started to talk about the weather. This precaution did not prevent ugly incidents. Those who thought Count d'Aché's arms hampered by the cloth molding his form quickly changed their tune. He rushed into encounters with unconscious bravery without losing anything of his infantile, apparently sincerely repentant look. He loved his long supple mustaches.

"You've been disfigured for life," he said looking at Angelo's wound. "Wounds on the forehead never disappear, and the scar will be ugly. It'll redden like a stigmata at the slightest emotion. You'll be a sight."

Carlotta shielded her eyes with her gloves.

"Did you lose a lot of blood?" she asked.

Carlotta had spent much of her childhood, all that counts in the forming of character, at the Castle of La Brenta. Her mother, Signora di San Martino, was said to be Duchess Pardi's most intimate friend. Carlotta's mother spent as much time in an odalisque's perpetual state of négligé as the Duchess spent at the beck and call of her exquisite and redoubtable nerves. "A woman has no friends," said the Duchess, "she has clients only. Caroline de San Martino stocks up in my house on everything that will help her manage her husband."

This husband, lugubrious by dint of prudence, was killed on February 5, 1831 at Modena, shouting "Long live liberty!" under the papal legate's windows. Although they found a simple soldier's corpse belted with cartridge cases, the police wanted to have the last word in such an unusual, imprudent affair. They discovered that San Martino had been going to the Carbonari meetings for some years; that he had never spoken out, but that without the slightest doubt he had resolved with a knife (and perhaps even "with his teeth") a number of delicate situations, especially the expedition of an inspector general of the Austrian armies whose death until then had been attributed to his horse shying on the slippery pavement in Turin. Word went round that Coriolanus de San Martino had been ambitious. The opposite side made him into a popular hero.

"It's the last word," said the Duchess, "but a king who's so hungry that he eats the corn bought for his hens won't think so."

"You should have told me," Caroline replied. "My situation is horrible. The court in Turin is the only place in the world where a widow is allowed to dance a bit. I don't want to waltz, or at least I can wait a bit longer, but where's the wrong in letting my legs walk to a little music, even in the form of a mazurka? Do you want me to tell you something? I need conversation, agreeable conversation. I'm not like you: as soon as they start airing major questions, I frown. I'm going to age before my time. Can you imagine me with wrinkles? And especially those that form above the eyes? I don't have a Roman face like you. You talk about liberty, but what about mine? I don't see why poor Coriolanus, who'll sleep the sleep of the just for eternity, would feel offended if a well-brought-up man held my hand and put his arm around my waist. Last of all, I've had enough of being looked at, ferociously at that, every morning when I'm still in my nightgown by my daughter who's less of a daughter than a little monkey aping you down to the very look you're giving me this minute. You and your revolutions are terrible! You're never happy. Well! The rest of us aren't either!"

"You're right," said the Duchess. "It's time you found out that Coriolanus was bored. Tell this to the world as I permit you to do, and your fortune is made. Now, listen, we're intimate enough to hit two birds with one stone. You'll see, I'm very indulgent. Give me your daughter. She will get in your way when you're in the company of well-brought-up people. And stop wearing those filmy nightgowns."

Carlotta was a thin little girl given to swinging her long arms. But it was not long before she noticed that the Duchess was particularly lovely on the days when gusts off the heights of the Cappezzone made La Brenta tremble. The castle had been constructed for a proud, resolute breed. The large rooms of the ground floor had been hewn flush with the bedrock. One day Carlotta discovered to her delight that behind a large Venetian mirror they had even neglected to hide the rough-hewn rock under any kind of finish. She was ravished by the idea of what was hidden behind the mirror, before which she secretly practiced gestures. Also she loved a circular staircase constructed of marble filigree by a Paduan architect whom she imagined first dying on the gallows, then murdered in the course of a riot in Ferrara, and finally as a monk burned at the stake.

The Duchess lived in the center buildings. Twisting corridors led to her room. It was such a large room that the lamps could not light the walls. They carried candles from one piece of furniture to the next. Carlotta's room was next door. Although three inches thick, the oaken door let through every noise. Carlotta forbade herself to listen, but she was forced to hear heroic conversations. She had loved her father's long nose, drooping eyelids, and gray face to the point of madness. "I'm destined," she said to herself, "to carry arms in the monarchy of Piedmont. Our republic will win its Jemmapes and its Valmys over all these little kings and dukes —lackeys of Austria who assassinated my father. As soon as I have a good figure—and I certainly shall because I must take after my mother at least a little—I'll win the love of the King's accomplices and Angelo will kill them." She went so far as to imagine herself the King's mistress in situations of extreme danger. She carried a little vial of mint water in her apron pocket on which she had written the word "poison."

She was in the landau with the Duchess for a review on the Polygon when she saw the King. He was a poor, obese fellow who on horseback seemed to have small, artificial legs. His double chin hung down below his mouth, which gaped vacantly. His medals and his grand crosses looked like knick-knacks. He passed before the troops, however. Angelo, who had only just left school, did not yet have his command. He was standing in the first line of the detachment, which, forming a square, flanked the squadrons. Even the blue of his overcoat seemed gold.

Carlotta began to have special ideas about the liberal party. She brushed her hair carefully every morning.

"Henceforth, you won't be the one to scratch me inside my corset," the Duchess said to her. "Your mother has never understood the first thing about the changes of the heart, but I love you too much to run this risk. For this operation I'm going to replace you with a girl who is very pretty but cold as marble and whom you'll end up by liking when you realize that marble doesn't catch fire. Moreover, you and I are going to be obliged to live in Turin from time to time: Angelo is going to receive a command. But you understand perfectly that he doesn't shine like a gilded candle in the reviews out of love for the King. We're the ones who need him, and we both should have a say in the matter."

"As soon as I'm anywhere near him," said Carlotta, "Theresa chases me away, shaking her apron as if she was keeping the hens out of the corn."

"Theresa has big ideas. Put yourself in her place. She nursed him. She has memories. Never say to Theresa that Angelo is my son (however, he is, I assure you, I'm still shouting about it); she'll scratch your eyes out or, rather, as she's a tigress, she'll scratch your soul out. Even I, when I go a bit far, have to bolt my door. She would come stab me in the night, and even twist the dagger. That's what passion is. I'm delighted. At least he will have inspired one."

"I'll tell you a secret," the Duchess added a few days later while the carriage was being readied to go to Turin. "Angelo has an iron faith in everything he says and does. Bravo! But loyalty never drove out a king. If you knew the incredible number of lies which must be told in order to create a republic! He'll never stoop that far, and neither you nor I will ask it of him. It'll be simpler if we lie for him. Our guests will be the people of Turin. Perhaps they will even arrive at night after the main door is locked. If Angelo talks to these people, he'll show his heart and they'll make fun of him; perhaps they'll even manage to make a laughing-stock of him. . . . And you know where ridiculed revolutionaries end up: in the potter's field. He's running a much greater risk. Let's say that in order to overthrow the King he agrees to lie. He's not stupid: he can see that it's a way to gain time. When hearts created for the truth consent to lie, they have a great advantage. What they still have of innocence and virtue makes them perfect hypocrites. We would never be able to be proud of him again. Whereas *we* can do anything, you know, being women."

"We'll make Giuseppe lie as well," said Carlotta, happy as a queen.

"Giuseppe's something else again," said the Duchess. "When Giuseppe wants to be handsome (and he always wants to be handsome), he looks at a portrait of Angelo. He has gotten so into the habit of it that he could shave looking at a portrait of Angelo."

The Turin house was as wonderful as the castle of La Brenta. You could watch passers-by from behind heavy curtains. They paced up and down the square. Some were ordinary citizens, others, informers. They all looked alike. You had to be pretty sharp. Carlotta had great fun.

In contrast she did not like the "guests" one bit. They waited till night to come scratching on the back door like rats. As soon as they were near the fire and had a cup of coffee, they became unbelievably proud. They leaned back against the chimney, stretched out their legs so that the costly material of their trousers held by straps under their feet was taut; they gestured to show off their ruffles, but at the slightest noise in the street or tremor of the *portière,* they were suddenly silent and showed faces which belied their words. They were handsome men; they knew it; indeed this was the only thing they did know—this and how to talk. The revolution was a way to get ahead; the important thing for them was to stay alive.

Carlotta had learned a lot in the solitude of the Piedmontese castle, especially all the delicious element to be found in a plot when you have the wit to make of it something heroic. "You're wrong," said the Duchess. "Such show-offs can't help believing in action, and their lives are so necessary to them that they're all the time inventing precautions against risking them. Exactly the precautions we lack: let's take advantage of their inventions. It would be too stupid to leave them an open field just because of a little bullet we didn't know how to duck. How do you expect to avoid being made a fool of, which is worse than death, if you don't know what they're like?"

Carlotta was critical of the liberals. She thought them niggardly even in their pride, which was, nevertheless, great.

One evening when there was no meeting, a knock sounded at the back door. Theresa went to open it as the knocking, although weak, continued and seemed to be a call. It was a boy who until then had passed as a simple collector of flowered vests. The vest he was wearing had been torn by a dagger which had just missed his heart. The wounded man was settled in Theresa's bedroom and little Lavinia was sent immediately to Doctor Paolo Bottachini whom they were sure of. He arrived a quarter of an hour later. Lavinia had been stopped two or three times in the streets by police patrols whom she had gotten rid of with a candid smile. The Duchess praised her by stroking her hair for more than five minutes. The wounded man had lost consciousness. Bottachini probed his wounds and announced that he was beyond hope. He even prepared an opium wine immediately. "If he comes round," he said, "he'll shout and struggle; the spectacle of his agony will terrify you. At the slightest sign that he's regaining consciousness, administer this potion. We must relieve his pain." After speaking these imprudent words, Bottachini was weak enough to let it be understood that he was listening attentively to the noises in the street. As everything was very calm in the environs, he decided to remain at the dying man's bedside. The Duchess thanked him for his devotion, insisting that they were only weak women and might lose their heads; she went out to get smelling-salts for everybody. She returned in a crazed state. "I don't know who opened the front door," she said, "but there are five riflemen in the vestibule downstairs and I saw the shako of an officer in the chasseurs coming upstairs. Come quickly. Follow Theresa. You know where to take him." Bottachini didn't need urging. Carlotta listened for the noises on the stairs. "They must be coming up like cats," she said to herself, "you can't hear a thing." She waited very boldly. She prepared a remark and a look for the moment a soldier would put his hand on her shoulder. She regretted that she did not have a knife. Theresa returned. "I got the point," she said, "and I slipped him out onto the shit. Just smelling his boots he'll be puking for a week."

"But this won't make up for our blunder," said the Duchess. "I should have understood right away that a dagger isn't a soldier's weapon. This boy was on his way from a meeting where I've been betrayed; he was coming to warn us. Bottachini had opium all ready in his fob and I'm sure that while exploring his wounds he did all he could to make them mortal. I let myself be touched by the poor young man's eyes rolled back in his head, and in our situation you must never be touched by anything."

She tried for several hours to get the dying man to speak, occasionally with great brutality. He gave up the ghost in her arms.

During the scenes which followed the doctor's hasty departure, Carlotta was often nauseated, but she made it a point of honor not to leave Theresa's little room. Finally, she said to herself: "Don't be more of a royalist than the King. This boy who had the strength to come this far could very well have stopped at some doctor's who was not a Carbonaro and trumped up something about a sneak thief. He passed twenty bells which he could have rung. He came and knocked on our door because he had something to say, and if we give him the means to do so now, he'll be content. Even if to help him do so, you've got to dirty yourself with a little blood." She had noticed that in pulling off Bottachini's bandage, the Duchess had gotten blood all up the sleeves of her blouse.

It was soon evident that it was fruitless to continue soliciting the poor young man for information. At daybreak Carlotta was drawn to the window by the noise of two horses peacefully crossing the Piazza San Carlo. Angelo and Giuseppe, whom Lavinia had gone to warn in the neighborhood, were approaching. They buried the body in the garden. Giuseppe was malicious enough to raise a large piece of grass sod with the shovel which he then simply let fall back on the grave. Two hours after this funeral, which was modest but full of dignity in the details, Giuseppe, wearing an orderly's uniform, drove the traveling-coach with all curtains drawn along the Susa road. He returned two days later about six in the evening. He went down the crowded Corso and returned to the stable. The coach was thoroughly besmirched by the reddish mud in which one often gets mired crossing Monte Cenis.

Bottachini was repaid by quite a long letter from the Duchess. "Things in writing last," she said to Carlotta. "He must stay scared for a while. Besides, he must be compromised. We must mention this letter I'm writing him all over town. His bosses will call him to account." After an affectionate reproach: "You did well to frighten us," she said: "We doubled our care and an hour after your departure, there was no need to have recourse to the little vial you left. The dear boy had recovered his senses enough to ask us to do him the service of getting through to France. As he seemed very courageous, we attempted the operation, which succeeded beyond our wildest hopes." There followed four lines in which great intimacy seemed to be concealed beneath the formulae of mere civility.

In the week following these events, Carlotta remained crouched on her bed for long hours in a state of charming disorder which she could see reflected in the mirror. Her heart was full of tender feelings. One evening she went down to the garden and tried to raise the carpet of sod that Giuseppe had let fall on the grave. But the roots of the grass had already gripped the earth once more. She began to look at Angelo with eyes whose languor, which she exaggerated, like a child, was somewhat comic.

Angelo was not pleased to see Carlotta and her husband.

"Steadfast in misfortune," he said to himself. "I can't claim that the castle isn't big enough for them and me too. They'd retort that there are thirty-four bedrooms—which everyone knows. Good-by to all the fine dreams in which I am myself so deliciously!" He had the table set in the main drawing-room. Despite its name, it was a room of modest dimensions; however, candles made a brilliant show thanks to a Venetian crystal chandelier.

"They're playing with words," said Carlotta. "There were engagements between advance guards, which are being called battles. They strut about all the time because three *bersaglieri* shot at something they took for an Austrian. When you know what really happened, there's nothing to crow about. Marcaria was occupied by a battalion of the Aosta brigade, a company of chasseurs and four cannon. The rest of the brigade camped beyond the Mincio. The second brigade was in San Martino. We got this from young Cervignasco, who's on Borda's staff. He brought more than fifty orders, all contradictory, to the supposed battlefield. A cavalry party had been stationed on the road, their picketed horses guarded by two mounted sentinels. Advancing in the open, Polish skirmishers fire a few shots on the horsemen. The sentinels retreat hastily, the other horsemen lose their heads, giving the uhlans time to run up and capture those who hadn't escaped. They thought that they were being attacked by the entire Austrian cavalry. 'I didn't see so much as a cat,' little Cervignasco told me, 'and I didn't see a single officer where he should have been.' This happened in the center of the Piedmontese army. On the left wing sharpshooters see a troop of peaceful miller's boys; they take them for dragoons of the guard and open fire hastily; a cannon shot is interpreted as a signal and a battalion and a cavalry regiment make way to leave the rest of the army room to deploy."

"You don't understand a thing about war, my love," said Gianpaolo. "An army is always a bit nervous; it always happens that way. Austerlitz began by grenadiers shooting hop-vine props for more than two hours. They were beginning to waver before these stoical wooden sticks when they met the Russians in flesh and blood and did marvels. That's not the point."

"I know very well what he means," she said. "The word games which I'm telling you about show their lack of desire to play the real game."

"I'm with you there," said Gianpaolo. "Charles Albert is an absolutist. He made common cause with the Revolution. He's waiting now for the end of the war, and he wants to finish it off without too many dismissals so that the revolution will be liquidated. It's not his troops that make him anxious. He knows very well that some of them will fly the coop like anyone else, but that they're better than most others. He's less certain when he thinks of all the free corps which have doubled his army. A crowd of twenty-year-old generals have been made in Milan. You're a field marshal at twenty-one in these legions; you skip from journeyman zinc-worker to lieutenant colonel. You won't deny that we're at the origin of these spontaneous promotions. It's our work and, for my part, I'm pretty proud of it. It's the only chance of getting control again some day but, just between us, all these crusaders, these *crosciati,* aren't worth the rope to hang them. Whether they come from the house of Savoy or the house on the corner it's always the same story: *Principi, principini, soldati cannoni, principi principini, palazzi giardini.* These tin-plate aristocrats think of nothing but installing themselves in the *Signoria* palaces. I know they've got to be in with us. But don't be surprised if you find them less flexible. They believe in their gold braid. The proof is that they keep adding to it. They've got sixteen-star generals. You'll see when they have to slip back into the ranks. I agree with you. We must strike. But do you know what I said? 'Strike, but coolly and very hard.'

"You know little Cervignasco? Little Cervignasco is very nice, but what is he? An aide-de-camp. He races on horseback from one spot to another. Perfect if you want to know what twenty Royal Cavalry horsemen or two rifle companies have been up to. And that's only what the horsemen or the riflemen were doing when he passed them because how could little Cervignasco know what they did afterward, running off as he does on his horse? I saw the Marchese Gerolamo Liamina. You don't like him, but he's a gentleman of the bedchamber. He told me that Charles Albert knows everything I've just told you perfectly. He named Allemandi general-in-chief of the free troops. He's sending them to the southern Tyrol, where, he says, they'll find a war more suited to their tastes. Charles Albert has known Allemandi for thirty years and distrusted him for thirty years."

"I had the pleasure of meeting Allemandi," said Angelo.

He recounted his adventure.

"You'll drive me crazy," said Carlotta. "What were you doing in Brescia? And especially the week of the uprising? Don't you know that at moments like that you must let the people cool off? That you can't touch them for two weeks?"

"I'd be in favor of treating them like the plague for a good month," said Gianpaolo. "You've got to think of the ones like your butcher's boy who discover hidden talents in themselves; they never stop. You can take care of them, but not till everyone's let go of them. I didn't think Allemandi so adroit. He's an arch-revolutionary. Generally they don't see details. I must admit that he put his finger on it this time. If you had been cut to pieces, he would have been in a fine position to liquidate his rivals."

Carlotta wanted to know everything Angelo had done since leaving Turin.

"I ran after Giuseppe who didn't wait for me and who took all my starched shirts."

"Stay with us," she said. "If I lose sight of you now, I'll die. There are still a hundred or so imbeciles who think they are doing business and will be irretrievably compromised in a week. To them you're just like any other man, that is to say, a means to success."

"I'll tell you why we came," said Gianpaolo. "The war everyone's making such a fuss over is only the fifth wheel. However, here are the facts: the period of naïveté is past; they thought that Radetzky was going to give them everything on a platter. They've changed their tune. Carlotta has just told us about the Marcaria affair, which happened three weeks ago. They thought they were taking Mantua. Finally, they took Goito and pushed the advance guard in the direction of Mantua as far as Sacca. The first columns of our left wing commanded by Lieutenant General Count Broglio and composed of Savoy and Savone brigades reached the Mincio only last Sunday. They took Mozambano; they rubbed noses in front of a hill, and the Austrians retreated peacefully to Verona. That was their plan. Radetzky hadn't the slightest intention of fighting between the Adige and the Mincio. They didn't force him to do so. Let them strut as much as they wish: he did what he wanted. They claim he feared intervention from France. He feared nothing of the sort. He feared a little strategy. But Charles Albert doesn't fight, or more exactly doesn't make his troops fight, except to make conversation. Why should France intervene? She has no interest in seeing Piedmont a great power. Charles Albert wants to talk. That's why Radetzky went quietly back to Verona. Each time Charles Albert arrives in front of a town or a fortress, as at Peschiera, he talks. He says: 'Surrender!' They don't surrender?

He's not terribly angry; he's bored. He says to himself: 'Another chance to start a conversation lost.' There is only one possible interlocutor: Radetzky. Who else do you think the King can talk to? Mazzini is indeed in Milan, but Charles Albert is a Faust whose heart has been disputed for more than twenty years by two irreconcilable forces: Mazzini and Metternich. One wants to rediscover the Carbonaro of 1821 in the King; the other, the grenadier of the Trocadero. Charles Albert has been serenading Mazzini for twenty years now, or rather they've been serenading each other. A king who has mobilized his equipment train and blown up bridges (because he does blow up bridges, but too late) no longer wants to serenade."

"I saw Semiramis," said Angelo. "I was at the barber's. I heard cymbals. We all went out, our cheeks covered with soap. She went by decked out as the Republic, followed by her Neapolitans."

"Belgiojoso? Don't laugh too hard at the Princess. Obviously, she's zero in Milan. The majority of the Milanese are monarchists. But the woman has a great deal of influence on these unfortunates. A doctrine which demands for the people the right to be as bastardly as a king has every chance of getting a hearing from those who have never received a thing. We'll have trouble with the Princess. You remember Bondino?"

"Brutus à la Rose?"

"Yes, Brutus à la Rose."

"He was in London."

"He was in London, and he's spent the last few years in Marseille staying with a certain Luigi Balluppi, an exile married to a Frenchwoman."

"Weren't there some rumors about this Bondino to do with the citadel of Turin? Wasn't he supposed to have sold it for a hundred thousand lire?"

"Pure calumny, that fatal sore, every day wider and deeper, favorite weapon of the tyrant. Even in our liberal party there is no lack of men unscrupulous in their choice of means. They lie and slander out of self-interest, ignorance, or incapacity—incapacity to find the men who are really to blame—and set themselves against men whom their violent passions discover and sacrifice. Remember what was said, even in our house, about Piero Marocelli when he came out of the Spielberg, even though badly hurt and with a wooden leg. Even Mazzini lent an ear. You never know when it will be worth while to start lending an ear. Bondino loves the people, but he loves them profoundly and not with this passionate love of effervescent youth which goes flat later with the deceptions of mature age and in the end, impregnated by bile, degenerates into ambition and loses itself in the violence of unprincipled demagogy. He loves the people; he never ceased conspiring for them, but with the defiance of an experienced observer and the calm of a philosopher studying men before delivering himself into their hands; he was armed with suspicious clairvoyance and circumspect in the choice of his allies, valuing their number far less than the sincerity of their devotion. He's a far cry from Mazzini, who wants to inaugurate a revolution based on love, to apply poetry to the seizure of power, and to draw inspiration from the school of tender Germany.

"You had other fish to fry at the time, but do you remember something that happened soon after your return from France? You used to go to Fenestrelle quite often, I believe, or, more exactly, to the first house in the hamlet of Agnelli, to a blond fellow's with a long mustache."

"You know as much about this as I."

"I'll tell you from whom I got it. Not Carlotta."

"I would, for that matter, have been incapable of saying where you went. All I knew was that you used to go off. That was the period when General Bonetto had decided to make us pay dearly for all the indignities he had swallowed at our house in the Piazza San Carlo."

"I did indeed go to Agnelli to see a blond fellow. His name is of little importance."

"Still less because I know it; it's inscribed on our lists. He's in our organization. That's not the point. We had not yet contacted him when you were in touch with him. One evening, or rather, one night (it must have been about three in the morning), you were coming down from Agnelli, on foot, naturally, and you went to get your horse in the stables of the Croce di Savoia, where you used to leave him. But you usually picked him up earlier; this time you were late. You knocked on the door. Fortunately for you,

you had agreed on a signal with the stable boy and you took care to knock the prearranged signal. Nevertheless, when the door was opened a crack you found yourself face to face with the barrel of a pistol. You must not have thought this worthy of notice, nor the fact that there were men in the stable in the process of unballasting the public carriage from Montgenèvre of four or five bales of paper which it had been carrying hidden under the floor of the coupé. These were Bondino's proclamations. And for us (for this was well before my marriage, although I had already been in the organization at least four years), for us, this—let's call it coincidence— this encounter of yours with the proclamation was, how shall I say? . . . In some way prophetic."

"Don't you find the word a bit grand?" said Angelo. "I can't see what a prophet could have to do with the encounter of a poor bastard and some bales of paper. I was a pretty poor bastard after my return from France. I had arrived here in no small state of exaltation. I thought I had found fraternity, which was described in our organizations by a formula which I still use a lot when I'm sad: 'The point of contact of circles of natural liberty tangent to other circles of natural liberty.' Above all I found that people thought they could act with impunity, that there was organized idolatry in the very heart of our meetings, and that the relation of superior to inferior in our liberal society prevented good manners."

"Let's say symptomatic if the word prophetic displeases you. But I'll stick to symptomatic because Bondino always wanted to meet you."

The crack of a gunshot, immediately followed by a second report, shook the echoes of the mountain.

"That's the master of the posting-station," said Angelo. "I found him this morning sawing off the barrels of a fine English gun. He wanted to put some venom into it. What *mylord* did he get this gun off? He came to show me how he had succeeded."

"I always wondered why there was a posting-station down below since there's no road from here on," said Gianpaolo.

"We're the ones who called it a posting-station. No stage-coach company would ever put an office in such a spot. It's a stable like any other—Michelotti keeps three mules there for hire at his own risk. You can go to Switzerland by the mountain path and the

Baranca pass if you really want to. Sometimes people really want to. There's a charge. The old Pardi who came to set himself up in these stones under Amé the Red or Hambert the Holy had, I believe, unique ideas about international trade and flights into Egypt."

"I was telling you that Bondino always wanted to meet you; he wants to more and more at present."

"Isn't this a bit exaggerated: he doesn't even know me."

"I mentioned the blond man with the long mustaches in the hamlet of Agnelli; I could mention your enterprises over toward Ivrea; those are far more secret."

"I have the maddening sensation that someone's been looking at me through a keyhole for years."

"I beg you, my love!" said Carlotta. "Go right to the point. Angelo suspects me and I can't bear it."

"Angelo doesn't suspect you, Carlotta; he's no puppet; he understands that it's not a question of spying, but of love. Bondino loves him. Angelo has known me long enough to know that I would have warned him twenty times if I'd warned him once had it been a question of anything else. You yourself, Carlotta, who are so fond of him and from whom, you must admit, I have no secrets, would have had no trouble chosing between Angelo and me if you weren't sure of Bondino and my intentions. I've been received in this house as a brother for more than six years now, and could I have been a malevolent dissembler for all that time? And you, my love, could you have been? Who would believe it?"

"I can't go so fast," said Angelo. "I'm still back at that love which confuses me."

"If you want to make me ridiculous," said Gianpaolo, "go ahead. Did I spend much time making idiotic statements to you on our journey to Rome?"

"We amused ourselves like two young dogs in the Papal States. But your old philosopher . . ."

"Giuseppe is his right hand."

"Giuseppe always has to be part of someone's anatomy. And what does Bondino, this circumspect observer of yours, want of me in exchange for his love?"

"It upsets me that you're taking it this way. Perhaps I was a bad messenger . . ."

"Not at all. The very best. Then I'll take it the way you prefer. What does Signor Bondino want of me?"

"Courtesy, that's all. He sincerely loves you as you are. He would like to have a calm, unhurried conversation with you here in the course of which he would explain certain things."

"I'd be greatly honored."

"Would it inconvenience you if he were accompanied by his secretary or governess (as he's an old man), and in addition, a Signor Cerutti who helps him with all the apparatus of his organization?"

"They'll be welcome with him. Nevertheless, as you saw, my household consists of Signora Michelotti. She did very well this evening for the three of us, but for a larger party, especially if there's a lady, Carlotta must be the mistress of the house and see that our guests are comfortable."

"Bondino will bring along his own servants; we knew that you were alone. I'm delighted by your decision. We have only one point left to discuss which could lead to argument if you were pusillanimous, but you're not. The leaders of the party are at present in a perilous situation. It's no hyperbole to say that they've got a bead drawn on them. Someone will have to succeed them and right now people are trying to get rid of the heirs. Bondino is adored and protected by his faithful followers. There are three or four of them, I think. They are good, simple fellows. We won't even see them. They could bivouac in the downstairs rooms where we never go. They'll get their own food and do their own cooking."

"We won't quibble over four or five men," said Angelo, laughing.

He got up at six in the morning. There was a ray of light under the door of Carlotta and Gianpaolo's room. As soon as Angelo's boots creaked on the landing, Carlotta peeked out.

"Where are you going?"

"To get the milk."

"I brought you some little cigars; come here; I'll give them to you."

"Is your husband still asleep?"

"I woke up. I found a charming little Ariosto in the cupboard."

"It's Lavinia's."

"I'm reading the story of the Knight near Damascus."

"You slept well?"

"Magnificently. What are those birds whose name you told me the last time I stayed here? They make a noise like a drum?"

"Fern owls. They make their nests in the eaves. There are thousands of them."

"Turn around," said Carlotta, "I'm in my nightgown, and slip your hand through the door and you'll have your cigars."

Angelo went down through the short cuts of the park. He crossed the Roman bridge. He found Michelotti cleaning his famous gun.

"What's up?"

"A thin bastard, from Novara."

"What was he up to?"

"Slunk off. He didn't like my gunfire a bit."

"You fired at him?"

"You think I'm that stupid? The coach dropped him beside the big beech before going up to the castle. Come on, now! He would have had to have done a lot more for me not to notice anything. He whittled matches all afternoon with his knife."

"What do you put in your gun to make so much noise?"

"Black powder. I've told you before, with short barrels, it even gives your fleas a shake. I aimed high. He didn't understand a thing. He wondered what the devil I was. Someone signaled to him this morning from a window. He left happy as a king."

"Four or five like him are going to be coming."

"Let them come."

The hawthorns were in bloom.

Climbing back up to the castle, Angelo met Carlotta.

"I wasn't joking yesterday evening," she said. "I haven't said anything about you. I never talk to Gianpaolo about you. I never talk to anyone about you."

"Where is Giuseppe?"

"In Turin, but not in the house on the Piazza San Carlo."

"He's going to come with . . . ?"

"No."

"What's he doing in Turin?"

"He's interviewing people. He has a very high rank. Well above Gianpaolo's."

"How long has he been in this . . . ?"

"He has one of the lowest numbers. One of the first ten. He was in the organization when he was still in France."

"What do you know about it?"

"I heard him talk about Manosque with Bondino."

"Perhaps because Bondino was in Marseille recently."

"No, it was about you. But Giuseppe saw my embroidered sleeve when I took a cooling drink from a tray that was offered to me. I was behind him. He looked at me and didn't say another word."

"How about you? Have you been in it a long time?"

"Since I was married."

"You were at the Ansaldis' in Novara?"

"Yes. Did you find the box of little cigars I left for you on the dresser in my room?"

"Giuseppe was at the Ansaldis'?"

"Yes. Lavinia is jealous. Sometimes she hides the poor little presents I leave behind."

"Whom is he interviewing in Turin?"

"People you wouldn't speak to who must be spoken to."

"What was decided at the Ansaldis'?"

"Nothing. There were a lot of people there. Only you were missing."

"And the police, I hope!"

"What do you have against the police? They belong to whoever pays them."

"What kind of money did you pay them with?"

"I don't know."

"But you're sure you have the police up your sleeve?"

"Absolutely sure. I took part in various conversations. You're prudent and I'm glad. I was afraid to find you'd flown into a passion as usual; I would have been unhappy. No one can block our path; there are too many interests at stake."

"Who thought of me?"

"Giuseppe. He has spent his entire life at your side in a subaltern position, and he did very well just loving you."

"Then even in the Agnelli period he was watching me?"

"The Agnelli period is the Agnelli period for you alone. You were amusing yourself. Your horse carried you down the valley gaily each morning. Some people have stuck to the idea of overthrowing the King of Piedmont."

"What have they done with that blond man?"

"Nothing. He signed up with us."

In the afternoon Gianpaolo suggested a game of billiards.

"I must go out," said Angelo. "Get some practice; I'm your man for this evening."

"You're going out?" said Gianpaolo, with the air of someone caught in an embarrassing situation. "I wish you wouldn't," he added. "Our guests may arrive any moment."

"As soon as all that! Where are they coming from, then? And how did you get word to them? I hear Michelotti beating on his anvil down below. He's the only one who could have carried a note to the posting-station at Cervatto. Are you a sorcerer?"

"No," said Gianpaolo laughing, "but I'm timid. Or say I'm timid with you. I know it's the most ridiculous thing in the world, but I can't help it—when I've got to admit something to you, I put it off and put it off, as if I had no pride at all, until I'm cornered. I always hope that Providence will get me out of it. However, I'm your friend. But it's hard to forget what you meant to us during the heroic period. I'm only a few years younger than you, but your education, the milieu in which you lived (when I was still cutting banal algebra classes at the Liceo Beatrice-Victoria you were already a cadet, and had even been in the famous square detachment of the review on the Campo Martio which so impressed Charles Felix after the attempt against the Austrian military attaché), your mother, your famous mother, everything to do with the passionate love which the soldiers had for you, your departure for France, our memory of a sort of Renaud, Roger, Roland gave to you . . ."

"Here we are back in the Ariosto you were reading this morning," said Angelo. "The book's full of flying machines. Nothing surprises me anymore . . ."

"It's much simpler than that. There was a man with us in the coach that brought us here. I never saw Bondino as impatient to meet someone. Usually other people beg to see him and he takes his time. He wanted to be told right away, and by word of mouth, of your acceptance or refusal (in which case he would have been inconsolable). And I didn't dare bring this man to the castle or admit to you that he was awaiting your decision outside or that I signaled to him this morning by waving a towel out my window."

"How romantic!" said Angelo. "You're right, it won't be long before they arrive, but since you assure me that they don't have a flying griffon at their disposal, I clearly have the afternoon to myself."

"May I accompany you?"

"Now you've hit upon *my* timidity," said Angelo. "I'll admit something to you as well. You must not go by the appearance of colonels when they're attacking at the head of their troops. There is no one more sentimental than I. Do you know what I'm going to do? I'm going to make a fool of myself over little field flowers. I'm going to stride across the moors and let the wind ruffle my hair. It would upset me to have you see me in such an unflattering delirium. Admit that your respect for me was severely battered (Thank God! For I prefer your friendship) during our official journey to Rome when I used to dismount to pick periwinkles. On this score I'd like to ask you a question: Were you already in the organization when you suggested that you accompany me to Rome?"

"I was still in rhetoric class when I signed up. At the Liceo we received secret proclamations and membership lists."

"That was clever."

"We were moved by the philosophical value of the arguments proposed. Others had made such an appeal to our feelings; these were addressed to our intelligence."

"By clever I meant your suggestion to accompany me to Rome."

"I'll be completely frank: I did make a complete, objective report of the circumstances and results of your mission. It was evident to me that Bondino held you in high esteem. I knew that we could not do without you."

"No need to make excuses, dear friend, I don't detest cunning— quite the contrary."

Angelo did indeed spend his afternoon looking for little flowers.

Early the next day he was in his room oiling the springs on his pistols with an oily rag when Gianpaolo knocked on his door.

"I wanted to ask a favor of you. What admirable weapons you have!"

"The best thing about them is their rapid trigger," said Angelo.

"I thought the saber was your favorite weapon; you use a pistol now and then?"

"When the game's not worth the candle. A saber pays homage. It gives your adversary a chance. These tools leave no room for chance."

"You've come to despise people to this degree?"

"It was hard for me to at first. Now I manage."

"Did you tell me that Michelotti was very devoted to you? Or did I invent that?"

"I don't remember having told you anything like that, but the owner of the supposed posting-station would indeed get himself cut to bits for me."

"What a shame! I don't want to deprive you of him. Is there no one else in the neighborhood?"

"No one else. You've got to go over the Cervatto ridge before you find a good strong man. Why?"

"Someone's got to fetch some papers in Switzerland."

"Michelotti will do the job very nicely. It's his line of work. You've only got to pay the tariff."

"I hesitate to deprive you of a friend for a considerable length of time."

"No scruples, old fellow. Duty above all else. He must go to Switzerland?"

"He must. And quite far there."

"Don't hesitate. If you have the slightest difficulty, tell me, and I'll intervene."

At table Angelo inquired about the success of the affair.

"He was very nice," said Gianpaolo. "He accepted right away. He's even left already."

The afternoon was calm. Only the wind hummed.

That evening Angelo, on his way up to bed, had reached the landing outside his room when he heard someone calling from the foot of the renowned stairs. He leaned over the bannister. At the bottom of the well of lacy darkness was Carlotta, golden yellow in the light of a candelabrum.

"You just called to me," he said, "in that charming voice you had when you were a little girl."

"You're talking with your tender voice too," she said.

"What do you want?"

"I must have wanted what you just gave me."

The next day Bondino arrived. He was an enormous man. He was crotchety about a cloth skullcap he had wanted to cover his head with which was not to be found in the carriage.

Finally he looked at the castle.

"It's even better than I'd hoped," he said.

He looked at Angelo.

"You're better than I hoped too."

His tone was coarse and natural. Angelo noticed a sudden flush in the cheeks of the governess.

"Recently I've been thinking myself a perfect hypocrite," he said to himself. "This woman sees immediately and clear as day that I take pleasure in the vulgarity of her master. That's not so good."

Bondino was authoritarian and flexible. Ugly, he had an exquisite smile.

"You must have heard bad things about me," he said when he and Angelo were alone together. "I've had enemies for thirty years. It's still rumored that in '20 I pocketed one hundred and fifty thousand lire for the surrender of the citadel of Turin. It's true, but with extenuating details. First of all, I received only one hundred thousand lire. Second, I was not holding the citadel: I was in Genoa when it surrendered. A re-enlisted sergeant was in command of the garrison that revolted. He asked no one for advice. He got taken for a ride: it was worth more than five hundred thousand. In his place I wouldn't even have taken the money, but securities, signed papers. Yes, it was too late. I returned from Genoa to explain to the sergeant that, according to the rules of the game, you don't get something for nothing. If I took two thirds of the loot from him, it's undoubtedly because I was too persuasive. It would have been better if it had been credited to me. You'll hear other stories, but it's the same thing every time."

He asked to have his room changed. He didn't like windows which looked out on too deep a void. Something else: he was in the habit of sleeping on his right side, but only if he did not have to turn his back to the door. Besides, he had to spend the morning in bed, on account of his painfully stiff limbs: he needed an eastern exposure.

Angelo was very interested by Cerutti. He was a debonair old man, dressed to the nines. You could feel that he was capable of irony.

"There are certain things people won't admit to a gentleman," said the old man. "They admit them to me. I'll let you profit by them. Even if you put the boss in an archbishop's room or in the Pope's, he won't shut an eye (and I mean it in the singular) unless I station a sentinel at his door. Not from fear, but from imagination. He lived too long in a country of policemen; he's no longer capable of tasting the charm of risks and perils and unexpected turns of events. Admit to me that this is no place for him."

His eyes sparkled. He was expecting an imprudent reply. Angelo played dumb. "Nothing is safer than this solitary castle. You can see people coming a long way off. Anyway, the only other inhabitant besides me for ten leagues around is the little blacksmith who lives down below across the bridge in the estate buildings— and Count d'Aché took care to send him away (to Switzerland), on some pretext or other."

"That's more than sufficient," said Cerutti. "Count d'Aché usually makes idiotic moves. This is one of them. He also made my ears tingle with those pistols, the works of which you were carefully oiling; everyone has the right to oil a pistol, and everyone does so, sometimes for esthetic reasons: I've seen weapons with charming engraving on the trigger guard, love scenes; if you don't oil them, they rust."

"Do you want to see them?" said Angelo.

He conducted him to his room.

"Here's what I've always dreamed of and never had," said Cerutti: "a little spot all my own far from everything: men, women, children, widows, and orphans. Your pistols won't be the thing that gets you into trouble. The boss will give you a speech which begins: 'I congratulate you for the glory with which you are covering the holy name of Italy,' and ends: 'Keep your spirit free of the illusions which come from false friends.' This'll just be the beginning."

"I'm delighted to have met such a powerful personality," said Angelo. "But what does he want from me?"

"There's where you're inimitable," said Cerutti. "He's no fool either. Despite his three-point speeches, he knows how to eat humble pie. He asked me one day how you managed to appear naïve. I told him: 'He exposes himself to danger.' He replied: 'He'll be ruined.' "

"I have a panic-stricken fear of what's called virtue," said Angelo.

"Yes, but the people in whom the spirit of the times is incarnate ask curious questions when they're about to give us the reins. They want us to bring them a nice calendar with all the saints on it. In a time of revolution, death canonizes you. You'll tell me that it's easy to collect dead men. You're still alive; you're a rarity."

This little conversation enchanted Angelo. "I was afraid I'd be bored," he said to himself. "What could be more ugly than gunfire within these walls, which are made to echo? To think that I had already chosen my barricades, especially the narrow door leading to the tower and plotted a whole scheme of flags to signal to Michelotti (who is less of a fool than Gianpaolo, and who has gone to Switzerland just about as much as I have) that the battle was on. What a wild good time I'm having! What a good idea it is to despise people! What other passion could ever give me such happiness!"

Bondino was clearly playing weak-like. He went so far as to take certain remedies against the gout. After dinner he demanded some music. One of Cerutti's men who had a little screeching fiddle was summoned upstairs. Angelo, who had been expecting simple good will, always rather difficult on a violin, was astonished by the man's virtuosity. Constantly evoking emotions, the below-stairs informer did anything he wanted with his instrument, even changed it's soul. This change was visible on his face: he lighted up with tender nobility. He played Beethoven's German Dances.

"This is why I prefer hatred to love," Angelo said to himself. "I can be mistaken in love. But I can never be mistaken in hating those who have forced this man to abase himself in order to eat, and the others who leave him in his abject state, or force him deeper into it, making him believe that things will change."

He noticed that the governess's face came alive also. She was said to be English, even the daughter of the illustrious Savone, who, from his residence at Colbeck House had shaken the courts of Europe for more than twenty years by waving Italian revolutionaries under their nose. Others said she had been the terrible old man's young Egeria and that Bondino had inherited lock, stock, and barrel.

Angelo needed action.

"And why shouldn't it be emphatic?" he asked himself.

Cerutti's man was playing a mazurka, and succeeded perfectly with his low chords in giving the illusion of hoarse hunting-horns. Angelo asked Miss Learmonth to dance. She seemed disconcerted and blushed very prettily. But she rose and he took her waist, which, despite her age, did not lack charm. She fell in spiritedly with the joyous step, keeping up with Angelo. He no longer thought of politics.

"Who would have thought that this woman's hips were supple?" he asked himself.

He thanked her for having been willing to forget for an instant with him her austere and worrisome responsibilities.

"I'm Scottish," she said. "They dance to everything in my country."

Carlotta wanted to waltz.

The spy played a very romantic tune.

"What a handsome couple!" said Bondino when the waltz was over. "You were brought up together, am I not right?"

"That's the usual expression," said Carlotta, "but in reality he was at the Prytaneum and I was home with his mother, which is another school altogether. I never saw him. Let me add that he carried on an indecent relationship with his nurse and that she stood guard over him."

"An admirable situation. Admit that you were in love with him!"

"Not at all. Of course I had feelings. Looked at this way I was in love with my father. Angelo was always a handsome knight. Obviously he interested me greatly. Waltz once around the room with him and you'll see what I mean."

"I'll get back at you for that waltz once around the room, my dear; you can expect a fine bit of mischief. It's not my fault if I aged in a harness which has given me a paunch."

"I see that I must ask your pardon as quickly as possible," said Carlotta. "I was indeed in love. Without knowing it, I was in love with what you finally brought us. When Angelo departed for France, I dressed in black from head to foot. If anyone asked in a low voice: 'Who is that child in mourning for?' the Duchess replied in a low voice: 'For a bit of grandeur.' I imagined that one fine gesture was enough to create a republic. Or at least I believed, and I wasn't the only one, that a hundred plots make a revolution. I get a taste for reality from my mother, I believe. I don't mean to say that the feelings I express now were those I had as a fifteen-year-old child; but knowing that Angelo had gone into exile, and knowing that we conspired unceasingly and that, nevertheless, the king very clearly would die in his bed, with a shrewd successor sitting ready in an armchair at his side—by dint of all this, without going so far as to ask myself of what use grandeur was, I began to desire more efficacious methods."

"You're stroking me as if I were a cat, but without looking what way the hairs grow," said Bondino. "You think you're giving me pleasure, but you're doing quite the opposite. If I understand you correctly, you like men of influence, even if they're damned funny-looking."

"It's hard to understand certain of your feelings," Angelo said. "In your place I would accept Carlotta's hommage. She has spoken with a boldness which to me at least is admirable. You had already been in exile for a long time when she was fifteen. In other words, you knew how to weigh pros and cons when she still believed in a frontier between good and evil. Her father died because he refused to be calculating. As for me, she watched me prancing about stupidly, but covered with gold lace. You've winged her; good shot!"

"Winged her! . . . You can go wing all of Piedmont! But joking aside, I've often wondered how you spent your time in France?"

"There's no formal answer."

"I've had long conversations on the subject with our friends. We had a thousand suppositions."

"Without ever guessing the truth, I bet."

"As for the truth, or at least as far as appearances go, we're not totally without resources."

"Trust appearances."

"I have some bits of paper with the names of the people you

saw in Aix. Then you disappeared."

"I had cholera. In such cases, one disappears."

"That cholera has been much embroidered. Miss Learmonth and I were in Marseille. The town hardly smelled any worse than usual. We burned punk."

"Maybe your informers didn't know how to write on punk. It's difficult."

"I was in Turin when he returned home in full daylight," said Carlotta. "We weren't expecting him. We had opened a window to listen to a barrel organ. A horseman crossed the Piazza San Carlo and came toward us. We were transfixed. He seemed very pleased with himself. We wondered where he had gotten it into his head that he was no longer in danger?"

"There she goes off on another delirious blast," said Bondino. "She has told me enough about you to fill volumes. All her speeches incline me to believe that she married out of spite, and that she's selling you out of spite; but let's be honest; she's giving you away; it hasn't cost me a soldo."

He rose heavily.

"Let's go to bed."

He managed to be alone with Angelo on the landing.

"You don't like me," he said.

"I don't like vulgarity."

"You're wrong; I feast upon it."

"Good appetite."

"Listen to me carefully. You think you'll succeed by maintaining a distinguished reserve; I'm the one who's succeeding, not as I'd like to yet, but it's beginning to come. You love Giuseppe? I use him; for fifteen years I've been wiping my boots on your little darling. I've taught him to have a fine opinion of himself. He would do anything to maintain his self-esteem. He does anything I order him to. But he's not what I'm after: I have a thousand like him; it's you. You have only to say the word. I won't pay you peanuts. It's no subordinate post I'm offering you: I'll go on doing the dirty work; you'll go on riding horseback. You won't even have to fight; we're not going to fight; we're just letting things ripen. You'll be the flag."

"I have the highest esteem for Giuseppe," said Angelo. "I believe as I told you about Carlotta, that it's difficult for you to understand certain feelings."

"I understand all feelings, and, to fill in a gap in your thinking, I experience them. But I don't believe in them. As for esteem, it's not a feeling, it's a lack of intelligence. Here's something to put in your pipe: it's not your flesh and blood I'm after. There's nothing finer than a victim if you want to found a church; with a flick of the wrist you could be it. And for free. Think that over. Your little friend has thought it over very carefully."

The next day Angelo went in search of Cerutti. He found him in the billiard room.

"You didn't show your entire hand the other day," he said.

"Certainly not."

"I should have asked pardon for killing a man who was perhaps precious to you," said Angelo, "but how was I to guess that sometimes you disguise them as lancer captains?"

"Ah! You discovered that all on your own!"

"Your boss helped me."

"He let the cat out of the bag? You must be hellish quick on the trigger. Well, what do you think of our little system?"

"Perhaps a bit too gingerbready for my taste."

"Obviously it was a carom shot; but, come now, you're not someone who can be gotten by a direct shot. And don't forget, we needed a nice neat package, with blue ribbons if possible. The people are very sensitive to the wrappings; it gets them in the imagination. We could have sent a bullet your way a hundred times while you were out on one of your nature walks, but where's the fun in that?—you can't boast about someone bumped off on the sly. And I always say, there's nothing more lovely than a good dirge. I don't agree with you. I think the plot was quite well rigged. And I have a right to say so: I hardly did any work on it at all. I just used what was given me."

"The first thing you needed was something to fill the coffin with. You had someone," said Angelo, counting on his fingers, "the lancer I supposedly killed with a pistol shot. Was he one of your men too?"

"Scarcely. He represents the original investment. You can't do without that."

"Two, my friend the artillery commander."

"He was the dupe. There's always one of those too."

"Three: that captain who exhaled ugly noises when I ripped his ticking."

"So few of our people have any manners," said Cerutti. "Besides, I never thought you'd get as far as him. Up to the last minute he certainly had no idea whom he was dealing with. Your artilleryman was the one who ruined everything. The minute you get amateurs into the act, all hell breaks loose. In principle, it was to have been a game of billiards, played off your temperament. We had your foster brother up our sleeve. He explained everything to us. He told us: 'He'll leap at any chance to meet us face to face.' I gave you a chance. The Piedmont cavalry love you to death: I have you murder a Piedmont cavalryman; I mount him on the head of a pin; I say about you: 'What a dirty scoundrel! To save his skin he murders a poor little soldier!' I organize a little chorus on this refrain. You come out to tell us: 'Pipe down there, I'm not what you think I am!' We catch you and hang you. While we're hanging you, you shout: 'Long live Italy!' Not in so many words, obviously, you can do better than that; I'll admit you've had the education I missed out on, and for the first time when you're on the gallows, you get some good out of it. That's all there is to it. We don't need anything more. You know how it is with a pig? You can eat everything except the squeals. Well, we've found a use for the squeals. All we needed was that artilleryman! Without him, in my system, there would have been only one corpse, not three."

"I would have preferred it that way," said Angelo.

"One corpse, and that one would have been you, naturally. Your friend knew you well. He had warned me. As soon as the artilleryman showed on the scene, he foresaw that you would get as far as the lancer captain. He wanted to go whisper a little advice in his ear. I said: 'No, no.' He told me: 'All right, but your fellow will get himself shriveled like a pancake.' He was right because in our work if there's one thing worse than an amateur, it's a zealot. My captain had your artilleryman in the bag; he just had to sit tight. But the beautiful burial had gone to his head. He'd have killed his own father and mother; everything was rosy. It's always better to stay cool."

"Good advice," said Angelo to himself.

At the lunch table they chatted about the temperature and the spring. The day was languorous with the first gust of heat.

Bondino spoke of the ivy covering the house. He said that it was unhealthy and disturbing; undoubtedly full of rats; perhaps even full of snakes. He praised English ivy, which was always agreeable. Miss Learmonth seized the idea so heatedly that there were several words she could not find to express her sentimental thoughts in their entirety.

They retired for their siesta almost on tiptoes. Angelo waited a good while before going out a little door which opened directly onto the rocks of the Mastellone. He crossed the brook on some stones and climbed the mountain. Tall hawthorns bordered the path; behind them he could make his way without being seen.

The hawthorns were in flower. Already April shone tenderly in the grass. After a full hour's climb through exquisitely fragrant pastures, Angelo went down into a vale toward a hut made of branches. Under this foliage Michelotti was plucking a grouse.

"I've been feeding off game birds for three days," he said. "They're easy to catch: they're making love. But they're thin. What have you been up to down there?"

"They were still talking this morning."

"Fun?"

"At first. Do you always feel like joking?"

"I haven't had much chance here."

"Four of them need calming more than the others. I intend to give a little speech to the others, and I want to save my breath."

"Do you want me to go look for my brother at Cervatto?"

"The less of your brother the better."

"May as well do without. If I'm free to explain the situation in my own way to those four characters of yours, they'll get the point right away even though I'm not a great talker."

While the grouse simmered in a pan, Angelo had a somewhat late but very enjoyable siesta.

It was already dusk in the valley when, after having eaten, they left the hut. They saw a rider also coming down the mule track.

"If that fellow made it over the Baranca on horseback, he's no slouch," said Michelotti. "Let's go see this marvel."

They hastened their steps. The rider noticed them and took something from the boot.

"The gentleman's nervous," said Michelotti.

He blew the man's gun from his shoulder.

The rider wheeled and then faced them. He had a pistol in his hand.

"I know him," said Angelo.

It was General Lecca.

"What's all this?" the general asked. "Are you reduced to waylaying people?"

He dismounted.

"Allow me to see what your animal is made of," said Michelotti. "Talk about roads, if you made it over the ridge with this nag, he's some parcel!"

"Just my dish," said Lecca, but he bridled.

He was delighted by the boy's astonishment. He explained that he was on his way back from Switzerland, but that on reaching the valley of the Anzo he had not dared ask for directions to La Brenta because of certain rumors, and that he had figured out the way by himself.

"Well," he said to Angelo, "is it true that they've gotten you in their clutches? It's rumored that you're hand in glove with Bondino, that he's staying with you, and that you're going to be the standard of this band of good-for-nothings. . . . I was coming to see you but all this shot the ground right out from under me. It seemed so extraordinary that I continued anyway, but without conviction, and if I hadn't run into you, perhaps I wouldn't have dared knock on your door."

"Bondino is indeed staying with me," said Angelo, "and he's made it quite clear that I'm under house arrest, but I came in search of the reinforcement of this little gun to do some house-cleaning."

He explained the situation.

"If I hadn't wanted to know the details of an affair which touches me deeply, I would have thrown out the whole works long ago."

"You're branded," said Lecca. "They tried to get you alive, then dead, and now they're making another small try, but what they want above all is to brand you with their own brand, and they've succeeded. Nothing's secret, especially when those who need publicity shout from the rooftops. It's rumored everywhere that Bondino is here with you, and he is. If you say that he came to do a little tatting, who'll believe you?"

"I sawed off the barrels of this gun," said Michelotti, "so that it will make more noise and that's exactly what it's going to do."

"Ah youth!" said Lecca. "I spent the best years of my life with a fellow who had guns, and when it came to noise, he was right up there with the greats, you can bet your life. But that didn't cut out the back talk. I'm with you if you want to go down, all three of us, and fill the old bird with lead; I'll pay my own way, but how will you go at it? Tell them they smell like rotten fish? They'll laugh. Kick them? It'd be like kicking a whale. You've got a public now. They've had two or three hundred agents circulating for a week now, publishing in advance the results of this famous conference. If you could see the mug on the guy they've got doing the job in the valley, it'd give you the shakes! Just let me tell you about my old friend Colonel Pardi; I'll stick my old comrade Pardi at the head of a column of good-for-nothings who are going to fly to assure the victory of the people (if there is such a victory!) it'll bowl you over (here I wink). Picture our good little fool of a friend Pardi pig-in-the-blanklet in compromise, should we ever need a nice little scapegoat. I got this blustering bully by the coattails. He turned to me. I'll be damned, but the fellow didn't stink of wine; his kind are lay priests and stink of printer's ink; they're worms that turn. He didn't like my 'Come now, young man!' one bit. But I held fire. There were a dozen mountain lads or so standing around, so doe-eyed and pure-souled that it made your mouth water, and they believed in this great plotter of a colonel. They were puzzling over his words, wondering whether they were fish, flesh, fowl, or good red herring. They didn't know which end was up. I said to myself: 'Maybe you're the one whose's the fool?'"

"Throw out Bondino, and they'll say you were greedy, that you wanted the biggest slice of cake; he'll label himself a gentleman with the biggest letters you've ever seen. Now, take your young friend who's playing rifleman with his gun (which he's rooked besides. Here, let me see. It was a fine English weapon. Why did you let him do it? You don't saw the barrels off a Hereford special, and a Brown into the bargain). All right, let's say that in a little while we get fed up, and he starts playing with that blunderbuss. If he demolishes the small fry, think how we'll look! We'll be classed for good and all as murderers of the people; they'll start teaching the fable of the aristocrat and the 'honest laborer' even in the primary grades. If he riddles Bondino's belly, it'll splatter all over everything. That fellow's always got a full gut, and he does business for too many people to be toted up pure and simple according to profit and loss. There are always high stakes behind this kind of socialist. Just between us, it's not up to you to do this clean-up job."

"Why not?" said Angelo.

"Because it'll be done by other people, specialists who don't work with a Brown with sawed-off barrels up to their ears in candor; manufacturers who deliver the goods clean and smooth because that's their business; men one must get rid of in the end, but that's another story. In a revolution, my friend, you've got to let the wolves eat each other. That's what Bondino's been doing up to now; and lately he's been trying to get you to be Little Red Riding Hood. You're worth more than that. That's precisely why I was coming to see you . . ."

Night was falling. The forest exhaled a deep sigh.

". . . you know my idosyncrasy," said Lecca. "You can't move a soldier anywhere near me without my having a mad desire to know how he's moving and why. I told you what I thought of Charles Albert. He doesn't trust his own military talents. He's right if he thinks of those who are going to criticize him from the first balcony, but he's wrong if he thinks about Radetzky. Fools are perfect in war. When he heard about the triumph of the insurrection in Milan, he should have advanced on Lodi as fast as possible and pursued the retreating Austrians. The Piedmontese were inferior in number, but puffed up like turkey cocks. Nothing was too good for them—sky's the limit—; they could have done anything, dared anything. It would have been a cinch. Even after uniting the garrisons and the detachments scattered on the shores of the Po and the Adda, Radetzky had hardly sixteen thousand men. Charles Albert, on the double, could have prevented the enemy detachments in northern and southern Lombardy from uniting on the Mincio. I would have stuffed a Piedmontese column along with a little nerve on the right bank of the Po and raced to Cremona.

The revolution would have caught fire everywhere (not Signor Bondino's revolution, but ours, the one where you can have a good time); on the way I would have picked up troops from Parma and Modena, Italian volunteers, and I would have stopped Wohlgemuth cold as he advanced on Mantua. A simple matter of imprudence. In war there's no keeping accounts. Either you throw your money out the window or else you do business and don't stick a whole lot of gold lace on your cap. This isn't my idea. Brune did it in 1800. With a flick of the wrist, he was on the right flank of the Austrian army, threatening their rear guard. There's real work for you! Not this smalltime stuff: send General Bès to Treviglio, push a cavalry regiment up to Cassano, have whole detachments of the army cross the Ticino, and thank you kindly, I'll wait for my escort before I make my triumphal entry into Lodi. To hell with triumphal entries! Expensive as short term loans, all of them!

"But that's not the point. The point is we know the gentleman in question—and without being mediums either. Whatever bender he goes on, he'll go home when it's over. If someone told me he had taken Verona, I would bet right off he'd lose it. Are we in agreement?"

"I don't understand the first thing about the movement of an army," said Angelo. "All I know, or, to be more exact, all I believe, is that the theory I learned in school is pretty useless in the field. But I've never been in the field."

"Stop there!" said Lecca, "I've seen you at work. When you came to hire yourself out at the Palazzo Borromeo, I took you for an amateur; the house was crammed with them. I stuck you with a job no one wanted. I said to myself: 'If he gets out of that, he's lucky!' You not only got out of it, but, I can quite literally say, you burned up the town.

"No, listen to me carefully: anyone can give orders, but to make oneself obeyed is something else again. I've had all kinds of bosses of all different stamps. I've been the boss myself. There's the kind that tells you: 'Forward!' when you know that for a trifle he would say: 'Retreat!' You'd attack like a crab. There's the kind that say: 'I'm scared shitless, but I'm going anyway.' That's the kind you follow and often end up leading. But you're being given a rag, tag, and bobtail; in five minutes all hell would break loose. Bondino is no fool. If he would have gotten his hooks into you, he would have used you for the same little game.

"But let's get back to the subject. I give Charles Albert three months. And at that I'm generous. Once this delay is over, he'll be sent back inside his own frontier with a kick in the . . . yes. I've gathered about a hundred men of your type and mine. Horses, supplies, and new weapons. No clubs and curule chairs. Just fresh air, leather saddles, well-furnished boots, and a little horse between your shanks. We'll make war on our own terms. To hell with everybody; we'll set ourselves up in a little corner of Trentino, and as soon as the Austrians cast off we'll give it to them on the right flank. The hussars of death if you wish. But something stylish and useful. Some little line that's a real parcel, as your friend who cuts guns to bits said."

He went into details. His little troop was in Bidogno at present, just beyond the Swiss frontier, two leagues north of Lugano; they were equipped, staffed with corporals, and ready to campaign. They had only to round the point of Lake Como, go up the valley toward Sondrio, and station themselves above Lake Garda. When the moment came, they could take off from there and not after sparrows either.

"You who always longed for the field of battle," thought Angelo, "here it is! War's what you've been preparing for for more than twenty years, and in particular one in which you won't have to subject your generous impulses to bookish strategy. Think of how upset you were, arriving in Milan, when you found that Hungarian courier with his pockets turned inside out. If you don't want to be reduced to this kind of murder, which is perhaps even profitable, don't let this chance slip by."

"I believe that it'll please you," said Lecca, who interpreted his silence correctly. "And you'll be killing two birds with one stone. You'll shut up Bondino and all his clique. If you strike at Verona, that'll show you're not on the side of the aggressors. There are quite a few young lads who would be happy to know this."

CHAPTER TEN

I'm with you," said Michelotti. "Besides, you need me. You can't go back down the La Baranca ridge. I know the little village you mentioned; good God, it must have taken you at least five days to get here; I'll take you back in three. I know all these nooks and crannies like my pocket and I have friends who will get us across Lago Maggiore. Show if you're really for the people. I too live on love and pure mountain water."

"I should be frank as well," said Angelo. "If Italy's to be made out of hot air, it'll be made without me. This'll be a picnic for me."

"My children," said Lecca, "imagine where we'd be if we had to stop and think of everyone's motives! I've always claimed that anyone having a good time does a bigger day's work than Napoleon. The day you cut the Austrian infantry to pieces, every thrust of your saber will be a fine one."

"I'll take you over the Rimelle," said Michelotti. "A good path for a Sunday stroll, but lead your horse by the bridle; easier that way."

A small icy wind enlivened the night. They climbed through pastures. The slopes of the Capezzone they climbed were entirely denuded. The other side, descending toward the Valstrona, was covered with beech forests. The trees, growing free at these high altitudes, reached gigantic proportions. They had no leaves as yet. Their buds, ready to open, reflecting the gleam of the stars from their varnished tips, magnified the scintillation of the heavens.

About one o'clock they reached a hut above the hamlet of Strona. Deepest night brightened the voice of the torrents. On all sides they heard the gush of streams. Far to the right above the shoulder of the mountains on what they took for the plain of Lombardy they saw the line of bivouac fires flaming.

"Those are Bava's reserves," said Lecca. "At daybreak, head us a bit more in the direction of Switzerland. I don't want to meet those people. There's no greater bastard than a territorial sergeant. If the patrols get wind of us, we'll have them at our heels all the way to the end of the world. Just try to explain something to a family man who thinks himself Julius Caesar!"

"They're not much," said Michelotti. "Of course there are patrols. That's not dogs you hear down there, now is it? But no need to fear. They're from Novara; they're scarcely even dressed as soldiers. Sweet as can be. Just look at me: I'm a deserter, and only lately I had a smoke with them, sitting right beside their guns. They talk about everything, except war. You mustn't think that everyone's screwed up so tight."

Angelo passed some exquisite hours on a litter of old beech leaves. Half asleep, he heard the roar of the streams and the rustle of branches in the forest. A murmur rose from below: the wind on Lake Orta.

Early the next day they arrived famished in Strona. It was a village of about twenty black houses. The walls were made of porous stone, which drinks in the smoke of the big soft wood fires customary in such small, sheltered mountain valleys.

"I have some gold in my belt," said Angelo, "but if I show it, we'll have our throats slit."

"Leave it be," said Lecca. "I have a few soldi."

"If we've got time to stop and chat five minutes," said Michelotti, "we can eat for free. Everyone knows me here."

He did indeed obtain a bucket of goat's milk. But the milk was full of hairs, and they had to pay two soldi to get a strainer.

"This is how you get the reputation of a milord," said Michelotti. "We'll never live down this strainer. Look at the fellow with the two soldi. His eyes are starting out of his head. We're going to be showered with questions. Let's drink up and get the hell out of here."

They had only to round the corner of a house and cut across a chestnut wood.

"I was intending to head straight for Stresa, but now that's out. A postilion leaves from here in a quarter of an hour. He'll undoubtedly carry your strainer with him and everything that's been imagined around it. One thing we can do is follow my first idea, settling for a bit more conversation, this time with the patrols, who will want to know why our throats are so delicate. We'll also have to explain to them why we have only one horse for the three of us. All in all, we'll have to explain a lot of things. But if you're big enough to hold a blunderbuss, what've we got to lose? Or else, we can go back up the mountain and look for another valley over behind there."

Angelo would have liked to meet a few good Piedmontese, even wearing reservists' caps, but the general preferred the mountain. "I hate to have someone cry 'Halt!' and 'Advance when ordered!' " he said.

The mountain they started up was steep and might have taken them three hours to climb. But after an hour the track they were following widened out and became almost invisible. When they reached the peak, they heard a little bell, and a spaniel bitch came to frolic about them. Following the small rust-colored animal, who lay flat at their feet every third step and then ran about shaking her ears, they reached a little sheepfold. The sky chirped larks. The sunlight was so beautiful that the sheep seemed made of gold.

They dropped the horse's bridle. He went to eat beside two donkeys. The shepherd gave them bread and cheese. He was a thick-set man so heavily bearded that only his twinkling eyes could be seen. To their prudent questions, asked mainly by Michelotti, he replied with a number of small enthusiastic exclamations. He licked his mustache vigorously.

A hundred paces off Angelo found the traces of a soldiers' camp. They had spent the preceding night there; the trampled grass had not yet sprung up. Undoubtedly they intended to return that afternoon or evening to the same spot. A stewpot and some pans were hidden under a tuft of hyssop.

The summit of the mountain consisted of a vast, entirely bare plateau, without shade or hiding-place. The path traced by the flocks crossed it in a straight line and was lost on the horizon in a soft azure haze.

"Let's look as small as we can," said Michelotti, "and keep walking. In an hour the sun will be beating down here like the devil. Nothing hides you better than sunlight."

They walked in the grass on the edge of the track, so as not to stir up the dust. About noon, behind a little undulation in the plateau, they discovered three stone houses built without mortar, white as old bones and deserted. One of these houses, however, seemed to be used as a church: a rough wooden cross was set on its roof. On the summit of another undulation, Lecca pointed out three red spots above the grass. The caps of the soldiers.

Michelotti wanted to go on as if nothing were there.

"We can go right under their nose. They won't see anything except the haze."

But Lecca preferred to stay hidden in the church.

"It's all very well for you and the colonel," said Michelotti. "You're gentlemen. But I don't like it; I've been watching you just now looking out all the windows. You think that if the soldiers come, they'll besiege us and we'll fight them off, make a lot of noise with our pistols and kill some poor bastard? Not me. Let's stay here if you want, but quietly. I have no title; I can't play big. You people know what Napoleon or the Pope would do in such a case; *I* only know what Michelotti would do, and those three fellows over there in their red kepis are three Michelottis, just like me. The last thing they're looking for is trouble; if we don't give them any, they'll take their siesta."

"I agree with you," said Angelo. "Admit to me that this flight from a strainer is pretty funny. It's already made us scale one mountain too many. All said and done, those soldiers are Piedmontese. Two of us three are Piedmontese, and you are a citizen of glorious Milan. We're all on the same side. As for Michelotti being a deserter, the Piedmontese adore deserters."

"Even when they shoot them," said Lecca. "I believe what you say, but they shoot them. What have you been doing in the last three weeks? There's no more Piedmont or Piedmontese: there are only people who shoot you in the back. You don't give a damn for anyone, but it's a miracle that you're still alive. God takes care of drunks and children. If you told me that the three red kepis were looking at each other like china dogs and that they were ready to exchange the desire to shoot each other for the chance of meeting other people to shoot, then I would believe you.

"But the golden age? Fat chance of that! This is the age of political parties. I thought Bondino had opened your eyes."

Finally, after waiting an hour in the cool little church, they saw the soldiers move off in Indian file.

"Now you're reassured just when I no longer am," said Michelotti. "They look as if they were returning to the sheepfold. The shepherd will paint us larger than life. Add to that the fact that they will be put out not to have seen us. Let's clear out as fast as possible."

They didn't slow down until they had begun to descend the other slope of the mountain through a very dark oak wood.

They spent the night in a village inn.

"I got some information," said Angelo the next morning. "The road that goes by in front of the door is the post road coming from Switzerland and going to Verbania on Lago Maggiore, two leagues from here. But at Verbania the lake is very wide. We've got to go up to Cannero to cross it. Let's rent a two-horse carriage, but with only one horse from the posting-station, and hitch up yours. Michelotti can drive. Two gentlemen driven by a coachman won't attract attention."

"You haven't digested what I told you yesterday in the church," said Michelotti, "but it's the truth; to most people, especially the people who may ask us questions, it would be much more natural if you weren't so chummy with me. Give me your soldi and I'll go arrange the deal."

"You've known him a long time?" asked Lecca. "How old is he?"

"Twenty-six. He's one of the numerous human beings my mother has impressed. I mean I've known him twenty-six years. He'll be very useful to us. He's a farrier and a bit of a veterinary."

Michelotti arrived with news. There was no danger of meeting soldiers on this side of the lake, but the roads were crowded with refugees from the other shore, where a number of skirmishes were going on, it seemed, as small Austrian garrisons clashed with partisans and the advance guard of Allemandi's troops. The innkeeper was taking advantage of the situation by refusing the horse and carriage until he got the wherewithal. Michelotti had brought him round, however, by talking shop, especially about contraband.

"I also said you were big wheels, but without saying anything specific. As he expects to get his knuckles rapped, and since he's made so much money lately that he doesn't know what he's up to, he was the one who uttered the word commissioner. I winked. We've got the horse and carriage. And we even have a ham and a demijohn of wine. But I give you my word of honor he thought of the ham all by himself."

The innkeeper came to bid them good-by. He was much impressed by Lecca's bulk. He pointed out that he had folded a large hunk of bread in a white napkin; he was completely at ease with Angelo whom he took for a clerk.

Half a league from the village they were obliged to look for a crossroad. They were in danger of death at every moment from the heavy traveling-coaches being driven at full tilt to Switzerland. One in front of them lost a chest which had been badly secured on the roof. It crashed to the road and just missed killing one of their horses. It was full of very richly embroidered women's petticoats which smelt good, even at a distance.

"They're really smoking them out over there," said Michelotti.

Thus they approached Verbania by roads bordered with flowering hawthorns. Thick weeping willows lashed the top of their carriage. The little town was full of noise. The church bell rang without haste, but without stopping either, with little well-spaced rings as if summoning the minister. They heard the rumble of numerous carriages rolling over the pavement, the nervous whinny of horses, the deep voice of coachmen, the bawling of a crowd which seemed to be composed of children crying in high-pitched voices.

Beyond the walls, the lines of sycamores bordering the road to Switzerland, which in ordinary times would have been used as a boulevard, were encumbered by every kind of vehicle. Certain low jaunting cars, on which were heaped bedding and even children, were drawn by big dogs who jumped in their traces and barked at the top of their lungs. Women of all classes, loaded with bundles or with their arms swinging free (which gave them a strange air, as if asleep), were walking along on foot. Certain of them, taking advantage of the fact that all the carriages were obliged to proceed at a walk, clung to the straps so that they were dragged along. Angelo noticed that the oval of their faces was far less perfect than in Piedmont. Some, although pretty, were square-jawed.

Here, too, the cross-country roads were deserted. A hundred paces from the highway to Switzerland, Michelotti could put the horses into a trot. In this manner they went along old crenellated walls, flanked by towers, and came into a neighborhood of kitchen gardens, vermilion vineyards, thick groves, and cypresses in which the morning wind purred like a huge cat.

From the top of a small rise and before going down onto its shores, they saw a good stretch of the lake. Furrowed by little pink waves, it was dotted by numerous flapping sails and black, flat-bottomed boats, slowly moving their legs like a cockroach on its back. All the furrows were directed towards their shore. On the other side the shore was covered with mist and smoke. There too bells rang without stopping.

After traveling along for more than two leagues, they reached the crowded road once more. Here there was no mob as at Verbania, but a long line of wagons, garden carts, tumbrils, a few coaches, and even elegant light buggies. The rapid carriages plodded behind the heavy vehicles for a long time before being able to pass them.

You could get to Switzerland on this side too. Not by the post road, but this suited people with something to hide. If you were not too loaded down and had the time to go slowly, you could reach Locarno this way. It had been rumored that the bridge across the torrent which runs along the frontier had been demolished by pioneers. That was why almost everyone was trying to take the post road, but anyone who was cunning, or at least could pay for sure information, knew that the bridge was intact and that, in any case, with a bit of nerve you could ford the torrent very nicely.

The road ran pleasantly between low, steep hills carpeted with periwinkles and the lake, which tossed up foam on the rocks.

"I'm going to stay at the tail end of the platoon," said Michelotti. "It's useless to go stuff ourselves into the middle. If things get complicated, we'd be in a Chinese puzzle."

In the course of the afternoon the veil of mist covering the opposite shore of the lake was rent, or rather, showed itself to be the
smoke of numerous brush fires and even hayricks shooting up high
flames as they burned. Several villages set back in the fields also
seemed to be on fire.

Michelotti stopped the hired carriage beside the lake near a boat
that three ferrymen, harassed and covered with black sweat, were
dragging across the sand. They had come from Porto-Valtra. They
had been on the go since the previous evening. They were exhausted. They intended to turn their boat over, keel up, and have
a good sleep under it.

They gave the ferrymen some wine out of the demijohn, and
ham and bread. Angelo noted that he had only one little cigar left.
He did not dare mention it.

Those were indeed villages burning on the other shore, especially Brissago, whose small Austrian garrison had been massacred
in the course of the night after a regulation siege. The ferrymen
mentioned a certain Beretta. He was in command of a detachment
of volunteers from Brescia, the spearhead of Allemandi's corps of
volunteers. Beretta was so far in advance that, having infiltrated
one small valley after another in a region scarcely controlled by a
few companies of imperial police, he had lost contact and had
started to make war on his own with about a hundred soldiers who
had painted large red crosses on their civilian jackets. Without
striking a single blow, he had taken a village on the heights; called
Rangio, it was on the edge of some woods in which they had hanged
four Croat chasseurs whom they had taken prisoner two days before and had been dragging along for the sheer glory of it. The two
or three hundred Austrian soldiers dispersed in the villages along
the shore had succeeded in gathering together under the command
of one captain and climbing up to Rangio where they had set fire
to the barns. Since then, people had been buying up huge quantities of flints. Allemandi was said to be coming.

"Allemandi is thirty leagues from here," said Lecca, "and it's
not even Beretta across from us over there. A week ago Beretta was
in Castelnuovo. There are twenty-five leagues between Castelnuovo
and your little burning hamlets, with too many pretty, peaceful
spots for a self-created general not to want to stop and rest in the

shade fifty times. Undisciplined volunteers don't cover twenty-five leagues on foot in a week with arms and baggage through countryside where wine is easy to come by just for the fun of setting fire to three little chalets which are of no value except to their owners. No. What's going on over there is our own men taking whatever they can get."

At Cannero, more bells were ringing. Reaching the village after nightfall, they found it overflowing with refugees. The bridge across the torrent between Cannero and the frontier was not destroyed but was so narrow that only one carriage could cross it at a time. A traveling-coach, hurrying across, had gotten wedged there. No one could free it until daybreak.

The master of the posting-station looked down his nose at these curious clients who claimed to be the owners of the second horse of their hired carriage. "Do you have a paper to prove it?" he asked. A mountaineer, strong as a horse, he had been dominating women, children, and those who were afraid all day.

"I have this excellent little paper," said Angelo, inserting the barrel of his pistol into the man's vest. "Don't play at flapping your big arms around that way or you'll flap them for the last time. And now if you want to be sure of one thing, that is, that you're a thief and we aren't, go turn your bug-eyes on the horse; hop to it, now! You'll see that there was never anything like that in a posting-stable."

"I agree with you, he's got four feet," said the fellow. "But you're not going to have him eat at table with you, and if you lose sight of him for five minutes he'll be whisked away quick as a wink. Much better if I steal him, since I'm in business and licensed. No use mincing words with you. Put away your little piece of paper; we'll be able to settle this."

He opened a shed which until then had been bolted. The straw was not very clean, but . . .

"We'll stay here," said Lecca. "Bring some oats for the horse and three buckets of water. You'll be paid punctually. And do you have any beef stew for us?"

"Are you joking! Of course. I've got some *boeuf en daube*. If you can call it that! When I saw the customers coming back for more, I went heavier with the watering-can than the demijohn.

Don't think you're going to get *boeuf en daube* fit for a prince. But I have a nice little pâté."

"I'd like something hot," said Lecca.

"Some soup then. I see that you understand: the pâté obviously . . . Now the cabbage soup with lard and pigs' feet, made for me and the household."

"I didn't know," Lecca remarked to Angelo when the owner had left them, "that you knew how to use a frozen face and a pistol as you did just then. It was thrilling."

"Do you think he'll make his fortune?" Michelotti asked.

"He knew the horse was ours. I detest dishonesty," said Angelo.

"Of course he knew, but I won't be as thrilled if you were really angry," said Lecca. "You've already caught me once with the real blood from a real wound. You get things too dirty."

The owner returned with an underling, who set up a table and chairs, pushing the straw away a bit. While he was stocking the horse's manger, a servant girl brought some silver and the soup, which smelled staggeringly good.

"Perfect," said Lecca, "but you too will be happy. We need you."

"You're no exception."

"Maybe our settlement of the financial question will be exceptional."

"Not even that. People would pay to breathe if I set a price on the air in my yard."

"Do lawyers refuse money?"

"Not exactly. But you've got to admit I was right about the soup. If there's ten lire to be earned, I should be the one to earn it."

"Maybe we'll make it twenty," said Lecca. "We want to get across the lake."

"Twenty lire! That's the price just to stay here! Without budging from your chairs you can see the forest burning above Luino."

As far as he was concerned, it wasn't Beretta, but Allemandi in person who was ravaging the entire region with fire and the sword. You couldn't be a tightwad if you expected people who were very peaceful on this shore to brave death.

"After we've eaten," said Lecca, "we'll take off our boots and have a little snooze in the straw. Let's sleep till daybreak and tomorrow we'll make out all right on our own. Perhaps tomorrow we won't want to cross any more and our lire will skip right out from under your nose. I said: 'Perhaps twenty.' For the moment, I'm only promising ten."

"And find me some little cigars," Angelo added.

An hour later he had found neither boat nor little cigars.

"You're asking for the impossible," said the owner.

"I'll go see," said Michelotti.

He came back empty-handed.

"It really is quite difficult," he said. "They've all got their pockets plenty full. All they want to do is sleep now. I thought I was talking their language, but you can have them! Different people have different priorities, and it takes a day to find out anything!"

"That's bad luck!" said Lecca. "As the crow flies, my men aren't more than five leagues away. But with the rumors that are going round and these bastradly fires, which are standing out like sore thumbs, they're capable of striking without waiting for me. Then we'll be in a pretty fix!"

Go round the lake? That was ten or fifteen leagues. They would have to cross the Swiss frontier. Obviously the Swiss were a push-over! The moment you were on the side of liberty, they winked at anything you did; you got through like a letter in the mail. But there was certainly a devil of a mess on the road between Cannero and the frontier. And they only had one horse! If only they had three!

"They'll ask the eyes out of our head for some stinking carcasses that will rot before we get there," said Michelotti. "Hold onto your centesimi. It's no use talking; we've got to find out whether it can be done at all. In normal times, with good animals, it's practicable, but even then it would take two days. I know the region and it's pretty rugged. If your men aren't fed up with sitting watching small fireworks with their arms at their feet, General, I don't know what Angelo and I can do with them."

"You think you can pick up Bayards by the shovelful," said Lecca. "You've got to work with what comes. I didn't come to get the colonel for nothing." He flew into a rage and explained what he had seen with his very own eyes at Ulm.

"It's almost midnight," said Angelo. "Let's agree on something.

I'm afraid Michelotti's right about going round the lake. Let him go look once more to see if there's not one victim of insomnia among all those sleepers, and if this millionaire is interested in a twenty-franc piece, let him say that we have one here at his disposal. If he draws a blank, we'll go to sleep."

Michelotti returned quite soon.

"I've found the impossible." (The impossible was a natty but taciturn lad.) "This lad has no boat. He's the crew on a little sailing ferry which goes back and forth all day. But don't give a thought to the owner of the ferry: he's not only asleep, but dead drunk. This boy is anxious because he saw flames a while ago on the spot where his house is across the lake. He wants to go see but he can't maneuver the ferry alone. I told him we'd help."

"If you'll give me a hand," said the boy, "and if you give me the money, we're off."

As for the horse, there were means to shackle him on the ferry.

"We take cattle across constantly in normal times," said the boy. "I know how to manage. They never budge."

Angelo wanted to leave a gold coin on the table to cover their expenses.

"You're crazy," said Michelotti. "Leave a gold piece on the table all by itself all night? The whole place would go up in flames. Take it easy. You don't joke around in wartime paying for a little cabbage soup. What are you trying to do? Put us back in hot water just when we've gotten into the clear?"

The ferry was roomy. Michelotti took up the oars.

"Easy does it," said the boy. "Don't make yourself puff. You've got a quarter of an hour's sculling ahead of you. We won't catch the wind until we've gotten out from behind the point. After that, at this hour there'll be nothing to it."

By the glare of the fires, and especially by one against the red light of which the dark silhouette of a belfry could be seen, they judged that they had between a league and a league and a half of water to cross as the crow flies.

The ferry didn't seem to move more than a few centimeters with each stroke of the oars.

"We'll never make it," Lecca said.

"I tell you we will," the boy insisted. "We'll catch the wind in just a little while. It's steady at night, off the mountains."

"What's going on over there? Do *you* believe in Allemandi?"

"I believe what I see, and if they've touched a hair of my wife's head, I'll know who'll answer for it. I can name names. Liberty has been declared. Therefore anyone can take it."

"I hear the wind," said Angelo.

The wind came first as a silence which had suddenly carried off the light crackle of the fires they had been hearing.

"So you do, sir," said the boy. "Look out for the sail; it's going to swing to the right. Pull in your oar, sir," he said to Michelotti. "I'll scull alone. There's just a bit more to go."

He pulled a little to the left; the mast cracked softly like a new boot; the sail swelled. The water slapped gently against the bow and the ferry began to bobble like a real boat.

The boy took the tiller.

"That's the Luino belfry you see," he said. "The town's not burning. What's on fire is the maize. We'll head up as far as possible. The wind seems to be of this opinion. This is the Dumenza ferry, and the pier is half a league above Luino. I don't think there's enough of a breeze to get as far as the pontoon, but I know a spot where the shore is much lower and sandy because of a torrent; we'll land in its mouth. We could have reckoned on this. There's a line under your feet; would you pass it to me, please, sir. Watch out for the horse, sir. Sometimes they're afraid and hurt themselves on the bolts. I've put oakum around them, but fear will get the better of anything. If those bastards have touched a hair of my wife's head, I'll drink their blood. Patriots or whatever else they call themselves. Joking aside, sir. The upper classes are the ones who are proclaiming liberty. Make out as best you can. I'll make the best of them, you just wait and see, the swine!"

"I've been observing you ever since we left your home," Lecca said to Angelo. "I bet you haven't thought of Bondino once."

"Bestow the palm for hypocrisy on me and don't bet," said Angelo.

"You do a good job of concealing. You turned heel on him without a single hesitation or murmur."

"What would I have murmured? And it was no time to hesitate."

"A matter of temperament," said Lecca. "I only know the pups of my own bitch."

"You want to know if I'm really Piedmontese?" Angelo asked, laughing.

"I know you are. Otherwise you wouldn't be in this Charon's skiff."

Now they could smell an enormous odor of bakehouses and the caramel smell of green maize burning. The gusts of wind extinguished and rekindled the tongues of flame and blew on the coals, sending quivering sparks racing up the slopes of the hills.

"I'm Piedmontese to my finger tips," said Angelo. "Give me the seven deadly sins and just see if I don't make them adorable."

The boy steered so as to catch the breeze running up along the shore. The ferry passed several hundred meters from the port of Luino. The little town had drawn its doors, shutters, and sheets tight down over its head and, all still, was silent in the dark. Now in the countryside cypresses, trellises, frames of buildings, and bristling forests—all incandescent coals—glared. The silence was completely beautiful. The velvet wind gave it vertiginous depth. A steady breeze bellied the sail; the mast hardly moaned. On the end of the promontory a few flakes of flame had almost finished devouring the arbors of a "fisherman's rest."

As a horseman, Michelotti marveled at their progress. Maneuvering the tiller and the mainsheet, the boy pointed as far as possible into the wind, taking advantage of all its little vagaries.

"I've been doing this for twenty years," he said. "With a light boat, we could go all the way to Locarno, fast too. But with this tub it won't be long before we're at the end of the line. Get back to the oars, sir, and backwater; I'll steer. The sand is two inches away on our right."

He dropped the sail, and after quite a long time (the ferry continued insensibly on its course) the bow touched the sand and tipped up.

"Let me pay this boy," said Angelo. "He deserves a bit of Piedmontese gold."

He wanted to give him a pistol too.

"No thank you," said the boy. "If they've done me wrong I want to get ahold of them with my bare hands."

He helped untie the horse and get him off the ferry.

"Cross the stream," he said. "There's almost no water in it. You'll find a road on the other side."

He disappeared without a sound. Here the silence was deeper than elsewhere. Suddenly a nightingale began to sing.

"He frightened me," said Michelotti.

The nightingale seemed to roll out his trills on a metal drum so that they resounded down the long corridors of the night.

After splashing about in the ford, they found the road and began to climb the slopes of the low hills overlooking the lake. As dawn was breaking, they were heading across meadows toward the edge of a dark forest. From these heights they could see the summits of Switzerland growing red.

The morning was calm and melancholy. The greater part of the sky was covered in the east with a large black cloud advancing slowly, encroaching little by little on the green dawn. From time to time, without apparent reason, the pine forest groaned. Below, the brown shining expanse of the lake creased evenly around the sand shoals and the shore. On the other side, water, shore, the wide strata of the mountains, and the shadow of the black cloud mingled in the opaque gloom.

They entered the forest. Night birds were rumpling their feathers in the branches. They came out in a clearing, on a thick carpet of mint which gave off a strong odor; they were approaching a little chalet when they were stopped short by the fire and report of a high-caliber gun going off right under their nose. Buckshot buzzed by them like flies. The horse gave a little cry. His neck had been grazed by a bit of shot. Lecca ran his hand quickly over the line of blood pearling on his coat.

"What's this?" he shouted. "They're shooting at horses now, are they? What's up?"

Silence. They saw the barrel of the gun aimed out the hole in a shutter. All three in a line, they advanced, step by step. The door was open. They entered somewhat hastily. Angelo had his hand in his pistol pocket. They found themselves face to face with a young peasant woman who was smiling stupidly. Her very beautiful eyes expressed absolutely nothing.

"Fine work!" said Lecca. "You'd be better off now, if you'd hit us."

"She's alone," Michelotti said after making a rapid tour and opening the cupboards.

The room smelled of sour milk.

"She must have good reason for what she did," said Angelo.

"You make me laugh," said Lecca. "There's no more reason in that noggin than there is in any other. First, an idiot doesn't get scared. She follows the fashion of the day. To hell with you and whatever you think of her! She's lucky nothing happened. Think what would have happened if this Joan of Arc had winged one of us; all three of us might have had to stay here. It would have been a historic event."

The girl was reloading her gun. She took black powder from a box with a soup spoon and poured it into the barrel. On the table was a small pile of round stones she was using as bullets. She rammed them with dry grass.

"We can't even tell her not to shoot any more," said Angelo. "If those bastards who are setting fire to everything come up this far . . ."

A cow mooed tenderly. The girl rested the gun on a bench, took a bucket, pushed open the door of the stable and went out. She continued to smile, not at the men who were there and to whom she didn't give a thought, but at some idea. Michelotti followed her.

"She has two cows," he said coming back. "She's milking them. She gave me some milk."

"Let's get going," said Lecca. "I'm about to lose my temper."

"Each time I see the way the world goes," he said after they had resumed their march in the forest, "I start to lose my temper. When I see the dawn, a bit of grass, milk, an idiot, and three fools, I ask myself if we wouldn't do better to pull the eiderdown up to our chins and smoke our pipes instead of trying to get them shot to bits along with ourselves."

At the first stream he washed the horse's wound. It wasn't serious: hardly a scratch with no danger of infection.

They had gone down the other side of the mountain through a countryside of severe but noble hills. Clothed with ilex trees, they bordered narrow valleys and little plains on which were ranged regular rows of the light "misty" poplars which sparkled and murmured at the slightest breeze. These "misty" trees opened, or rather evaporated, before the facades of beautiful farms well white-washed with oily lime. Stylish balustrades of small castles could be seen just above pine groves. At the bottom of a narrow gorge of gray rocks covered with Spanish lilacs, a post road made its way. A brook, so green that it was almost black, accompanied by gilded willows, crossed the meadows. At intervals they heard the melancholy cry of a peacock. It was about to rain.

Here no one believed in Allemandi. They knew he was on Lake Garda and in great difficulty. They got their news from Varese. Allemandi had gotten a licking at Castelnuovo from a dry-farting Austrian general who had given him all the cannon-fire he could take. You can pick up what's left of Allemandi with a shovel, along any road, like horse turds. He had three or four thousand *crosciati* with him. Some said ten thousand. Why not a hundred thousand? A hundred thousand or five hundred thousand, it makes no difference when its *crosciati* we're talking about. They're all snot-nosed wretches who paint crosses on their jackets and call themselves volunteers. Volunteers of the school of grab-all-you-can-get, volunteers to steal pigs or suck the wine out of kegs; but if you want volunteers to stand up to cannon-fire, especially when it's being aimed by professionals, then you won't find a soul. Allemandi is Piedmontese.

"Corvi con corvi non se cavan gli occhi," [1] said Angelo laughing. "Look out, I'm Piedmontese too."

"Allemandi would dry snow in an oven and sell it as salt. You're not going to tell me otherwise, if you're really Piedmontese," said the man. "I'm the mayor of this little town. I take the parish poor; I dab a cross on their vests and if I think them even bigger fools than they are, I go so far as to give them a bit of a line about Italy: I'm as good as Allemandi. I'll eat my hat it wouldn't take me a week to get all the sheep in the entire town into my fold. But as for making war on the Emperor of Austria, that's another kettle of fish.

"Here's what's going on in Luino. What did Luino have that we

[1] "Crows don't peck the eyes out of other crows."

didn't, so that they're in flames down there and we're peaceful as could be here? Clacking tongues. Perhaps even sincere ones. And where does that get you? It puts a different kind of coin in your pocket and that's precisely all. Making Italy? I guarantee to you it didn't fall on deaf ears. Everyone has set to it. But I haven't seen many who've forgotten to take care of themselves first."

He was a notary and mayor of the commune. He went on to explain that he had simply bought the records from the heirs of the last lawyer (to be really accurate, his father had bought them and had given them to him in advance as his full inheritance). "For as you see, I'm a cripple. My two brothers divided a magnificent piece of land, cut exactly in half by a little stream and the wisdom of God the Father. A third robber threw over the whole business and got the hell out. We stressed my bad pin, and I got the papers. Let's say I was jealous (it happens I've done very well for myself); now Italy's being created; this is a sacred cause and since to put Italy together you first have to take her apart, I rip the bits which in my opinion are badly sewn. The world's not going to stop turning if one brother or even two unfortunately happen to be in the path of a bullet, or even several if necessary. Then I'd be the natural heir. What would you have to say to that? And if I wasn't, I'd work it out so I was. Now mind you, by the greatest of luck I love my brothers and they love me; I don't want what they have. But are most men like me?"

He served them the local wine.

"From my own vineyards, or at least from the estate which is so well divided by the famous brook and the care of the Lord."

In spite of his peasant clothes he had great dignity; the wine was served by a girl who was incontestably his mistress as well as his servant, nicely gotten up and with beauty suitable to her circumstances. She looked at him tenderly. He was between fifty-five and sixty with thick pepper-and-salt hair and good eyes. His little mustache was exquisitely fine and of a very handsome black tint.

"I allowed myself to stop you on the square just now and bring you here," he said, "because one cannot speak the entire truth. Even that which consists of proclaiming that you want to buy two horses. We have horses to sell, but if you ask us for them (and especially if you're on foot when you ask) we charge a very high price. But, without repeating what I've already said, my brothers want to sell exactly what you want to buy. I have a little clerk as well who's in the notary office because he's a hunchback. (In reality, he's the one with the degrees; *I* never studied law). You have only to give the word and I'll send him to get the beasts. It'll be a matter of two hours."

"I like to choose my own horse," said Angelo. "I'm the only one who knows what I'm going to expect from him afterwards."

"My clerk is a hunchback, but he's noble," said the man. "His arms are two plugs of tobacco crossed with the motto: 'God bless you.' Never go for a cripple when you see him holding his own among peasants. It means he's tough-skinned and has a good liver. Let this cripple do what he thinks best and he'll find you a horse capable of anything, even carrying Alexander to the tip end of Asia."

"How do you know we want to go to the tip end of Asia?" said Angelo.

"I wasn't born yesterday and I know this gentleman," said the man, indicating Lecca. "Isn't he the general who, three leagues from here, organized a party of horsemen for a campaign? What I said about the crusaders only goes for the crusaders on foot."

The clerk was sent to get a few horses. He departed, mounted on an enormous, fiery horse which he further excited by shouts worthy indeed of Alexander.

"You who know everything," said Lecca, "do you know what our little family man, Charles Albert, is up to?"

"That all depends on the way you look at it."

"You don't need to sugar the pill for us. You must play the market a little. In that kind of work you need real information, not gossip."

"Don't speak ill of gossip; sometimes it's really good. But it's a fact that if you're going to put your three soldi on history you've got to know what you're putting them on. When I said that it all depends what way you look at it, that's not what I meant. Some believe that Italy is a great lady dressed like a statue and crowned with laurel before whom everyone bows respectfully and that the Austrians (who don't bow) are badly brought up blatherers and bunglers."

"Don't bother yourself with allegory," said Angelo. "We want to be the masters of our own country."

"Who's we?" said the man. "And masters of what? But I won't contradict you. You want to know what they're saying in Varese? First, they're talking about the business in Mantua. That happened last week. Bava looks as if he loved women made of marble dressed in the Roman style. He said to himself: 'I've come to stroll under the walls of the town; it will rally at the sight of my beautiful eyes.' Note that he had twelve thousand men. He came within cannon range of Fort Belfiore. He danced attendance, with his little bouquet of violets in his hand, waiting for the town to revolt. He would be there still if the garrison on the square had not undertaken to send him away with the honors of war."

"Good," said Lecca, "but that's Bava for you. I told you about him," he said to Angelo. "I was face to face with him after the arrival of the Piedmontese. It was a question whether Borromeo, the Prince, was to have a say in the matter or me. He pulled his handkerchief out of his pocket fifty times if he pulled it once. And the handkerchief was perfumed."

"You want to know about Charles Albert?" said the man. "That's day before yesterday's news then. I warn you: there's a victory involved. At the end of last week I signed a deal with the commissariat about some forage to be delivered in Varese; they loaded it on baggage vans heading for Brescia. At the beginning of this week General Sonnaz (you know him? *He* doesn't pull his handkerchief out of his pocket, I guarantee you; he doesn't pull anything out) General Sonnaz, at the head of twelve infantry battalions, a brigade of cavalry and two batteries, one horse-drawn, crossed the Mincio at Monzenbano. While the infantry searched the heights of Montevento and its foot hills, the cavalry advanced across the plain as far as Villafranca. That takes care of Sonnaz. That was Monday. He moved Monday evening; he retreated to his position Tuesday morning. He met no one in front of him. Tuesday evening the Duke of Savoy crossed the river near the Volta mills on a pontoon bridge. The next day the Piedmontese army with thirty-seven thousand infantrymen, four thousand horsemen and eighty horse-drawn field-pieces crossed the Mincio, and off they went. I'm not drawing the numbers out of thin air; I got them from the commissariat. I still had two hundred and sixty vans to load. They had cut off all payments. I go to see what was up with my little paper signed by Sonnaz. They tell me: 'Sonnaz, much good he'll do you, he's with the Tedeschi!' They tell me the whole story. The two hundred and sixty vans go to Monza. As far as I'm concerned, Brescia or Monza, what difference does it make? . . . But I say to myself: 'What are they really after?' I see perfectly well that they want Verona; except that between will and can . . . I don't need to have gone to a military academy to understand that they've got to march past Peschiera. Major General Rath is in Peschiera. When he sees the Piedmontese left flank there for the taking, he'll jump on it.

"My clerk says to me: 'Boss, we're in this business up to a hundred and ninety thousand florins worth.' You've never had a credit of a hundred and ninety thousand florins parading its left flank in front of Major General Rath's cannons? I assure you it's a funny feeling. I say to my clerk: 'Let's go to Milan.' I get there. In Milan I go to see one of my friends. He's the meat contractor. He's in deeper than I am. I say to him: 'What do you think of what's going on?' He answers: 'The figures are wrong. Sonnaz is not the only one on the other side of the Mincio; Charles Albert's there too. It's not a question of thirty-seven thousand men, it's a question of sixty-three thousand.' I say to him: 'That settles nothing.' He says to me: 'No.'

"I go to see another contractor. He says: 'It's a simple case of heads or tails. The battle's on at Pastrengo.' 'Where did you get this from?' He replies: 'You can believe me; I'm in up to my eyelashes.'

"Do you know Pastrengo? It's impregnable, even if you're on the ground with your cannons and I'm up above defying you. Well, can you imagine, our sturdy Piedmontese countrymen took it!"

"And then what?" said Lecca. "What did they do next?"

"You're the kind of person who's never satisfied, General. Next? Next, I'm selling you horses."

They were splendid beasts, full of fire and tenderness. Somewhat astonished, they looked attentively at Angelo and Lecca. They sniffed Michelotti's shoulders while he felt their hocks and looked at their shoes.

"I have a hundred or so of them, all the same," said the man. "Just what you need, General. There's not an infantryman alive who could look these horses in the face."

"I'm not rich enough," said Lecca. "We'll take these three."

"Come over this way a minute," said Michelotti to Angelo. "I thought we were only taking two: one for you, one for me. Lecca already has one and he's getting another. How much have you got in your belt? No need to tell me exactly. You're not going to support this old trickster, are you?"

CHAPTER ELEVEN

They reached Bidogno that very evening. The site was well chosen, even exalting. The mountains, pasted one against another, the tallest in the background, as is only right, raised their bronze earth skyward so that it shaded from dark green to dark blue, from dark blue to pure blue, and from pure blue to the light green of approaching night. A sort of dawn, but shadow-shrouded as the soul of the hero, glorified a thousand upward-yearning poplars. The entrance to this setting was down a triumphal way of elms.

The three horsemen advanced abreast. A trumpet sounded the curfew. Angelo's horse broke the pace and began to amble, as if to criticize the others and assert his independence. He had already shown at various moments in the course of the afternoon, always very agreeably, his faculty of getting fun out of everything. This time he was in agreement with his rider who, at the sound of the trumpet, had contracted his knees lightly.

Lecca led them to his headquarters in a bourgeois house.

"I wasn't the one who drew the portrait of the young Verdi on the top of the piano," he said. "I found needle-point slippers in every closet and the owner of this shed has the courage of a lion. He's lending me his ground floor for my staff work."

"Don't let them put anything over on you," said Michelotti to Angelo during a moment they were alone. "While you were thinking of glory, I was keeping my ears open. Do you know what the man in a blouse who stopped the general at the entrance to the village wanted? He wanted money. If you want to be a great man, you mustn't say you've got any. Anyway, you don't; you have just enough for the two of us. Let's try to find out what we're getting into. From what I understood, they haven't paid for the week's forage. You mustn't let them take you for a banker. Ask to see the sabers they're going to give us."

The storm which had threatened all day broke in the course of the night. It played to its heart's content in the mountains where unending echoes resounded. Angelo was greatly enjoying these full, beautiful sonorities when, by the gleam of the lightning which crashed brutally against his windows, he saw the door of his room open. It was Michelotti.

"Have you a scapular to lend me?" he asked. "The thunder frightens me."

"Go put your pants on," said Angelo. "Nothing is more dangerous than to wander around flapping in a storm. Your shirt tails are making wind . . ."

". . . Now that you look human, we'll have a little cigar," said Angelo. "Nothing keeps off lightning like smoke. You know it never strikes chimneys where there's a fire. We left La Brenta too fast; I didn't have a chance to explain things to you. You think I'm full of theories; I don't have a one. Six months ago I would have died for my ideas; today if I die it will be for my own pleasure."

"Let's not talk about death right now," said Michelotti. "Don't make two devils out of one. I'm not that interested in ideas; I don't understand a thing about them. Holy Virgin! That one didn't hit far off. Did you hear the trees crack?"

About four in the morning the storm grumbled away. Michelotti went back to his room.

"Perhaps I'm a simpleton," he said, "but that's because lightning strikes so suddenly. They say that it jumps like a dog on top of those in a state of mortal sin. And this seems reasonable. On the other hand, I never believed in Italy. She can't bless scapulars like St. Ursula and she doesn't protect you from anything. What good was all your schooling if you ended up with as few ideas as I have?"

After the night's torrential rain the sun rose in a laundered blue sky. Distance no longer existed. On the horizon they could see the smallest details on the mountain peaks, and especially the pines sparkling like crystals. Around the village the sainfoin grew bright blood-red. Poplars glistened and the air resounded with the dazzled song of a thousand larks.

The meadows, where large puddles of water crushed the narcissus, gave off a musky odor. Bees buzzed about the flowering lindens.

Cascades rumbled in the mountains. The least noise rang out in the limpid air. Long before reaching the camp, Angelo heard the clatter of curb-chains, the whinny of the horses, and the rub of saber scabbards.

The cavalrymen were drawn up in some stubble. Lecca had been finicky about the meeting. Despite their civilian clothes the men seemed to be wearing uniforms. A large cross of black wool, four inches wide, was sewn on the left side of their jacket. They sported feathers on their hats and stood impeccably at attention. Five triangular, bright red flags floated above their heads.

When Angelo came out of the willow grove the trumpet sounded *Ai Campi*. The order "Present arms!" was given. Sabers were unsheathed all at once with that noise of a flight of birds so dear to the heart of any soldier who is a bit of an artist.

"Their actions are a matter of honor," he said to himself. "Yet they're all deserters like me."

He passed slowly in front of the troops. His horse, understanding the game, was even more serious than he. Following the rules of the trade, Angelo looked into the eyes of each man he passed. With pleasure he saw gleams of malice in them.

"Ah! Dear Italy!" he said to himself.

Most of these cavalrymen (Lecca had exaggerated; there were not a hundred of them, but sixty at most) were young or in the prime of life. They all wore mustaches thick as a finger, rolled and even reddened by daily use of a little curling iron. Some wore their beards in fan-shapes, rounded, spread in bibs, or wedge-shaped.

Lecca made a little speech, the rhetoric of which went marvelously well with the singing air, the dancing poppies and leaves, and the joyous sunshine. He said that now everything was possible. He spoke of charges with sabers bared as you speak of Sunday afternoon walks. The horses, which obeyed the lightest movement of their riders' hearts, began to shake their manes and undulate their rumps. The trumpet played a charming little tune in which were both a marching-rhythm and a little melancholy.

"It's in the bag," said Lecca.

"How are they armed?" asked Angelo (they were returning to the bourgeois house). "I certainly saw sabers and I even thought I recognized the equipment of the Piedmontese army. I saw boots but what's in them?"

"Nothing. They all have first class blades, polished and sharpened. Perfect as to weight and length, and their arms are splendidly strong. Naturally I see what you're driving at. But that was the only thing in the little commissary depot we broke into a month ago. Up to now I haven't worried too much about firearms. While I was alone, I didn't want to furnish important arguments for action to men who curl their mustaches so well. Besides we're going to have to get the hell out of here as fast as possible. The news is so good I can't believe my own ears. I want to go have a look for myself. We must find some little carbines on the way. I admit that a carbine with a bandoleer dresses up a cavalryman very nicely. I'm like you: I find them somewhat naked with only a saber."

It was said that the Piedmontese had given proof of extraordinary courage at the battle of Pastrengo.

"I'll admit a bit of strategy was used, but not a grain of common sense; an imbecile can easily win a battle, but he'll never win a war. We haven't seen the whole story yet."

"Since you're the first to bring up common sense," said Angelo, "there's a question on the tip of my tongue. We're good enough friends for me to ask it straight off, without being flowery. Where's the money coming from? In other words: who's paying for our victuals or forage?"

"No one. I live off the country, my friend. I know my business. Your war college seems to have lacked qualified professors. We're campaigning for all the stay-at-homes. And let me tell you, they don't let it bother them. So let them foot the bills."

"He takes us for ninnies," said Michelotti to whom Angelo related the conversation. "I'll go along with what he said about our soup and our stew, but have you taken a look at the saddles and the harness? I must admit you were perfect; it's too bad you couldn't see yourself. You can't imagine how the lads have taken to you. With the exception of four or five to whom I wouldn't even entrust my old grandmother (and then some!), they're good bastards. I don't know whether you noticed the little carrot-top. He's from Genoa. He served in the dragoons, but he fancies himself as a chasseur, don't you see? He was a tinker. He's always dreamed of fanfare. His kind always suits me right down to the ground. With your style you could make anything you wanted of him . . . But to get back to the saddles—it's a good job of faking, but they're not from the army. The seamy side of this business must be something incredible."

The troop assembled for departure next morning at dawn.

"Who's in command?" asked Angelo.

"You," said Lecca. "You're now in a situation where you can let your heart speak. Go to it. We ask only one thing of it, and that is that it tell us everything it knows. Consider me as a simple technical advisor. I'll be in the rear guard."

Angelo summoned Michelotti.

"Ride boot to boot with me at the head of the troops," he said to him. "You can act as liaison officer if necessary, and if it isn't, you can help me smoke my cigars."

He summoned three other cavalrymen to complete the little advance guard and, in particular, one of the bearers of the very beautiful red flags.

As often happens in the mountains, the weather had abruptly changed for the worse: yesterday's radiant morning had been succeeded today by a tormented dawn. Driven violently by a high north wind, clouds unfurled against the summits. Nevertheless, when the sun rose, it sent bundles of burning rays, starring the landscape with splashes of moving gold through wide rents in the gray sky. Thus at various heights in the distance there rose out of shadows solitary poplars, groves, willows, grazing land, pines, small castles, perching villages and, on the horizon, through breaches opened in the blue mountains, the leopard skin of the Lombard plain.

It took the cavalry about two hours to cross the Bidogno basin along roads bordered by willows which on this windy morning exhaled a strong sugary smell. On the other side the ascent was quite steep, but they held their ranks easily, concealing effort with pride. Angelo extended the trial a little longer on slopes covered with small round stones which rolled under the shoes of the horses. They continued to climb for a long time toward a forest on the edge of which Angelo stopped and watched the troops pass. He had listened all the while to the noise of the shoes on the stones: he knew that everyone had kept his rank. He wanted to pay the homage of satisfaction to these most sympathetic, proud men.

"Gentlemen, I commend you," he said. "Now let's have a little fun."

The wood was not thick. Through the trunks could be seen a large plateau, bare and deserted. Sunlight and shadow mingled and frolicked with the wind on the close-cropped grass.

Angelo put his horse into a trot and turned the corner of the wood. "Let's get the greatest possible happiness out of this situation," he said to himself.

He started to gallop. They followed him in good order. He ordered them to deploy to the right and left. They obeyed him, this time without pride. Out of the corner of his eye he saw the outmost riders, more thoughtful of their position than of intoxication. Finally, extremely black clouds began to move across the sky with sweeping, dramatic gestures.

"Let's not push these nice boys to extremes," Angelo said to himself. "It's gloomy; they'll imagine a terrible future."

He ordered them to proceed at a walk in a column, two abreast.

"Have you tried out your saber sufficiently?" asked Michelotti.

"Yesterday morning in the washhouse on an oak washboard. Mountain housewives like dazzling linen; they beat it for hours with good strong arms, using a beetle. The board was as solid as iron."

"You saw the trade name on the guard? It's English steel."

Angelo almost replied: "It'll be an Italian arm wielding it."

"These clouds incline even me to exalted thoughts," he said to himself. "Or else, is it the fact that I am at the head of a certain number of men who obey me?" He would have been annoyed to have spoken pompously. He made a few brief, icy remarks about the comparative value of the different steels of the various sabers he had used.

The rider to his left had his own ideas about the value of English steel. He was a hairdresser's assistant. His round head, full pink cheeks, gray eyes, and nicely drawn brows gave him an infantile air which he had corrected by growing and very carefully caring for an enormous ink-black mustache. He, too, was from Genoa and was a friend of the carrot-top Michelotti had mentioned, friend and even neighbor. They lived next door to each other on the same alley consisting of a flight of marble steps in the old town. They had left together out of boredom.

"His legs are short," said Angelo to himself. "He must be very short when standing; and with those mustaches which are hard to wear."

The hairdresser said he was a bachelor. His horse rocked him in a most restful state of pathos composed of clouds and scudding shadows. He talked about women, saying that they were far from being the most fascinating thing in the world and that if you walked along the Corso among the carriages (since you've got to go out a bit in the evening) you were in danger at every step of being insolently crushed, and all for nothing.

Angelo explained to him how to test a saber on a washboard or, better still (if possible), on a chopping-block. The hairdresser was intensely interested by the fact that it was necessary to hang the board at the chest level of the imagined adversary.

Little by little they made their way up the mountain. They went along halfway up, going from one small valley to the next. All around reigned somber, thick woods. The weather had darkened for good and all. Wind squalls even sprinkled a little cold rain.

Tramping through ferns, the troop was traversing a long stretch of woods in silence, when Angelo, riding first, almost bumped into a peasant crossing their path with two mules loaded with lumber. Since it was an accomplished fact that he had accosted the man, Angelo questioned him more out of politeness than defiance.

The peasant looked at the horsemen assembled around him and was confused from the very moment he started to speak. He showed a paper.

"I know," he said, "that my permit is not valid for this spot since it's made out, as you see, for Monte Garropoli, but I didn't find what I was looking for down there. If it's a question of adding a little something so that you can drink to my health, officer . . ."

"To whom did you pay the two hundred lire I see marked on this paper?" said Angelo. "Who signed this? I can't read the name. And where are you from?"

"I'm from Pagnona. I paid M. Luigi."

"Who is M. Luigi?"

The peasant looked disappointed.

"Surely you know M. Luigi?" he said.

"Go get Lecca for me," Angelo said to Michelotti.

"Luigi?" said Lecca. "No, not from Adam. But I bet he's a commander!"

"A general," said the man.

"I didn't dare go that far," said Lecca. "And he sells papers, does he?"

From what the peasant explained, Signor Luigi sold just about everything: roads, God's good fresh air, the right to be born into this world and the right to get along in it. He was installed at Pagnona, with twenty crusaders and he was doing Allemandi's requisitioning.

"Where is Pagnona?"

"Behind these woods, five leagues away."

"We're going to let you go scot free, but keep your trap shut and don't say you've seen us."

"He's going to sell us for a song," said Michelotti in Piedmontese dialect.

"I won't sell anyone," said the man; "it won't be in my best interests. If they knew I was strolling around these parts, they'd fine me."

"Where did you learn my dialect?"

"I was in the pig business before the war."

They let him go despite this last remark, which was open to various interpretations.

"We'll halt when we're out of the woods," said Angelo.

From the edge of the forest they had an unlimited perspective. A sawtooth of blue mountains level with the ground hardly stopped the eye in the distance. The deserted plateau was covered with heather. Here and there the silver hatching of scattered rain-storms erased the horizon.

"Those mounted on horses provided with oats—there are six of you, I believe—step forward!" said Angelo. "You'll scout for us. You can take advantage of this to feed your beasts at the first barn you come to. Get them used to fresh grass, but slowly. Pagnona, which the man spoke of, must be ahead in that direction. I want to know exactly where. I want to know as well if he spoke the truth about the size of the garrison, and I want to know all this without anyone making the slightest noise. If we could only march heavy shod like Allemandi's men, we would be soldiers under Allemandi. But we're not under him. We must prove that we're right not to be. Come back before nightfall. It'll come quickly in this weather. I'll bivouac a league from here, but pay attention: I'm going to order the sentinels to engage in combat with sidearms. So you'll do better to get back while there's still a bit of daylight."

Angelo commanded the others to dismount and inspected the horses carefully.

"What do you think of them?" asked Lecca.

"Fine fellows," he replied. "They seem to know that there's a difference between a horse and a dog. But, it's been a Sunday stroll up to now. From here on we'll see which it really takes, a wink or a whip, to get them moving."

"You're under the same impression that I am?"

"I've got to know your impression and what it's about first."

"The peasant was a fake, wasn't he?"

"He didn't speak like the real thing. And he let himself be trapped by Michelotti's dialect. You didn't know Allemandi was so near us?"

"Not the vaguest. I thought we could go on galloping for two days more."

"We just missed falling in head first, with our eyes closed. You were sure of the people you got information from?"

"All the more sure since they were called public opinion. Public opinion has no interest in deceiving. I was careful not to ask direct questions or to let them think I needed information. Perhaps I don't know where Allemandi is, but Allemandi doesn't even know that I exist."

"Allemandi's making war against Austria, and that's exactly the war I want to make too. There's no reason why I should conflict with his plans."

"If he doesn't conflict with yours. Logically you're right, but these days no one fights for his lady love's big beautiful eyes. He just tries to pull through in the best shape he can. What do you intend to do with the people of Pagnona?"

"Leave them in peace, if they leave me in peace. I intend to go down into Lombardy as quickly as possible. I was intending to march east for two days to pass the top of Lake Como and then choose among the valleys to the north of Brescia the one which would give me some leverage on the rear or the flank of the Austrian corps fighting over toward Salo. We're only a little swarm of wasps but if we choose the place to sting carefully . . ."

"Long live theories," said Lecca. "I'll remember all my life that I won the battle of Waterloo in a taproom in Lens on the 17th of June, 1815, at nine in the evening with three little stem glasses, a little pitcher, and some fine bread crumbs. I had even taken Wellington prisoner. Your idea holds water. I can even say it has only one fault, which it shares with all ideas; it thinks itself the only one in the world. But it's got to live with other peoples' ideas. This man Luigi (with a Luigi idea in addition) is in Pagnona because Allemandi has an idea. Our sixty horsemen have sixty ideas; the six men you sent as scouts have six different ideas, and even I have one. I won't mention the ideas your King of Piedmont threw at the Emperor of Austria; there are a hundred thousand of those of which we don't know beans about except that they exist and that they're strong as a horse. Remember the Palazzo Borromeo. You had blown up the engineering-depot. It always blows up five minutes too soon for someone and five minutes too late for someone else. And the person for whom it blows up at exactly the right minute uses it, not as a liberating explosion, but like the croupier's rake. Allemandi doesn't want to defeat Austria; no one wants Austria's defeat; no one wants to be over-harsh. Everyone wants to seize fortune by the forelock."

"So you came to La Brenta to get something to help you out on a rainy day," said Angelo.

"If I had half your talent, I'd be Pope," said Lecca.

The men had pitched camp and were stirring their polenta. Angelo walked up and down a little to limber his legs. The vast, gusty plateau inclined him to triumphant melancholy.

At the end of an hour Angelo realized that he had completely forgotten Italy. The men had eaten their polenta and even smoked their pipes.

"They think I'm cooking up trouble for Signor Luigi," he said to himself, "and I was far from it . . . perhaps even in France."

He gave the command to strike camp. He ordered a judicious formation with a detachment of three riders on each wing. These scouts were to forage on the flanks, nevertheless staying within shouting distance. He placed the rest of the platoon in a compact mass in lines of four, and ordered complete silence.

"Indeed, this is the least kindness I can do these men who have three times too much mustache and are as wildly happy as I am," he said to himself. "They'll be delighted to prove to themselves thus that they are no longer dreaming on some side aisle of the Corso."

A palpitating red dusk struggling against downpours on the horizon safely authorized a tragic attitude. The horses themselves began to march through the heather as if on the stage of a theater. Finally, after a half hour of lofty deambulation, the happy men consented to find a site for a bivouac under some oaks.

Angelo awakened about midnight. He had been fast asleep. He went to see the sentinel he had posted on the Pagnona side.

"All's well, Colonel," the man, who obviously took a foppish pleasure in the moaning of the night, said, "but if you look straight ahead of you, you'll see lightning that the good Lord never had anything to do with: it's the cannons of Peschiera."

Angelo would have located Peschiera farther to the left.

"I'll bet my life it's there ahead of you," said the man. "I know the region like the inside of my pocket. I went on a bender in these parts four years ago, Colonel."

Angelo supposed that he had been one of those peddlers who carried political tracts in the false bottom of their candy boxes.

"No," said the man, "that wouldn't have suited me. I've met that type: they're all walking on eggs. And they work their asses off, and for nothing. The papers they're hiding have them in a total state of funk, and you can have every damn one for all the happiness they'll ever get you! They think of nothing but the day quail will drop from trees already roasted."

He spoke well of forests and the art of getting an immediate profit from their gloom and melancholy depths.

Angelo was too content to meet a kindred spirit: he allowed himself to confide in the man several times.

"The truth of the matter," the man, who was now ill-at-ease, said to him, "is that I had plenty to crow about. Does the name Vincent Panici mean anything to you? There was a good deal of talk about me. I had a vineyard over toward Lonato and, one day I hired four young saw-pit workers to bludgeon a priest to death. My motive was good (he had abandoned my sister), but afterwards, I had to take to the hills."

The lightning from the cannonade continued to leap above the crests of the hills to the east.

"Hold your breath and listen," said the man. "You can't hear the cannon—it's too far away—but there must be one hell of a stir going on over toward Brescia: the noise comes up the valleys. Just now something exploded, down there to the south."

"That's toward Mantua."

"But what could be exploding toward Mantua? There's nothing but water there. The snows are melting, Lake Garda has overflowed, the Mincio is wider than the Po. There's water as high as the tops of the willows. It seems some general has sent his cavalry into these marshes. Somebody said something about the Piedmont cavalry."

"Must I admit that this is the first time I've fought?" Angelo asked himself. He found the murderer very agreeable.

The scouts returned at dawn. There were only five of them left; the sixth had deserted.

"He said that with you things were never going to be plushy, Colonel."

Angelo was naïve enough to ask precise questions.

"We went to Pagnano," a tall lad told him, apparently thinking the whole matter a good joke. "You didn't want any noise and there wasn't any. We made less than if we'd beat about the bush. We entered the village sedate as could be. We told a few fibs, but they didn't take. They've been on to what we're up to for some time now, and it effects them about as much as a poultice on a wooden leg. They're like pigs in clover: they've got everything they want. When they run into the slightest difficulty, they bat their eyes, and it's just like rolling off a log. You wouldn't run into trouble with them unless you wanted a piece of the pie; then of course they'd show their teeth. But according to what they say, it's a big country, and if we want to gallop through it, what's stopping us?"

"He would have left us anyway," said Lecca. "It's better that it's over with rather than still ahead, and he'll be more useful down there than here. He's going to make a real fish story out of it. He'll say that there are at least two thousand of us. That'll set him up much more than if he told about two ragtails and a bobtail."

"Do you see that thin dark fellow down there in the seventh line with the crazy eyes?" Angelo asked Michelotti. "I chatted with him last night while he stood guard. He knows the country. Go tell him to come up front with us."

"Just before enlisting in General Lecca's troop," said Panici, "I ferreted all around these mountains. Lake Garda's ahead of us. It's two days' march to the east. You can't see it, but if it weren't for the iron box in which you keep them, your cigars would be just like the lake: getting wetter every minute. What I mean is that after Milan fell, there was one hell of a jumble in this region. One part of the Austrian garrison took off for Verona at top speed. The other part which was in less of a hurry (I must admit too that they were trying to transport some small arsenals) was caught short by Allemandi; whether they got a licking or gave one, in any case they turned back to barricade themselves in the towns and villages they held at the time and still hold. The whole country is sizzling with patrols. Any moment we could fall into the fire."

From the heights they had reached they could see the fortress of Cosenza, the hospital of Paterno, Montalto, and Cervecato. An immense chestnut wood covered the hills opposite. The valley was dotted with fields, cottages white as snowflakes, meadows greener than ivy, bouquets of trees, plantations of olives in neat rows, figs, and fruit trees. But two somewhat hoity-toity *cassine* were burning. The smoke which the damp air weighted down dragged through the orchards.

They passed two hundred meters from Cosenza as the crow flies, but under heavy cover and without making any noise. The boulevards which they saw from the other side of the ravine were deserted. Sheets were drying in the windows of the hospital.

"I'd fight single combat with a superior officer to get a spyglass," whispered Lecca. "I wish to hell we knew who's holding that damn village!"

The trees they kept beneath were somber and thick-piled. The wind had dropped. The clouds moved only enough to tear slowly and let through a long straw of sun.

Going along a mill stream, Angelo, Michelotti, Panici, and Lecca, who were marching as an advance guard a hundred paces ahead of the platoon, caught up with three peasants who didn't even try to hide. Angelo questioned them. They were taking their money to eight brigands who were, they said, in the valley of the Macchia. It was nobody's business but their own. They were allowed to continue.

After fording a torrent which, thinking itself a river, was putting on airs, with a sandy bottom, osiers, and, here and there, deep water, they crawled up the long spine of a gently sloping mountain. Despite the absence of any visible habitation, numerous kitchen gardens were squared off along the ash groves; a few rows of vines, and some hedges of naïve but robust roses made the walk pleasant and even made the ring and clatter of sabers a little ridiculous. When they had climbed higher, they saw that the cultivated plots must have belonged to the villages of Cervecato and Montalto, toward which an entire little group of peasants seemed to be hastening.

Passing the summit of the mountain, Angelo saw a half league ahead of him across the valley a hundred or so soldiers reconnoitering in the beech woods. He sent Michelotti to order the cavalry to be silent. Happily they were just then in a heroic mood and were singing in low, noble voices which didn't carry far.

The sharpshooters were executing with a great deal of discipline a maneuver which had been well planned. They were searching each bush with a bayonet and were moving slowly in an arc of a circle, weapons at their hips, ready to draw. He recognized them as Croats by their red epaulettes.

"We can't charge on this peak in these trees," Angelo said to himself.

The men were immobile; the horses, made of marble.

"And what if they discovered us all of a sudden, petrified as we are, right under their hunting dogs' noses?"

He imagined the astonishment of the Croats.

"But," he said to himself, "that's for an opera and not for a military operation."

The phrase gave him pleasure.

The Croats went down into the little valley, but instead of climbing the slope leading to the cavalry, formed columns in fours on a little road and moved off in the direction of Cervecato.

That night, they chose the site for the bivouac with great care.

"I know very well," said Lecca, "but a gun costs forty-six lire, powder forty soldi a kilo, and a bullet, a centesimo. Just add it up. That means a dead Croat costs more than fifteen soldi. The general public thinks war is waged like one big binge; anyone in the business knows that you're firing bank bills every time you shoot. You asked me where the money came from: the truth is that it comes from nowhere. There are only two alternatives: either we mortgage our sabers to some Bondino or other and get carbines to get the chestnuts out of the fire to our heart's content or we do everything on our own and learn how to pinch our buttocks. Afraid? Old man, I'm always afraid. It's horrible, but that's the way it is, take it or leave it."

Angelo thought of the little arsenals Panici had spoken of.

"I understand," said the latter chewing his mustache, "I don't like being reduced to contempt any more than you. I know of a little supply of arms. If they haven't been moved, they're at Balvano. But they're well guarded by reserve grenadiers. These old soldiers can't be maneuvered; we'll have to lay ourselves open completely. Remember that my information is two months old, but if you order me to, I'll go check. There's something else; Michelotti has inspected the horses: three have dysentery. Their bridles have been shortened to keep them from eating grass, but we need oats. The fetlocks of five others were a bit hot. There's no more maize flour for tonight."

About four-thirty in the morning, there were smothered noises in the bushes and the men jumped for their sabers: it was a little boy from ten to twelve years old, mounted on a she-ass, which one of the sentinels was driving ahead of him. He claimed to be going to the convent of the Madonna dei Carmini.

Angelo asked for information about this convent, and especially if it had any granaries. The little boy, who was not in the least impressed by the bare sabers and the red glare of a pine torch, replied that there were certainly granaries where there were monks.

"Besides," he added, "they sell masses for six centesimi, and they sometimes say five of them. I'm just going to buy one for my mother who has strained her back."

Angelo sent three cavalrymen with the little boy to ask for maize flour and a sack of oats.

"I'll go along too," said Panici. "I'll be damned if I can't find out something about Balvano in this convent."

At seven o'clock neither the cavalrymen nor Panici had returned. They had heard the bells ring the angelus, and the convent didn't seem to be more than an hour away from the bivouac.

Finally they arrived, bringing everything that was needed.

"In a sense I drew a blank," said Panici. "Once burned, twice shy, and those Croats we saw yesterday have scared them. That company searching the bushes was looking for the troop of a certain Carmine Crocco, who is in possession of the woods in these parts. He's a peasant who said to himself: 'Why don't I get in there and clean up too?' He's gathered two or three hundred colleagues with whom he's collecting taxes. I've heard of him before. They didn't say a word about an arms depot. But I have an appointment this afternoon with a Capucin who likes wines at the inn of Santa Maria al Tufo. It's at a crossroads two leagues from here. I'll go in civilian clothes. This time I'll get something out of them."

Angelo wanted him to take along one of his little pistols.

"If I'm taken and they find such a lovely weapon on me, they'll shoot me dead on the spot. Besides it has your monogram on the trigger guard; allow me to tell you you're not prudent. You don't know me; perhaps I'll desert and use this marked pistol as a passport to people who would certainly pay a big price to prove you're a knave."

The mad spring storm seemed to have calmed down. Large

creamy clouds floated across a seraphic blue sky. The wind blowing off the Alps was still cold, but as soon as it dropped, the heat
made the insects chirp and the birds sing.

Angelo asked himself the same question ten times: "Am I
happy?"

Panici arrived at nightfall.

"The depot is still where it was," he said. "However, the bulk
of it was moved out three weeks ago. The Bade infantry's guarding it. A hundred and fifty men, they say. They've got their thumb
in the scales obviously. I say a hundred. I know Balvano. You go
all the way to the village gate under cover: that's a cinch. Afterwards, you go along little streets; that's bad. But the Bade infantry
is not the top of the pile, far from it. I couldn't find out who's in
command. The Capucin says a certain Francis. That's pretty vague.
And the Capucin is not a Capucin. Or at least he's just enough of a
one to deceive fools. As the questions I asked him were not stupid,
I showed that I was pretending to believe he was a Capucin without really doing so; this way I didn't seem too underhanded. Who's
he working for? A mystery. For the Austrians? No. But I wouldn't
bet my life on it, because my life's quite a lot to bet. The inn
people are in with him. They know where we are, who we are,
and how many we are. I could have gone there with a trumpet."

"Nevertheless, you did right to go there in your shirt sleeves,"
said Lecca. "We're not in a position yet to skip the amenities.
Where is the arms depot in Balvano?"

"In the Bargello, in the cellar."

"There's an answer to the question I've been asking myself con-
tinually," Angelo said to himself. "I love cellars. Even more, I love
the alleys leading to them in which you have to slip along, saber in
hand, while the Bade infantry snipes at you."

He saw such a happy future for himself in these combats which
would have been frowned on by the war college (especially the
idea of dismounting cavalry to attack a fortress) that he said to
himself: "Halt there! This is fine for you, but is it fine for all these
sturdy lads asleep under the pines, near their campfires? Some of
them will kick the bucket."

This popular expression horrified him. He increased this horror
by saying: "They're going to get their ticking burst."

As soon as they were alone, he told his scruples to Lecca.

"You're strangely egotistical," said Lecca. "I've pointed it out to you before, but this time you've gone too far. I've seen you chat with four or five of these fine lads, which is excellent. But what have you learned? They've told you they used to be house-painters, waistcoat-makers, hairdressers, or masons. There's even one (I don't know whether you've come upon him in your efforts to win the love of the entire world) who is a valet, or, more exactly, was. But they hid the main point from you. And this is precisely that they jumped at the chance not to be. In their new social situation, which allows them to view the world from the top of a horse, death exists. Well! perhaps this isn't any too funny (to put it mildly!). Don't worry, they'll do everything to avoid it."

Angelo ordered them to strike camp at midnight. According to Panici, in half a league they would have to cross a deep river; he said that only the peasants could show them the ford. At dawn a storm broke with such violence that the horsemen were obliged to take shelter in a shed near a cassino; the cypresses and the statues around it appeared in the lightning. They were somewhat lost. Panici seemed curiously embarrassed. To every useful suggestion for finding their way again, he opposed bad reasons without even trying to make them sound good.

Angelo summoned Michelotti.

"Take it upon yourself not to tremble like a leaf each time it thunders," he said to him. "I'm not very sure of Panici. Go knock on the door of that house and ask a peasant to take us to the ford."

"*You're* virtuous," said Michelotti. "*I* can't afford the luxury of being an atheist. Without paradise, and consequently without hell, I don't know what god to call my own. You can be glad I'm scared of the Heavens. It's proof you can count on me."

The cassino belonged to an old bourgeois woman who loved soldiers, but as one loves boiled eggs. When she learned that her shed was sheltering cavalrymen, she suggested to Michelotti that they open the drawing-room, light the candelabra, and organize a quadrille for the officers with her two daughters, niece, and serving girls. As for her peasants, first of all, she had only one, a man, and he had left the previous evening.

He returned at daybreak, but muddied up to the knees. This added to Angelo's suspicions.

The man played the fool and called for his coffee.

"I'll give you some, bad at that," said Angelo. "You're going to march five paces ahead of me, and this man" (he indicated Panici) "is going to prod you in the ass. As for me, take a good look at me and look at what I have in my hand. I'll blow both of your brains off if we're not across the river in ten minutes."

"Bravo!" said Panici, laughing. "You've caught on, but all the more reason not to get angry. I simply wanted to furnish good merchandise in return for a florin I was paid, and you won't hurt anyone. We would have been across the water in a quarter of an hour. We'll be across in five minutes. It won't give us any trouble."

Nevertheless, Angelo pushed the two men ahead of him across the ford. He had the satisfaction of noticing that as they went deeper into the water, Panici's look grew wilder and wilder, and even became imploring.

"You're not sure of the passage?"

"Of course! But it's impossible to know all the holes this river digs in the sand, and I see that if I lose my footing you'll leave me to drown. I think that's cheap for a florin."

On the other side of the river, the horses found it hard going; the rain still fell, soaking the sticky grass.

Toward evening, when they had reached a mountain where the north wind blew disagreeably, Angelo looked for a sheepfold as shelter. He found one in which there were a shepherd and two young boys. It had rained all day as they passed by obviously hypocritical villages.

Angelo ordered the shepherd (who said that his name was Nicolo Provenzano) and the two boys not to move from the shed without his permission. He bought five large lambs from them, and the horsemen made it their business to prepare everything necessary for eating meat.

In the morning the shepherd and the two boys had disappeared. Angelo deployed his troop in small platoons reconnoitering reciprocally. Lecca stationed himself beside Angelo.

"I'm staying with you today."

Panici approached as well.

"No joke," he said, "you'd be grossly mistaken, Colonel, to think that I'm a complete traitor. I accepted the florin because it was a florin. It was that troop commanded by Carmine Crocco. They're far from wanting to cut the ground out from under us, quite the opposite. All they're asking is that we slow down a little."

"I prefer this to the look you gave me when you had water up to your armpits."

"That's because I don't know how to swim," said Panici, "whereas I can make out fine with a saber."

Angelo sent him to command the platoon on the right wing. Michelotti commanded the one on the left.

He came galloping up to ask:

"What shall I do about that village down there? Do you want me to enter it?"

"No, bypass it to the left. Keep under cover. Continue to advance under the trees. Send one of your men to tell Panici to search the grove ahead of him. When you see him come out, trot to the line of cypresses and open out toward the mountain. I'm going to wheel to the left in a moment, and I'll whistle to Panici so that he'll fall back toward these slopes covered with juniper."

"Are you anxious about the horses? You let us ride along a road surrounded by hedges which could be full of leveled guns," said Lecca.

"The horses are fine. You noticed the hedges," replied Angelo. "Did you also notice the little walls? If there are peasants ambushed anywhere, they have it very good, and their trigger fingers must be itching. We're a perfect target. The enemy must show himself."

"A funny way of going about things. I admit that if they fire on us, it will eliminate the misunderstanding, if there is one."

"They'll aim at cap feathers. You and I don't have any, but it's not for nothing that I hold myself stiff as a sentry. Your roundness makes you stand out. If I'm picked off, you'll know about it. If you are, don't worry; I'll finish the work."

"It won't be the first asinine thing I've done," said Lecca, "and I haven't been killed yet."

He didn't like allusions to his stomach. Besides, anyone had to admit that despite his age and corpulence, he had what it took.

"I retreated on the 15th of April in Tuscany with Murat. One day . . ."

Someone was shouting over Panici's way.

"I'm going to see what's up," said Angelo.

He jumped the hedge and put his horse into a gallop.

"You mustn't let anyone see the movements of your heart," he told himself.

He was still thinking of the need to dominate he had shown at the ford.

Nothing important was going on with Panici. The platoon had simply flushed a rabbit and gone shouting after it. Everyone was excited by this march, which at least was something military, in a landscape which the light fog made mysterious.

"A quarter of an hour ago," said Panici, "behind this chestnut wood, I discovered a shed in which I found bread and an empty bottle."

He was farther from pleasure than his men and ready to do anything that could be taken as zealous. The submissiveness of his look was disquieting.

"He's still thinking about his 'four soldi treason' or more exactly his 'florin' one. I can't tell him that it doesn't disturb my happiness in the slightest: he would detest me."

Angelo went nonchalantly along, bridle-rein slack, through the fine rain.

"Am I to follow Michelotti's movement?" asked Panici. "I see he's pulling away."

"Go pivot around that farm with a yellow dovecote and gallop to the summit."

"Do you really believe we'll be ambushed over there?" Lecca asked when Angelo had rejoined the center platoon.

"No, the platoon which had the florin given to Panici must need guns as much as we do. He wanted to slow us down to have time to assemble his people and be on the spot at the same time we are. I'm giving him the impression I'm looking for him, saber bared, so that he respects me."

"And what about Balvano? How are we going to take it? I warn you: there is no precedent in Roman history . . ."

"Perhaps I'll have some infantry. I'm not in any hurry. The

town is still more than seven leagues away. The peasant knows I'm going there. He's going there too. We've got to decide him to put his footsoldiers under my orders. They have hunting-guns. That's plenty good enough for me."

Puffs of mist rose from hayricks, groves, and forests; the hide of the horses and the damp clothes of the horsemen exhaled steam.

"What's Michelotti doing?" Angelo asked.

He saw him, recognizing him by his brown serge jacket, which looked almost red in the rain, galloping in front of his deployed platoon. The horsemen disappeared behind a fold in the terrain.

"Go see," said Angelo to one of his men.

With a disconcerting lack of hesitation, the man kicked his horse and was off at top speed.

"Proud as a peacock," said Lecca. "He's a former postilion from the Genoa stagecoach stables. It's curious how these fellows from the seashore are good riders when they don't become sailors. All a question of pride. But what the devil is your *alter ego* up to over there?"

"We'll know soon enough," said Angelo.

He had the trumpet sounded several times to recall Panici, who had a tendency to go off, and he ordered a trot to get them away from the walls of a large farm which they had just by-passed.

"They've captured three peasants who were taking shelter under a green oak," said the postilion from the Genoa stagecoach stables when he returned. "What do you want done with them? They're three men in the prime of life who are rather inclined to think us handsome and to be polite. As soon as you stop frowning at them, they smile nicely, and you would think they wanted to stroke us like cats."

"Go say to free them. And say to smile at them four or five times as well. Tell Michelotti to go to the summit as fast as possible right after that. Tell him to wait up there till Panici and I reach his level. Stay with him. You can then come and give me an account of the maneuver."

Angelo used the trumpet once more to give Panici a push; his platoon seemed to be laboring along in Indian file in plowed fields a quarter of a league to the left. Pigeons flew up from two or three pigeon cotes. Panici made some sweeping gestures to show that he was navigating some heavy terrain. Michelotti's horsemen rose from the fold of the hill which had hidden them. They were foraging in perfect order in the direction Angelo had sent them. Michelotti's red jacket was, as it should have been, at the point of the marching wing.

"Nothing simpler than to be a general," Angelo said to himself. "This is how . . ."

"Do you still have one of those little cigars left?" (Lecca had taken out his short pipe.) "No more tobacco. This rain freezes the old gullet. Give me one and let me stuff it in my pipe."

Angelo ordered a trot and then a gallop when he saw that Panici had gotten free and was galloping toward the summit.

From the top of the hills they overlooked a descent which led to a wide valley.

"I understand why the old corporal who taught me at the Prytaneum swore by the exercise field and nothing else," Angelo said to himself.

His imagination roamed joyfully as his horse swayed.

Panici (whom they could no longer see; Michelotti's platoon had disappeared also in the thickets of this wide, flat valley, in which dusk was coming fast) asked for orders.

He was, he sent word, before a large barricaded farm. But, in the twilight, which had deepened a great deal, he saw light through the cracks of the shutters. Moreover, a thread of smoke was coming out of the chimney. This didn't seem to be according to the rules. Should he flush out the people who were obviously watching? How bold was he authorized to be?

He also sent word that Balvano was only three leagues away; that if Michelotti was still on the right, he would soon cross the road from Brescia to Balvano.

"Column left!" commanded Angelo.

And he ordered silence. Crossing meadows which muffled the steps of the horses, he and his men joined Panici's platoon.

The farm had the appearance of a fortress. The shadows of evening exaggerated the strength of its walls.

Lecca said that they would lose some feathers, and all for nothing. In addition he shook his hat, which was heavy with rain, and settled it on his head.

"Don't touch your sabers," said Angelo in a low voice. "I only want to check if my suspicions are correct."

He dismounted. He approached a small barricaded window. Panici followed him. He looked through the cracks in the shutter.

He saw the main room of the farm lit by a fine open fire and by a few candles, especially two stuck to a table. He counted six, seven, eight bearded peasants, the knees of a ninth, the hands of a tenth; others must have been seated or even lying down in spots he couldn't see. Those he saw were armed—daggers, butchers' knives, and pruning knives slipped into their belts. They had hunting-guns. Despite all these weapons and equipment, they were sleeping or drowsing, dulled by the heat.

"Why aren't they guarding themselves?" whispered Panici. "There aren't any sentries."

"They know we have nothing but sabers. They're safe behind the doors. Besides, they're not squarely opposed to us, you know."

"I don't know anything. I only know the man who gave me the florin, remember? Would you accept my word of honor?"

"Of course, it's always of the best."

"They want war guns, just as we do, and they won't spit on a chance to give us a hand. Here's my plan."

"I no longer need a left wing," said Angelo. "It will only be constantly giving our scent to all the little posts they must have furnished this side of the plain with. Join your men to mine and come lead me to that Brescia road which you mentioned."

He got back in the saddle.

"What you've just done, my little lambs, is ten times harder than charging behind standards," said Lecca when they were far enough away from the farm to be able to speak aloud. "Forty horsemen who don't make any more noise than a carp . . . I take off my hat to you. If you like compliments, my children, my shop is open."

Night was falling.

"I've only been this way once," said Panici, "and I was running for my life. I must find a little knoll where there's a calvary."

It was difficult. Finally they heard a horseman. He was coming toward them; he was speaking boldly to a horse which was slipping in the mud. He was one of Michelotti's men.

"I've come to get you," he said. "We're in trouble with some priests."

They marched indecisively for still another half-hour through squalls of wet wind which had grown cooler before they made out the dark flame of a torch.

The man carrying this rustic torch was a bourgeois in a redingote. He had subjugated his opera hat with a scarf knotted under his chin. He stood beside a priest in alb, stole, and casuble who was awkwardly lifting a beautiful monstrance. Behind these notables could be seen faces beneath hoods attached to mozzettas and other faces under top hats subjugated with scarves too. This entire assembly faced the dazzled horsemen.

"Thank God you've come," said Michelotti. "They were even speaking Latin to me . . ."

"We also spoke a language which any Italian heart should understand," said the priest who was holding the monstrance as one holds an ax. "We're not carrying the Corpus Christi for pleasure in the midst of these gusts, but in order to touch your heart. We've been parleying for three quarters of an hour."

"We're wet to the skin," said Lecca. "A quarter of an hour more or less won't change a thing. But explain yourself clearly. I warn you that at the first adverb, I'm clearing out. I may not be taking the Corpus Christi for a walk, but I've got my own body with me, and it's beginning to have had its fill."

It was a matter of life or death. Without the slightest exaggeration. A horrible death for women and especially girls. Carmine Crocco had seized Salandra last week. Everything had been exposed to fire and bloodshed; everything! and especially virtue and modesty. Stupration, lasciviousness, and even cynicism of the most shameless kind had spread their filth beyond repair over not only the most respectable houses, but also the squares, crossroads, milestones, stoops. It was as bad as Sodom, and right out in the open in the same way! But, for the last twenty-four hours Crocco's advance guard had been occupying positions on the outskirts of Balvano.

"You have an Austrian garrison?" Angelo asked.

"We have an Austrian garrison. Not a strong one; in case of attack, it will withdraw to the Broletto and leave the town open to every depredation. They'll be content to resist in their redoubt. But we know a great deal, like everyone threatened by misfortune, and in particular we have learned that Crocco would never have dreamed of attacking us without his conviction that you're going to move in. This evening about five o'clock, our friend Count Berlini, who has a cassino on the road you took, sent us a message to warn us that, judging by your maneuvers, you were a regular troop who would probably accept our supplication kindly and perhaps even with friendship."

"I have a farm right near here where we can get out of the wet," said the bourgeois, who was carrying the torch.

It was more than a farm; a hamlet rather.

"How far are we from Balvano here?" asked Angelo.

"Almost three leagues, Officer," replied the bourgeois. "And across hills where brigands never venture because they're separated from their hide-outs by plains they would have to cross in the open."

"Naturally we protect widows and orphans," said Lecca, "and, as the case may be, chastity. But only on certain conditions, of course."

He spoke of the arms depot. The old canons wanted them to light a bit of a fire first.

"The subject is hot," said Lecca. "You must warm yourselves around it, until we've reached an agreement which satisfies my interests. I've left men for whom I have the affection of a father out in the rain. We must come to the point, and quickly."

"This Austrian garrison," said the bourgeois, "has been with us since well before the war. You know what it's like: you can't go on forever looking at each other coldly like so many china dogs. Add to this the fact that we're not far from the frontier, that our dialect has always been a sort of low German: in short, there's not one of these soldiers who hasn't been our friend, often our ally, either openly or covertly, for some time. As for your men and your horses, I have sheepfolds which could shelter double the number."

They were indeed very roomy, old-fashioned sheepfolds.

"Take care of the horses," Angelo said to Michelotti. And to Panici: "Take ten men with sabers bared and have them enter the salon where we're parleying. Station five pairs of sentries outside wherever you choose. You take a small patrol of three men and scout around the neighborhood. To show you I trust you, I'll tell you what's in the back of my mind. I'm not afraid of Crocco; I'm afraid of a nice little bit of German-style treason with sharp-shooters hidden in the bushes. So patrol on foot with your sabers ready in your hands. And before being killed, shout like the very devil."

He was ashamed of all these precautions when he returned to the drawing-room where Lecca was continuing the conversation. Everyone's face showed consternation. The general was talking shop.

"That bewildered air can't be put on," Angelo said to himself. "And you don't bother to fake it (with a prodigious artistry that would be needed) when you have one or two companies of good riflemen posted in the bushes. This is the idiotic look of innocence."

"This is a bit beyond our means," said the priest. "How can we get these guns?"

"By any method except prayer. Surely the virtue of the ladies is worth a bit of an exertion!"

A gleam of vanity appeared in the faces fashioned by trade and by the ceremony of the Mass.

"If you want me to talk of patriotism, I've got my phrases ready," Lecca continued. "But let's keep things down to earth. I have my plan; you have yours, because it is a plan to want a nice clean dining-room and authentic 'children of Mary.' I need the arms which are stored in the cellars of your town hall. I was coming to take them by force. You tell me this force will break the glass bells covering your clocks. You know, I hope, that I love bronze figures and respect them; Cupid and Psyche look very nice on a mantle. I wouldn't touch them for anything in the world. But guns are another matter. Give me those guns and I'll go find out for you whether it's raining fifty leagues away.

"Come now, Father, you've got something up your sleeve, haven't you? You don't want to betray us, do you? What? Friend-ship, common interests? Come, come, a careful negligence, that's the way to go at things. In order to escape vulgarity one falls into the most abominable affectation."

This Balvano affair was quickly concluded. At dawn, one of those heavy dump carts used to transport manure arrived, grinding along the foggy roads. It carried a hundred or so guns, chests of powder, sacks of bullets, boxes of grease, and pipe tobacco in kilo packages.

"You forgot my cigars," said Angelo coldly.

"Yesterday, I was happy," he said to himself. "I thought constantly of winning us glory through force. This bit of sleight-of-hand couldn't be more stupid. Lecca will tell me, and he'll be right, that instead of spilling blood we've spilled saliva. But I'll never be happy unless I take part in great events."

In the course of the morning, torrents of black smoke rose above the woods. Crocco was avenging his discomfiture by burning a few farms.

CHAPTER TWELVE

Summer was coming. The plains of Lombardy exhaled a life-less odor. It was rumored that the Piedmontese had taken Peschiera. To the east and the south, the horizon was leaden. The sun had to cross behind smoke-heavy clouds before rising, and autumnal dawns preceded the dazzling days. Even when the rays of the setting sun struck them head on, these clouds did not glow. Only in the dark of night did a rosy coal breathe from beneath their ashes and occasionally crackle thunder over the chirp of crickets.

"It's in the gardens," Lecca said.

He meant that the battle was receding toward Mantua.

Since they had rounded the north of Lake Garda and started down toward Verona through the valleys of the lower Tyrol, Lecca no longer remained back with the rear guard, but trotted along with the head platoon. He was now on familiar terms with every-one except Angelo.

"You impress me," he said. "I expected passion; instead I find you cold as an Englishman. But although you impress me, you don't deceive me. I see you don't want to fritter away your courage. You know you're going to have to pay it out all at once, and you remain polite: this is rare."

Not a single *franc-tireur* remained in the mountainous country they crossed to reach the battlefield. The villagers said that the volunteers from the Tyrol had been ordered to go to Brescia and Bergamo to join the regular troops. But for the most part they had gone home, not caring for army discipline. Allemandi, who had been accused of treason (the word was much in use), had been arrested in Brescia and conducted to Milan—fortunately for him, as the populace would have cut him to bits.

"Like Carthaginians," said Lecca. "They're going to crucify conquered generals. With such people one good gun is worth all the prayers you can say."

They found foothold on the slopes of Monte Baldo; they slipped down into small, wild valleys; they threaded their way to the osiers of the Adige. Across the river the road linked Radetzky with Trentino. Hidden in thick chestnut forests, they watched detachments of imperial light-infantry pass on their way to reinforce the garrison at Riva.

"You don't need to look longingly at me," said Angelo. "I haven't the slightest desire to attack those footsoldiers. They don't even have cartridge cases. They may be good with a bayonet, but it'd take them a quarter of an hour to understand what's happening and get in position. They'd be no more than a mouthful to us, not worth the feathers we'd risk losing. Anyway, some thirty men less won't worry Austria. What she won't be able to stand is a threat to this road, which she must be guarding with her life since it leads to Innsbruck. We'd have five or six squadrons on our neck, and that would be the end of us!"

"I've got to admit you take a load off my mind. People like you often want to end their life as a pyrotechnic sun. I've known many such."

"On the other hand, I'd like very much to do them out of a courier. We saw two pass yesterday. There must be something juicy in their saddlebags. But it's got to be a clean job."

"It's getting you down, isn't it, waiting around like this? You need a bit of free rein. Don't you like these mysterious woods?"

"I'm curious. I'd like to see in black and white what's going on in Verona. You sound as if the forest were good enough to eat, but I've known you to gobble down official papers in your time!"

After several days' Sunday stroll through a countryside which, no longer knowing what god to call its own, met each requisition with almost religious fervor, they had reached the hills bordering the plain. Before them were the cliffs skirted by the Adige on its way to Verona. Beyond, in thickets and villages, orchards and tawny fields, the Austrian army stirred. Smoke rose from the bivouacs. The white uniforms of the Francis-Charles infantry dotted the meadows like flowers. Gathered in the shade of trees, in formation along embankments, escorting baggage-wagons, shoulders to the wheels of cannons, patrolling Indian file or in squads, flying about from farm to farm, the white redingotes blossomed over the whole country. From a belfry which Panici said was that of Pastrengo, floated Wohlgemuth's emerald-green standard; the towers of Parona, Avesa, and Quinto bore Clam's orange flames. In the distance the sun gilded the walls of Verona.

From the south there no longer came the slightest sound of the battle. The horizon, still smoke-darkened, paled. The bickering of Piedmontese trumpets sounded only in the early morning hours. It was very hot.

Angelo departed with two horsemen: Michelotti and a small, thin man nicknamed the "little hairdresser." Giosuè seemed to be his real name. Angelo found him congenial. "These people who aren't much to look at," he said to himself, "are generally warmhearted."

Together they continued on the road through the chestnut forest they had traveled with the platoon the previous days. Across the Adige the Verona road ran through orchards.

They did not want to use fords known to the peasants. At the foot of a rock they found one on which the ruins of a black tower rested. This crossing, now abandoned, had probably been used in the old days and finally given up as too difficult. It was only practicable on horseback, but the hard bottom held safely. The tower marked it—a distinct advantage, since they might need to find it again quickly.

The sun began its ascent. The cool flowed away with the dew. The trembling aspens shone in a light mist.

They heard a baggage-wagon rumbling away toward Trento. Toward Verona, magpies in the apple trees chattered that their part of the world was free of soldiers. The horses, calmed by the stream across which they easily fought their way, drank playfully with little thrusts of their muzzles.

They rode ashore on the shingled beach of the left bank. When the sun entered the valley, it would dry the marks of their passage.

Since the dispersion of Allemandi's bands, the Austrians supposed the region entirely free of *franc-tireurs*. However, they could not allow the hoofprints of their horses to be too much in evidence. A state of siege had surely been declared on both sides of the river. The peasants could move about only individually and on established routes. Wohlgemuth's patrols, composed for the most part of Croat light infantry and uhlans from the Taxis brigade, rarely ventured on the right bank. They did not like the silent forests, which until just recently had crackled with snipers' gunfire. They made only a few forays there in full daylight, in compact columns, and on unwooded roads, to assert that they were more or less taking possession of the place. They withdrew well before the blue dusk.

The Austrian detachments, although undisturbed for three weeks, still found this dark bank a bit hot. Settled astride one of the high branches of a chestnut tree, Angelo had again and again seen chasseurs and uhlans come to sniff along the Adige. They seemed interested in the tracks left on the sand and among the osier thickets.

Instead of spurring his horse directly on across the meadows toward the road, he went upstream along the pebbled shore. A green wind swept down from the mountains of Trentino. The horses were joyful. Dazzled by the many shining aspens and birches and interested by the silence which the light patter of leaves heightened, they made sport of a bit of fear.

Three or four hundred paces above the ford, Angelo found a rocky path leading to the road; after winding a short way along the bank, he turned toward an apparently abandoned mill. The carcass of the building showed through its stripped thatch; the wheel turned uselessly, shaking big tufts of moss. There lingered, however, the burned-wood odor of a now extinguished fire.

The three horsemen stopped behind a thicket of alders and rose in their stirrups. The odor, undoubtedly that of a campfire, seemed to indicate an only occasional bivouac, for a rainy day perhaps, but certainly deserted today. The horsetails which encircled the cottage, although fragile plants, were all intact. Besides, at this hour a small post would be busy making coffee or, at the very least, smoking. But they caught no smell of tobacco. Toward

Verona, magpies still jumped from apple tree to apple tree. Toward Trento, circling crows wheeled peacefully above land that was completely silent and surely deserted.

Across the road, they found spacious, blond oak forests. This bank of the Adige, open to the west, favored agriculture more than the other. The obstinate mountaineers had bitten small vineyards out of the black, rubbly stone. A few villages had taken root and had even bought elegant steeples for their hunchbacked churches. They had leveled terraces around their houses and treated themselves to a few very blue cabbages. The timber stood high and the forest floor was polished clean as a new penny. It was difficult to find cover in such light, airy woods.

They had to go deep into the forest, climbing into the mountains. They saw that soldiers had passed through the area frequently, obviously at ease.

The sun was still rising when Angelo, going first, came out into open pastures. From this high land he could hear the dull clamor of the bustling camp entrenched at Verona.

Michelotti was familiar with the region. He knew every nook where a four-footed beast in the form of a horse could be found.

"Beyond that ridge is Santa Clara: the horses there are ragtails and bobtails, but they've got beautiful little mules—short, rugged animals. The only hitch is that their hindquarters are poor; used to rough ground. If you rode over to that juniper tree, you'd see the houses right below the ridge. The fields are rotten, full of rushes, with water everywhere. You remember the time I took back a big red-silk handkerchief to my mother? I was coming from here. They have a fair in September. This year they'll be out of luck."

The engineers had obviously been busy at Santa Clara, which they examined cautiously: a few trenches had been dug on the edge of the hamlet.

"I'll bet whatever you name that there isn't so much as a cat in those holes," said Michelotti. "In theory, digging trenches down there is a cinch; in practice, you dig down two inches and it fills up with water."

To be on the safe side, nevertheless, they retreated toward the summit visible beyond Trento.

They soon came upon wilder country where the ground was

slaty, denuded of grass, tufted only here and there with lavender, box, low juniper trees and, at long intervals, minute pines. Big grasshoppers, thick as a thumb, sprang up between the hoofs of the horses.

They needed a lookout from which to survey the road. Michelotti remembered an abandoned house on the slope above Borghetto, but, beyond the fact that Borghetto, being a stage-stop in the valley, probably harbored a garrison, the site did not suit them. The house would have been a convenient shelter, but the oak forest from which it scarcely peeked out greatly restricted its view.

It was broad daylight, and their unusual stroll through open country could be spotted; they had to find cover as quickly as possible.

Finally, at the mouth of a small valley full of fallen rock, Angelo was moved to tears. He had feared that he would have to settle for something less than perfect, but now he had found an ideal spot. He could see at least two leagues of the road toward Verona and, toward Trento, as far as the eye could see, to orchards soft as cotton wool in the distance. They could go down an easy incline through the heather; there was even a track to entice them.

He was cautious and scrupulous enough to patrol the immediate environs himself. When he returned, Michelotti and Giosuè were making a meal of some goat cheese. He shared the food. He hadn't thought to bring along anything but cigars.

"This isn't, strictly speaking, a military operation," he said to himself. "It's the kind of sally they try to persuade me one can no longer indulge in. For such a sally, cigars are sufficient."

The wind still blowing off the Alps cooled and refreshed them, but the valley had filled to the brim with sunshine. The Adige sparkled. The aspens, trembling and flashing, vied with the shining flow of the river. Sparks flew even in the orchards. Heat rose in gusts. Then the wind shifted and blew from Lombardy. It was sultry.

The road was deserted for a good while. The sun dissipated the mist of the river. In the distance toward Trento, they saw a high belfry rise, thin as a thread, in the midst of gilded vineyards, violet gardens, and russet maize.

It was hot. Giosuè took off his jacket. He had on a livery vest, striped red and gold. Little by little a cloud of dust smudged the line of the road toward Verona. The wind was not stirring it up. Although it seemed to stay in one spot, the cloud was in fact advancing at a walk.

"Look at that black fellow," said Giosuè, "just below us, to the left of the poplar."

He appeared black because they were looking at him from a great height. In reality he was slate-colored, especially in the full sun. They thought he was a dismounted uhlan. He left the road and took a path toward the Adige. He was followed, then joined, by another. The cloud of dust reached a line of willows. It stopped in their shade. A third uhlan rounded the poplar and started toward the Adige.

"There must be a patrol somewhere down there," said Angelo to himself.

"A horse," said Michelotti.

But it was a work horse, and the shadow no bigger than a pea following it was doubtless that of a small boy. They came from the direction of Trento. They turned up a mountain road which ran between vineyards.

The cloud had disappeared. In its place a detachment of Hungarian infantry, recognizable by its white uniforms, was resting in the shade of the willows.

After a good hour's observation, they knew that there was a small cavalry post just below them on the edge of the woods bordering the road. The uhlans who had gone toward the Adige had returned; others had taken their route. They counted five in all. They finally noticed the corner of a house which emerged from the woods; the sun had until then disguised it, striking its rough-cast wall and making it appear one with the white of the road.

"Don't be anxious," said Michelotti. "If you want, we'll get them tonight. At two in the morning. I'll nab them all alone, if necessary. They'll fall right into my hands. They're dug in there. They'll be caught with their pants down."

The Hungarians had resumed their march and were approaching. Through the dust they could make out the black points of the shakos and the straw-gold of the guns.

Angelo tried to decipher a tattoo on Giosuè's forearm: a cross;

the motto was partly hidden by the fold of his elbow; it seemed to be: "Neither God nor master."

A man was coming on foot down the road to Trento. He had probably been on the road a long time, hidden in the shade of the orchards. He came out into the sunlight a quarter of a league above the post of uhlans. A soldier. He had no gun but carried on his back a pack which, polished black, reflected the sun. He was a chasseur. The rays reflected from the pack lighted up the green feathers of his *bicorne*. From time to time the green plume was clearly visible. There was something disturbing about this little figure. He had no gun (this was now plain); he was consequently not on duty; anyway he would have been wearing a cap. What was he doing on the road? He had a mountaineer's walk and swing of arms, the air of someone who knows where he's going and who, moreover, has no time to dawdle. A liaison officer with areas out of reach on horseback? He would have had a gun . . . Unless he had rough ground to cover and was armed with only a pistol and dagger so as to be less encumbered. In this case, he had to be kept in view. At any moment he could enter the woods and climb up to where they were. Where had he come from? If he had set out this morning at dawn (at the pace he was going, he covered a little more than a league an hour), he had probably come from the village whose belfry they saw, thin as a thread, in the distance.

"What's that steeple?" Angelo asked.

"Nothing much," said Michelotti. "If the fellow came from there today, he spent the night in a hayrick and started from someplace else. You think there's something there because you see a steeple, but that's all there is except a barn split open like an old straw mattress. The church is a chapel vowed to ward off the plague. Even if they've stuffed four footsoldiers and a pot of coffee into it, it's the end of the world and not enough of a set-up to send out liaison officers. But I'm dubious about the four footsoldiers. And the liaison officer too. It's a pretty strange fellow who travels like that. You've never seen his like in the army. Just watch him. If he gets out of sight, we've got plenty of time to go meet him halfway in the forest. After all, he's only a man. But you'll see, he doesn't give a damn for anyone."

They could make him out better and better.

"And upstream from your church vowed against the plague, what is there?"

"That depends on you. What do you want to do? You can amuse yourself up there all you want, but you won't find a damn thing. On this side, there are a few more cabbage patches; on the other, nature herself. Ten leagues to Rovereto.'

The chasseur was approaching the uhlans. He left the road and struck out across the fields, toward the Adige.

"I like this fellow," said Michelotti. "You see, he hasn't the slightest desire to get anywhere near a master sergeant. You've never understood the first thing about second-class soldiers."

The detachment of Hungarian infantry had come closer. In the dust they stirred up, the lines of four, the swinging dirks, cartridge cases, and guns slung over shoulders could now be distinguished. The chasseur disappeared over the bank of the Adige.

In the course of the morning Angelo understood little by little the entire activity of the road. It was peaceful. What he had taken until now for small squads of troops going to reinforce the garrison at Trento (especially the detachment of Hungarian infantry which, after passing the sentry-post of uhlans, marched away toward the north) were no more than strong parties of footsoldiers (about a hundred to a hundred and fifty men) who had the task of going very slowly from Verona to Trento and from Trento to Verona, to see that all was safe. Once each league they halted, smoked their pipes, and looked about. It was as simple as that. To supplement this somewhat slow but steady police force, small posts of more mobile uhlans had been scattered at intervals along the road.

Angelo took pleasure throughout the afternoon in making sure that this system had made no provisions for any act of caprice. Once the detachment had passed, things went on as usual. The uhlans rode about a little and made a small tour around their camp. They seemed neither nervous nor curious.

Just when they were no longer thinking of him, the chasseur with his shining pack (it was more than three hours since he had disappeared over the bank of the river) came out of the osiers along the Adige, rejoining the road three-quarters of a league from the post of uhlans, at least two leagues behind the detachment on foot, which continued to march toward Trent. He seated himself calmly at the foot of a tree and undoubtedly had a bite to eat. Some crackpot, they thought, watching him.

Toward evening six artillery caissons went down the road in the direction of Verona, making a great deal of noise and stirring up a great deal of dust. Then night fell. The wind still blew from Lombardy, bringing with it noises that were hard to identify. At moments, it sounded as if people were shouting in unison. At other moments, the firing of platoons seemed to reverberate in the air; but such cannon-fire was an illusion, for the only fire was that of the stars, which blazed out as usual, one by one in the night.

The river raised its voice. A lantern strolled along the road. It hesitated for a moment. Then it circled in one spot, as if carried by someone who had turned around something, undoubtedly a traveler hidden in the darkness, a nocturnal horseman making himself known to the post of uhlans. This maneuver was repeated often for a good part of the night. In the gathering stillness the Adige roared with increasing magnificence.

Angelo closed his eyes without intending to. He would have been annoyed if anyone had told him he was going to sleep on the job. Michelotti was snoring soundly. Giosuè yawned.

"You don't sleep?" Angelo asked, somewhat formally.

"I should be more familiar with him," he said to himself. "He's going to think I'm stand-offish, whereas my formality is a matter of politeness and even, in this case, of affection. Why wouldn't he deserve such treatment? It's specified in the Rights of Man. But, does he want to be treated formally? That's what I should ask myself."

"No, I never sleep, at least, rarely, as little as possible," said Giosuè. "I can't afford the luxury. My bed is the only place where the King's not my cousin. It would be a sin to waste time sleeping."

"You're a hairdresser?"

"'They call me the 'little hairdresser' because as you see I'm not a big man. No one imagines that small people can ever do anything big. But a hairdresser—that's pretty fancy. I was a butcher."

"In Turin?"

"Yes, on the Lungo Po. I had a tripe scullery."

They talked about the King of Piedmont; they agreed there was no resting their hopes on him. Giosuè had ideas for using the large squares of Turin, especially the Piazza San Carlo. He imagined festivals there of women and girls dressed in white, their arms full of lilies. Angelo asked him why he wore a livery vest.

"I got it from a fellow who used to buy brains from me. He would come round every day punctually for three sheep brains. While I split the heads, he would stand there with his thumbs in the armholes of his vest. Finally I said: 'Three heads free for that vest.' Three heads split, mind you. It was a deal."

"I don't know what Lecca told you to win you over," said Angelo, "but whatever it was, it must have been a tall tale. I'm certain of only one thing, and that is that we're no angels of liberty. Other than this I have no theories."

"Me neither. I've never known why I want the things I do."

At dawn, a long convoy drowned out the roar of the river for some time with the noise of its passage. Then there was a moment of complete silence before the larks began to chirp. For some time it was very difficult to distinguish the larks' chirping from the firing of muskets in the distance. Angelo, lying on his back, drowsy and yet spellbound by the intense early morning odor of the sparse meadows, followed with half-closed eyes the flutter of black wings in the sky. He said to himself that a bird hardly bigger than a thumb could make a great deal of noise when drunk. He woke up abruptly. The green dawn was splashed with red. An instant later he heard the detonation of a cannon. An entire battery began to spit. He understood that what he had taken for a lark's voice was the noise of gunfire, which sounded like sheets ripping.

They had not yet saddled their horses when loud reports of fortress artillery resounded. Fieldpieces began to fire faster and faster, especially several batteries which could not have been more than ten leagues away. Also in that area, platoons fired rapidly one after the other. High on their horses, they saw that a sharp action had been initiated in the direction of Rivoli. But, far to the south, the horizon was shaken with flashes of light and, in the direction of Lake Garda, whirlwinds of black smoke, shot up thickly as if by the draught of large chimneys, rose above the mountain peaks and began to thin out in the wind. Under the noise of the cannon and the crackle of muskets coming from Rivoli, drums rolled.

"It's wrong to stop and think," Angelo said to himself.

He knew that in a moment he would begin to idealize the battle.

They had just entered the woods when they heard the whistle of a fife. It was a company of imperial chasseurs. Doubtless the Santa Clara garrison going to battle. They went along the edge of the woods in Indian file. The soldiers were smoking large porcelain pipes.

Angelo thought it very fine to smoke on a morning shaken by cannonades. He lit a little cigar and offered some to Michelotti and Giosuè. They slipped the little fifes of tobacco under their mustaches—somewhat mockingly, for since the battle had begun to be noisy, Angelo's gestures had become a little pompous. With these toothpicks they could play the Piedmontese gentleman in fine style.

Now they had to make their way into the darkest part of the forest—a labyrinth of old oaks. If surprised, they had only to stand still; the tangle of low branches would conceal them. "*But the bad part comes on the way out said the fox who swallowed the razor blade*," murmured Michelotti. They had put their foot in a confounded ant hill. The waters of the Adige seemed all of a sudden to flow furiously. From the north the clamor of bells and the nasal shrill of trumpets winged down upon them like ducks in flight.

In the last hours of the night, on the basis of a note from Trento which reached Broletto at eleven in the evening, all the troops cantoned in the valley of the Sarco and those getting ready to move toward Vicenza by the mountains above Borgo—that is, the entire third corps of the army—ebbed back into the valley of the Adige. Brigadier General Thurn, stretched out on the grass of a knoll a league and a half from Trento, was eating a snack beside a hurricane lantern. He was awaiting news of the Geppert battalion cantoned in Vezzano. He did not want to give the order to march and engage the bulk of the corps in the roads of a narrow valley, before being sure that Lieutenant Colonel Lentzendorf wouldn't crowd his flank on the mountain paths. He knew Lentzendorf. The fellow was a romantic Bavarian. Thurn was eating an excellent roast of sow. The light of the lantern made the grass a fairy-story green. Through the crystal of the carafe, the white wine was rose-colored.

Thurn requested his box of cinnamon bark. He loved wine, but with a little something extra: cinnamon was just this little something.

Before him Trentino was a constellation of campfires. Despite a hot night, soldiers like flames. They burned bushes along the roads while waiting for orders. Hummocks, thickets, and strange rocks in the shape of medieval castles stood out black as ink against the glowing smoke.

Thurn was in a good mood. He had a weakness for troop movements. He organized them with unequaled pleasure, and nothing was better than this moment when everything was ready, in suspense, at his service. With one word he would set fifteen thousand men marching, two thousand horsemen, fifty-four cannon, twelve commissary wagons, and two hundred drums. In the gloom which encircled his lantern, beyond the epaulettes and chests of his staff shining with gold lace, he saw the fires of his first brigade, ready to march into the mountains of the Margola. First he would speak with Lentzendorf, then he would have them sound the requisite blasts of the bugle.

Lentzendorf was brought before him at three in the morning. The Bavarian had remained very matter-of-fact. Several hours before he had received his instructions; the distant rumble of a considerable engagement to the south, echoing up the gorges of the Sarco, had put him on his guard. He was thus in a frame of mind to resist his own whims. He had ranged knots of troops along the road from Vezzano to Trento and was waiting for orders to fan out as a rear guard.

The noise of the engagement echoing in the gorges of the Sarco disturbed Thurn for five minutes. The attack on the entire Piedmontese front by Radetzky was not to start before daybreak. That was still a good hour off. Lentzendorf explained that the gorges leading to Lake Garda could have swallowed and swollen the uproar of Mantua, where it was known that big cannons thundered from time to time.

Upstream from Trento, the second brigade slept beside dying fires. Its commander, *Feldzeugmeister* [1] Nugent, had been alerted over Thurn's head by a special fast messenger from Verona. In the

[1] *Feldzeugmeister* is a brigadier general in the Austrian artillery service.

early hours of the preceding day Radetzky had sent Nugent, his youngest aide-de-camp, whom he had personally ordered to cover twenty leagues in the Alps in six hours. The poor fellow, a lieutenant in the mounted light-infantry, flew over the hilly tracks of Monte Tondo. Toward ten in the morning, in the vicinity of Santa Clara, he was trotting headlong down rough footpaths among fallen rocks when he noticed, on the edge of a beech wood, three unsaddled horses sniffing the wind . . . If he hadn't been pressed for time, he would have gone to examine the beasts, which appeared fine and were unaccountably alone: they were Angelo's horses.

Nugent was ordered to move five hours before Thurn. He had battalions, companies, squads, and even small lonely posts scattered over more than forty square leagues between Trento and Bolzano. At his order drums rolled, trumpets blasted, torches were brandished on the heights, and couriers galloped off at top speed. At eleven in the evening, when Thurn was beginning to move, Nugent had been under way for two hours. Moreover, the battalion quartered at Bolzano had been on the march for more than six hours, and the footsoldiers of the Francis-Charles infantry had reached the level of Bronzolo, having covered more than a third of the road to Trento.

Nugent could not control his troops as strictly as Thurn. He had to go along with whatever his officers initiated, even when they exposed scattered contingents along the side of the road. "Basically," he repeated to himself, "what I'm doing is pressing a sponge. So much the better. If the juice runs between my fingers, the important thing is not to lose too much."

The night was dark, and, with a lantern hanging from his saddle-bow, he scaled the thicketed slopes of the left bank. He had no imagination; he was like St. Thomas. But he climbed higher and higher on the rounded hills in vain: he could make out nothing of the movement of his troops.

They were making their way along the narrow valleys of torrents, without either flares or torches. However, he had had enough experience as a simple captain of troops mustered in the high Tyrol to know that his infantry was dragging its feet; that oaths and kitchen utensils resounded among the rock falls, rich meadows, and bogs; that his cavalry fumed about in the obstacle-filled dark; that his baggage wagons were breaking the muzzles of the mules; that his artillery teetered on the edge of deep ravines: what he didn't see didn't exist. He felt uncomfortably alone.

His staff was worn out. For hours everyone, even his experienced commanders, had been hounded for news by the couriers he continued to dispatch at a gallop.

Finally, two squadrons of lancers were pointed out to him as they came out onto the Ora road. Then he heard the rattle of his ammunition wagons. Having twisted and turned without stopping for hours in the steep labyrinth of the Menandola, the battalions of chasseurs, exhausted, halted on the heights of Caldar. Nugent saw their bivouac fires light up a league away, all along the road which led down to the Adige. He cherished his anxieties for moments like this.

At five in the morning, he had ranged his entire brigade in marching order along four leagues of the road, and his advance guard was encamped in the suburbs of Trento. He accorded everyone an hour's rest. The orchards were full of horses standing stockstill, with heads lowered. Infantrymen with their shoes off slept on the banks.

Nugent changed horses. He would have liked to change his staff as easily. His senior officer had disappeared; his aides-de-camp had still not returned. He thought of his daughter dying of tuberculosis in Vienna.

Thurn had departed. He had had his Croats march past to the clash of cymbals. He was sure of Nugent. He had no need to see him. He had received a report, moreover, that the advance guard of the second brigade, having traveled like greased lightning, was now cooling its heels a quarter of a league from the northern suburbs of Trento. He did not like the Tyrolean chasseurs. He thought that with their thick mustaches glued down on their beards, they had the mugs of bulldogs. But he knew they were intrepid marchers.

The air was perfumed with the rising sun, summer, and the mountains. The Croats quickened their pace. They were glad to go first. They knew that an army stirs up a lot of dust, that you choke in the middle of a column caught in a narrow valley. For hours they had been asking themselves: "Will Thurn think of us?" They knew his weakness for them. They shouted "Hurrah!" The cymbals struck violent black sparks.

At noon Thurn was installed in the castle of Besseno. His engineering-battalion was building quite a considerable structure in the valley of the Nomi, on the right bank of the Adige. The sappers worked stripped to the waist. Uniforms no longer mattered. A pick and shovel are congenial tools. They could believe themselves free. They were singing. They dug entrenchments and redoubts in the San Giacomo pass and, on a height commanding the Rovereto road, they established a strong blockhouse equipped with infantry and artillery. Cannon-fire could be heard.

Getting settled in the castle was not as easy. Thurn wanted twenty rooms. The old lady was stubborn as a mule.

She faced down the most stylish of the staff. But she was a baroness and, judging by her accent, Hungarian.

"Come now, Monsieur de Latour; you've got to take that away for me, child. No, wait, I'll do it myself. Give me my cane."

"Madame," said Thurn, "Colonel Zobel has been attacking the Corona Plateau since this morning and I'm going to attack Rivoli this evening."

Suddenly worn out, he turned on his heel.

The Baroness curtsied.

Zobel, having left Ovio, had come up for the assault with eight companies and three detachments trained to set off rockets. To his right he had Colonel Melczer, who had left Brentanico with four companies and two cannon. Zobel and Melczer were fire-eaters, Zobel especially. He made war the way an old gardener plants vegetable beds. He fell on a line of skirmishers backed up by a large reserve. He didn't hesitate. He made his men jump right in. He lost a third of his force in two hours. He kept up his attack until noon without winning an inch of ground. He broke through and then stopped to catch his breath. He asked himself what the hell Melczer was up to with his cannon. Melczer had lost one and was defending the other at sword's point. Zobel's soldiers were from Vienna. Driven, with a sword in the small of their backs, they forgot modern ideas like anyone else. Dug into trenches, they felt themselves down-at-the-heel and debated their situation (inwardly, an important point but, alas, no guarantee against the firing-squad). But indisputably he should have withdrawn. The corpses of the morning were ugly, black with flies. Nothing resists gunfire like a cloud of flies. Toward evening, he no longer had any doubt: Melczer was giving way. They were going to be turned to the right. Zobel awaited nightfall and gave the order to retreat.

The scarp of Besseno was traced with gardens of boxwood. The cool of the moat and the night suited the odor of the bitter shrubs. The large map, a lantern at each corner, was unrolled on the gravel of the terrace.

"The Baroness agrees to give you the second floor."

"I don't want any more rooms. I want oxen."

Thurn ordered one sixteen-millimeter cannon and one seven-millimeter howitzer hauled up onto Monte Pastelio with oxen. He summoned Colonel Wocher who was in command of the second regiment from Banat. Wocher was a pure Banatian; he pronounced mute gutturals badly. The map impressed him. His soldiers were ploughmen. Thurn knew Wocher liked the inside of his own pocket; with the end of his cane, he traced small circles on the map. Sufficient unto the day is the evil thereof; a battlefield must be limited. The end of the cane lightly tapped well-defined cantonments.

"Besides, I'm going with you, Wocher."

A white glimmer tore the night; a peaceful roar rolled echoing through the valley.

"What is it?"

"A storm, Count."

"Pack up," said Thurn. "I'm going with the Banatian. Give us two five-millimeter fieldpieces. A general move for the Bade infantry; Croats nine batteries, sixteen baggage-wagons, immediate departure. The rest at midnight, that is to say, in an hour. The Kinsky infantry in the lead, then the uhlans, the mounted batteries, etc. I want order. We're in a narrow corridor. Tell Nugent to follow."

The lightning and thunder surprised Angelo as well. Like Thurn, he had been following the noise of the cannon for hours. He was astonished by this roar brusquely introducing a sovereign majesty.

"This is a pretty pickle," he said to himself. "Michelotti's going to want to hide in my fob."

At nightfall the three horsemen had dismounted. They had extricated themselves from the thickest part of the forest, pulling their horses along by the bridle. They had found stopping places where every sound echoed beneath the high-branching trees.

"How many men are there in an army?" Giosuè asked.

"Very few."

"Offer cigars," Angelo said to himself. "Now's the time to use their idea of a gentleman. A Piedmontese, cigar in his snout, keeps his head high, even if it's being cut off. I've done so a hundred times. Besides, our situation isn't bad. If the entire platoon were here, it would even be good."

He saw himself all of a sudden charging the flank of the convoys and columns whose passage he heard.

He wondered what Lecca was doing.

"Anyway, he won't be able to use me for show. He's going to have to win his deputy's sash on his own."

The idea that the Napoleonic general was "hard-pressed in his political entrenchments" pleased him very much.

The Piedmontese cannon were no longer firing. In the clamor of the battle, Angelo had recognized the report of the four-millimeter pieces. Their mechanism had interested him greatly in the days when he dreamed, on the steps of some church of Saint-Roch, of riddling things with grapeshot. He had been told that in theory the four-millimeter fieldpiece was "dainty" and could be called the carbine of the artillery. He knew that it weighed three hundred kilos, that it fired a ball one league with five hundred grams of powder; that at three thousand one hundred meters it easily hit a man on horseback; that at this distance it could wipe out a cavalry corps; finally that the explosive force of its hollow ball was terrible. All very nice on the Polygon in Turin, on a spring morning, with new boots on, a docile horse, and a kepi with a pompon. But in darkness out of which the specter of a patrol might appear at any moment, it was another matter. The fact that Piedmont possessed an instrument capable of killing a horseman three thousand one hundred meters away (besides, why *one hundred*?) was not at all comforting. All the more because these instruments seemed to have positively shut their traps for the day. And troops still continued to flow down the valley of the Adige. It was now or never to wipe out the cavalry corps—the range made no difference.

They had to joke their way through this.

Muskets seemed to flare up again for a moment in the area which had been feverish all day. (Zobel's rear guard, somewhat nervous, was shooting at the bushes from which the hailstones of a sudden shower had just ricocheted. In reality, Zobel's retreat was not followed up. The three horsemen listened attentively to the fusillade. They were shooting in an echoing ravine.)

"Just because you don't like eating larks' tongues yourself, don't turn others against them," Angelo said to himself. "Since that thunder a while back, Michelotti's been expecting the devil and his host to come tumbling down on his back . . . If it's only a question of the Austrian army, he'll see easy enough. As for the little hairdresser, if I got him a good curling iron, he'd friz up one of their mustaches! . . ."

It was impossible to see to the end of one's nose.

"We've got to be friends," said Angelo. "When there are fifty or sixty men, a commander is a good thing. But three, I can't see why they need to be spoon-fed."

"Speaking of spoon-fed, it's going to be time for a bite soon."

The whole point was to know who the peasants were for in this neck of the woods.

"For their own interest."

"If Piedmont's getting them down, we'll make them understand that their interest lies with us three."

"Piedmont won't get them down the minute they can do some horse-trading. If you want to teach them anything, you'd better get started. They've got ears as big as cabbage leaves. They know who owns those cannon. If you've got them, you're it. If they belong to someone else, you won't get anywhere."

"I know how to talk with my hands," said Giosuè. "When I want something, people understand me fast. I can go explain to them what we want. We're not asking for the moon."

"You'll be sent packing like a leper. Do you think they've been waiting for you to arm themselves? You have a carbine and a saber, and what else? They have popguns. They ram them full of shoe nails. You think they're going to open up to you? These are hard times. You'll find a gun barrel as big as the neck of a bottle sticking out of a hole in the door. Try and talk with that staring you in the eye."

"I have some nice little gold pieces," said Angelo.

"Your tongue is the longest thing you've got, I've always told you so," Michelotti commented.

"We don't really need to eat," said Giosuè. "At least not right away."

Angelo was of the opinion that they should spend the next day traveling rapidly north. By then it would be easier to see what was happening; the mere passage of time would resolve the day's action. The affair at Rivoli would turn one way or the other. If the Piedmontese had the worst of it, this entire army corps going down the valley of the Adige would scatter through the mountains in little groups. That would be the moment to get into the act, to hell with lost squads, patrols, and foragers. When such people have had a beating, they don't kick up much of a fuss; we'll kick one up for them. If, on the other hand, our little friends on the road to-night take Rivoli, they'll have just one idea: to ride about in the plain and try to settle their accounts. At that moment, if we're in the neighborhood of Rovereto, perhaps even a little higher, big boys like us can get through the rear guard. They have soldier's bread in their packs, and sausage too, but anyone who's gobbling his food is a cinch to hit. Finally, in spite of the inky night and some storm rumblings, he described a situation in which there was still room for a little initiative.

"I must not let them see I'm in my element," he repeated to himself. "Even Michelotti (especially since hearing the thunder) would not like to know I'm trying my hand at war as one tries on a pair of gloves."

Day was dawning when a violent explosion shook the heights of the heavens. They were dumbfounded to see the peak of a completely rocky, blue mountain smoking. Thurn, by using oxen and caning his artillerymen's backs, had succeeded in installing a sixteen-millimeter cannon and howitzer on Monte Pastelio.

Michelotti undertook to conduct them to Rovereto. They were now in pastures where they could gallop.

"They don't need my talking to them anymore," Angelo said to himself. "It's daytime, and Michelotti's certainly going to hide us on those wooded hills. I can afford the luxury of a little solitary melancholy. On a beautiful morning like this with golden light and a landscape washed clean, making fools of kings, it'll be staggering."

After crossing the large floor of lustrous grass, they climbed the second story of the mountain. On peaceful summits the beeches had established the order and cleanliness in which they are accustomed to live. It was very open beneath the trees; pleasant riding. The springy soil hardly crackled and deadened the noise of the hoofs. They could let the reins hang loose. The horses, delighting in the cool, fresh air, made small feminine moans and walked at a measured gait. The leaves sounded like a sea asleep. The very light was at ease.

If the battle had recommenced, its clamor did not rise so far. The explosions continued regularly on the blue peak across the valley, tumbling down the hot corridors of the clear sky. The noise was that of a deep bass voice with undertones of thundering bronze.

The other slope led as well onto a floor of grass. This vast gilded pasture extended as far as the distant sawtooth edge of a pine forest rising from the slopes of the mountain.

"Down there, there's a road," said Michelotti. "When you go from Verona to Vicenza, it's the one that turns left at the entrance of Soave. It climbs this far passing by Tregnago and peters out in some forgotten spot. It's a little like the roads in our part of the world: it fizzles out, but if you go on after it fizzles, you pick up the road from Vicenza to Trento. Go down into the valley, turn left and you come out just where you want to, in Rovereto. Anyway that's the way it used to be in normal times. I did it in '42 and again in '46."

"What do you mean normal times?"

"When you could buy a soldo's worth of bread and two centesimi's worth of sausage wherever you went, first of all. I came into Rovereto with six old nags hairy as Popes, and bridles made of old bits of string. I went to the Piazza dell'Orologio and borrowed a bowl of beef stew as big as a foot bath. I sauntered about with my hands in my pockets; I stared at people; I said good day to the ones I liked; I turned up my nose at the others and went home with my nags singing *La Mère Godichon*. Try and do the same thing now with your saber."

"If I offer them cigars all the time," Angelo said to himself, "they'll soon think that I want the impossible. But the only thing I want is short-term happiness, twenty-four-hour pleasures or maybe even twelve-hour ones. If need be, I'll burn the candle at both ends, as a convinced apostle of liberty. But, in reality, I'll do it so I can afford a sun, an entirely artificial pyrotechnic one, as Lecca used to say."

When they halted, he spread his cigars on the grass. Rummaging in all his pockets, he found thirty-four.

"You must have more in your boot," said Michelotti. "I saw you put a package there which had three left in it."

"I've often seen Michelotti act like a hero in Ariosto," Angelo said to himself, "and so naturally that it made me envious. But I was wrong: he feels the need to smoke a little cigar when in danger of being caught short in banality. He watched me: he feared that he had not taken sufficient precautions."

He divided the cigars in three equal parts (he found a few more in his pistol holster and his cartridge case—but these were in pieces). Michelotti carefully gathered the bits, claiming that "you could chew them" (which he immediately did) and divided them with Giosuè (who likewise crammed the tobacco into his mouth with evident satisfaction). It was three in the afternoon—a long time since the previous morning's small piece of cheese.

Angelo gave a third of the cigars to Michelotti, a third to Giosuè, and kept the rest.

"You might want to smoke one sometime when I didn't think to offer you any," he said. "And, if you want to go so far as to eat them, what's stopping you?"

"Let's not waste the stuff," said Michelotti, "chewing-tobacco is the poor man's meat. Cigars are for show, and what a show!"

He stuck a cigar in the corner of his mouth and moved it about with his lips in a virile manner.

They now had to descend the northern slopes, no small undertaking. The mountains sloped sharply down to shadow-filled bottom lands, through landslides which had uprooted beech trees and gathered up boulders.

"No harder going than in our part of the country, Colonel, but what does the little hairdresser have to say about it?"

"If I'd wanted a highway, there were plenty around Turin."

Giosuè rode well. His horse was plainly too big for him; but it was clear, not only that he had chosen it, but also that he had desired it (he had perhaps even wanted it to be bigger). The nickname "little hairdresser" was understandable. A dried-up, not very red-blooded, finicky man, he always seemed to be chinning himself.

The valley was so narrow that the air was cold as in a cellar.

After more than an hour's fight with their self-respect, which made them forget Austria completely, they reached less treacherous slopes. A road ran a hundred meters below, at the bottom. They looked down on a house with large stables. Smoke rose from the chimney.

"You know what that is?" asked Angelo.

"In normal times it was a posting-station."

The smoke smelled good: wood, burned fat.

"Above all, no gold pieces," said Michelotti. "I know you— you've got bad habits. You've never gotten used to the idea that war's a time for giving people the slip and getting by. But I'm starved, and I want to know what indigestion is like. I'm told there is such a thing. If you pay, you count for something. I don't want to count for anything."

He proposed that they enter with sabers bared.

"It's true," Angelo said to himself, "that we haven't unsheathed our sabers often. Why wouldn't hunger be a good pretext?"

They were, in spite of everything, in the midst of planning a little trick when they heard the sound of wheels: a traveling-coach was drawing up at a walk, four lancers escorting it.

The carriage doors were closed off with leather curtains. Angelo noticed the bars of wood wrapped in cloth attached between the axles to support the springs and keep the carriage from rocking. The coachman drove as if he was in charge of the Holy Sacrament.

"That must be some bigwig they're lugging."

However, the lancers did not look as if they were escorting "top brass." One of them was even smoking a pipe.

The coach stopped in front of the inn. The innkeeper came forward. He spoke to someone who must have raised the curtain, but on the other side of the carriage, so that they could only see that he took off his cap and bowed slightly several times. The lancer smoking a pipe patted the necks of the draft horses. Another lancer dismounted and, pulling his beast, went away toward a small thicket of elders. The coachman raised his head and looked at the mountains, which undoubtedly seemed lofty to him. A young girl with thick red hair took various poses, standing so that she was framed in the doorway of the inn. A lancer went up to her and, leaning on his sheathed lance, bent down to talk to her. She stepped aside to let the boss pass carrying a basket covered with white linen, which he placed on the seat beside the coachman. The innkeeper then withdrew, taking the red-headed girl with him. The lancers returned to their posts. The coachman shook the reins, but kept the bridle-rein carefully in his hands. The horses started off again.

"It's too bad we can't charge in this narrow valley."

"Charge four lancers? That's a dream of glory for you! All we've got to do is advance, stare them down, and take the basket."

"I'd like to see the bigwig."

"What's preventing you if you ask politely?"

"I'd like to ask in a pretty setting. You don't know any nice spot which could do us honor?"

"Quantities of them. The one with the most class is up there."

Michelotti pointed out a wide gap in the profile of the mountain. It was a ridge over which the road passed.

They had to climb through the rockfalls once more and make quite a long detour. The ridge was indeed a nice little battlefield.

"Lecca was mistaken about me," Angelo said to himself, "but that's because he's blinded by politics, especially ever since he started pushing me ahead of himself. Without the basket, which probably has some ham in it, I'd never have the self-conceit to order anyone to charge, especially the little hairdresser, who still thinks I'm a real colonel and, consequently, would make me responsible for any orders I do or don't give. I don't want to subject anyone to my own conception of happiness. Not out of sentimentality, but because I refuse disagreeable thoughts which I'd have if someone died through my fault because he thought he had to be on my side. Fortunately, there is the basket and everyone, even the Church, talks about 'daily bread.' 'Work or you'll perish of hunger in the street.' These grassy slopes, this dark red sun, this brisk air, and even these lancers with their nice uniforms covered with gold are well worth a tripe scullery where you splash around in cow dung."

The sun was a little lower in the sky. The shadows deepened the echoes. They heard a fox yelp. Angelo noticed that they could still hear the cannon thundering from the summit of the mountain.

After a half-hour's wait, during which Angelo thought of the Rights of Man and of the Citizen, the traveling-coach appeared. The lancers did not show the slightest surprise at three horsemen stationed on the heights. Angelo advanced at a walk. He had imagined a pitched battle and even a sort of Fontenoy.[2] He had told himself, too, that the general, or perhaps even the field marshal, in the coach would undoubtedly station himself at the carriage door, a pistol in his hand. Thus Angelo's motives were lofty. Seeing that they took him for a peasant, a tradesman, a strolling bourgeois, he made his horse rear, drew his saber and shouted savagely. He regretted this cry immediately, but he was already passing at a gallop right in front of the draft horses, before the coachman's gaping mouth. He wheeled as sharply as possible to charge once more. The little hairdresser was in the thick of things with a saber which seemed gigantic and, in any case, was literally throwing off flashes of light. A thrown lancer remained prudently stretched out on the meadow in a somewhat bizarre position. Finally Angelo was confronted with steel and, behind this steel, a thin face, an ironic laugh, a *shapska* shaking gold lace and golden medals.

"He scorns my *crosciati*'s vest; he's right: it's ridiculous."

He was astonished to have done without thinking what was necessary to split this face in two. His adversary fell from his horse like a sack of wheat. On the other side of the carriage, the battle was over. Michelotti and Giosuè, dismounted, looked at the dead and even kicked them about. Angelo understood quickly that "they were not touching the pockets."

[2] Fontenoy, Belgium, the site of a "classic" battle in which the French, led by the Marechal de Saxe, defeated the English and the Dutch. Louis XV came out to watch the battle. Each side urged the other to fire first.

The coachman had disappeared, as had the fourth lancer, who, it seemed, had been hit in the shoulder. Angelo wondered why the field marshal was not to be seen. The leather curtains of the coach had remained lowered: he went to raise one. He prepared a Piedmontese phrase, that is to say, ultra-Napoleonic. He saw violet silk: a woman! He was caught short.

She was curled up in the far corner of the carriage, her knees tucked up under her chin, but she had a little dagger in her hand. Her hand was delicate and the dagger like a jewel. Angelo was still trying to understand what this elegant woman could be doing in a military area when he saw that she was seated beside a litter on which lay a young man in a uniform covered with gold.

Angelo tried to reassure her; she plainly did not understand Italian. The gilded young man spoke German vehemently but he hadn't much strength and let his head fall back on the cushions.

"We've attacked a wounded man?" Angelo said to himself.

"What do you want us to do? It's simple," said Michelotti. "We've got something to eat, that's the main thing. You're always looking for trouble."

The basket which had been filled at the posting-station contained chickens, ham, bread, wine, and potted meats.

"Don't fall on the food like roughnecks," said Angelo. "This woman is obviously of the best society; let's show her we're men of honor who've seen chicken before."

"You know too much," said Michelotti. "When I'm hungry I don't feel like joking."

He went to look at the wounded man.

"One in a thousand," he said. "You saw the crosses he has on his chest? Some are as big as your hand. He's lost one of his pins, but he's certainly a bigwig."

"At most the son of an archbishop like me," said Angelo. "They keep the bigwigs under glass. It's a long time since Vienna let her waltzers make war."

"I don't agree. Since the populace began to break windows in palaces, the archdukes have a tendency to get themselves assigned to the front. You don't give a damn, you pay cash; I pay attention: I have only my skin. I can smell out the top men; this is one of them. He went to see for himself what was happening to that precious equality and he met a heavy-handed cannon. We've got him and we're going to keep him. We're going to keep the prize! You've seen the little lady? She's got the eyes of a dead fish."

Angelo remarked that they were not going to spend their entire lives on the road, beside three dead bodies. Michelotti and Giosuè dragged the corpses into the underbrush. The coachman and the wounded lancer would sound an alert, but they had some way to go before reaching Rovereto.

While they caught the three Austrian horses, which had not had time to warm up in the quick skirmish and had not gone far, Angelo watched the prisoners out of the corner of his eye.

"She was carrying off her glorious young husband to some retreat. Like La Brenta, perhaps, in the mountains we can see from here," he thought. "She thought herself safe with an escort of four lancers. How firmly she held her little dagger when I approached!"

He thought again of his shout before attacking.

"It's true that swaggering made it easy for her to despise me. Hardly fifteen leagues from here the fighting's very different and, even if you believe in the justice of no particular side, it's always virtuous to rub up against a cannon (heavyhanded, as Michelotti calls them). Then if you make your own fanfare in your gullet, you can get away with it, a little ironically if absolutely necessary, but to attack a traveling-coach which is going along at a walk on a highway . . ."

He even imagined that at the moment he charged the lancers had been smoking their pipes.

"You no longer believe in liberty? Very well. But, the wounded young man (especially if he's an archduke) certainly had stopped believing in his blue blood long before he discovered it was red. Nevertheless, he went to an area where he risked losing a leg. And he lost one.

"Women whose lashes cast a large shadow are generally light in spirit. This one must imagine you are one of these self-made men who have the happiness of humanity on the tip of their tongues like a salesman's smile; a kind of Bondino, but stupider, because Bondino doesn't shout extravagantly and one can, if not respect him, at least fear him for what he is. Besides, do you care so greatly for people's esteem? Aren't you, on the contrary, trying by all possible means to make yourself loved, even at sword's point? And nothing is stupider than to say: 'Love me, I'm worth it!' "

"Are we going to wait all day?" Michelotti asked. "We've got the horses and all the junk. Let's go."

He knew a road at the base of the ridge, on the Vicenza side, which climbed among woods to some sheepfolds where he'd be damned if anyone came in search of them. They'd give them the slip and get by. If they hurried.

"Are you in charge?" Angelo asked.

"No, but you're fluttering around like a wet hen. All of Austria will be on our tail in five minutes."

"Then you can have it out with Austria. When you take something, you've got to be able to pay for it."

"Pretty fine, aren't you! I buy on credit."

"No one's giving credit any more, didn't you know? Climb up on the seat and turn the carriage around as gently as possible. We'll go to your sheepfold, but at a walk."

After more than an hour's climb under cover of large beech trees, they came out onto moors surrounded by the stars. Night was falling.

"If I was that woman, I'd be nitwitted and speechless," Angelo said to himself. "There's no choosing one's own heart. Am I at least able to enforce this walk which must please her, since she's caring for her husband?"

The sheepfold to which Michelotti had led them was a long building of gray stone, concealed in the grass like a hare. Inside, it was one long shed all of a piece with a floor of beaten earth. The grease from the wool of the flocks had tarred the walls of uncut stone more than a meter up. Its wide door easily swallowed the coach and troop. Giosuè closed the folding door and slid the bolts into place. The silence smelled of large rats, birds of prey, and flint. The Austrian horses sneezed.

Michelotti lighted a lantern, and unharnessed and attended to the horses. Giosuè found a niche (from which he pulled out an old pack saddle for a mule and ram's horns which had been used for gunpowder) full of fagots and even logs. In the middle of the sheepfold he made a fire on a flat stone intended for this purpose.

The leather curtains of the coach had remained raised. Angelo saw a tapered hand resting peacefully on violet silk. Finally, the hand moved, the young woman bent forward undoubtedly to reach for a piece of her baggage. The reflection of the fire put a gleam of flame in her eyes.

"I haven't searched them," Angelo said to himself, "and I certainly won't search them. Let her take the pistols she's surely got in that box and kill me. It will be a beautiful death. If she arms her husband, it'll be easy for them to fire on Michelotti and Giosuè, who aren't expecting a thing and will bolt. The woman would then be capable of saddling the horses, climbing onto the coachman's seat and taking her husband home *at a walk* through the forest, in spite of all the outlaws in the world."

He wanted very much to be killed by her. He posed suitably and in a good light.

She had put the money box on her knees only to take out a candle. Angelo approached with a brand and lighted it. The wounded man looked as if he was in pain.

"Can I help you in any way?" asked Angelo.

Her wide eyes looked at him, but her mouth remained closed (it was well-formed and large); she turned away to the money box, which contained bandages, lint, and phials.

Angelo returned to his place.

"I should have helped her," he repeated to himself, "at least to hold the candle so that she had two free hands."

But he didn't see how he could have done it without appearing to intrude.

"What are we up to?" said Michelotti. "Are we going to eat something more?"

"I'm glad that I thought to divide my supply of cigars," Angelo said to himself. "If I hadn't done so, and if I did now, they would think it was to keep them under my thumb. I don't need cigars to make myself obeyed."

"Eat if you want to," he said, "but go eat outside while you take the first watch. The patrols looking for us must have already left. Get it through your nut that if the patrols ever make fools of us, the first cut of my saber is going to be for you, while I'm still good and alive. Warn the little hairdresser; the same goes for him.

As long as it was only a question of liberty or Piedmont, I didn't mind a little horseplay. But now, we're the ones at stake."

He gave very strict orders.

"They're not going to come after us with lanterns," said Michelotti. "Don't think that. Even in full daylight, you've got to know where the sheepfold is to find it. You can go right by without seeing it. I've had it happen to me. The lancer and the coachman who escaped must have told terrible tales saying that there were at least a hundred of us. They're not going to put four or five guys on our heels with their heads in the air. It'll be squads and companies, perhaps even platoons of lancers stuffed full of fool stories. Do you think the three of us can engage in a pitched battle? The main thing is to stay clear."

"You're wrong; staying clear isn't the main thing."

"Then, allow me to tell you that you dumbfound me! Don't worry, I'll keep my eyes open and my ears flapping. But, in my opinion, listen carefully to what I tell you: a little shame is quickly past."

The young woman had succeeded in sticking the candle to the cover of the money box. She was talking to the man, who seemed to be more comfortable. Their conversation in low voices was like doves cooing.

Angelo, searching the basket of provisions, found an entire chicken, some potted meat with its cover still on, and a ham which had been cut into, but cleanly. The bottles of wine were intact; perhaps two at most were missing.

"I've got to admit," he thought, "that the loneliness of La Brenta, the rocks, the beech trees, and the brisk air have given Michelotti a strong backbone. A gentleman, hungry, would not have done better. He took just the minimum. And that's as it should be. You mustn't force others to enjoy things as you do, or else back you go to Bondino. With him everyone is fitted into the same mold. But if you believe in quality, you'll find it in the fact that he didn't let himself muck up the whole basket. As to the little hairdresser, he came here to change his station in life, and he hopped right up the easy way. In short, it will be easy for us to behave virtuously if we must."

He folded the chicken, the potted meat, and the ham in clean napkins; he put two bottles of wine under his arm and went to take the food to the prisoners.

The woman did not understand. The man managed a small smile. He had blue eyes; the smile hollowed a charming dimple beside his whiskers.

"Naturally," said Angelo aloud, but as if speaking to himself, "I need a silver platter, plates, flat silver, and glasses, but I'll be damned if I'm going to search your trunks."

He had never seen such complete incomprehension display itself on a human face. The woman looked at him as a cat would have—an unfamiliar cat. She experienced emotions, it was clear, from her glances at her husband, at the vast carcass of the sheepfold in which flames stirred the shadows; her mouth, which was beautiful, deep red, and set in scarcely tinted amber (she was a brunette), trembled almost imperceptibly, but there was no way of understanding her feelings.

Nevertheless, she rose, got down from the carriage, as if Angelo did not exist (besides he had drawn back), and approached the trunk.

"If she is to stab me, this is the moment," Angelo said to himself. "My back is turned."

He derived immense pleasure from not moving. He responded to the wounded man's smile.

"What an admirable death!" he repeated to himself. He was thinking of the little tapered hand.

But the young woman returned quite simply with dishes of silver plate, flat silver, and goblets.

Michelotti was keeping watch as he should. He had settled himself in a hollow in the grass, twenty paces in front of the entrance door. The starlight was so clear that he could see the tops of the forest trees standing out on the slopes of the mountain a quarter of a league away.

"I'll go take a little turn over there in a while," he said, "to relieve my conscience. As I see it, the last thing they'd think is that we've carted off their archduke up here, bag and baggage. There's not many would do it and you're lucky to have me along, especially at the pace you made me keep. How I cursed you! They won't get the picture for two or three days. Tonight, they're looking for us on the roads. Besides, look: to find the sheepfold, you've got to fall on top of it. Certainly, rummaging around, they'll find us, but between now and then a lot of water will go under the dam."

He had a plan to take the prisoners as far as the Piedmontese lines. He rejoiced in the expression Lecca would have on his face.

"That's how we differ," Angelo was saying to himself. "He thinks of the future; I don't. He has desires which the present never realizes."

Giosuè was seated on the grass, his back to the wall, smoking a little cigar.

"You should get some sleep. You'll have to relieve Michelotti in a little while."

"It's too beautiful out. It would be stupid to lose any of it."

Angelo went indoors to put some wood on the fire.

"People like Michelotti," he said to himself, "lay the blame on things, never on themselves; their choice lies between peaceful servitude and restless servitude only. As soon as they discover this truth, it reduces them to asserting their power. I, too, have never seen as many stars as tonight, nor more brilliant."

The wind roared like the sea. It even thundered as the roofing of chalky clay tiles swallowed it up. After a moment, Angelo heard in this thunder that of a large cannon. It was doubtless the battery which had for some time been making the summit of Monte Pastello speak. It was fired without haste; its arguments seemed incontestable.

Angelo had made himself a seat with the saddles. From where he was, he saw the interior of the coach with the young woman, her closed face, her tapered hand, and the wounded man who had raised himself on his cushions. They had not blown out the candle stuck to the cover of the money box. Having finished eating, they were talking; not a connected conversation, but a few words, cooing rather than talking.

"They, too, hear the cannon," he said to himself, "a cannon which seems to be winning."

He pulled out his watch and rubbed the case on the cloth of his trousers. He looked at his reflection in the steel. His face was haggard (the convex mirror accentuated his thinness).

The man leaned his cheek against the young woman's thigh covered with violet silk. At intervals he spoke one word, always the same one, in a gently pleading tone. She seemed to take pleasure in refusing, in making him wait; finally, she smiled. Angelo averted his eyes. He burned with shame as if he had just taken something which did not belong to him.

When he dared look again, the young woman was singing in a low voice. The wounded man had closed his eyes.

"At the age when in France, for example, a young man with a pure soul can devote his time to saying that he loves something other than the colors of his flag without being rudely checked by his conscience, I was in the Prytaneum at Turin," Angelo said to himself, "and under false pretences: I was learning from those I wanted to destroy the trade which would permit me to destroy them. For a long time I believed that liberty was a conquest, and it's a condition. I pursued nothing more than a hare, imagining according to a naïve (but handy) principle that this hare in the hand was happiness. But, nothing touches me more than melancholy (as for all those who usually most enjoy happiness they don't possess). Her song, of which I don't understand a damned word, certainly speaks of deep forests where one is happy. What must be the charm of melancholy for two alone together!"

He noticed that the young woman had not been singing for some time and that he was listening to memories. Soon she fell asleep. He approached on cat's feet and blew out the candle which she had left lighted.

"If it's only a question of getting oneself a woman with all the trimmings and elegant enough to do me honor," he thought, "I have only to return to Bondino as one returns to a badly cut redingote which nevertheless keeps one warm. Carlotta will be only too glad. I'll even have a salon, and a salon which will be sought after whatever the result of this war. I know how to use pride, and the disgust which d'Aché and company will inspire in me (which I will not even need to hide) will give me an enticing originality. They'll recognize my right to press a loving hand before going to sleep. So loving, even, that it will tremble each time it betrays me. Yet it will only betray me for political reasons and I am guaranteed faithfulness in the contract. If Carlotta ever lost her taste for me, they would remind her that it was her duty. They will be so glad I'm asleep that they won't haggle over the few drops of opium I demand. Rather they'll send for it all the way from China!

"But will I have the right to the essential if it is not in an attractive body and a well-disposed heart? The day I need a bit of soul, what'll I do? That's the moment I'll miss the serving-maid who was so nice to me in Milan. She hid nothing behind her adjectives: they came completely naturally; she would never prefer my equestrian statue to me: she knows that marble is cold. But am I as vital as a brewer?

"I raised a carriage curtain and found myself before a completely justified dagger. That woman was within an ace of striking, and she's capable of finding an artery instinctively on the first try. I was expecting a field marshal; I knew I'd done better the moment I saw her eyes. People say that on such occasions they flash lightning; actually they were icy. They showed no warmth until she turned to look at her beloved, or more exactly to make sure that he was still there, under her protection.

"Carlotta will never have her elegance. Not that she'll scrimp trying; she'll think of a thousand little devices. As for everything else, she'll be perfect. But everything else, the girl in Milan had that, plus added advantages: with her I could smoke in bed.

"No matter how long they turn me on the spit, I'll never make an edible dish for the gentlemen in the government. They don't know that six days out of six I make fun of myself, especially when I have that look which Carlotta would like to see modeled in bronze on all the public squares of Piedmont.

"Everything is disputed; which comes down to saying that no subject is sacred anymore; this hasn't fallen on deaf ears. Debates are so fashionable that ideas are sold in the streets. The cannon which annihilates the plateau of Rivoli is no longer anything but a charlatan's chest. A few years from now (the time needed to understand fully the value of four or five words akin to *social* for the figure they want to cut in the world) frontiers will no longer lie along rivers and mountains; they will cut down the middle of dining-room tables and even between the occupants of marriage beds. Everyone will be playing politics. It will be the new, less extreme way of getting out of oneself. A tripe butcher from Turin will no longer be obliged to ride a large horse, he'll gargle with *social* and exhale patchouli. No more *little hairdressers;* no more *big hairdressers.* But, I'm very finicky about the direction in which my hair is brushed!

"If I have no *loving hand* to hold in mine at the tragic moment of drowsiness, I'll grow sour. Unless I want to be absurd (and full of aches which my temperament will make insupportable) I'll have to stop chasing the hare I've been going after all this time. But could I ever get used to a vast horizon? (Now there's a thought that would upset Carlotta.) What pleased me about vast horizons when I saw them on either side of the hare was that they seemed constantly bathed in morning light. Not that I fear melancholy suns (even as regards the liberty of the people) or *del cammino alto e silvestro,* but I distrust irony. However, I'll be forced to use it.

"You fear the withering of the heart?" he said to himself. "Well, that's easy. In two months you can be in France."

He remembered moments when he could have had happiness like that he longed for now.

"Even when you're excited (you evidently were when you charged the coach shouting so ridiculously), you never have an air of tragedy—you're simply bug-eyed. When you raised the leather curtain of the carriage door, you must have been as pretty as the plague. It was easy to confront you with the point of the dagger, easier than gripping a horse pistol, loaded, moreover, with a ridiculously large charge, and leveling it at those hypocritical peasants whom the plague had shown how to live and who wanted a courageous woman's rings and my boots. And she fired. She had even fired a few days before at a crow which was accustomed to eating carrion; she used to say that it approached her body like a conquering lover.[3]

"This idea of the crow has more in it to make me happy than all Signor Mazzini's theories," he said to himself after a while.

"Do you know what's been going on tonight?" said Michelotti. "I didn't see you outside. I bet you slept like a log. I'll tell you what I've been doing: I glued the little hairdresser to the door as a

---

[3] Angelo remembers the bravery of the young woman who accompanied him on many of his wanderings in *The Horseman on the Roof.*

sentry; I pointed his eyes to the four corners of the compass and I went to make a little round in the woods as far as a high spot overlooking the bottom lands, toward Rovereto. All the scum of Rivoli are up in first-class farting fire. No more playing around; it's the real thing. Somebody's getting it. In our area, from what I saw, they're still marching into the low lands. Austria must be pouring into the plains of Mantua like a stream of shit. In my opinion, we're the ones who are winning in the whole deal. But, in any case, it's a cinch for the three of us. We'll see later how we can get into the act. The important thing is that the little archduke's no problem. They don't give a damn for him. In peacetime they would have been after him; they would have flung twenty patrols on our coattails. But today, we're free—they've got other fish to fry. I have a plan. Let's leave right away. I'm sure we'll get through. We'll take the two turtledoves to Brescia, to the boss, just as sure as one and one make two."

"I have another plan," said Angelo. "Let's leave right away, as you say. But when we're back on the road below, you get down from the coachman's seat and this noble woman (whose eyes are not cold) will take your place. We'll give her a pleasure she can appreciate. She'll take her husband wherever she wants, post and packing paid."

"I've always known you were crazy drunk," said Michelotti, "but, this time you've gone too far. We didn't fight our guts out for nothing . . ."

Angelo allowed himself to make light of the previous day's little combat.

"Perhaps you're no great warrior," said Michelotti, "but you're going to have to prove that you want to give your damsel liberty."

He drew his saber.

"How stupid he is!" said Angelo to himself. "He uses his saber as if it were a fly swatter. Yet he's my only friend. If I disarm him, he'll bear me a grudge forever."

He kept up the fight, dead serious, using all his skill to make the crude and even base attacks he parried appear cunning. Michelotti was the first to tire.

"*Basta!*" he said, "you're right, but admit that we've got good blood in our veins! And admit, without spite, that all the junk they tell the people, is a lot of crap. One guy who knows is always better than a hundred searching!"

Michelotti drove the traveling-coach down through the woods very gently. He spoke to the horses with intelligent brutality; the animals made it a kind of point of honor to brake the heavy carriage with their full weight.

CHAPTER THIRTEEN

Thurn spent the night in a windmill. Without closing his eyes, he listened to the large howitzers rumbling down on Rivoli like heavy birds. He felt old. He breathed with difficulty.

As soon as daybreak came, he buttoned his tunic and went out. His medals were heavy. He was impatient with his buttons decorated with eagles. Outside, shouts and the distant crackle of gunfire mingled with the song of larks. His orderlies turned away from him abruptly to hook their collars, then faced him and saluted.

"Why are they red as tomatoes?" he asked himself.

"You look strange . . ."

"It's hot, Your Excellency!"

That was it, it was hot. That was why he was having such trouble breathing.

And the dawn did not make it any cooler.

The brigadier general did not like things which grew. He looked indifferently at the hawthorns, the holly surrounding the hillock, the top of the low forests, and the blue flock of mountains to the south where the fighting was.

Thurn seated himself on a wheat-roller. An aide-de-camp unfolded a map and extended it at his feet. Generals came out of the bushes. Thurn motioned to them to stand behind him.

"My cane!"

He rested the end of his cane on a locality on the map and then looked at the real place on the horizon. Someone offered him his binoculars. His silence questioned them.

"Surely Nissel has not yet reached his position, your Excellency. The valley bottoms are in bad condition; yesterday's storm filled the torrents; I had trouble crossing, and he has six cannon. On the other hand, Hohenbruck engaged the enemy ten minutes ago in the center of the front. You can hear him."

"Hohenbruck is a wag," said Thurn.

He was anxious about Zobel. Zobel had his finger on the Sanctum Sanctorum of the story. The fate of the day was in his hands. If only Zobel would break through just three centimeters into the Piedmontese left flank, as far as Vola, for example, even without taking the village; if he would just hurl two companies of chasseurs into the vineyards . . . Thurn tapped the map with his cane. The lancers should stand by to exploit Zobel's smallest success.

"They're not out of the Incanale pass yet, your Excellency."

"Why?"

"The Piedmontese abandoned the lower entrenchments, but they've dug themselves in on the heights where the monument to Napoleon is located. The 4th Banat regiment, a battalion of the Louis regiment, and the 6th Tyrolean chasseurs have been on the offensive the entire time. The Banat is missing officers."

"Where are they?" said Thurn.

That was quite a question, and they were silent for a full minute.

"All right," said Thurn.

He asked for his portfolio. He wrote an order. A sergeant held the ink well.

"Not much ink left in this phial," said Thurn.

His voice was affectionate; the enlisted man swelled with pride. The high-ranking officer continued his report.

"The troops from the Alps, which are still snowbound, are exhausted. Their resistance to the heat is low. They've been walking for five days under the Italian sun with arms and equipment. They're short of food. The beasts of burden were unable to follow the columns. There's half a league of steep slopes before reaching the entrenchments of Incanale."

"Yes, it's very hot," said Thurn.

He called for a courier who was walking away with the note. He crossed out *lancers and hussars;* he wrote carefully above the crossed-out words: *dragoons, especially those of the Kerpa brigade.*

If possible under the orders of the leader of the Wurbna squadron.

"The lancers are too light," he said to himself. "They leap about, and it's not fencers I need. I need heavy carts. Not intelligence, weight. The heavier my cavalry, the better it'll get through."

He asked how many cannon Zobel had taken with him. He hadn't taken any.

"Acting like the Hungarians," thought Thurn. "He hasn't digested his retreat of day before yesterday."

Once again he saw Zobel scratching his whiskers with long thin fingers. He took up his binoculars. The center, drowned in smoke, seemed to be securely locked with the enemy. On the right Nissel had, it seemed, reached his position. A few sounds could be heard. You had to listen carefully to distinguish them from the larks, but it seemed that they were indeed the noise of an engagement with sabers. Finally, Thurn pricked up his ears: something had grumbled on the left.

He turned toward the generals looking for the eye of the man who had been making the report.

"You told me, didn't you, that he didn't take any cannon?"

"Yes, your Excellency, but the Piedmontese have them on the spot."

Thurn smiled: the joke was a good one.

"To horse! Let's get a little closer."

The more he thought it over, the more content he was to have thought of the dragoons. "No need of intelligence," he said to himself. "What could be more stupid than the apple that fell on Newton's nose!" He like his silent staff. Gilded but mute. Difficult to organize, but he had succeeded; ordering them all to wear monocles had been a great help. The blow he wanted to strike in this battle was going to succeed too. He watched for a let-up in the firing toward the center. Without this horrible heat . . . He was pleased to enter the shady forest.

Thurn came out of the woods about ten o'clock. He had breakfasted under cover, but the heat had been insupportable, not a breath of air and full of flies, especially the tiny, very annoying ones. As soon as he had passed the edge of the woods, he beheld the entire plain of Rivoli a hundred meters below him and about a half a league away. Nothing was happening there, or more exactly, nothing was happening there any more. The air still smelled of gunpowder.

At first sight, the plateau seemed covered with corpses, and *white corpses* at that—that is to say, wearing the white tunic of the infantry of the line and of the Hungarian grenadiers. But when he looked again, these *white corpses* were in curious positions, although they were indeed stretched out on the ground; they were talking an Innsbruck dialect. The air was so calm that voices rose like smoke from a charcoal-burner's fire.

They were what was left of Nissel's column. They had taken the plateau of Rivoli.

"Let's go!" said Thurn, while pulling at his horse's mouth (making him waltz and he acted as if, on the contrary, he wanted to constrain him).

The Viennese volunteers, the Tyrolean chasseurs, and the grenadiers had scaled the steep precipices and had thrown themselves on the enemy, bayonet in hand. Exhausted, the soldiers were resting, lying on the grassy heights they had just conquered.

Nissel was dazzled by a victory which, all in all, had been rapid. The head of his column had done all the work before even receiving help. His losses had been incurred mainly in a violent fusillade while they were scaling the precipice. The enemy had withdrawn toward the village of Rivoli without continuing resistance.

Thurn drew Nissel aside, going so far as to be familiar in a most flattering way.

"Do you have a change of linen?"

"Yes, your Excellency."

"Could you lend me a shirt?"

"At your service, your Excellency."

"I'm sweating like a pig," said Thurn, "and (he unbuttoned his tunic) it's very disagreeable. It makes me itch. I lose time scratching. My baggage is back on the road with the convoy. I didn't think to have it loaded with the artillery."

Thurn had a thick fleece of gray hair on his chest.

"Strange as it may seem," he said, "I get this hair from my mother. She was a Battenberg, and they claim that once upon a time a Battenberg accorded her favors to a bear. A Swiss bear, what's more. The pride of one of my grandfathers was his beard. It came down to his knees."

"Allow me, Your Excellency!"

Nissel rubbed his back with a handful of grass.

"That grass smells very good, Nissel, what is it?"

"I don't know, Your Excellency. In Italy, every grass . . ."

"Send three companies off in the direction of Spiazzi. You may take them from behind. What's ahead of you?"

"The 14th of the line and probably a Tuscan battalion."

"I don't understand a thing about those people," said Thurn. "So much the worse for me. In principle, the spearhead toward Spiazzi should be making them anxious. Go see. In any case, you'll open up the Incanale outlet a bit. Is that little village down there fortified?"

"Yes, Your Excellency. They defended it yesterday; today they abandoned it without a fight."

Thurn wondered whether the easy time they were having on the right wing didn't conceal a trap. He went to the village (it was Zuanne) and climbed the belfry. He couldn't see much from up there even with the binoculars: thickets, the edge of the plateau and, beyond, small valleys the cannon had filled with smoke.

Under this smoke the 14th Piedmontese of the line withdrew through the bottom lands toward the village of Rivoli with all its guns and equipment. They took with them carts full of bearded wounded who made it a point of honor to consider the blood like a fine spot of color in a painting.

The wooded heights which formed an amphitheater around Rivoli were covered with Piedmontese on the march. A squadron of hussars from Sardinia with sabers bared was waiting, massed beneath the willows. A multitude of artillerymen and horses were hauling fieldpieces up a hillock through turpentine trees. The gilded helmets of the Genoa dragoons danced in the dust. The royal rifle battalions were crawling along the slopes of the hills in battle formation. The *bersaglieri,* their cock feathers shining in the sun, wound in Indian file along the peaks.

A sudden engagement on the left sounded like a sheet tearing, and then the next instant, as if many were being torn. Above it all, you could hear the Piedmontese muskets, recognizable by their resounding reports (a new powder from France was being used). The rifle battalion nearest this side seemed to shiver to bits and scatter in the thickets. They deployed as sharpshooters, flashing silver scales: each soldier was drawing his bayonet. They became blue: they were charging. The trousers of the uniform could be seen better when the soldiers were running. The white Croats emerged from the forest. The fusillade of the Austrian platoon crackled like dry wood.

General de Sonnaz had just reached the battlefield with the 16th of the line. Zobel's advance guard had worried him during the brief hour in which his flank had been exposed. That was the risk of the maneuver he had undertaken. The alternative was simple: lose a half a day or rub up against Thurn's right wing. He knew Thurn; he had met him before the war . . . no, before the insurrection, for if at last it had turned into a real war with dignity, flags, trumpets, this war had begun as a wagoners' brawl (that is to say, a bad way to begin). He had not wanted to get mixed up in it. He had only gone into Milan in order to buy some gloves. (If they understood the allusion, so much the better!) He had met Thurn before the wagoners' brawl in a drawing-room; which duchess's drawing-room? Or arch . . . with diplomats, Hübner and . . . and anyway I was in civilian clothes; a simple Piedmontese gentleman. I had come from Paris, fashionably dressed: a gray redingote, most noticeable among those bedecked uniforms, grand crosses, decorations. Nothing much on me: simple as could be. You never know how Piedmontese pride will show up. In Thurn that Austrian assurance based on weight . . . The heavier an Austrian is, the more sure of himself he is. (De Sonnaz was slender, delicate as an iris leaf, with a thin mustache, like a whiplash, floating a bit.) Thurn with his right wing clinging to the slopes of San Zeno di Monti. I marched past him this morning at the head of my troops. How many of my men did he kill? Two hundred? That's the end of the world. When the Piedmontese want to get through, they get through. Go ahead and kill them.

The 16th of the line marched down the street of Rivoli. De Sonnaz was right: these men feared only one thing, "And that is to pass unnoticed," he said to himself. Piedmontese from Coni: mountaineers dry as oaks; this battlefield was ideal for them. The battlefield had another advantage to judge by the peaks Sonnaz saw rising above the roofs of the village: it was probably all within view like a stage. De Sonnaz gently urged his horse between the lines of soldiers and marched with them in order to get out of the narrow street and see the landscape.

It was magnificent. The amphitheater was beautifully rounded. They could maneuver there as on the war college blackboard. At the end of a road bordered by mulberries, the spearhead of the 16th's advance guard still going past reached their battle position. They were climbing the slopes. The soldiers broke their pace and entered the thickets with their weapons in their hands.

"What are we fighting up there right now?"

"Croats, General, battalion strength. We're trying to find out if they're being supported."

Once more it was Thurn's right wing. De Sonnaz understood the maneuver clearly. During this march this right wing had been prodding him with its tip ever since Castelnuovo. The troops must be drawn up very deep. They were now executing a face-left maneuver so that they would be aligned on his left.

He sent a courier to the Novara lancers. He wanted to have two squadrons on hand. He put his horse into a trot to climb a hillock. He asked the little aide-de-camp, who was brown as a nut and had such pretty eyes, for a cigar. He was new. This was the moment to win his loyalty.

Over the sound of the firing and the rumble of the 4th artillery caissons, the Novara lancers blew a few blasts on the trumpet, just enough to say that they were pleased to be on the move.

They arrived in platoons, coming out of the cedar groves and from around the corner of a wood of green oaks, by-passing houses and small vineyards. The pleasure they took in moving was visible even in the sparkle of their lance blades.

De Sonnaz granted himself the luxury of deploying his battalions in the form of a checkerboard. He loved a formation which in itself was certain. The mountainous terrain did not perhaps lend itself very well to this deployment, which requires rhythm (one dreamed of having it executed at a measured pace), but it added a kind of romanesque touch to the golden rule. The infantry uniform was not piped in amaranthine for nothing.

They were locked with the Croats up there. The gunfire was thick and fast, and despite the smoke covering the battle, it was easy to see that they were giving way, foot by foot; but the oak wood from which the attack had started seemed to overflow with white uniforms. It sweated them from every pore.

De Sonnaz didn't want to enter a serious engagement on the left. There he would have to cope with Thurn's right, and I wouldn't touch Thurn's right with a ten foot pole. The prisoners had said that it was commanded by Zobel, and anything to do with Zobel is immediate slaughter. Zobel is myopic as a bull: he lunges head lowered at any moving object. He's simply been put there to kill my men and get my battalions to run his way.

De Sonnaz wanted to pivot a quarter of a circle toward Rivoli to block the passes to Osteria del Dogana and Incanale, which the uhlans he knew to be massed on the Verona road did not yet dare enter.

He called the little nut brown fellow (who was very swarthy indeed and chubby).

"Sir," he said, "go reconnoiter the ravine behind those low hills. If they can contain a battalion, send the third there. They're over there, climbing. Hide them in the ravine and explain the maneuver to them."

He was going to give way before the Croats until the edge of the ruddy heath where the cannon balls had lighted the dry grass. There the enemy's flank would be exposed; the 3rd would then show itself, wouldn't attack (De Sonnaz stressed these words and stroked his mustache), wouldn't attack, and would climb on the double toward the wood in order to outflank their assailants completely. Zobel was myopic, but when circumstances so demanded he put in his monocle. They would give him a chance to use it.

"Leave the initiative to the company commanders. You'll be supported by the lancers I've brought up."

"Fine boy," he said to himself.

He watched him gallop away. The young man rode in the new style. He wasn't a career officer or a "political": undoubtedly a nobleman's son. At the present moment, nobles were staking a lot of money on their sons. What up to now had constituted nothing more than a boulevardier's elegance was now a means to success.

The 14th of the line in retreat came out abruptly on the peaks at the center. They advanced along a front a mile long. They were driving their carts of wounded ahead of them. Their rear guard was undoubtedly being harassed. Their surly firing still continued. They tried to stand fast on the summits in order to give their sanitary corps time to reach shelter. They were fiercely shaken. He could see their ranks wavering. Finally they gave way and tumbled down the slope. The peaks were instantly covered with white.

De Sonnaz loved the enemy because he could understand them by hints.

"They're going to entrench themselves there," he said to himself. "As soon as they're on a height . . ."

The Austrians had indeed stopped. And "they're bringing up cannon." Mounted batteries appeared. The 14th regrouped further down, sheltered by hedges and thickets.

De Sonnaz called an aide-de-camp.

"Go tell the 16th that they're going to be taken to task by the artillery. Tell them not to move. Tell them to hold their ranks even if they see our first line giving way badly."

"I need two battalions, not one in the ravine," he said to himself. He summoned another aide-de-camp.

"What's the name of the swarthy fellow I sent off?"

"Peretti, General. Orlando."

("Ah! The young Peretti! I should have known: the spitting image of his mother. Why didn't he introduce himself, the fool?")

"Go join him. Take the sappers, the pioneers, and the *bersaglieri* reserves. The same orders as before. Make the lancers march in the direction of that large red farm. Tell them to wait there."

He called him back:

"Restrict yourself to transmitting the orders. Leave the initiative to the company commanders."

He himself departed at a trot toward a grove of willows in which the drums had assembled. He took the greatest possible pleasure in putting his horse through his paces. He understood General Bès, who could not think of the simplest things except with his legs apart as if in the saddle.

He lined up the drums. Hurrahs came from the enemy lines. They got under way at a walk and began to go down into the amphitheater; the Croats, regrouped into lines, were marching along, pushing ahead of them a shining fringe of bayonets. The mounted batteries unyoked on the peak began to fire.

Good old general Bès! How right he was! (De Sonnaz raised one arm.) The whole reason for being on top of a horse was in order to think. He glanced to his left. The lancers were reaching the red farm. A heavy volley burst out ahead of him: the front lines engaged. He lowered his arm. The drums began to roll like thunder. The 6th corps of the Piedmontese army showed itself.

In addition to the retreating 14th, the waiting 16th, the riflemen engaged on the left, the *bersaglieri* deployed as sharpshooters, the Novara lancers, the Genoa dragoons, and the hussars, the 6th corps included five thousand other men. Battalions of the Savoy brigade, Royal Piedmont, Queen's brigade, Aosta brigade, and light infantry had been hidden until now behind hedges, hayricks, and walls. They surged up suddenly, shouting.

Six fieldpieces flanked Rivoli on each side; a mountain battery of four pieces had been installed forward in the ranks on a small round hill beside a hermitage. All these cannon spit at once.

De Sonnaz touched his horse with his boot and rushed forward. He heard his staff following behind him. He saw the galloping hussars opening to the right; to the left, the dragoons. The smoke of the cannon and the muskets rolled across the sun; the bullets raced across the fields like rabbits.

At six in the evening, the Austrians had been repelled and were beginning to flee along the entire length of the front. Zobel was retreating step by step, making his first line slip behind his second, and so forth. The center, broken through repeatedly by the bayonet assaults of the 16th of the line and by the charges of the hussars, had been pursued as far as San Martino.

The left, its Banatians falling back on its Croats, its Croats on its Viennese volunteers, dazed by the blows of all of Piedmont, yelling and bristling cock feathers, ebbed back in disorder into the narrow defiles, its rear guard hard pressed by the Genoa dragoons, its flanks harrassed by the Aosta Alpinists clinging to the heights.

The body of a Hungarian general was brought to De Sonnaz on a stretcher. With the sleeves of his tunic turned up and his collar unhooked, the corpse was that of a man who had been willing to put his shoulder to the wheel. They searched him. He was called Matiss.

"Don't know him," said De Sonnaz.

He was anxious about his horse. The one he had started the battle with had been killed under him; he had replaced him with this black one he loved; this horse had received a bomb splinter at the base of its neck. He had it examined by a veterinary.

"The elevation of the base of the neck permits the free movement of the two elements of force in the animal machine," said the expert. "It is the principal point for the readjustment of equilibrium for the mounted horse . . ."

Which amounted to saying that he would have to bemourn such a spirited beast. Night was falling. Darkness never improves things. He knew that "the horse carries his rider, supports him, and concentrates all his strength at the base of his neck." The bivouac lanterns which lighted the stable did not disperse the shadows; quite the contrary. At midnight, De Sonnaz received a note from Charles Albert: "What you've run up against is only the advance guard of a corps of twenty-five thousand men," said the King. He ordered him to beat a retreat.

"Twenty-five thousand men; no doubt that's quite a few," De Sonnaz said to himself. At Rivoli he could hold out against very strong forces, but had had only nine thousand men in all. And he still had to regroup them. Daybreak came at four. "It's easy to talk about leaving on tiptoes. We'll give it a try; that is, on the condition that we strike camp immediately." He was going to withdraw toward Peschiera. He sent couriers to all the battalions.

"Where is the young Peretti?"

"I don't know, General."

If the King's information was correct, he would have Wohlgemuth's four brigades and the entire first corps of Prince Schwartzenberg's army on his neck. The note also mentioned five squadrons of lancers. That was a bit much. And where had Austria stuffed the footsoldiers and horsemen all this time? He had thought them occupied with Bava or with Bès. Was he, De Sonnaz, the only

one making war? Couldn't the other Piedmontese generals put in
a few extra hours?

The setting of Rivoli was very lovely in the summer night. The
soldiers were extinguishing the bivouac fires; the echoes had become magnificently hollow; they gave back in a noble tone the
movement of the caissons, the squadrons, and the battalions. Too
bad they had to clear out. You could hang on here till kingdom
come. Obviously, if the information was correct, it was better to
pack up, especially if Nugent was going to appear out of Trentino
with all fresh troops from the Tyrol. But you've got to explain a
wise action (if you can get anyone to listen to you), whereas
heroism strikes the imagination; then all you have to do is to walk
down the street with head held high.

At daybreak as De Sonnaz was lining up his troops on the plain
along the route from Castelnuovo to Garda, a four-stripe doctor-
major cautiously opened Nugent's bedroom door in the Palazzo
Malipiero in Rovereto.

"I'm not asleep."

"I'm sorry, your Excellency, I would have thought that the
theriac or the extract of juniper . . ."

"I'm in less pain. The pain is wrapped in cotton, but if I move
. . . I had to call the sentries just now. All three of them carried
me to pee."

"Sciatica, your Excellency . . ."

"In my case wouldn't there be . . . you know my daughter's
illness? My chest hurts a great deal; like knife jabs. My mouth
tastes of iron."

"The electuary, your Excellency. As for your chest, it's a classic
example; the intercostal muscles. I know it's claimed . . . obviously, in line with modern thinking; but we're more positive."

All that was left in Rovereto were a few members of the staff
and those in charge of organizing the hospitals. The last brigade
which had passed entirely under Thurn's command had been completely engaged in the attack on Rivoli. The wounded were arriving in wagons.

The little mountain town had resumed its peaceful life. Nugent listened for hours to the buzz of a hornet which had caught its legs in the netting of the window. His fever made him long for quantities of soldiers. He told himself that his regroupment in the Tyrol had been a success. This was small consolation. He clearly heard that the streets were empty.

Angelo, Michelotti and Giosuè had furtively crossed the Trento road a league north of Rovereto on the evening of the battle of Rivoli. The weather had been fine all day, even a little hot.

The valley of the Adige was deserted. No peasants in sight. Something not to their taste must be brewing. They went so far as to leave the orchards loaded with apples to get along as best they could by themselves.

Without being entirely duped by this bird-filled peace (nothing imitates peace better than the very edge of an ambush), they thought it a cinch. They had only to stretch their necks and take a peek, cut across every road, come out of one wood only to go into another.

Surely some Austrians still remained tucked away in certain corners. Nevertheless, there was no guard at the little bridge of Isera. They crossed to the right bank of the river. They made their way around the village. Michelotti knew a hostler there. A house near the willows. If only he had, how should *I* know what, it doesn't matter what, bread more than anything else; they'd get four or five hunks of bread . . .

"It'd be better to wait for night, to leave the river, to go up into the mountains. In any case we've got to go around the end of the lake."

As for Giosuè, he could go without bread indefinitely, he "was still nursing." Go around lakes on horseback! And night was falling on the mountain which it was proposed he climb . . . It became very dark and the roads worsened. But with the exception of noises (and not one of them suggested war), night remained quietly in its lair.

Just before dawn they made out Torboli, which is opposite Riva. But unless they made a wide detour to the north of these two little towns, there was no way to cross this peaceful land without being noticed. There were people in the olive groves and even on the lake, in boats that didn't move or moved just enough so that the cool of the air would be agreeable. Sabers hanging from bearded scarecrows would surely be of general interest.

All three indecisive, they were standing on the edge of a wood ruminating unhappily (not far from feeling themselves ridiculous before these laborers, and especially these lazy fishermen—who, moreover, were singing, and very rightly), when a man in a black lounge-jacket, sheltered under a sunshade, came out of a thicket.

The newcomer hardly paused; he approached without appearing to be the least bit frightened.

"If you had no beard . . ." he said to Michelotti. "But no, even if you hadn't a beard, you still wouldn't be the man I thought now that I've had a good look at you."

He explained that he was looking for his wife's young brother, who had left three months before. At first he had come home to sleep every evening. Since good weather had come, they had not seen him. He must have gone north. Angelo pointed out that the battle was to the south.

"Obviously," said the man, sponging his forehead.

As for food, he had none with him. He was going to spend the day in a little cassino which he had on the other side of the wood, to see to a few feet of trellised vines, to keep himself busy.

"It's right near by. Come on. I have some hens. There'll certainly be some eggs. Unless they wanted . . ."

But they would have to cook them and there was neither bread nor salt, although maybe they could find some salt if they searched the little boxes on the mantle.

They preferred to gulp down the eggs. They were in a hurry. This haste disturbed him; especially their modesty.

"I've given you the rope to hang me with," said the man. (He had turned white as a sheet.) "You aren't *crosciati*?"

Angelo reassured him.

"We're Piedmontese," he said.

He was moved to tears by the grace of the vine which enlaced the trunk of an olive tree. He pointed it out.

"I understand everything, even pride," said the man who was getting his color back, "but I no longer have any use for anything.

I succeeded in marrying a girl a few years ago who could have done better for herself. She had only to say the word and I would have sold all the land I own around here and we would have gone to town, to live off some small tyrant, or perhaps even off an idea, for as you can clearly see, I'm no peasant; I regret this, and it's harder to forget that one has learned Latin than to learn it. I too have dreamed of saluting the rocks of Salamis and kissing the sacred earth of Marathon. Instead of saying this one word which would have made her my companion, my wife had other things to say. I began to love parasols and to live off the open air. There are three of you. Wouldn't you be happier if I made it four?"

If they were really headed south, it was useless to go around to the other shore of the lake. This shore would do just as well, and the road was shorter. "You can march all the way to Peschiera without fearing a thing. The Piedmontese left is supposed to be around Garda. That's ten leagues from here. You'll be there this evening."

At dusk Angelo was indeed stopped by a "Who goes there!" It was firmly spoken by a tall, thin young man in an alpaca redingote with a wide ribbon of the new colors of Italy across his chest. He was the sentry of the outpost of the student corps from Lombardy. They had fought the day before against Zobel's Croats. They had aged twenty years in ten hours, and they were in the process of enjoying their recently acquired maturity . . . They were holding a small front behind a brook. They did not understand why the retreat had continued all night and still less the rumors which had reached them according to which they had to retreat still more. They recounted their battle; it was incontestably a victory. With their own eyes they had seen Zobel giving way and even reeling under their blows. They had put themselves voluntarily under Sonnaz's command because they liked his attitude . . . They could find no praises high enough for the thin Piedmontese general; he had been seen everywhere on the battlefield. It was said that four horses had been killed under him; that he had been wounded in the shoulder; that nonetheless he continued in command of the corps. Nevertheless, opinion was divided on this last point. It was also said that De Sonnaz had died of his wound on a cart going down to Rivoli; that General Bès was now in command and that they were withdrawing because the general was too fat for this war.

The little village of Albisano which the brook defended was overflowing with these young civilians in university caps who, moreover, were grouped according to their field of study. They had no uniforms except for sashes with the colors of Italy slung crosswise over their shoulders above the belts and bands which cinch the jackets, redingotes, boleros, and even the black smocks of the second year science students. There was also an extraordinary collection of beards.

Angelo noticed among them men who were already formed and, without the slightest doubt, formed by something other than yesterday's battle. These mentors were almost unarmed, at least as far as he could see. "They must certainly have pockets and something in them, but they've learned not to show them off first thing." These gentlemen also wore sashes, but casually, without smoothing them out, sometimes even rolling them into a string.

"We have only to stay in this corner," said Michelotti. "They're nice. A little cavalry won't do them any harm. If anyone had ever told me that one day I'd be a grandfather . . ."

"They're your age. Some are even older than you."

"Yes, but look at their eyes."

The fact of the matter was that Angelo was melancholy, even when he was among blustering show-offs.

"Italy is too beautiful; she's in the process of making cuckolds of them."

"That's life," said Giosuè. "Long live egotism!"

About three in the morning there was an alert. Angelo rushed out with a dozen or so students who were already chewing open cartridges. Large black clouds were speeding across the moon. The sentries had seen large tarpaulined boats in the shadows of the lake. A rift in the clouds made them clearly visible. They were slipping along quite near the shore. The moon remained uncovered; the boatmen noticed the confusion and shouted that they were transporting supplies to Peschiera.

Angelo did not go back indoors immediately; he smoked a little cigar. Dawn was not far off; it was going to be very hot again.

The heights where the Austrian army were marching were black as ink.

Thurn had forbidden fires. Pipes and cigars were severely forbidden too. Court-marshal for any battalion commander who . . . He had permitted himself the luxury of one of those outbursts of anger from which he recovered quickly, but which had their effect.

". . . I shoot immediately."

"I don't understand the first thing about people who fight like lions and then clear out."

He advanced step by step in what he did not allow himself to call "the conquered territory," demanding perfect order of his men, down to their very formation in lines behind him, walking on foot like everyone else in the center of the front line. He overwhelmed Zobel on his right and Wohlgemuth on his left, who had been sent to him from Verona, with foot messengers carrying orders requiring signed receipts, the signatures of which he carefully deciphered in the moonlight, adjusting his spectacles.

"It's like the battle of Lutzen on the wings," he said to himself. "But I have a lake on one side of me and on the other Wohlgemuth, who doesn't like me. It was right here that Napoleon broke through our center."

He was reassured only from minute to minute as he saw the white chest of his battalions more than a league wide come out of the woods.

He was on his way down into the Rivoli amphitheater when a glow, rising to the left, put him on his guard.

He thought immediately of some insubordination on Wohlgemuth's part.

"Dawn, your Excellency."

He wanted to beat to death the young officer who had spoken. Then he grew envious of this free spirit which could recognize dawn immediately.

Day brought peace to him. He stopped to sleep at the village of Rivoli. At three in the afternoon he rode to see Zobel.

"Have your scouts found any springs?" he asked before leaving.

"Yes, your Excellency. Two very abundant ones. Enough for the cavalry and the convoy."

"Tell the infantry to fill their canteens," said Thurn. "The commanders will be responsible. They'll be court-martialed if I find a single canteen empty when I return."

The heavy air was heaped all around. The mountains themselves seemed cloistered within walls of storms.

Zobel was entrenched on the peaks overlooking the lake. His Croats were asleep, lying in groups under the ilexes. He was a small man. Something in his personal life had made him frown when a young man; he had never been able to get rid of his scowl.

"Have you thought of water?" Thurn asked.

"Yes, I had the canteens filled."

Thurn lay down on the grass beside Zobel. They were on a lookout. A half a league below them the thin ribbon of stubble and vines touching the root of the mountain unfurled; then the lake stretched out, leaden, reflecting the dark sky. On the opposite shore mountains of blue rock emerged from the heat mist.

"It'll be hot in the plain."

"We're going down there tomorrow?"

"I don't know."

Thurn had received orders from Radetzky on awakening. He had kept the aide-de-camp waiting. People seen just waking up are never handsome. The marshal was going to leave Verona.

"A classic maneuver," said Zobel, "this business in the center."

Thurn did not trust the classics. They were dealing with nervous types. Zobel didn't remember ever having met De Sonnaz before the war. Thurn spoke of a ball at Countess Hübner's. "Yes, I was there," said Zobel.

"A thin man just back from Paris."

"The Piedmontese are all thin, and they've all just come back from Paris."

"What's opposite you?"

"Come and see."

Zobel led Thurn to a spot from which a village could be seen below on the edge of the water. With a spyglass they made out the men occupying it.

"Lombards, students. I don't like them much," said Zobel. "They've already made me lose my temper."

It was very hot. The darkness of the storm weighed them down more than the sun. The heavens, darker and darker as dusk drew near, were in commotion, weighted with the load of clouds which rose all around the horizon. The wind blew in sudden dry gusts.

A downpour started as Thurn was remounting. The Rivoli cantonment smelled of pigeon droppings. He called for a table, his portfolio, and candles. He began to write out orders very carefully, forcing himself to write legibly, without flourishes, except the signature in the form of a ducal crown: a flourish he had learned from a calligraphist, but had sharpened on his own. When he had finished writing, signing, rereading and correcting, he noticed that the storm had broken. It was making a lot of noise. Lightning streaked in unending zebra stripes across the sky. The rain was so heavy that he could hear the tiles of the roof tremble.

Thunder rumbled in Verona. With its streets bordered by arcades and its circular stairwells, the town was an instrument admirably suited to this kind of music. All booted and spurred, Radetzky had been waiting an hour in the vestibule of the Palazzo Maffei. Someone had brought him an armchair. He had stuffed cotton in his ears.

The staff surrounding him opened its ranks to let through the little Ardelinda, Princess Windischgraetz, his hostess's daughter, with whom he was in the habit of playing grandfather. She was dragging along an enormous footman's umbrella. He unplugged his right ear:

"You haven't gone to bed yet?"

The chinstrap restricting his jaw changed his voice. The child looked at him with astonishment.

"You're not afraid?"

"I'm afraid you'll get wet, Excellency."

He took the little girl on his knees. She wanted to keep her umbrella. He put the umbrella between his legs beside his saber. He replugged his ear.

"Tell Princess Marie that the child is here."

Lightning struck the column in the Piazza delle Erbe.

It rolled like an orange over the paving-stones. By the light of the flash more than a foot of water could be seen boiling on the square. The thunder clap shook the palace and seemed to swell the vestibule with a breath of wind sufficient to burst the walls. A strong odor of phosphorus spread.

Radetzky stood up. He deposited the little girl on the ground and took her hand.

"Come," he said, "we'll go upstairs."

The child was still dragging the umbrella. The staff drew aside to let them pass, scabbards clanking one against the other. On entering the first floor drawing-room, Radetzky took the wads of cotton from his ears.

Princess Marie Windischgraetz was a round little woman with a very rosy complexion. The mourning she wore suited her to perfection.

"A bad start," said Radetzky.

"On the contrary," said Princess Marie, "I consider it very good."

"Tell me why, I beg you."

"The Lord wants to strike our enemies blind. They won't be expecting us today."

"You're right, no one would think of putting so much as a cat out in a night like this, and I've put out forty thousand men."

"It's thundering and raining on the Piedmontese too."

"That's their business. Mine is to know how battalions soaked to the bone and frozen to the marrow are going to act tomorrow morning. Have you ever spent a night in the rain?" (Radetzky loosened his chinstrap and took off his helmet.)

"Women suffer other trials." (She did not succeed in looking as if she was really in mourning. She was too rosy; her bare throat made her jabot too vermilion; a large knot of black-and-white-striped faille pinned to her bustle gave her the look of a pharaoh hen.)

"I've recalled Wohlgemuth," said Radetzky, unbuckling his belt and unbuttoning his heavy cavalryman's cape. "Thurn will be able to make out all right on his own. At present he has a river on his left. Thurn certainly prefers a river to Wohlgemuth. But Wohlgemuth has been marching toward Somma Campagna since seven in the evening with three infantry brigades of the most ordinary kind, men from Vienna who think in the stupidest way that 'if you go out in the rain you get wet.' The Prince was Hungarian; you're

Hungarian: it's natural for you to see divine harps in the storm. On that score the Piedmontese are Hungarian too, Marie. Why are you laughing?"

"At your harps. We would see dulcimers, not harps."

"But for the Viennese who count by hundredths of a florin, rain—especially rain that makes a noise like this evening—is an excellent pretext for lending an ear to the modern ideas according to which, believe me, the dulcimer no longer exists unless it's of the kind that pries up paving-stones and hurls them through windows. I have seven brigades, six squadrons, all my fieldpieces— two entire corps on the march in this devilish night. At my age, I see things as they are. I have just ordered everyone to halt where he is. But what's it like where they're halting according to my orders? Soaking fields in which my artillery is going to sink up to the naves? Swamps in which my cavalry is going to bog down?"

"You know that God protects a just cause."

"I don't know much along those lines any more, Marie. Don't stare at me. I know what God gives me, and I thank Him for it. I pray to Him and I love Him. But, I wouldn't have much self-respect (nor would he undoubtedly) if, instead of swearing like a pagan, I started to pray. Please send someone to find out what's happening to the weather."

The storm seemed to have moved on toward Peschiera. Unfortunately. News had arrived from Prince von Schwarzenberg who was commanding with Wohlgemuth. He had stopped on the Castelnuovo road.

"That wasn't the direction he was going in. He was marching toward Custoza."

He had chosen this road because it ran along an embankment above the fields. The streams had overflowed.

"A league too far to the north."

Colonel Wyts had also succeeded in sending a lancer. He wrote in his note that he was already in position when the order reached him and that he was staying there, not budging.

"Bring me the lancer."

He had arrived in bad shape. He had been taken to the infirmary.

"What does he say?"

"That it's raining, Your Excellency."

The lancer was right. Yes, it was raining.

Princess Marie remained still for a long time. The marshal had slumped in his armchair. He was asleep.

She took off his shoes, went and opened the door carefully, asked for some boiling water and powdered coffee. She did her cooking on the corner of a console. She liked small housewifely tasks.

"What is it?" asked the marshal.

"I'm making some coffee."

He had gone back to sleep.

He awakened abruptly. The thunder had ceased about a quarter of an hour before.

"Day is breaking."

The continual grumbling and the convulsions of lightning were moving away to the south. A large expanse of green sky opened toward Venice.

The marshal buttoned his cloak.

"Each time I put on my helmet I think of my father. He used exactly the same gesture to put the glass bell back on the clock."

He tightened his chinstrap.

"Where is Ardelinda?"

"Mme Delobelle came to get her when you were talking to the officer last night."

"Give her this little penknife. She wanted it. Be careful, the blade is very sharp."

He mounted his horse and dictated orders to attack while going down the streets of Verona at a walk.

Once out of the Porta Pallio, he could see that the weather was going to be fine. The east was entirely clear. The storm was moving off in the direction of Mantua.

Charles Albert was galloping along the road from Mantua to Castiglione. He was dressed in black, without either piping or braid. No one could have known he was king. It was raining too hard to wear his feathered *bicorne*. On his head he wore the *cuir bouilli* kepi of the Sardinian artillery. He had taken along only two aides-de-camp. He was on the point of joining the rear guard of the Savoy regiment, which was on a forced march to Somma Campagna. Dawn was just beginning to break.

The soldiers watched the thin artilleryman go by. The sky was clearing in the direction of Verona. Here the storm continued to agitate the poplars and shiver the darkness to bits.

Charles Albert didn't like people who ostentatiously sported beards (and, in consequence, a proud look). He saw in this a manifestation of liberalism. He was always ready to take anyone down a peg who not only grew the hairs on his chin, but also lost an infinite amount of time trimming them in the shape of a top, a chess bishop, or a French-clipped tree.

Three thousand six hundred bearded men were marching along the road hunched under the rain in rows of four with trumpets, flags, cartridge cases, and drums.

He shouted to them: *"Avanti! Avanti! Presto!"* going by at a gallop. They all told him to go to hell. The infantry wasn't going to knock itself out for a cavalryman.

On the other hand, he loved the saltiness of their language. He sucked his mustache with pleasure.

At the crossroads of Castiglione, General Aviernoz and the staff were waiting with fresh horses. The King entered the inn and changed his tunic behind a screen. The fresh one was black like the first and without either braid or decoration (with the exception of a little *moiré soutache* trim on the pockets) but it was dry. He drank some coffee.

Aviernoz was from Chambéry. He made his report. He had sent *bersaglieri* to Monte Piona, between Soma and Madonna del Monte, to look out for the enemy. He was going to join this detachment in person. General Broglia was holding the small wooded hills and the vineyards from Soma to Somma Campagna with ten thousand men: Tuscans and Piedmontese. Toward Mantua the troops were advancing along three roads. There was hope they would be on hand in two hours. No news from De Sonnaz. The last news, received evening before last had said that he was standing fast on a line from Garda to Castelnuovo, in front of Peschiera. There were difficulties in the commissary department. No bread for the last two days.

While Aviernoz was talking, hussars passed on the road at a fast trot. As for the positions of Soma and Somma Campagna themselves, they were holding them with two battalions of the Savoy regiment, volunteers from Parma, and a company of *bersaglieri* with a battery of cannon. At the Bosco inn there were another battalion of the same Savoy regiment, a Tuscan regiment, and some seige cannon. The Aosta cavalry was pivoting in a region he pointed out on the map; it was undoubtedly maneuvering with difficulty because of the storm in the night. The streams had overflowed. He had climbed onto the roof of the inn at daybreak. You could see expanses of water sparkling in the fields. It would be ideal if the movement of the Aosta cavalry could be completed in an hour at the most. It was five in the morning. The squadrons would be facing the Villafranca road at this moment.

The King departed across country with an escort of three chasseurs. He was riding a black horse entirely to his taste. The storm had withdrawn to the west. It was already very hot. The water-gorged earth was smoking.

On the summit of the hills an infinity of people could be seen moving. They were peasants leaving the battlefield with their carts and their cattle. All night the hamlet of Albisano below the heights of Rivoli had been agitated by the preparations for this flight which, in the morning, emptied towns, villages, and farms along the entire length of the front.

Angelo had kept Michelotti company ever since the first thunderclaps of the storm. He had seated himself on the straw at his head. He searched his mind for ways to reassure him. He had made him feel his heart under his vest. "Feel," he said, "how regularly it beats. Count for a bit and you'll see. This thunder and lightning is making a lot of noise although there's nothing to it; but if it puts us in any danger, my heart would be ready to give up the fight."

"That proves nothing," Michelotti replied. "Your heart especially. *You* live off defiance; not me. Now the little hairdresser's heart, maybe . . ."

He put his hand over Giosuè's heart.

"Ah!" he said, "worse still. Then you've never eaten cabbage soup?"

The only way he could calm himself somewhat was by going and lying down beside his horse.

Angelo went upstairs to smoke a little cigar with the peasants.

He found them packing up their goods and chattels. "Our cousin who lives in Castelnuovo has just come five leagues as fast as he could to warn us," they said. "When the lightning flashed, they saw a great many Austrian horsemen standing stock-still in the fields. The vineyards are full of Croats; their waxed kepis are shining in the rain. It seems that lower down toward Somma Campagna it's the same story."

In the other houses candles gleamed in the windows. Shadows gestured wildly. There too, people were tying up mattresses and putting hens in baskets. The rain was so heavy that the splash of the lake water could be heard above the echoing rumble of the thunder.

Angelo questioned the cousin. This Austrian army, immobile in the storm, seemed true. The cousin's devotion was explained too: there was a cow here which belonged to him. The cow was led on board a big barge where bundles were being piled. Each flash of lightning revealed other boats without sails which were being loaded.

As dawn broke the cow could be heard mooing out on the water, but the boats were hidden in the mist hanging over the lake. The window out of which Angelo watched overlooked terraced kitchen-gardens and olive groves which scaled the mountain like the rungs of a ladder.

"You've seen the new cartridges?" Michelotti asked. "Very handy. Imported from France. But they cost money. What are you looking at?"

Angelo pointed out white uniforms visible in the thickets above the olive trees.

"Hungarians."

The houses of the hamlet had become singularly silent. The window was large enough to allow them to aim their three guns out of it.

"I liked the old way," said Giosuè. "I did the loading myself; I was sure of my shot. Now, how am I to know it won't go wild?"

The Hungarians were out of range. They were everywhere in the wood; this was no patrol. Besides, they had their equipment with them, especially a little mortar on a gun carriage.

"Come closer, my little lambs!" said Michelotti, "come to us,

we have a little surprise for you. You think the French cartridge
capable of picking them off over there?"

"Don't risk it," said Giosuè. "It's a novelty like the sewing-
machine. It's made for sewing with a hot needle, for fast work,
but not for enjoyment. In a hundred years when the taste for enjoyment is lost, then maybe, but now while we still have it, don't
trust the little bastards."

Angelo was pleased by the silence. He could see guns protrud-
ing from the windows of the house opposite. The students were
as bold as hardened criminals.

"More than half of them cleared out last night," said Giosuè.
"They even fought to steal the boats."

Suddenly the Hungarian sharpshooters leaped very rapidly from
terrace to terrace and threw themselves flat down in the grass.
Immediately a volley burst from all sides. The little mortar did not
fire grapeshot as Angelo had thought; it spit some kind of stew,
which first splattered the street, spreading an oily, incandescent
substance, then struck the walls, and finally began to fall on the
roofs.

"We're going to be cooked on a spit."

"Loose the horses! Open the stable door; they'll save themselves."

Angelo jumped through a dormer window of the stable and took
shelter behind the walls of a pigsty.

The entire mountain was covered with Hungarians. About ten
small mortars were concentrating their fire on the village. To the
right, the enemy sharpshooters were already in the plain and were
forming companies.

Michelotti and Giosuè brought sacks of cartridges. Several
houses were going up in flames in Albisano. Small groups of students came to take refuge behind the pigsty, which had thick walls
and resembled a small fort.

"We're going to be outflanked," said Angelo. "We must make
for the vineyards."

Their retreat was greeted by a volley of bullets, but the enemy
had not yet entered the village and was firing from a distance.

The position in the vineyard was better, sufficiently withdrawn
in any case so that they would not be passed by the Hungarians,

who had gotten a foothold in the plain. This company was fighting at close quarters with a troop of small black soldiers who were protecting artillerymen pushing the wheel of a fieldpiece.

Beneath the smoke pouring from the barns where the stew had set the old straw on fire, the remains of the Albisano garrison leaped into the vineyards. A few officers were waving swords with gold tassels.

Angelo was ambushed at the foot of a small elm. He was firing on the Hungarians threatening the cannon . . . He saw Giosuè strolling between the vines as if in a palace. He shouted to him:

"Don't be a fool!"

"Why can't I be more familiar with him?" he asked himself. He noticed then that the din was deafening and that there was undoubtedly a major engagement on the right in which several pieces of artillery were engaged.

Suddenly it seemed that the elm sheltering him was struck by hail; bullets fell in its branches, hacking to bits its wood, leaves, and the leaves of the vines it supported. The Hungarians were charging. They seemed enormous, and their mouths gaped wide as ovens. But, caught by a fusilade, they were stopped twenty paces from the edge of the vineyard. They threw themselves to the ground and finally withdrew, crawling and then running, leaving the stubble heaped with dead and wounded.

"How many are we?" Angelo wondered. He asked himself too where Michelotti was. Before him he saw no one but three students who had lost their caps. He leaped beside them. The three were delighted about the way in which the Hungarian charge had just been repelled, but they didn't have much ammunition left. They were fastening their bayonets to the barrels of their guns.

The mortars began to spit grapeshot. Angelo crouched behind a willow stump. He thought that these bits of metal flying about at random cutting vine-stocks thick as an arm were stupid. He called students and signed to them that they should clear out.

On the other side of the vineyard, stubble fields one after another made a plain a half league wide as far as the small, monotone hills covered with the smoke and commotion of lively engagements.

Scattered remnants of the Lombard student battalion were trying to cross the open land against the resistance of the cavalry.

"Don't run," said Angelo to his companions. "You have no chance against cavalry. Stand fast if they charge. Fire at half-range at the horse. It's infallible . . ."

"Are you a professional soldier?" a small blond fellow asked him.

"No, this is the first time I've been in battle, but I was a hussar."

They could see the Wurmser dragoons taking prisoners and massacring. They were galloping along fifty or sixty paces from one another, trying to encircle as many fugitives as possible. When there were enough to make it worth it, they disarmed them, and one dragoon alone led them away as prisoners; but when the footsoldiers allowed themselves to be taken one at a time, they killed them so as not to be slowed down.

Suddenly the little troop was charged by six horsemen, sabers bared. Angelo knelt on the ground to show clearly that he wasn't going to flee.

"Here at least it's not a question of *accidents* as it was a while ago with those bits of lead," he said to himself. He was glad to wound a horse in the neck and kill its rider with the first bullet. The dragoon toppled over in a spectacular fashion throwing his arms up in the air and hurling away his saber. Another dragoon, hit in the back at the moment he was turning, was thrown with a piercing shout. The others cleared out.

But there was only one student left with Angelo. The two others, the little blond and a tall fellow, had lit out. They were scampering away, each in a different direction. The little blond was immediately hunted down and sabered; the tall one turned in his tracks, fired and felled a dragoon whom he finished off with his bayonet. He ran to rejoin Angelo and the other student.

"That was close," said Angelo. "I warned you. I know that a cavalryman is terrifying when he comes at you at a gallop, but, believe me, he's only a man and remember, they all shout when they charge. Not because they're ferocious, but because they're afraid like you. But your friend . . ."

He was dead, half decapitated, and his hands were hacked to bits.

"We must take his cartridges," said Angelo. "We have hardly any left. And his gun too; it may come in handy."

He went to pick up the saber belonging to the dragoon he had killed and slipped it, bare, into his belt. Since crouching to escape the grapeshot, he wanted to fight with a saber.

The Wurmser dragoons ("two platoons at most," Angelo said to himself) had not captured or dispersed the entire Lombard battalion by a long shot. In the beginning, their shouting and galloping had been in their favor. But two companies had regrouped and were marching in a square formation.

"Let's join up with those reasonable men."

To join them they had to go the entire length of the plain; they reached them just as the square, regrouped into a column, was starting up the hill. Angelo looked for Giosuè and Michelotti in this troop. They were not there, although there was a little bit of everything: *bersaglieri,* chasseurs, even dismounted hussars and artillerymen.

Angelo began to march along beside a large soldier of the troop in leggings. He asked him what had happened. The man said he didn't know a thing, that he had been in convoy on the Castelnuovo road when the Austrian cavalry had enveloped him. They had fired between the wheels of the vans. The only weapon he had left was a whip. Angelo offered him one of the two guns he was carrying. The soldier gave him a funny look.

All the detachments had crossed the little plain; only dead and wounded in red-and-black uniforms and bare horses galloping at random remained there. The battle raged in the distance on the outskirts of a little town drowned in cannon smoke.

Trumpets blasted and sabers sparkled through the rows of trees and above the foliage of the vines where cavalry fought. The sky was entirely clear; it was hot. Almost all the soldiers had put their handkerchiefs under their kepis so that their necks were covered.

Angelo understood how ridiculous he looked carrying two guns among these men who were definitely getting the hell out, although in good order. The hill was steeper than it seemed from a distance; the small round stones on its slopes slipped under their boot nails; the troop, sweating in their heavy uniforms, increased the heat tenfold; above all, he was thirsty and felt fatigue coming on.

"You're from Castelnuovo?" asked a hussar who had unbuttoned his overcoat and shirt, showing a handsome cushion of dark hairs on which shone a medal of the Virgin. "I ask you this because I was cantoned there last week."

The soldier took him, or pretended to take him, for a bourgeois who can be screwed out of his filthy lucre by a mere fib. He stated bluntly that he was thirsty, that on a day like today you had to pay for everything, in short, that in civilian clothes it must be easy to find a bit of tin. He saw the saber slipped through the belt and added:

"Look out for that, it cuts. If the krauts take you with that, they'll back you up against a wall . . ."

"No," said Angelo, "I'm not from Castelnuovo, and I'm taking a little stroll for my health because the weather's so fine and the landscape pleases me. I haven't a centesimo but I'll give you some scraps of cigars: chew them, they'll stop your thirst. That's what I do."

"I was just noticing that you're wearing the saber like someone in the trade," said the hussar, "but someone who isn't going to take any unnecessary risks."

He had charged three times in the course of the morning. First on the road from Castelnuovo to San Ambrogio to free the field-pieces. The Austrian dragoons had outflanked them: they couldn't have held out long. They had been reduced to nine hundred men. A fair number had been cut to pieces. What was left had regrouped under the command of "monkey's ass," a sergeant major: a Signor . . . ugly as a flea, but what a man! There was someone who knew what it meant to talk! After that they hadn't stopped moving. They had flown head on into the feathers of the chasseurs from Carinthia. That was over by Somma Campagna. They had faced right. Our infantry had taken a beating over that way. Face right, face left; in short, it had turned out badly. It seemed that now they had to go to Peschiera.

On the other side of the hill they found a village entirely submerged in soldiers: a jumble of footsoldiers, horsemen, and wagons was trying all at once to get into the village and get out.

"They've taken care of themselves all right down there," said the hussar. "Do you want to try and elbow your way in?"

"No," said Angelo, "but I want very much to get in there and do some fighting; that would make me willing to overlook a great deal."

"I agree with you. The only kind of Austrian I like is a dead Austrian. They told me to go to Peschiera, and that's where I'm going. But to get there maybe I don't need to glue my nose to the ass of some fellow who calls himself sergeant. We have only to take a tangent. You have two popguns; give me one. We're plenty big enough to make ourselves respected even by lancers."

They left the column and went around the village. They went along the flank of the hill, taking care to veer away from the lake shore where villages were burning. A gunboat was taking the garrisons of the little fishing ports to task. The Peschiera cannon was bombarding it abusively. It approached, buzzing like a gadfly, spitting salvos and fleeing, escorted by jets of water. On the road on the edge of the lake several platoons of red dragoons wheeled this way and that in the cross fire.

At the end of an hour they had lost sight of the lake. They were a league from a town toward which an infantry regiment was making its way.

Angelo and the hussar were dying of thirst. It must have been noon. The sun was unbearably strong; the stone of the hills was burning. A kind of silence had fallen, in which the tramping of the troops on the march, the crackle of bushes which bullets had set on fire, and the snore of flaming corn-shocks resounded. The air had grown thick with dust and smoke.

"This is the moment to be quick on our pins if we don't want to do without a drink altogether."

They were the first to arrive, but the town was already full of soldiers besieging the fountains. Riders were urging exasperated horses through the mob. Everyone was battling his way with his fist.

"I'm certainly not going to use my fists," Angelo said to himself. "If I wedge myself into this mess and anyone starts roughing me up, I'll draw my saber."

Fatigue, thirst, and tobacco juice intoxicated him. He noticed, nevertheless, that the soldiers battling their way along were unarmed. He scraped the bottoms of his pockets: he didn't have many bits of cigar left.

The hussar was not hard to please. He had already lost his

helmet, but he was drawing near the basin.

"I must find men who . . ." Angelo said to himself. He was thinking of Ariosto.

He left the market town; the sun blinded him. He started to chew tobacco again. He lay down in the shade of a willow. Almost touching his feet, caissons, baggage wagons and footsoldiers went by, part of the troops moving toward Peschiera.

He wondered where Michelotti and *Giuseppe* were. He slept for an imperceptible instant before realizing that in his heart he meant Giosuè and not *Giuseppe*.

A voice awakened him. "You snuck off on me." It was the hussar; he no longer had his overcoat or his gun, and on his head he wore the helmet of baggage-train men. He had had to go without anything you could call a real drink. He had just been able to plunge his head into the basin and swallow one stinking, shitty mouthful! He was much thirstier than before.

And the stories they're telling! General d'Aviernoz, well, he's dead, old man! He was holding Soma—well, at that. He had dug trenches all around, bastions. Inside he was like a pig in clover. He was killing off all the Tyroleans and Hungarians you could wish. The others put their handkerchiefs on the end of their guns. They shouted: "Long live Italy!" The fool thought they wanted to desert. He ordered a cease-fire. A Tyrolean captain came to shake hands with him and at the same time, mind you, he got two bayonets in the stomach. They took Soma. And Somma Campagna and Villafranca. There are uhlans everywhere.

Angelo's loss of consciousness in the shade had set him up; he could enjoy the taste of tobacco again. He was not displeased to see the hussar, who was obviously getting all he could out of the war once more.

"It would be one thing if we were malicious," the man said, "but look at it this way: are we malicious? . . ."

"Don't count on me for malice," said Angelo, "as you see, I'm a civilian. I can get the hell out of here without being accountable to anyone. If I stay here, it's because I like it. I don't like to bolt."

"First, it all depends what you're bolting from," said the hussar. "Then I wonder where the wrong would be if I hitched a ride on the baggage wagons as far as Peschiera. That doesn't mean I'm yellow. Do you see a fly in the ointment, my civilian friend?"

Angelo was going to answer him crudely when soldiers marching between the baggage wagons began to shout their heads off. On the enemy side fifty or so red cavalrymen poured down the slope of the hill. He ambushed himself behind the trunk of a willow and aimed carefully at a tall gangly rider bearing down upon him like a bat out of hell. His bullet hit the lancer square in the forehead. He was proud of this tricky shot and of the two or three that followed, carrying with them the same will to give a good performance. The volley coming from the bank beside the road toppled four cavalrymen; several others, wounded, dropped their lances; others danced a kind of very rapid Hungarian quadrille at a respectful distance and fled toward the hill.

The convoy had cleared out as fast as possible. Angelo found himself back on the deserted road with a squad of footsoldiers from Cuneo who seemed angry.

"Those cowards have left us in the lurch," said the sergeant. "If the lancers come back, we're in a pretty fix!"

"We can repel two hundred," said Angelo, still exalted by the attack. "We have only to hold our ground."

The retreating soldiers gave him a funny look.

"I was a hussar," he added, "I know how those birds maneuver, and I remember what I used to fear when I was on horseback. I served under one of Napoleon's generals."

"Unfortunately, we have no Napoleon on hand," said the sergeant. "Or else we wouldn't be in the spot we're in."

He stated bluntly what he thought of the generals and the King, speaking as a non-commissioned officer in command of twelve men who's been through the mill.

"That foolish bastard Aviernoz!" he said.

He seemed touched by the latter's death; there was something tender in his insult.

"If I don't watch out, I'll get tied up with these professionals," Angelo thought, "but it's a fact that the lancers could have gone to fetch some comrades on the other side of the hill. If they come back, and if these game fellows give even one damned inch, we're lost. And to be cut to pieces in such conditions would be to die an accidental death, which is what I hate most."

He risked pointing out that they were in open country and that in the little oak woods on the crests they would be protected from anything the cavalry might attempt. They listened to him, even nicely.

All together they cut across the fields toward the woods.

The sergeant gabbled on like someone who has just had a narrow escape. He was called Arturo, was a farmer in civilian life, and had won his stripes in the battle of Caffaro. He said, with a touch of ostentation, that he had under him notary clerks and even lace-workers.

Angelo noticed that these notaries and lace-workers trampled the lancers they had killed. But he didn't have time to be ironical about what he had noticed. The lads were looking for crusts. They were starving.

Angelo, who had thought himself the master of men's souls ever since the squad had closed ranks behind him, wanted to be agreeable. He asked for a bit of bread.

"What have you found, Luigi?" said the sergeant.

"Flesh! These characters are fat as tuna; they must have eaten in restaurants. They aren't thinking of the future."

"They haven't touched a thing since Friday. They've been tightening their belts for the last four days. We were hoping for a little something this morning when the Ostrogoths jumped on our necks. Talk about soup! We vented our anger on the fellows opposite, if that's what you're after, but anger and edibles are two different things, my lad, and in the long run, you look to the oats, like a horse."

What the devil did the King think he was doing? That was the point. If he had arrived this morning while they were holding the little grove, they'd be in Verona right now. Maybe not that far; in any case in that direction. They had charged six times. Hadn't he seen them give them a run for their money? Afterward, of course . . . There had been fifty of them, and only twelve were left!

The plain they were crossing was covered with stubble. The sun flashed off it as if from a mirror. Angelo even wondered if the woods toward which they were moving were not the shadow of this light, plain and simple. Toward the enemy the heat dimmed the horizon, but on the peaks of the hills a sort of orgeat white could be seen spreading: the Croats. They were more than a league away and looked as if they were advancing prudently. The noise of a crowd marching had replaced both cannon and musket fire.

"The men in this battle," Angelo said to himself, "hardly make as much noise as people coming out of a theater."

The sight of the Croat infantry made them hasten their steps.

"We're not much afraid of the footsoliders," said the sergeant. "We know how to keep them busy. The question is to find the right spot."

He had them count their cartridges as they marched along. Finally they reached the woods, which were no shadow and very thick. They had already been fought in, moreover, probably in the course of the dawn engagements. There were dead in every nook and cranny. Most wore the insignia of the Aosta brigade and some the number of the Pignerol battalion. The Austrians, according to the sergeant, who pretended to know what he was talking about, were Viennese from the Clam brigade and Banatians. They looked for bread in their capes and pockets, but found none. On the other hand, there were quite a few cartridges in the cartridge cases. The sergeant had them collected. "We'll have something to shoot with anyway."

He was of the opinion they should halt in the woods. He admitted that he had had enough.

"This courageous man fought a *good bit* of the morning, yet he looks at me all the time and wants me to give my opinion," Angelo said to himself. "But look out: it must be an opinion suitable for exhausted notaries and lace-makers."

"We can now see the Croat patrols," he said. "There are about twenty men in each, and there are three of them, without counting what they precede and what must be on the other side of the hills. They're not moving fast, but in an hour they'll be at the foot of our knoll. If you want us to fight, I'm your man and I'll stay with you. But it's easy to see that this position which has been taken and abandoned is worthless. Therefore, what's the good in fighting?"

Perhaps they could explore the woods. Down at its southern extremity, how were they to know whether they weren't in danger of falling on several bits of the Piedmontese regiments? That was toward Mantua. Troops might be coming from that direction. That would help them out nicely. In that case, yes, he would be in favor of coming back and telling the Croats off; but, strictly retail, twelve or fifteen at a time. Short term loans.

"What the hell is the King up to?" the sergeant asked, yawning so wide that he risked unhinging his jaw.

Through oaks which bit by bit became taller and thicker, they threaded their way along the stifling but dark floor of the forest, in shade that made them drowsy; but they heard cannon fire once more from a few fieldpieces which clattered dryly in the distance.

The wood was cut up into small valleys in which poplars and aspens shot up; they went down into them in the hope of finding water. There was some at the bottom in the puddles left by the storm in the night and in the fold of what, in winter, must have been a small stream. Their politeness, so much in accord with the imperials, mustaches, and eyebrows of the entire troop, went straight to Angelo's heart. He took out his tobacco and put it in the lining of his hat.

"When you throw it away, think of me," said the soldier who was next to him.

"My kingdom for a cigar," he said to himself. He would have given him a whole office full of tobacco.

"Let's not go to sleep on the job," said the sergeant. "Let's get moving."

They were approaching the edge of the wood when they heard firing quite near. They came out of the trees to see a small mounted fieldpiece careening toward them at a gallop, pursued by dragoons.

"This is a job for us!" said the sergeant.

They ran to get within range. Angelo recalled trick shots. He knelt in order to be really sure. He saw with pleasure that the squad remained in formation, putting a taste for their work well ahead of many other considerations. For five minutes he was extremely happy seeing the cavalrymen tumble to the ground.

The dragoons yielded almost immediately before this well-organized attack, which fired a rotating volley. They cut up a bit more, but far off-stage, and turned their horses.

The cannon and its caisson had stopped on the edge of the wood. The horses, covered with foam, were chewing their bits furiously. It took the six artillerymen and the corporal some time to catch their breath. They were black with powder.

"We were in position along the Sandra route. They made us run to the Bosco inn. We had to fire grapeshot. The Hungarians were twenty feet away."

"You had Savoyards with you?" asked the sergeant.

"I had Savoyards and Parmesans."

"The Duke was with you?"

"Of course! The whole works. They lost half their fellows. We were covering their retreat. We just missed being outflanked."

"We were outflanked," said one of the artillerymen.

"We were betrayed. But it's not over yet. From the Bosco inn we went to the Madonna del Monte. We got back on the Sandra road. For the life of me I can't tell my right from my left any more. We had to fight with bayonets. They were up to the wheels. The Regina brigades were the ones who got me free. It's one hell of a *pastaro;* men from everywhere are everywhere, but in little bunches like you. Without you children we would have had it."

According to the corporal—and he said that it was an order—they had to regroup at Peschiera; above all they must not go wandering around Somma Campagna. That was the center, and the center, believe me or not as you like, is stuffed solid with cavalry. They had tried to poke their noses there: all red and blue: dragoons, uhlans, lancers. You see farms and villages drowned in cavalry like stones in a brook. The dragoons were on our tail in no time.

The artillerymen had no bread. Their horses, harnessed one behind the other, were chewing the bark off trees. They went around the hill to continue on their way to Peschiera.

"Ask them if they have any grapeshot," said Angelo to the sergeant. "The patrols we saw a while back must have come up. If they heard the noise of the engagement, they'll be in the wood."

"Of course I have some," said the corporal, "but today, I prefer to whip on the horses rather than unhitch them."

He didn't like the smell of the Croats in this neck of the woods.

"It's Zobel," he said. "We came up against him this morning. You should just see what's left of the Visconti regiment."

Angelo could not stop looking at the corporal's hands. They were enormous and calloused.

"We're a long way from the victories of a young republic over an ancient tyrant," he said to himself. "But what is one to think of these 'liberals' who have a king for general-in-chief?"

They had passed the place where the hill joined another among the poplars of a small vale when the Croats came out of the wood too far away to be a serious threat immediately. Despite the distance, the patrols fired shots which could very well have been signals.

"Jump on the caissons, lads; we'll show them our heels."

"I don't have the slightest desire to clear out," Angelo thought.

He stood still while the others scaled the standard-sides. Circumstances made him seem a little ostentatious. He noticed this too late. The sergeant looked at him with disdain and turned his head.

Angelo was about to excuse himself ridiculously when the artillerymen whipped their horses with all their might.

"And besides," he said to himself, "what you were going to say is dumb as could be. How do you expect them to understand that you're afraid of dying an accidental death?"

He hid behind some vines. The Croats had stopped on the edge of the woods. They were not worrying about the small, fleeing cannon. He could hear their gibberish and the calm commands of the officers. They came out into the open, guns slung over their shoulders. Some were smoking pipes.

Angelo was fascinated by their strangely circumspect gestures. They behaved like people who have a certain manner to maintain in the eyes of the world. He was not displeased to note that they all seemed unnatural. He, too, slung his gun over his shoulder and marched under the trellises to the edge of a little pigeon cote. He found a handful of maize in the cote which he crushed between two stones. This quid of Indian corn somewhat sweetened his saliva; it had been very bitter ever since he had drunk in the mud. Raising his collar, he saw above the foliage of the vine-covered apple trees. Croats were slowly invading the plain, completely unopposed. He put his hands in his pockets and began to follow, plain and simple, the little path which passed near the pigeon cote.

He was not certain that it led in the direction of Peschiera. There were orchards all around him.

Coming out of the orchards, he found a burning village before him. The bright color of the flames told him that the blazing July day was about to close.

CHAPTER FOURTEEN

The moon had risen when he made out in front of him the silhouette of a construction with the look of a fortress. He was astonished to find Peschiera so small; it wasn't Peschiera. He should have known. Peschiera, where the entire routed left wing had converged, must have been full of hubbub and bivouac fires. It was silent here, except for the noise of running water which aroused his thirst, and shadowy, except for the red gleam of a lantern beneath a portal.

A soldier was seated in the dark, smoky light, his gun between his legs. When he heard Angelo's step, he shouted: "Pinerolo?" and whistled the first bars of the march of the 108th.

"No," replied Angelo, "neither Pinerolo nor Savoy."

"Savoy must be much farther to the right," said the soldier, "but where the hell is the Pinerolo?"

He ushered Angelo into a little guard house. There were five or six men there, all pioneers. The little fort (which was a fortress only in the moonlight) was called Benaco. They had come to build a bridge across the Mincio, which flowed at the foot of the walls. The bridge was in position. They were waiting for the Pinerolo regiment.

"If they begin to cut up like everyone else! . . ."

According to what they said, the attack in the afternoon had been right and proper. There had been a bit of a rout, but basically the best thing to do was to line up behind the Mincio and wait there in fine style for the Ostrogoths. They had been there since ten in the morning.

Angelo told of the Croats marching this evening across the plain with their guns slung over their shoulders. They counted on their fingers all the regiments and even the divisions posted behind the Mincio, from Peschiera to where they were and from here to God knows where! . . . De Sonnaz had all his men, separated from the rest, of course, but not by much: you can't make an omelet without breaking eggs. The Duke of Genoa! They had seen the Duke of Genoa, seen with their very own eyes, as the saying goes. He had crossed a league farther up on another bridge (not as well made as ours, vanity aside). The Duke had I don't know how many, but at least five hundred, men with him already. And that was only the start. Savoy? Savoy was farther to the right; they had crossed about three or four in the afternoon. No, there are ups and downs obviously, but it's all going along all right. And the Pinerolo regiment was coming.

They had bread and water in a pitcher. Angelo ate and drank. He awakened. One of the men was shaking him.

"You have cartridges?"

"Yes."

"Give me two or three and come see."

The moon had traveled far in the sky. It was setting in the west, giving off a red light. Angelo could not hear anything at first but the moaning of the Mincio.

"Listen," said the pioneer.

The same noise as in the afternoon.

"I've lost faith in the Pinerolos," said the pioneer.

The team was not commanded by a corporal or a sergeant, but by a master carpenter. He came to have a look. As far as he was concerned, carpentry aside, orders were orders. Noise? Well, what about it? What the hell did he have to do with noise? He listened, nevertheless, and signaled with his hand for a bit of quiet.

"We didn't even think of bringing along cartridges."

"You make me laugh," he said. "Have you ever seen a bridge built with cartridges?"

He didn't want to clear out. It was hard to resist his kind of command: "Clear out if you want, but I'm staying."

"Here is madness at last," Angelo said to himself.

The moon was slipping behind the hills. A reddish darkness extinguished the glitter of the poplars in the countryside. The noise increased; it was no longer necessary to listen with care. The master carpenter, the *boss,* had gone out with his pocket knife and was whittling a stick.

"I lose virtue dreaming of great maneuvers," Angelo said to himself. "It consists in the stubbornness of this workman who wants to deliver the goods to those who ordered them."

The nights were short; dawn was about to break. The boss got up and went to blow out the lantern.

Angelo counted his cartridges. He had some in every pocket: enough to supply seven scantily. He was pleased with himself. He enjoyed all the comedy of the situation. He was somewhat disconcerted when he heard Piedmontese being spoken with an inimitable accent in the bushes at the foot of the fort.

It was a troop of wounded. They were wearing the feathered hats of the Regina brigade. The strongest were carrying the weakest as hunters carry deer. Their bloody bandages were most touching in the green light of dawn. Out of breath, with uhlans hard upon their heels—"They're right there!"—they wanted to throw themselves into the fort, and hide in rat holes.

They supplied everyone with a magnificent excuse to escape. They pushed them onto the bridge; they made them cross the Mincio.

"Cast off," said the boss.

He leaped to work with his ax. A uhlan appeared on the other shore. His surprise at the river, which suddenly blocked his path, made him into a magnificent equestrian statue fit for a palace square. He wasn't there long enough to lose his beauty; all the pioneers and Angelo fired on him at the same instant. He toppled into the water with his horse.

The boss had hacked the cables which held the bridge below the fort. He delivered several more very judicious blows as he withdrew. The entire edifice was reduced to several large casks eddying in the current, capsized floors, and poplar trunks which, being green wood, sank immediately like lead.

Everything had happened so fast! They didn't have any clear

idea of what had made them cross the Mincio. The uhlan bobbed to the surface of the moving water two or three times, peacefully, as did the horse, which still moved its legs feebly while drowning.

The carpenter was proud as a peacock.

"It was indeed an extraordinary bridge," Angelo said to himself, "as perfect as the theoretical 'easy to destroy' ones."

Now was no time to dally; the uhlan was not alone. The wounded had been part of a rear guard. They had held out against cavalry and infantry with swords and daggers for a good part of the night. They were carrying their captain with them: he had died on the way. They didn't want to leave him: he had been quite a man. They didn't want the pioneers to help them with him either; they were big boys.

The cannonade had recommenced toward Peschiera. The battle was being resumed.

"Peanuts! a poultice on a wooden leg," said a little soldier of the Regina brigade.

He had gotten a bayonet in the arm, but he was wearing a swashbuckling hat and sporting a virile bad temper. Nothing existed except the Regina brigade. And he had seen the Regina brigade melt like a lump of sugar in boiling coffee. De Sonnaz thought himself an eagle. Why the man was as thin as a board! What was he hoping to prove at Peschiera?

The large cannon of the fortress thundered to the north at regular intervals. To the south, daylight had not succeeded in piercing the thick violet mists, shot through with flashes of light and grumbling like a train of tumbrils. This was in the direction of Goito.

These men had fought all night and were full of extraordinary news. The King had fought too, at Goito where the mist was. They pictured him in a stance a thousand times more *equestrian* than that of the uhlan. At the same time, they accused him of everything and said that he was a fine figure of a foolish bastard.

According to one wounded man whose beard was bloody, they were out of luck if they thought Goito was going to fix things up. What a joke! The bigwigs, bastards one and all, had plotted the whole thing. It was easy to prance about in a battle with a gold sword at the end of one's arm. "You saw the King that night?" He was in the sack snoring. He didn't come lend a hand. You're the biggest fifth wheel his cart ever had. What does he have to lose, do you think? When he's had enough, he'll go put the squeeze on from the other side. He'll give us all the slip and come out on top."

The wounded man breathed with difficulty. He seemed to have been hit in the chest. A little fresh blood flowed from his mouth.

Angelo was surprised not to be moved by this blood and by that which spread in a star-shape on the bandages of the other soldiers. He saw in it the badge of a freemasonry.

"They must have lived through some bad moments," he said to himself. "They were terribly afraid. They'll never be yellow again. They're going to make everyone else pay dearly for this."

They carried the captain's body a little too pompously. Was he not simply something to barter with?

"Since you've resolved to be egotistical," he said to himself, "remember you're not *paid* to escort these people; they undoubtedly have the very stupid idea that the mere fact of having a hole in their chests justifies anything. I don't want to be there when they invoke the highest gods on the corpse of this captain; it will have stiffened into the arc of a circle so that it looks like a stuffed rabbit. I know violent combat only by hearsay . . ."

He dropped behind and left the troop. He had all the fewer scruples because, across the open fields, he saw a small village where they could obtain help.

He headed right toward the cannon.

He had been walking for more than an hour in this direction when, having crossed a willow hedge, he found himself in the midst of fifty or so civilians armed with regulation guns, but seated in the shade in the field. They were a detachment of the provisional reserve. The men had no uniforms: they were wearing jackets, redingotes, and even top hats. They were pretending to be ambushed. One of their battalions and two cannon were up front guarding Borghetto, whose bridge they had blown up.

"Here's why no one worried about my civilian jacket and my Bolivar hat," Angelo thought. "Nice to know. If anyone asks me what I'm up to in the area, I'll say I'm in the provisional reserve."

Up to now, despite his finesse, or perhaps because of its *Piedmontese* quality and the subtleties that it made him see in everything, he had stupidly feared that his right to be on the battlefield would be contested. He was not far from believing that he would have to show his ticket.

He was not ashamed to ask for a little tobacco. Someone gave him a handful. He stuffed a good piece of it into his mouth.

The field in which the reserve detachment was enjoying the shade was a pretty square of grass enclosed by willow and aspen hedges. Beyond the hedges Angelo crossed other enclosed fields before coming to the edge of close-shaved, undulating terrain where a road bordered by tall silver poplars wound.

The entire region was deserted: everyone had been drawn north, where cannons rolled their fire like bass drums. All alone, a small buggy with its top up trotted down the road. Angelo and the carriage reached the intersection of the highway with a dirt road at the same moment. The carriage contained men of "the right sort" dressed in their Sunday best; three of them. They stopped to ask if he knew where the King was. Their faces were astonished but official.

"He's certainly not in the direction you're going," said Angelo. "You're headed for Peschiera, and they say the King's in Goito."

One of the three men, the one in the middle, wanted to know if this information could be trusted.

"Not at all," said Angelo, "but if I had to look for the King, that's where I'd go."

He explained why.

This explanation seemed to addle the honorable gentlemen somewhat; they asked for information on the battle in progress.

"I have none, except that there's some fighting going on everywhere and that up to now the encounters don't seem to be turning to our advantage. If you go to Goito, make a large detour back on your steps: this morning the uhlans had reached the Mincio, and that's hardly two leagues from here."

"Our mission is of the highest importance," said the speaker. "We must give the King a flag embroidered by the women of Milan. It would be too bad . . ."

This embroidery did not make Angelo laugh. He thought of Milan and hastened toward the cannon. The heat was insupportable. He took off his jacket and finally, after emptying its pockets, threw it away. Even his vest was too much, but it had fobs which were handy for cartridges; he contented himself with unbuttoning it, unhooking his collar, and rolling up his shirt sleeves. The sun bit deep. Angelo heard the blood beating in his ears, multiplying the hollow echo of the artillery. He was hungry again. "I've turned into a tobacco-eater," he thought. He wondered if this heroic nourishment, joined to the delirious light and the moist air, wasn't dimming his sight and if, indeed, it was the battle which was shaking sheet-iron behind the hills.

Coming out of a hollowed road he fell *fortunately* upon a village which had almost finished burning. The walls had been clawed by exploded bombs and bullets. He found a stupefied peasant emptying a drawer and putting iron forks in a sack.

The Austrians had crossed the Mincio out there this morning. They had swallowed down those little schoolchildren, the students, in one mouthful. You should have seen it! Who would ever have believed such a thing on the other side of the river! There's a villa belonging to the Marquise Bevilacqua in the trees: you should go see how they served that up Hungarian style!

Indeed it was a slaughter of Louis XV armchairs and statues. They had even succeeded in mutilating the reproduction of the Venus de Milo; Diana, Minerva, Juno, and the Vestals were lying on their side. Beside them lay the corpse of the kitchen maid.

Are you in the 43rd *bersaglieri*?" asked the peasant. "They left here an hour ago."

"The 43rd suits me," Angelo said to himself and doubled his pace.

He was soaked with sweat and out of breath when he reached a sort of little rear guard or, more exactly, ten or so laggards. These men were as determined as he, but as tired. They didn't have enough strength left to be astonished at the advent of this recruit running as fast as his legs would carry him: they were doing all they could not to lose contact with the tail of the battalion, visible through the dust, four or five hundred paces ahead.

Finally, the battalion paused and the rearguard was able to catch up. Many soldiers were in their shirt sleeves and wearing civilian hats. Nevertheless, he went and introduced himself to a lieutenant.

He was a thin dark man, who had kept his clothes cinched tightly despite the heat and who was resting on his feet, closing his eyes and chewing his mustache.

"There'll never be too many of us," he said.

He looked as if he didn't like enthusiasm. Angelo, however, had not put much of it into his offer to serve, just enough to be polite.

The roll of a drum started everyone marching once more. Angelo fell in with a line, beside a tall, lanky fellow who must have been from the valley of the Aosta.

"Chew?" the mountaineer asked him.

Angelo gave him a pinch of tobacco.

"We've been tightening our belts for the last three days. Have you eaten?"

"A piece of bread with the pioneers last night."

"Those fellows! A pack of thieves . . ."

The battalion obviously consisted of the debris of other battalions; there were even Neapolitans from the volunteer corps.

They crossed the Mincio on a bridge guarded by two batteries of light artillery. It was not the Peschiera road.

"We're going to Villafranca."

"A cinch," Angelo said to himself. That meant going back to the places he had seen the Croats marching with guns slung over their shoulders.

An order to hasten was passed along. They tried to, but began to lag almost immediately, stirring up a great deal of dust. The sun weighed upon them too heavily.

They were flaming hot as furnaces when they reached Villafranca. They had left more than a third of their force along the road in the shadeless fields. A sergeant had been detached to organize these laggards in case they were charged by groups of cavalry. Resting in the shadow of the houses, they bandied a phrase about, despite their exhaustion, until they realized that it meant just what it said, dead from heat.

The little town was overflowing with soldiers. It was even claimed that there were four generals there: Bava, Olivieri, Robilant, and the Duke of Genoa. In any case, Robilant's and Olivieri's cavalry were there, patroling around the edge of the suburbs.

They looked for fountains. They were all dry. The military

authority had first had them guarded by sentries, bayonets affixed to their gun barrels, and finally, because of the riots, had had the faucets hammered shut. Water was being given out in the school yards, but you had to stand in line.

About two in the afternoon (the heat had overpowered all the soldiers and imposed silence on them; the town was quiet as a cat when the clock struck), there was a noise at the southern gate, near the Benedictine monastery. Two brigades of Cuneo guards had arrived from Mantua. They were worn out. Lying in the shadow of the walls, the men rested at the entrance to the town. A short time later, it was said that the King had just arrived. Immediately the silence became heavier.

Angelo had already heard similar silences and sounds like the stifled noises now floating in the sky. He looked in vain for crows flying. According to his comrades in the 43rd, the Austrians had occupied the heights; what you heard were the blows of their mallets; they were sinking piles, fortifying their positions. Nevertheless, something was flying over the roofs: chain shot, destined for the foraging cavalry.

These balls played cat-and-mouse with the small, intensely blue hussars for a good while near the walls of the town. Smoke, dust, and the shying of the horses gently animated the dazzling light.

A drum rolled. "On your feet!" someone shouted. They had to cross Villafranca. The 43rd followed in the footsteps of three thousand men of the Lombard legion. It was indeed the King on the porch of a small palace; his black uniform, without any gold lace, mingled with the shadows. Only his face, cut in two by his mustache, could be seen. The cannonade had begun on both sides.

Once out of the streets, the 43rd deployed. The battalions preceding it had already deployed. The valley they were entering was covered with smoke in which blocks of earth could be seen leaping up but the forest of bayonets which emerged from it advanced, holding its line. All that showed of the officers as they caracoled about on horses engulfed by the smoke of the cannonade were their feathered *bicornes* and the thread-like swords they brandished ahead of them.

Angelo asked for cartridges; they were passed to him by the handful. He greeted several bullets which struck cloth around him. He heard a campaigning footsoldier's tinware clatter to the ground. He put his foot on a soft but living body. He jumped. People were shouting: "In line, in line!"

Suddenly he saw an Austrian leather cap rise a few steps to the left. He hurled himself forward, aiming his bayonet. The small section of the battle he saw was filled immediately by about ten dragoons' helmets and by sabers raised and then slashed down. The tumult of cruppers, manes, and heads of frenzied horses dispersed the smoke, and he could see a narrow corner of the valley; cavalry and white Croats were giving way and then fleeing toward a grove.

He heard someone shout "Forward!" They were now marching toward a hill tufted all the way to its summit with poplars and cypresses. The caterpillars of several regiments were crawling across the blond heights. They twisted in the arc of a circle before the puffs of smoke coming out of the woods.

Angelo noted with pleasure that the balls traced (as he had always imagined) visible trajectories. But he was surprised by the shaking of the earth beneath his feet. Moreover, some of the balls, filled with powder, burst after hollowing long furrows in the ground. The explosions made horrible wounds; he saw one send a dragoon's arm and half his shoulder flying into the air. He found the whole thing relatively easy. He scaled the hill, running like the others. He was expecting some major difficulty. He was far from thinking that the bullets miaowing by were the real thing. He was astonished how few soldiers reached the summit with him. Beside him a lieutenant, completely surprised, had lost his nerve and kept opening his mouth without emitting a single sound and pointing his sword in the direction of the enemy. He fired at the white suits fleeing between the trees.

The 43rd had in fact just conquered, by what is called main force, one of the hills commanding the valley of the Staffolo. Cries of "viva" rang out from the Piedmontese ranks. In the surrounding tumult they made no more noise than a little oil in a frying pan . . .

Other cries of "viva" rang out on other summits. The Austrians were being hunted from hill to hill. The green river of the five thousand men in the Piedmont brigade with the Duke of Genoa in command flowed, feathers in their hats, through the valley bottom, pushing before them the old plaster and chips of the white Croats. The cavalry trumpets began to sound the small, sour, hurried notes which encourage horses. The cannon sang with the beautiful voice they have when heard from the right side.

Angelo wanted to march in the van. He was carried away with things. People said to him: "Take it easy!" the 43rd had finished its job or, at least, gotten the real dirty work over with. Their orders now were to hold their line. The position was a fine one; the soldiers were in ecstasy as they looked at the steep slopes they had scaled under enemy fire. Everyone looked as if he was about to be promoted.

"Here is still more freemasonry," Angelo said to himself. "They'll never forget from now on that they climbed steep slopes to take this height. Must I too become a member of one of these secret societies?"

He looked with compassion at the twenty or so Croat corpses lying under the small green oaks.

"I've no sooner won than I'm on the side of the loser."

He was disappointed: first, by this rapid victory; second, not to have once felt that he was in any way useful. The knapsacks of the dead furnished only meager nourishment. His share was a biscuit hard enough to break his teeth; by dint of chewing it, however, he tasted a bit of cumin-flavored flour.

There was nothing to do on these heights except watch the battle move away in the direction of Somma Campagna. When the sun went down, he saw the helmets, breastplates, and sabers of squadrons on the move sparkle in the plain. At eight in the evening Somma Campagna was taken. The light artillery batteries changed position at a gallop.

At a certain moment there had been some question of waiting for the victualing wagons. The 43rd had even sent a fatigue detail to the base of the hill. At nightfall the detail had not yet returned. The officers declared that no one would eat, but that it was a good sign and the proof that they were dancing faster than the violins were playing. They would have been pleased by this violin tune if they could have found something to drink. The night was not even cool. The valley the Piedmontese cavalry had trampled for hours smelled of manure.

Someone awakened Angelo to give him another Hungarian biscuit. He had gone to sleep looking at the smoke from the gunpowder passing in front of the moon and repeating to himself a hundred times: "Will I find happiness?"

At dawn the order came to break camp. "We're advancing," people said.

At the bottom of the hill they entered fields covered with vines and elms. The regiment had melted away; a hundred or so men were left at most. The tall, lanky fellow from the valley of the Aosta was nowhere to be seen, nor the mustache-chewing officer.

The heat was already intense. Angelo was astonished by the march forward: several times he recognized spots they had been the day before.

They had been under way some time when a peasant lying in the grass rose and ran toward them. The Austrians were over there, in the village they were approaching.

Ready to snipe at the enemy, they slipped along under the trellises. Armed with his staff, the peasant came with them. He yapped brief phrases to guide them. Finally, through the foliage, they saw the enemy. They were grenadiers and Hungarian chasseurs.

Angelo, thinking that they were going to play it shrewdly, was greatly astonished when they began the attack, or more exactly, a disordered volley.

"There's more passion than tactics in this," he said to himself. "We're no longer fighting; we're insulting each other with gunshots. What are the officers up to?"

The peasant shouted as if he had been flayed alive. With his staff he pointed out a large red farm a hundred feet from the vines.

The column had been surprised by the fusilade; a few grenadiers bowled over like ninepins made the surprise a bit disorderly. But under the bullets which continued to slash them, the Hungarians closed their ranks and executed an impeccable maneuver.

"There's a machine for you," Angelo thought. He was delighted to see it functioning finally. It functioned very well. The grenadiers hurled themselves into the attack. The men were six feet tall, swollen by belts, straps, and pompons which made them seem even taller and bigger in comparison with the sharpshooters kneeling or lying behind the vinestocks. These giants, when they were hit, toppled with a crash.

The 43rd's firing was now much more satisfying; nevertheless, certain grenadiers had fallen hardly five or six feet from the position. One wounded man, sheltered behind the body of one of his comrades, began to fire with his barrel nearly touching the body of his adversary. His shot blew off the head of a swarthy man. Angelo saw the blood spurt; he even thought he could feel the heat. He continued to fire but less sedately than usual. It was no time to be finicky.

The grenadiers gathered for a new assault.

At last they understood what the peasant was shouting: the large red construction could be used as a fort. They had to get there as fast as possible. It would even have been better if they had run there a little sooner. While they were executing the maneuver, the grenadiers' shots heaped the vineyard with dead and wounded.

Angelo hastened under the shed, behind a pile of fresh straw. He saw a corner of the road, the entrance to the village where the Hungarians were setting up a little mortar. It seemed that there was nothing to do but to sell their lives dearly.

The first discharge of the mortar sailed over the roofs like a flight of partridges; the second made tiles and bits of timber jump. After a quarter of an hour's bombardment, so much smoke had been vomited by the little snub-nosed piece and so much dust had been loosened from the walls of the house raked by grapeshot to the bone, that it was like trying to fight under water with a sword. The sharpshooters on both sides fired with their eyes closed; the fusilade harrowed the smoke-house at random.

"This place is fit for smoking hams; the first idiot to come along could run me through with his bayonet sight unseen," Angelo thought. "There's no longer any merit to be gained here. One dumb thing follows another more absurd every time, all luck and no courage. I never said I wanted to play in a lottery!"

After several such clear-sighted thoughts (he saw himself committed to the most perfect of those accidental deaths which he dreaded above all else), he rose and was about to let himself be carried away by his need for imprudence when he heard the Piedmontese trumpets ring out. They were teasing on the men attacking the village, probably a detachment of the Regina brigade; this brigade liked trumpets a great deal. He checked his bayonet and hurled himself out of the farm at the same moment that the garrison poured out of it tumultuously like rabbits from a hutch.

Although he had received the blast of grapeshot head on, he had imagined the mortar to be the Devil himself. He was surprised to stumble almost immediately on the bodies of its servants. The smoke dispersed. There were no more Hungarians. They were under fire to the right and the left, but more to chase them than to fight with them. The detachment of the Regina brigade had surprised them at the moment they were dragging a small fieldpiece by hand destined to breach the walls of the farm. They had abandoned it. Victory was complete; thus even their artillery had been swiped.

The reinforcement which had arrived so opportunely was, however, far from showing external signs of the military virtues which this victory seemed to suggest. Angelo saw to his amazement that the soldiers were throwing away their guns. They had taken aside the lieutenant of the 43rd; they reproached him for this combat in which quite a few of them, they said, had kicked the bucket, and all for nothing.

Angelo wondered where these kicked buckets might be: they were nowhere to be seen. "This great battle," he said to himself, "has cost them just three blasts of the trumpet, and it lasted only five minutes. Yet they were twenty to one." Indeed, the men of an entire regiment were present. It seemed as if they were no longer commanded by man or beast, but by a feeling which drove them to accompany their virile gestures with high, piercing voices. Those wearing gold braid bobbed on the surface of these disputes like corks on a stream; except for one dumpy little captain mounted on a mortar carriage who insisted on shouting over and over again with his arms raised to the sky: *"Chi ha mangiato il diavolo, mangia anche le corne!"* But they told him that, after eating the devil, the horns were just what they didn't want to eat. Masks of the most sordid fatigue were on every face.

"What's going on?" Angelo asked of those around him.

"It happens that we're super-done-for and had," said a big bold fellow who had hairs even in his ears.

Despite his goat's head he too had the voice of a counter-tenor.

"That's the voice of defeat," Angelo said to himself with astonishment. He was still on the hill he had climbed so happily the day before. How had the regiments which had flowed through the valley of the Staffolo wearing such beautiful feathers been *turned inside out like the fingers of a glove*?

Everyone spoke of the church of Volta as if it were a holy sacrament. But what was the church of Volta?

"Where were you that night?" asked the bearded man. "Then stop where you are," he continued when he learned that Angelo had remained on the hill (which he identified as the hill of Mondatore if it overlooked the entrance of the valley). "You didn't see a thing."

They had attacked (they and a thousand others—what am I saying, a thousand! A hundred thousand! The entire army!) and taken Volta, and lost Volta, and retaken Volta, but not the church; that was impossible. Zobel's Croats were inside, and even Zobel (this was less certain, he knew nothing about it, they said it was so). In any case, taken, lost, retaken, relost, but never the church: they couldn't touch it. On foot, on horseback, by carriage: whatever they did, nothing worked. Repulsed with losses and tumult. Bayonets broken. (This was no metaphor; Angelo noticed that most of the soldiers' bayonets were indeed broken, and their stumps even covered with dried blood.) Night time. You couldn't see the end of your nose. They fired at an Acqui regiment taking them for the Ostrogoths and vice-versa. Our own cavalry cut us to pieces. I was so full of smoke I was puking my guts. We weren't just sitting on our asses. We slaved for seven hours without having a bite to eat. In the morning along came some fellows from Mantua who had really had it, with breadbaskets empty as ours. These and more landed on our ears, and so *barca*!"

He heard someone shouting: "Bread!" He interrupted himself to shout: "Bread! Bread!" with his voice of defeat.

Now the soldiers had thrown away their guns. They were divesting themselves of their equipment. The captain, who had climbed down from the mortar carriage, had resheathed his proverb; he had begun to float about like the other officers. They avoided looking at each other. Besides, their misery showed in their eyes and they could hardly stand up.

Angelo did not know that his face was sad and bearded too— that is until he heard the men talk of bread and even of beef (roast) as people who haven't eaten for four days can talk. Hanging was too good for the Lombard contractors who feared Radetzky worse than the plague because he was putting his foot right in the middle of their cashboxes simply by advancing in the plain; they had fled, taking their herds of cattle with them; peasants had even taken the rope out of their wells!

There was a moment of ironical confusion in the midst of these evocations of food stolen by cowardice and panic. A strong troop was coming down the hill. They were marching with the resolution of those who wish to carry all before them. Men began to flee on all sides without trying to pick up the guns which they had thrown in piles against the walls. It was only De Sonnaz's three regiments departing, without their equipment and disarmed, the tunics of their uniforms already unbuttoned like civilian jackets.

They brought excellent news: an armistice had been requested; no one was fighting any more; hostilities were suspended. They were repeating this last phrase everywhere because, since it was not of their own making, they found in it a little royal air behind which they could take shelter as behind an order.

They knew where the food was. They were going after it. People followed them in lock step.

Angelo abandoned his gun. He was afraid of being taken for a coward, but he kept his saber. He feared one of these fine fellows who thought themselves already in the clear might vex him. "Now that they're no longer afraid of anything," he said to himself, "they're capable of coming and asking me to my face why I'm fighting as an amateur. I must be able to answer them without making a speech."

It was easy to see that everyone had put this famous spot where the food was on the other side of the Mincio. Many flocks of soldiers, all with the same idea, were marching across the plain toward the poplar grove from which emerged the piles of a bridge made of iron wire. A platoon of Genoa dragoons came out from behind a barn and went trotting along, bringing up the rear. They were shouted at and stoned. They made room. Driven back on all sides by the shouts and the stones, they departed to ride alone far off in the stubble fields. No one had forgotten that in the course of the night they had done a dirty job of sabering several Piedmontese regiments without recognizing them. They too were marching toward the bridge, but before reaching it, they halted and waited to bring up the end of the column.

"There are the first culprits," Angelo said to himself. "From now on people will be making them up out of whole cloth!"

As soon as he imagined himself endangered by society, he assumed a disdainful air. Anywhere else the look in his eyes would have brought him trouble. But here everyone had a disdainful look.

The strange thing was that there were indeed supplies, even regulation ones, across the Mincio. An outdoor butcher's had slaughtered some steers.

"If this isn't treason," Angelo said to himself, "it's a good facsimile thereof. Who will remain drooling at his post if there's a wedding banquet here?"

One large loaf of bread and three pounds of meat were handed out for four men; wine was promised in an hour.

Angelo suffered a moment of terrified panic before this meat; he felt himself capable of eating it raw. The three soldiers with whom he made up a team got out of this fix with plebian elegance: they put the pleasure of rustic cookery before their ravenous hunger. They made a fire of straw and kindling. Other similar fires blazed up all around. Their part of the countryside soon twinkled gaily.

The cannon no longer thundered. You could hear the wasps buzz and the grinding of the axles of a long convoy of wagons carrying away the wounded. A horseman, who hadn't the least intention of stopping, left news as he went by about four o'clock. The negotiators were not yet back from the enemy camp. In his opinion they shouldn't expect a gift. The Austrians had stacked arms, but were lined up, right wheel, everywhere, up hill and down dale. You couldn't see the ground any longer, but only an ocean of leather caps and ten thousand statues of uhlans.

The dumpy little captain climbed onto a drum and shouted: "Soldiers!" He shouted once more: "Soldiers!" and then began a discussion with two lieutenants who had approached; the general indifference forced him down from the drum.

There was no further news in the evening; they went for information through the curtain of poplars. The contingents of the Casale brigade, the Lombard regiments of the brigade of guards from Cuneo, Aosta, and Pignerolo and the corps which the day before had still been under the walls of Mantua were camping disarmed on the plain. The baggage convoys were moaning along all the roads. The cavalry was passing in Indian file, on the sly: they wouldn't be easily forgiven!

They got wind of quite a bit. *Primo*: within a quarter of an hour of one another a courier from General Sommariva and an orderly from General Ferrero had come to say that at about five or six they should withdraw across the Ollio. They had replied: "There's time for everything; we'll eat, rest, and after that we'll see." *Secondo*: it was only a rumor, but people were saying that Radetzky himself wanted them to withdraw further than the Ollio, back of the Adda; and to hell with them. Why not? Now, this much was certain: the artillery had no more ammunition. The King (what do you know, someone mentioned the King!) had said: "I prefer to die with my weapon in my hand." Much talk on this score: easier said than done. He had to say something. Besides, all this was nothing but words.

Night fell.

Angelo noticed that everyone was leaving for Piedmont in little groups. "Why should I be more royalist than the King?" he asked himself. The King's tossing in his chips. The people are it. Join them!" But he swerved somewhat from the road everyone was following. He was sleepy.

After marching for three good hours, at the moment the night was calmest and all rustling with the song of crickets, he entered a little market town. He was the only traveler in the place. The people were out in the street, enjoying the cool and waiting for news. He told them what he knew and asked for a bed. A woman of about fifty who had listened to him, her hands on her belly, said: "Come with me."

CHAPTER FIFTEEN

S omeone was shaking him. He awakened.

"What time is it?"

"My dear sir," said the woman, "it's the day of the week you should be asking, not the time of the day."

He learned that he had slept forty-eight hours at a stretch.

"I came at leasty twenty times to tell you the Austrians were coming. Every time you replied: 'They're stupider than we are.'"

"Then I'm witty when I'm asleep," he thought. He remembered nothing.

Now the Austrians had arrived. He could hear their hubbub in the streets.

"First there were five of them, then ten, then a thousand!"

The regimental wagons were passing under the windows. He asked for scissors to cut his beard. His right foot was stuck in his boot; with blood. He discovered a wound on his calf. It had bled a great deal and taken care of itself. He left an inch of beard. He was very pleased by an infantile question which he asked himself while listening to the shouts of the Hungarian drivers: "How do the horses understand the Kraut they talk?"

The woman gave him some coffee. Night was falling.

"The moon rises at nine," she said.

He intended to slip out of town at dusk.

They had fought at Goito. It seemed that it had been a catastrophe. A lot of Piedmontese had fallen. Poor lads! The others had arrived subsequently: five, then ten, in no hurry.

"And what's been going on around Brescia, Bergamo?"

"Not a word."

"Nevertheless, the region is easy to defend," Angelo said to himself. "All the roads are bordered with canals and deep ditches; the fields are palisaded by trees and hedges. The cavalry can't maneuver on such terrain, and the artillery come upon obstacles at every turn of the wheels. It's because we don't want to. The King has thrown in his chips."

He went from the kitchen into a croft; he leaped a low wall and followed a path which ran along the stables. He had kept his saber.

The night was still dark. The Austrian campfires were easy to avoid; besides, they had posted no sentries. They were cooking soup, smoking their pipes, and speaking calmly out loud.

When the moon rose, he had traveled some distance. He was traversing the area where the regimental convoys, the baggage wagons, and the artillery were coming into the territory of the cavalry and the infantry. It was also the hour when the campfires die down and only a live coal remains; sleeping forms suffice to conceal them. But most of the roads, bordered by poplars, were black with shadows. All he needed was sharp ears and a good nose. The night was full of noises, from the surf-rub of the army still settling down, to the rasp of a pipe-smoker clearing his throat and the rattle of a dreaming horse. Arresting his catlike steps from time to time, he could also easily interpret the smell of the cavalry drill fields, coffee, tobacco, and the footsoldiers' sour leather.

He had tried at first to climb up in the direction of Brescia with the idea of crossing the Milan road and climbing into the mountains. But he realized he could not keep to any plan. At every moment an unforeseen obstacle forced him to change his course. A door opening into a farm kitchen in which Hungarians in police caps were roasting fresh pig over big fires pushed him left into the shadows. The voices of a small post made him retreat into the shadows on the right. The important thing was to keep slipping along; to hell with mountains.

When the moon set before dawn, he no longer had any very clear idea of where he was. He had crossed the gravel bed of a river, wide but almost entirely dry, which he supposed to be the

Chiese. He felt he had been pushed quite far south. He expected to find the bed of the Oglio at his feet or—who knows?—the walls of Cremona.

Day dawned, revealing an unknown plain covered with poplars, aspens, plane trees, sycamores, meadows, and orchards.

From a peasant who had spent the night in a hayrick and was timidly making his way back to his household gods, glancing like a hare in every direction, he learned that what he had crossed was not the Chiese but the Mello. Consequently, he was far from Cremona. Besides, there was fighting at Cremona. He could not believe in this battle. The peasant agreed that battle was saying a lot: there was tumult in that quarter, that was the truth of the matter. It could have been created by the confusion of a retreat across the Po which was throwing a little powder in people's eyes and at the sparrows. "But," added the prudent peasant, "be careful, this area is full of patrols." He advised him to take the dirt roads which cut through the willow brakes.

The roads were very nice, but they threw him off, especially in the indecisive light of dawn. Rounding a curtain of trees, Angelo found himself face to face with a uhlan who had also lost his way. He was a young man, apparently only recently recruited. He called out to Angelo with the triple violence of youth, surprise, and pride.

"Ergib dich, du bist gefangen. Geh, sei ka Tepp!"

"I don't understand a word you're saying! What are you talking about?" said Angelo, drawing his saber.

The uhlan also drew his saber and tried to maneuver.

"Was? Willst du mit mir spiel'n? Diese piemontesischen Schweine glaub'n alle, sie san mit'm Herrgott auf aner Schulbank g'sess'n! Hast no immer net gnua? I werd' dir geb'n!"

"I must stand up to him," Angelo had said to himself, "and he won't know where to turn."

So, instead of lighting out, he advanced until he could touch the cavalryman's thigh; in an instant their sabers were flashing, guard to guard.

"Jessas na! Was hat er denn g'macht!"

Angelo easily disarmed the uhlan.

"Basically," he thought, "this is a horse gained."

"Dismount!" he said.

"Schaun S' Herr, i hab ja nur g'macht, was ma ang'schafft word'n is! Sie brauch'n si' do net glei so aufreg'n!"

"You don't understand? Wait, I'll explain."

Angelo seized the horseman by the neck of his boot and, pushing him violently upward, made him fly over the top of his horse. He jumped in the saddle and gave the horse a kick.

"Mei Pferd! Mei Pferd! Du Gauner!"

For more than an hour Angelo was intoxicated by the horse. He marveled at this beast, which, although unfamiliar with him, obeyed his least touch or look. Prudence no longer counted; pleasure before everything else. From afar he saw bivouacs, infantry tents, columns on the march, foragers, artillery, and baggage wagons. His childish stunt did him a great service. Now that they were the victors, the Austrians were giving in to the heat too: they had taken off their tunics and their overcoats. All cats are gray in shirtsleeves. Obeying Angelo, and even joining in his game, the horse could do nothing but a uhlan trot, walk, or gallop. The victors were too victorious to imagine that this rider amusing himself was one of the vanquished.

He slept at a little farm. The peasant had seen him enter their courtyard with terror. But after his fear, the Piedmontese accent and two or three natural gestures a Kraut would have been completely incapable of imitating so reassured him that he would have given Angelo the shirt off his back.

They settled the charger in the stable after admiring his blanket, harness, and good temper.

The peasant, a good Lombardy man, no more from the Danube than Angelo, said: "Come in. I've hidden all the lucre and edibles, but I've got plenty of ham and eggs for you. All the more because I've got to eat too. If I didn't fill my belly, I'd stop being afraid, and it's fear that stops me from joking with people who don't joke. Some of my neighbors were too trusting: they thought a soldier-boss was a man like any other. To make a long story short, you can go see them: they're lined up at the foot of a wall full of lead while I've still got my guts."

He had sent his wife and children off to the hill where there was always a chance for anyone who can stay crouching in a bush. They had three or four more days before the reserves, who are less peremptory about booty and with whom you can always make a deal, arrived.

He thought Angelo better informed than he actually was. He never once supposed that this thin warrior with the look of an operatic hero had been cavorting about through the enemy lines all day on a stolen horse.

The day before the King had addressed a proclamation to Lombardy. He had said: "Take up your arms!" He had spoken of the ultimate sacrifice and humiliation.

"Take up your arms! What arms?" said the peasant. "What does he want us to use as weapons? Patience? The first Piedmontese saber I've seen in the last week is hanging from your belt. However, God knows how many of your King's men have gone by here, hundreds and thousands of them. And they've all tossed their arms over the nearest windmill. Don't you see, there's no worse humiliation than to see the wicked making hay while you're eating humble pie just because you tried to fart higher than your own ass. If you find a Lombard peasant ready to go cut Zobel's beard with his sickle, come and tell me about it, I'll go with him. But I'm alone, and I have my hay to get in."

In the morning when Angelo was leaving he counseled him to avoid the towns and stay away from roads. He could make out best across country. Straight ahead as long as there was no one there, and get the hell under cover as soon as he saw anyone. And remember to be afraid; he insisted on this: "They're savages!"

Obviously Angelo wanted nothing more than to go straight ahead. But he realized that little by little he was entering a region mired in troops, halting or marching, and far from being in their shirtsleeves. He almost stumbled on an entirely gilt-edged staff. He just had time to slip into a lane and stand still as a pillar of salt under the willows. It was a general (he seemed to be asleep on his horse) and his escort. The procession was marching along at an extremely slow and silent walk.

"I'm remembering to be afraid," Angelo thought, "but that won't prove much if my horse recognizes some colleagues and begins to whinny."

He used all his knowledge and then some to make his beast understand that they were playing a game and that he had to play too. It never moved except to twitch its ears.

Angelo spent the night on a hill. By the bivouac fires he came upon and their alignment, he judged that at least four divisions surrounded him, all perfectly disciplined.

At dawn trumpets sounded reveille without skipping a note and even with the flourishes of a casern.

Angelo remained on the hill all day. The bushes in which he was hiding were grazed over and over again by flank guards and scouts. He had taken the precaution of tying his horse to a pine a hundred paces from the bushes. If the beast was discovered, it could pass for the mount of a horseman who had gone to take a leak.

The army was advancing prudently. To anyone who knew the state of the Piedmontese troops, this slow and circumspect advance was ludicrous. The maneuvers were, nevertheless, extremely noble. The infantry was marching in battle formation along several leagues of the front. They were carrying flags and driving a dust cloud of foragers ahead of them with flames on the tips of their lances.

Toward evening Angelo remounted his horse and chanced it. At nightfall he found a bourgeois in Russian stockings airing his feet under a willow.

"I've had enough," the man said. "I left Goito day before yesterday in the evening. *You've* got it made. But if they catch you on that jade, under you'll go without so much as a ripple."

He had friends in the region, and this very morning he had been told a way of getting by the Austrian army.

"Thurn's the one strolling through these parts. He's not the man to risk bothering his legs by running. He takes one step at a time. He's going to Lodi just the way you've seen him. If you're going my way, that is to where it's safe, go up north."

He hadn't the slightest desire to accompany Angelo. Life and death, those are personal matters. A question of individual temperament. In any case, he seemed well informed. Before moonrise, Angelo heard in front of him the hollow sound of a countryside without bivouacs. In the morning he caught up with the stragglers of the Piedmontese army. They were lying along the road. Peasant women, disconcerted but full of good intentions, were trying to comfort them and even to prod them on with the words they used to drive cattle. These housewives, with their instinct for order, made pyramids of sacks, epaulettes, shakos, and the litter of weapons. The intersecting roads, villages, farms, inns, vestibules, and churches were encumbered with soldiers either fleeing or resting . . .

These men, freed from the yoke of discipline, no longer knew what peg to hang their hats on. They looked at the horse the way children look at candy. Angelo would have preferred violent gestures. He would have been delighted if they had unseated him, giving vent to their desires at least. This lack of character irritated him. He began to gallop. He passed some officers fleeing in a calash, insulting them as he went by. Finally he heard the sound of an engagement back of the hills; he spurred his horse still more urgently in that direction and drew his saber. He thought of the hangdog looks he had seen, fearing they were catching. But when he reached the summit from which he could see part of the plain, he couldn't make out a trace of the combat. He could no longer hear the gunfire. However, it was no illusion. Often in the course of the day, volleys crackled to the right and the left of him. Each time he tried in vain to satisfy his pride. Against his will he sheathed his saber.

He was still wondering whether these scattered salvos were the sign of excessive cowardice or of a burst of courage when the dusk was shaken and splattered by blazing light and an enormous detonation. Shortly afterward he met a little abbot gaping at the heavens. According to this man of God, this thunder out of a serene sky had occurred in the direction of Pizzighettone, and it was twenty to one that the powder magazines had just exploded.

Angelo passed through Crema, which was crowded with wounded, none seriously. He had been disgusted by the weakness of the disbanded soldiers; he was still more disgusted by those who shouted like creditors. Moreover, they offered their bandages as their stock-in-trade. Certain of them already talked through their noses like protesting bailiffs. Angelo, expecting them to demand his horse, lingered in the streets. But he didn't find the argument he was looking for: they passed too easily from arrogance to moans. Nor did he find anything to eat. He heard them saying that the King was going to Milan. He left the town right away, quickened his pace, and entered Milan by the Porta Roma with the first rays of dawn.

He returned immediately to the inn where he had rested after the uprising. He expected to find the little servant in the midst of her morning tasks. Everyone was asleep. Just above the trellis, the window of the room in which he had spent nights of dreamless sleep was open. He called out in a voice which he was surprised to find his own. He heard someone jumping out of bed, barefoot. It was not Lucia, but a tall, somewhat madonna-like girl who was delighted to show herself in her nightgown. She said that Lucia had gone, but that she was not the only girl in the world, and she called Angelo "handsome."

"I'm her cousin," said Angelo, "and I've got news from home for her."

The madonna winked to show that she understood the nuance. Lucia had gone to work at "Il Tordo d'inverno" on the Corso del Bocchetto behind San Stefano in Broglio, but she added that if Lucia had had that kind of cousin she would have bragged about him; all this to show that she wasn't born yesterday.

"Il Tordo d'inverno" was a hoity-toity inn. A delicate-legged thoroughbred was being rubbed down in front of the stable. They had not kept Lucia: "We don't put up with that kind of a woman here." The porter also showed that, in his opinion, it was very early indeed to be looking for her. Angelo spoke exactly as was necessary in order to obtain first politeness and then information.

Nothing sure, mind you, but nine out of ten Lucia was serving chianti in one of the slop-houses around the seminary, in the Via Bagutti maybe.

The February revolution had left its mark in the quarters around the seminary; half the houses were gutted or showed wounds patched with boards. Angelo drank some chianti and in the end ate a bacon omelet. These people spoke willingly and unreservedly. They knew nothing about Lucia; in any case, she hadn't made any impression on them; maybe she had come and gone without anyone noticing her.

Angelo returned to "Il Tordo." His demands for hot water, a razor, clean linen, and new boots made him immediately appreciated. He was given a room which smelled of Farina toilet water.

Except for boots for which Curzio, the Milanese Sikorsky, needed three days, he had at his disposal by four in the afternoon two soft shirts, trousers with straps under the feet, a scarab vest, and a long alpaca jacket. The shoemaker had brought him Albanian-style low Souvaroffs with which in any case he could stroll sidewalks.

The streets were entirely deserted. At the corner of the Corso Francese and the Via di San Pietro, Angelo went up to a poster some citizens were reading attentively. It said: "The army is conserving its numerical superiority. Sixty thousand men should inspire great confidence. The royal army is strong enough for anything. The Austrians will soon be forced to retreat. Volunteers should stay to one side and wait to annihilate what remains of the enemy as he retreats."

He looked in at the cafés for a half-hour and then went home to bed. He did not feel in the mood to face the *table d'hôte*. The softness of the sheets kept him awake a long time. He thought of the "loving hand."

Day had scarcely dawned when the respectable house was animated by unusual hubbub and coming-and-going.

"Well worth paying six francs!" Angelo said to himself.

He tugged playfully at his bell rope, but pulled it more than ten times before someone came. It was the stiff valet who had ushered him in the previous evening, but now his hair was standing on end and he had a wild look in his eye. From the outset the man spoke rapidly in Lombard dialect; his slow, well-brought up roll of the throat was gone.

It was no longer a joking matter. They were lost! Some . . . A hundred . . . bands . . . fugitives, wounded, heads covered with handkerchiefs, torn clothes, bare feet! . . .

Finally he found words which restored a shred of his dignity.

"You must shake off your lethargy," he said. And he went out, clicking the door.

Angelo's first care was to shut his saber in the closet.

The streets were now full of a tumultuous crowd. The news of the disaster was like a stick plunged into a damned ant-hill.

"Admirable," Angelo said to himself. "They all have packages under their arms. They all have something to save, but instead of holding their ground, they're looking for a hole. Where do they hope to hide their goods and chattels?"

He stopped in a group looking at something on the sidewalk: a pool of blood. The course of egotism didn't run smooth, whether in small things as here or, undoubtedly, in great.

In the afternoon he bought a hundred cigars and, box in hand, went to a café.

The morning's panic had been provoked by the arrival of the first fugitive soldiers. The town, with its shop fronts, well-brushed redingotes, cotillions, and women's faces—on which it was delightful to imprint the marks of terror—gave their tongues back to these defeated men who needed accomplices and scapegoats. It was a big come-down for Milan. That explained the blood on the sidewalk. No longer did people make a mystery of feelings which would have seemed unsuitable the day before; nevertheless, they were not yet very bold, for from minute to minute they realized that danger was not immediate and that there was still a way to save face.

With his *acqua d'amarina* before him, Angelo listened to the people conversing around him.

They needed a strong government, a dictatorial magistracy to see to the defense of the town: they had clipped their whiskers in February and they'd clip them again this time (an allusion to Radetzky, who had cut his mustache the morning of the revolution). A committee of public safety had been created, consisting of General Fanti, the lawyer Rastelli, and Doctor Maestri. ("What's become of my Prince Borromeo," Angelo wondered, "and what's Lecca up to? If he isn't dead—and I don't think he would have been so imprudent—he'll get back here as fast as possible.") There was a lot of talk about Garibaldi. Also about Fava, the chief of police. He was arresting, apparently without commotion, the most ardent patriots in town, especially a certain Franini, Cattaneo's friend. Cattaneo had accosted Fava and had insulted him sharply in front of his *sbirri*. He had called him "a royal tool of defamation, discord, and confusion." Frattini had been liberated. He had been accused of having spoken against the government. On this score, they would have had to arrest everyone.

In the evening the proclamation emanating from Bozzolo, in

which the King, calling all the Milanese to arms, urged them to be ready to die rather than lose their independence, reached Milan. He assured them that his soldiers would spill their blood down to the last drop for their fatherland. Children ran in the streets with sheaves of printed proclamations; they threw handfuls to the right and the left; the sidewalks were heaped high with them. The phrase "last drop" was wildly successful.

Back at "Il Tordo" Angelo thought everyone looked heroic. They charged through dinner, and the seamstress told the gentleman (who was simply asking for his candlestick) from the top of her starched collar, which the haughty carriage of her head made look like Bradamante's gorget, that their quarter alone had a hundred and thirty-five kegs of powder, twelve chests of cartridges, and as many caps.

Angelo checked the fastening on the cupboard in which he had put his saber and put the key in his pocket.

Day broke early, and people could be heard in the street early too. Since everyone was talking over the head of his interlocutor, especially to reach a "third party," the "third parties" were reached in their beds.

Angelo resisted the enthusiasm of this second day far less well. The Milanese were exalted with a bitterness that pleased him. He was tempted a hundred times to take up a pick and shovel and help the people excavating public squares or preparing paving-stones for barricades. The pharmacies were making gun cotton; printer's lead was being melted to make bullets. But he saw Garibaldi and his followers leaving for Brescia.

"There's a little dish of butter under each of those extraordinary red caps," he said to himself.

Would Curzio deliver the boots? This artist did him one better: he sent a sort of protonotary to "Il Tordo" carrying a top hat like a lord. This eccentric character drew an apron of green cloth and a little wool rug out of his bag; having put on the first and spread out the second, he knelt down. Angelo, however accustomed to astonishment, stared wide-eyed. He had to try on the boots; they were only mounted on the vamp.

"Shoemakers are all anarchists," Angelo said to himself. "Does this man realize that these boots are my flag?"

The lord was a cobbler to his fingertips. He accepted the sparkling wine Angelo offered him in the drawing-room.

"I'm going to ease the neck of the boots the least little bit," he said. "You mustn't even know you have them on."

Then he came to the heart of the matter.

"At present every novelist is extolling heroism; it's old hat. I have five children who don't always get their noses blown when they run; the wife is no doe, and I live in a building where they boil cabbage on every floor year in and year out. I carry my liberty in my pocket, in my wallet. My master is my enemy. They say the people are going to get control? Nothing could suit me better."

He had had a fine peek at the cards.

"Did you know they went to France? Who do I mean by they? Those who said: 'Italy will make out all right alone,' for God's sake!"

The next day or the day after, Angelo saw the man called Cattaneo in action. Milan had taken Cattaneo to its heart. He was the man of the hour. He had shot his entire bolt against the provisional government. Irresponsible criticism was his line. He was a St. John Chrysostom. He had been strolling *at random* through the crowd. Someone had shouted: *"Viva!"* He had gotten up on a chair. He had first advised them to dam the streams in the environs of the city, thus forming a vast swamp which would prevent the movement of artillery and horses or the organization of a siege. He also wanted to give the national guard war leaders, experienced war leaders, instead of those who had been chosen out of party spirit. And he cited, as replacements, names from his own party.

"Everything can be summed up in this 'Come in my boat,'" Angelo said to himself.

But suddenly they heard a cannon.

It was not a big cannon. The Piedmontese infantry was camped outside the city from the Pavia Canal to the Adda Canal. The cavalry was in town on the parade ground. Since seeing the suffering caused by the lack of supplies, the committee had comforted the soldiers with white bread, cheese, wine, a double ration of meat and cigars. They had distributed forty thousand shirts donated by the citizens. Thanks were in order, but how can soldiers show thanks? They promised to conquer or die. That was the least they could do.

From the first slow, rounded detonations, which rolled peacefully to the end of their echo, the people demanded barricades furiously.

"They're not a thing you can demand," Angelo said to himself.

He went to see the battle. He climbed the ramparts at the Porta Romana. From the houses across the road people shouted to him to get down, that he would be killed.

"Mind your own business," he replied. "I'm English."

The English were highly esteemed. The English ambassador had gone to lunch with Radetzky at the outposts in order to recall to him the Rights of Man and of the Citizen.

He couldn't see much. The fate of the city was being settled by a few puffs of smoke and several cracks. A line of infantry was moving through the gardens; a platoon of lancers, all hunched over, was going along the canal. A sluggish cannon sounded from time to time.

However, about four o'clock carts of wounded arrived. It was said that the soldiers had fought with ardor one would not have supposed them capable of after so many disasters. The Piedmontese entered a town and camped on the boulevards. They said the King had taken part in the battle, that he had been so close to the Austrian chasseurs and artillerymen that their grapeshot had killed or wounded three officers and several riflemen beside him. When this rumor had circulated all around, the King, too, entered the city and took over the Greppi house.

"It really seems they were after something other than victory in this battle," Angelo said to himself. "Let's see what happens next."

It had begun to rain.

In the middle of the night he was awakened by the tocsin and the light of a blaze.

"Death to the Croats!" the valet he met on the stairs said to him.

For an instant this exclamation made Angelo hope that chance had foiled the plots. He was already searching his pockets to find the key of the cupboard.

"No, no, don't trouble yourself," said the old man from whom he had not been able to hide his ardor. "We're the ones burning the country houses. The King said they impeded the defense of the boulevards."

The conflagrations continued all night. In the morning they were still throwing off fire and flames, and even flaring up in new spots. It was a very special decor; the smell too; both impelled you to sweeping actions and the prudence which follows upon them.

"Milan is not Moscow," Angelo said to himself. "These small market towns contiguous with the city are not constructed of wood but of solid stone. I would like someone just to tell me how the burning of the doors, windows, furniture, and roof can keep the enemy from hiding behind walls which are still upright, and from making loopholes in them? Who are they trying to kid? And what about?"

The tocsin continued to ring. The Piedmontese soldiers marched past. They took possession of all the gates of the city. They were evidently preparing for battle. Angelo saw his suspicions confirmed in this.

"Why didn't I think of that? You can burn houses with two aims in mind: to make the Austrians believe you want to resist at any price and to make the Milanese fear that this price is high, and thus intimidate the property-owners."

He was at Curzio's paying for his boots when the noises in the street took on a particular note.

"Here on the other hand is something real!" he said to himself.

"They don't want to be sold at auction, sir, and they're right," said the cashier. "The Piedmontese engineering-corps burned the houses around the Porta Nuova this morning. They wanted to set fire to a merchant's office, but he intervened and said that they could at least spare an honest man's books since the King had capitulated."

Angelo ran to join the agitators. They were madmen crazed with anger, but there were tears in their eyes and they were shouting: "We want to die!" Piedmontese soldiers and even officers who had torn off their epaulettes joined their ranks. These men also wanted to die. "And I too want to," Angelo said to himself. He no longer feared to be made a fool of. He had found men of spirit.

The King, surrounded by generals, was on the balcony of the Palazzo Greppi. He was making a little speech. All his gold lace and his thin voice falling from above made gunshots burst out. The staff retired indoors hurriedly dragging the King with them.

The people shook the doors of the palace and succeeded in breaking down the main one. They hastened into the courtyard and vestibule, but the stairs were guarded by riflemen and the national guard fifty lines deep. Besides, citizens who had stepped out of the crowd calmed them with reasonable talk.

The King returned to the balcony. Angelo could not stand the spectacle of these faces, magnified a moment before by anger, now raised imploringly to the sky.

He returned to "Il Tordo." It was just as difficult for him to stand the solid bourgeois setting of the dining-room where platters of roasts were circulating.

"The capitulation was signed," the boy told him, "but he tore it up."

Angelo pushed his plate away.

"My mother's right," he said to himself, "the real fighting's in Turin."

He had his horse saddled. He passed down streets where useless virtue contended in torchlight. He was obliged to struggle against his heart. As soon as he was out of the city, he started to gallop.

But the routes to the Ticino were blocked with convoys, artillery ranges, and baggage wagons also returning to Piedmont.

"How can a king who promises to enclose himself in a city to defend it send his artillery and his munitions away?"

The officer he had called out to replied insultingly.

He reached the Ticino long before the convoys. The larks were beginning to tremble. His house was across the river among the trees.

"Why don't the birds awaken in the park as well?" he asked himself. "They're silent as if there were someone there, but Lavinia isn't there. I don't smell the fires."

He tied his horse to a willow. Noiselessly he entered the woods. He knew what he was going to find. The guard was indeed hidden in the box ten feet from the entrance gate of the house. He couldn't miss his target. Besides he had rested the barrel of his gun on a forked branch to make his shot certain.

"They don't know me any more," Angelo said to himself. "They don't yet know that now I'm resolved even to grapple like a carter. If I liked to bet, I would win. For example, it would be easy for me to get up there behind that man without his hearing me and strangle him. But he's a small fish and it's the big ones I have a grudge against. I must get to Turin."

He retraced his steps and remounted his horse. He made a wide circle of the house and picked up the road beyond Novara, hurling himself into a gallop. He changed his foundered horse for a fresh one at the gate of Vercelli. He kept up a hellish pace all day. He dismounted at nine in the evening in front of the Bonafous diligence office. The street lamps were not yet lighted. Turin was enjoying a bit of savory melancholy in the summer dusk. He slipped down the little streets. He bought two soldi worth of grapes. He was picking at the last bunch slipping along the walls under the arcades of the Piazza San Carlo when he was seized by the arm. A hand drew him into a half-opened door. He was about to kick out when he heard a voice coo: "Colonel! Colonel!"

It was Giosuè. Their embraces continued for five whole minutes.

"I've been standing guard since yesterday morning," said the little hairdresser. "I thought that if you were alive, you would come back as fast as possible. I watched the windows of your house from here all day."

"What's become of Michelotti?"

"When I lost sight of him, he was hopping like a frog in the smoke. Oh! he has nine lives like a cat. Don't worry."

He related several battles.

"And what's going on here?"

"I've seen some buddies. They all think we've had it."

"The King's coming back?"

"There are a hundred kings. As soon as anyone mentions the word republic, a hundred come out of the ground."

"What are *you* going to do?" ("Finally, I treated him as a comrade," Angelo said to himself.)

"Go on, Colonel; I'm going with Garibaldi. Once you get a taste of fresh air . . ."

They kissed each other on either cheek and then solemnly three times more.

"A brief moment of happiness," Angelo said to himself.

He strode across the square. As he approached his house, he saw the door open. He entered without needing to push it. Lavinia was behind it.

"You were expecting me?"

She replaced the bolt without replying. She checked the latch as if this was the only idea left in her head.

He went up to his mother's room. He knocked.

"Come in."

"You knew it was I?"

"Lavinia clicked the bolts. It couldn't have been anyone but you."

The master bedroom was full of shadows which a night light was agitating softly.

"Where are you?"

"Here, on the couch. Lavinia has been watching for three days. The child is no longer anything but a double sentry."

"Why isn't she with her husband? Giuseppe must have some high post?"

"Steep, my dear, but she doesn't want to break her nails scaling it. I hope you're going to see Giuseppe?"

"I came here on purpose to see him."

"He's out in the fashionable world tonight, I believe."

"I don't have time to wait."

"I wouldn't be angry if the fashionable world saw you."

"Must I ask your pardon for having left you to fight all alone?"

"No, I had an amusing time. They use big words; I use big remedies. It's charming. You would have been in my way. I had to act without scruples."

"I've lost mine."

"God be praised, my little one! I've always wondered what gave you any fun."

"Anxiety. Never for you?"

"Yes, certainly! A metaphysical jam, imagine! I've tasted it. Where would pleasure be today without it?"

"May we speak of love?"

"What do you think we've been talking about since you were born, my little one? Come lie beside me a minute."

He stretched out beside her on the couch.

"We make an Etruscan tomb right now," she said.

He smelt her exquisite vanilla perfume.

"I need a loving hand."

"Don't take mine, my dear."

"I'm going to return to France."

"If you found it there, leave right away."

He stood up.

"Do what you have to do," she said. "Don't think of the consequences. I'll join you wherever you are."

He heard the little bibelots clicking as he walked to the door.

"Blow out the night light, little one."

He passionately loved the perfect silence of the stairwell. He went up to his room. The candelabra were all lighted and placed, moreover, in front of gilt and mirrors as if for a party. He saw that his suit had been laid out on his bed.

He couldn't have chosen better himself; he preferred this short black-velvet redingote with its very fitted waist to every other coat. The choice, undoubtedly Lavinia's, of shirt, trousers, and boots interested him somewhat more: they were what he was accustomed to wear for fencing-matches. And he saw, resting on the arm of the chair, a green canvas case from which two saber guards emerged. He drew the blades from the scabbards: the two weapons had been sharpened to a fine edge.

"Even today," he said to himself testing the points, which pricked like needles. Finally he noticed a note resting on the glove box. Lavinia had written: "At the Ansaldis', Palazzo Barbieri, Porta Susa. Go in through the garden." He added below: "And why not by the main gate?" He placed the note thus appended well in evidence against an opaline carafe and went to choose ("myself") his most arrogant top hat.

When he went downstairs, the house was profoundly silent as before. Nevertheless, the state chandeliers had been lighted, especially those which gleamed in a tall mirror with feet. He saw in it the advancing image of a man whose height was doubled by his hat, carrying a green canvas case under his arm.

He wondered who had sharpened the sabers. Lavinia must have thought of it ("my mother, too, although with scruples, even though she pretends not to have any"), but the material for the operation and the brow bent over the grindstone demanded muscles which only the she-wolf, Teresa, would have had. "Our nurse has given Giuseppe and me the essentials," he thought, "bread and knives."

Whole families of little shopkeepers had come to look at the illuminations around the Porta Susa. The Ansaldis had put a few Venetian lanterns in the trees. Enough to stir the imagination: the least gleam, repeated, makes a king's cloak of the night. All the lines of the Palazzo Barbieri were outlined by little lights in colored glasses.

French-style lackeys crowded the park gate; they drew aside to let the top hat pass. Starched shirts were smoking cigars along the garden walks. The musicians of the orchestra were getting a breath of air on the front steps, violins under their arms.

Angelo went up to a window. Smoke from the branched candlesticks still whirled from the last waltz. The women were fanning themselves. Among them, emerging from lemon-yellow furbelows, was, naturally, Carlotta.

Giuseppe crossed the drawing-room. His steps were too big. "He's been warned," Angelo said to himself. He climbed the front steps rapidly and went in to meet him. He saw him coming toward him, open-armed, from the end of the hall. "Trousers too wide," Angelo said to himself, "waist too high, and why that Titus haircut?"

"At last you're here!" said Giuseppe and he clasped him to his bosom.

He pulled him into an antichamber adjoining the ballroom. "What's the good of speaking?" Angelo asked himself. He rested the green case on a table and unbuttoned his redingote. They were stripped to the waist at the same instant.

Giuseppe delivered the first thrusts but against dazzling steel. He searched for an opening angrily and even with a touch of genius. His fury rose to a strange beauty. "Bravo!" said Angelo. At the same time he thrust with all his might. Giuseppe stiffened, still standing, and fell all of a piece.

. . .

"No," Bondino had said, his arms folded, in the doorway, "let them do as they wish!"

Now he rushed in.

"Marvelous . . ." said Cerutti pushing ahead of him, "what a marvelous young man! He understood that here he was not in danger."

He repeated his sentence two or three times at the top of his lungs.

". . . the only place in all Piedmont where he risked nothing," he added pushing back Bondino. (He was covering even Angelo with his body.)

"It was a bit much, but we appreciate it; believe me, we know how to appreciate . . . I've never loved anyone as much as you. Come on."

". . . no, no, never," he said (he was helping Angelo slip on his redingote). "I was overwhelmed! Thank Heaven! That such joy was promised to me! And to have it all this very moment! You can't imagine, come on!"

He conducted him to the door.

"From here on I imagined nothing more," Angelo said to himself.

He passed the Porta Susa and marched at a good rate on the road to France. He knew a posting-station in the suburbs; in a quarter of an hour he could have a good horse. At the end of the street, the moon lighted the Alps; beyond, the heavens were open.

He noticed that he was being followed by shadows slipping very cleverly from arcade to arcade as they drew nearer to him. Others were coming to meet him.

"Ah," he said to himself, "it's a long way to France!"

Manosque, January 6, 1957